PRAISE FOR SPENCER ANDERSON

"As a fan of Spencer Anderson's War Bird Trilogy, I am hooked on his books. I can't wait to get a copy. It is another page turner that will appeal to everyone who reads it. He builds a story that appeals to everyone, both male and female, veteran or historian. His stories teach not just the history of the wars or adventure, but the people who are involved. There will be a great love story, along with great lessons of family relationships and life's lessons. I will never forget the night my wife started to read 'Avenging Angel: A Pilot's Story.' She was shocked to find she could not stop reading. She thought she would never like a book about wars and airplanes. Fooled her! I can only say, if you don't love to read, you should not start one of Spencer's books, because it will change your life. I, on the other hand, love to read, and have read many of the best novel authors in the country, and I truly believe Spencer Anderson is among them."

– MICHAEL J. MCFARLAND, AVID READER

"World War II history of untold POWs' plight to survive in Germany. The book brings the life of an American pilot to survive against all odds. A must read for all Americans. This is our time to believe in the USA."

– SAMUEL ZYGNER

"I have read his three previous, war/flying novels and am salivating in anticipation of #4. The cover of *Survive the Night* says it all... one can't wait to see how their B17 was attacked, who will survive, and the process by which the inevitable rescue takes place. Anderson's details about flying and the realistic interchange between pilots, the crew, and the tower is most engaging. Bombs away!"

– BRUCE RODIN

SURVIVE THE NIGHT

Spencer Anderson

SURVIVE THE NIGHT

First Edition

Published by Tactical 16 Publishing

Colorado Springs, Colorado

www.Tactical16.com

ISBN: 978-1-943226-78-8 (paperback)

ISBN: 978-1-943226-77-1 (hardcover)

PROLOGUE

On the morning of July 18, 1944, what started as a decisive attack that would break the back of the German Luftwaffe, ended abruptly in the skies above Memmingen, Germany … setting in motion a ten-month nightmarish odyssey for the pilot of *Addie's Armor*, Gus Bodine.

Captain Bodine put *Addie's Armor* into a climb rate of 550 ft per minute on a heading that would bring them to the marshalling point 15,000 ft above the Italian countryside. He knew that things would get very busy … very soon.

"Sergeant Richardson, I need to talk to the fellas. Put me on the intercom."

If his crewmen were half as jittery as he was about their biggest combat mission to date, they needed his leadership and reassurance.

The radioman flipped the switch. "You're on the air, Skipper."

"Captain to crew: You guys are ready. We are only one plane among over two hundred. Your knowledge and commitment to excellence are as strong as any of the crews up here. Just remember, we're more than just a crew. We are brothers. Things are going to get busy, and I want to give each of you a chance to speak whatever is on your mind to say. I'll start. …I made a promise to my wife that I would return to her. I intend to keep my word. The only way I know of to do that is to focus every thought on the job.

"Spud, how about you? Are you good to go?"

"Radios tuned in, and I'm anxious to get back to Sterparone, sir. … Nervous as a long-tailed cat in a room full of rocking chairs, though. …Over."

"Copy that." Gus chuckled at the time-worn joke by the Idaho potato farmer's son turned B-17 radioman.

"Sergeant Clayton?"

The ball turret gunner (the ball turret is the plexiglass sphere attached to the belly of the airplane – arguably the most dangerous position on the plane) keyed his mic. "I'll never get used to the idea that there is a man inside every plane I shoot at. I'll do what I need to, though. I always have. I'm with you guys all the way. Oh, and be sure to lower the landing gear before we land so I don't get road rash, Skipper."

"Again with the jokes, eh, Clay?" Gus and his co-pilot, Hank Barenz, had a good laugh.

Every noncom and officer echoed the sentiments of commitment, duty, and brotherhood. They all wanted to be home again. Hank ended the round-robin conversation, "Lieutenant Barenz here. I've been flying next to Captain Bodine and you knuckleheads since our first wheels up as a crew. He is, without a doubt, a man I trust with my life to get me back to my bride, Linda."

"Gentlemen, what we know, what we've trained for, and what we've put to use for our missions so far, is our best chance of getting back home. Bodine: Out." Gus returned his mic to the mounting clip.

The raid on the Memmingen aerodrome began with the largest armada of B-17 Fortresses ever assembled. Two hundred seventeen of the "Forts" of the Mediterranean Allied Air Forces (MAAF), started the mission from various bases in the area around Foggia, Italy. The newest addition to the group, three dozen B-17Gs, including *Addie's Armor*, of the 483rd Bombardment Group, arrived in-theater at Sterparone Army Air Force Base in northern Italy in March 1944. Known for their excellence in bombing accuracy, the new B-17Gs were ordered to form up in the rear echelon as they flew to the intended targets.

Bravo Flight Leader to flight: Watch your separation distances. Stay on my wing. I'll guide us into position.

Capt. Bodine flew his plane into her assigned position as his two wingmen tucked in close off either wingtip.

Whang! The ear-piercing metal against metal explosion, caused by a nearly direct hit of an exploding 88 mm shell burst, momentarily deafened the crew. First one engine burst into flames, then another. *Addie's Armor* nosed down in a death spiral as a squadron of German Me 109s and Fw 190s swarmed overhead witnessing the destruction.

CHAPTER 1

SUMMER 1936 / PROVO, UTAH

Gus Bodine charged through the mudroom door and into the kitchen where his mother was busy preparing the evening meal for the family. She slid a pan of dinner rolls into the oven and closed the oven door.

"Shhh. I don't want the rolls to fall. What's got you into such a tizzy, sweety?"

"I got it! I passed my driver's test mom! I can't wait to tell Addie!"

Gerry Bodine entered through the same door and strode into the kitchen. "Mmmm … smells good in here. Is that a pork roast I smell?"

"It is. Your son said he passed his driver's test. I guess it's time to let him start driving now." Anna Bodine was not keen on the idea, but Gus had kept his word to keep his grades up, help around the house with chores, and help his father down at the car dealership on weekends and summer breaks. He was given a substantial allowance as a reward, but truth be known, he would have worked with the mechanics at *Bodine Chevrolet-Buick* for free. In two years, he had grown into a "fair to middlin' apprentice mechanic," to quote "Bo" (short for Beauregard) Taggart, the boss of the company's repair and detail shop. Gus loved learning about the mechanical details of cars, and had grown to like listening to Bo's thick Georgia accent as he taught him the inner workings of the internal combustion engine.

"Hey, Mom, I'm going to run down to the park for an hour or so. I'll be back before nine, okay?" Gus was out the door before his mother could say anything.

Gerry walked into the living room and sat down on the sofa next to his wife. He had a conspiratorial look and a certain smile that Anna knew all too well, an expression that usually made itself known on birthdays, anniversaries, and Christmas.

"Is there something that you want to say, my husband?" Anna placed her crochet hook and yarn on the coffee table and smiled warmly. "What have you done, dear?"

"Bill Farley traded in his car for a new Buick Special that we just put in the showroom. I had Bo Taggart give Bill's Ford a once over. The engine sounds like a bucket of bolts rattling around, and the clutch is shot. I offered him three hundred on trade for the Buick. He accepted the deal after the usual dickering. Anyway, Bill has his new Buick, and I have a Model B Ford with a near-death engine and clutch."

"Hmm, dear. Do I sense an early Christmas present for Gus about to evolve in your story?"

"I suppose so. After all, you've known me for the better part of twenty-three years—over twenty of them living under the same roof. Sometimes I think you know what I'm going to say before I do! Anyway, I thought I'd sell the Ford to Gus for a hundred bucks."

"Sell?" Anna looked at her husband with a raised eyebrow. "He's your son, not a customer."

"Of course, dear, but just hear me out. I'll charge him one-hundred dollars for the car. Gus can do the repairs himself. I could probably have it fixed and sell it for a tidy profit, but I'd rather see the smile on Gus' face when he hears he has a 'new' car! That'll be worth the price of admission, right? Besides that, when he puts his own sweat and money into it, I think he'll appreciate it much more than if I were to simply give him the Ford. In my own defense, it's no different than what we did for Russ two years ago when we helped him buy his first car," Gerry added.

Anna Bodine chuckled, as she recalled Russell's 16th birthday. He and Gerry found a 1928 Plymouth Model Q Roadster (powered by a 4-cylinder, 170.3 cubic inch power plant that produced a whopping 45 hp at 2800 rpm) owned by Keith Salisbury, apple farmer. The car was in pristine condition but was too small and under-powered for a family of four. So it was, that the Salisbury family became the proud owners of a year-old Oldsmobile Special 4-door Touring Sedan, and Russell Bodine came into possession of his dream car, a '28 Plymouth Model Q Roadster.

Addie and Gus sat on a bench beneath the canopy of the gazebo in the center of Pioneer Park. Gus reached for Addie's hand and sighed deeply.

"These are the memories that warm my heart the most … sitting here with you. Do you remember the first time, Addie? Our first dance?"

"May … I think it was Friday the thirteenth. Yes …" She let her head rest on Gus' shoulder. "We were in the seventh grade. We walked up Center Street from Dixon Junior High toward the park when I saw the Gazebo through the trees." She squeezed Gus' hand.

He picked up the story from there. "You asked me to carry you to the Gazebo. I remember feeling so … so grown up. It was silly, I know, but I was twelve going on 'grown up' in my mind. I never wanted that night to end."

Gus and Addie reminisced, reliving the memories of the four years they had been best friends. Now, at 16 and much more than mere friends, they couldn't imagine being apart … growing apart … ever.

CHAPTER 2

SUMMER 1941 / STANFORD UNIVERSITY

Gus began packing for his summer break. He had written to Addie in May that he planned on spending the break in Provo like he had the previous summer. He regretted not having written to her more frequently. The letter in May was only the third letter since September. The fact that there had been no reply, caused him to feel disappointed but not overly concerned. The telephone was no help, because Addie was attending full time at BYU (Brigham Young University). Private telephones were not allowed in the dorms, so making regular calls was not practicable. Truth be told, with so little communication between them, both Addie and Gus had grown distant from each other … but not because their feelings had lessened. Both of their hearts ached from want of being in each other's arms.

Gus Bodine's academic advisor during his second year at Stanford University was Dr. Prescott Day. Gus had met with him on two previous occasions but was unaware that Dr. Day's interest in Gus went deeper than that of a mere academic interest.

Late in the spring of 1941, as classes were being readied for final exams before the summer break, Gus found a note taped to his dorm room door. It read, "See Dr. Day at 3:15 p.m." It was almost 3 p.m.

according to the alarm clock sitting on the nightstand next to his bed. He knew he should settle into jamming for a final exam in metallurgy, but instead, he left the dorm, jumped on his bicycle and rode across the quad to the administration building.

He arrived at Dr. Day's office at exactly 3:07 p.m. He tapped lightly on the door and was rewarded with a hearty, "Enter!"

The bespectacled sixty-something professor wore a bow tie on the collar of a pinstriped dress shirt. The gray woolen cardigan sweater he wore gave the man the paternal grandfatherly image of a wise family patriarch.

Dr. Day motioned to a chair, removed his spectacles and place them on his desk. "Mr. Bodine, I have something to tell you that may be of some use, given your interest in the new science of aeronautical engineering. First, I need to ask, is that discipline still of interest to you, and if so, have you made plans for your next year of study?"

"Yes, sir. I see a need for engineers in the design and fabrication of aircraft to meet both military and civilian demands far into the future. It's an exciting field and one which fires my imagination. I would like very much to be a part of that endeavor." Gus fidgeted in his seat, his imagination filled with wonderment. He sensed a crossroads approaching, beyond which lay the reality of his sought-after desires of a career in aviation.

Dr. Day introduced Gus to two opportunities that would begin the adventure of his young life. First, he directed Gus to Palo Alto Airport where the 20-year-old undergraduate soon discovered his second greatest love: the world of flight and particularly the Stearman YPT-9. The recommendation was by no means a spur of the moment bit of advice to a student whose head was in the clouds about his outspoken desire to become an aeronautical engineer. The professor hoped to see the day when Stanford would add the field to its curriculum and dedicate an entire school to that endeavor. He had been closely monitoring Gus' academic performance. The bright young man's first two years at the University were exemplary. Dr. Day's interest in Gus was ignited by his first paper, *Warbirds: The Future of Air Warfare.* The paper reflected a budding sophistication of the principles of aviation engineering that would, one day, lead man to the edge of space.

The second opportunity would introduce Gus to Spartan Aviation in Tulsa, Oklahoma. Spartan was set to pioneer the first college-level graduate program in aeronautical engineering. Underwritten by J Paul Getty, the program was intended to boost lagging sales of the Spartan inventory of aircraft and would be competing head-to-head with Lockheed, the California-based aircraft design and manufacturing company whose chief research engineer, Clarence "Kelly" Johnson, was gaining fame as an innovator in aircraft design.

After half an hour of pondering how to tell Addie he would not be coming home for summer break, he opened the drawer to his bedside table, removed a composition pad and pen, and began writing.

> *Addie, my love,*
>
> *Hi, sweetheart. By now you're probably wondering why I'm not in Provo, or at least not on my way. I was packed and ready to go when I got a note to see my academic advisor. My meeting with Dr. Day resulted in a big course correction for my ... our ... future, that is, if (and it's a mighty big IF) you still want a future with me. Please, let me explain.*

Gus went on to tell Addie the plan he laid out for the next school year, including his hope to earn his pilot license before he transferred to Spartan Air in Oklahoma. He promised Addie that he would see her over the Christmas break. He would write at least once every week, and, if they could schedule their telephone time, he would call twice a month (they would both be attending classes and telephone availability would be scarce at best). He closed his letter with a heart-felt confession of his deep love for her and his hopes for their future together. Short of a written proposal of marriage, which he hoped to do in person at Christmas, he ended his letter.

The route from Stanford University to Palo Alto airport was a four-mile straight shot down Embarcadero Road. Gus covered the distance in less than 20 minutes on his Schwinn bicycle. His Ford Model B was stored in a shed in the back yard of a young Stanford professor of chemistry. Professor G. Sutton Parks had posted a note in the student union building advertising rental space available on his property. As it turned out, the shed was what was left of an old carriage house. A new padlock and re-setting of the door, both accomplished by the hand of Gus Bodine, bought Gus a month of free storage and an ongoing rental fee of seven dollars per month.

———

His first visit to the airport had proven no less than monumental in shaping his career choice as a pilot and engineer. First, he met the affable Fred Wick, himself an experienced pilot. During World War I, he had flown with the American contingent of pilots known as the Lafayette Escadrille. Now, at age 42, he owned his own crop-dusting and aviation touring company, Bay City Air. He had two airplanes, both were Stearman YPT-9s. One was currently on a job and flown by Gene Cummins, Fred's partner. The other biplane, the one used for flying tourists around the Bay Area, was parked outside the hangar and shone brightly in the afternoon sunlight with its yellow wings and olive-green fuselage.

Fred was sitting behind his desk in the small office at the back of the hangar when someone knocked on the door frame. Bookkeeping and the other paperwork required to operate his small company were the least pleasurable aspects of his work, and Fred happily dropped his pencil to the desktop, glad for any interruption.

"The door is open. Come on in."

Gus entered and closed the door behind him. His eyes flitted about the room taking note of everything: aircraft engine maintenance manuals, books on agriculture and crop dusting, and technical manuals on the YPT-9. Framed photographs occupied a shelf behind Fred's desk. One of them showed a group of men standing in front of a British built biplane, known as the "Sopwith Camel." The other showed a younger Fred standing next to a beautiful young woman. *Wife? Girlfriend?*

Gus introduced himself and took a seat in the wood-framed folding chair offered him.

"Well, young man. What can I do for you?" Wick asked.

Gus took a deep breath, released it, and fixed his eyes on the blue eyes of Fred Wick.

"Sir, I have recently finished my second year at Stanford. I intend to learn everything having to do with flight. Additionally, it is my intention to learn to pilot an airplane. To that end, I would ask, do you offer flying instruction, sir?"

The two talked for the next half hour. Fred would ask the questions and Gus would offer succinct answers with no *ifs*, *ands*, or *buts* attached. He knew what he wanted and was determined to do whatever was necessary to obtain it.

"Well, you seem to know exactly where you're heading, young man. Assuming you are as committed to learning to fly as you are to your schooling at Stanford, I don't doubt that you'll achieve your goals. Aeronautical Engineering, eh? ...I don't normally take on flying students unless I know that they are willing to work their butts off to stick with the program."

"Mr. Wick, I have one hundred and fifty-six dollars. It's all the money that I've earned in the last two summers working at whatever odd jobs I could find. Is that enough for a start?" Gus offered a nervous smile, uncertain whether he might be laughed out of the office.

Fred thumbed through the bills: tens, fives and ones with the couple of twenties thrown in. He stood from behind his desk and extended his right hand. Feeling much relieved, Gus took the offered hand in a firm grip and gave it a brisk shake.

"What do you have scheduled for the rest of your afternoon, Gus?"

"Nothing in particular, sir." Grinning inside, Gus sensed something exciting was coming.

"Let's walk outside … and cut the formal speech, kiddo. You sound like you write for The Wall Street Journal or something." The pilot-owner of Bay City Air smiled at Gus as the two of them left the office and walked across the empty hangar floor to a side door leading to the tarmac outside the hangar.

"Meet the Stearman YPT-9. She's been upgraded to a Jacob R-755, 7-cylinder, radial engine, with a little more power than the original Continental. Climb on up to the forward cockpit, Gus."

"You mean we're going up now?" Gus' heart leapt in his chest as he stood open-mouthed before his new instructor.

"You want to start your lessons, don't you?"

"Yeah, but …"

"No *yeah-buts*, Gus my boy." Fred showed him the handholds and the right places to put his feet. There's a leather flying helmet hanging on the control stick. Put it on. You'll need to use the handheld microphone if you want to talk to me, but for now, raise your hand and give me a 'thumbs up' if you hear me okay. Got it?"

"Yes, sir." Gus followed Fred's instruction and soon found himself sitting in the cockpit of a real airplane. He was thrilled, nervous, and a little frightened.

Gus felt the biplane shift a little as Fred climbed into the rear cockpit. A few seconds later a voice came over the speakers embedded in his leather flying helmet.

"Do you hear me up there?" The sound of the crop-duster's voice came through loud and clear. Gus raised his hand and gave a thumbs-up gesture as instructed.

"Good. I'm going to fire her up. You'll hear some noise, and the plane will shake until the engine is running smoothly. Sit back and relax. I'm going to teach you about the controls of the airplane: rudder pedals, control stick, and throttle. You'll have a chance to fly this lady, but not to worry. I won't let you crash." He laughed loudly. Gus chuckled nervously.

Gus' first flying experience was to hold the biplane in straight and level flight. With a bit of gentle coaxing from his instructor, Gus soon was able to hold altitude and direction of flight in a proper level configuration. Next, Fred demonstrated a series of "S" turns and altitude changes. Gus' first attempt at a shallow left turn resulted in a loss of 300 ft of altitude. Fred did not take the controls from him, but simply said, "Bring your nose up a tad, Gus. Add some power. Keep it on the horizon. Good. ...Good. You've got it."

Whew! was Gus' silent reply.

After 45 minutes of turning and weaving their way through the skies above Palo Alto, Fred took the controls and brought the Stearman down to a perfect three-point landing. He shut down the engine and instructed Gus to chock the wheels. Side-by-side, the two "pilots" walked back to the hangar.

Fred sat behind his desk in his chair and folded his arms across his chest "We're in early June, Gus. Your classes start up for you pretty soon, don't they?"

"Not until the first week of September." Gus didn't miss the pixyish half-smile that lit up Fred's eyes. "Why? What are you thinking?"

"I'm thinking that we can help each other. Tourist season is picking up as are the big AGRA-company contracts for crop dusting. I could really use some help around the hangar. What you say?"

"I don't know. Could we arrange some flying lessons, in lieu of cash salary?" Gus became suddenly excited about flying lessons and working around airplanes. He could learn a lot about aviation, and with a pilot license under his belt, he would have a substantial head start on his advanced degree program in aeronautical engineering.

Fred and Gus sat on opposite sides of Fred's worn-out steel desk and hammered out a deal.

"I'll teach you everything you need to know about the Stearman: electrical system; engine components; flight characteristics: lift, drag, pitch, roll; flight instruments; ... everything. By the time you and I are done, you're going to be a good pilot— not a great one, but a good one. Now, there's the question of how much all that training is going to cost you. You have any thoughts, pal?"

Gus focused and maintained eye contact with his would be boss. He knew he could not—and would not—sacrifice his perfect academic record at Stanford. "I should be able to give you four hours a day three or four days a week. If it's all right with you, I could trade whatever salary I would earn for my flying lessons." Gus waited for Fred's reaction. He knew that he would be taking time away from Fred's crop-dusting work to teach Gus how to fly. Keeping the hangar clean and organized would be the least he could do as payment for flying lessons. He never expected or even thought about earning money to work around airplanes. His eagerness to get started was palpable.

Fred smiled and chuckled a little at Gus' willingness, as naïve as it was, to offer free labor in return for a few flying lessons.

"I don't do work for free, and I don't expect you to provide a valuable service to my company free of charge. So, I will pay you a dollar-and-a-half an hour as paid salary. The lessons will be the other half of your earnings. We will fly twice each week for two hours per week total. I figure by the middle of August, you will have twenty hours of instruction—maybe more if we can work it out. That should be enough to take you well past your first solo. Deal?"

"Deal!"

Gus head was filled with visions of his "new" future as he rode his bike back to the dorm.

Two weeks of hangar cleaning, flying lessons, maintaining the YPT-9, filling the spray tanks with either pesticides or chemical fertilizer passed quickly, and on June 21, upon arriving back to his dorm room, he sat down, exhausted, at his small desk and wrote to Addie.

Addie, my love,

I'm dreaming of us together … sitting in the gazebo or lazing in a hammock near Lost Creek.

I have exciting news to tell you …

AUGUST 5, 1941 / SOLO

Twenty-year-old Gus Bodine checked his class schedule for the beginning of his junior year at Stanford: Intermediate Metallurgy, Physics, Advanced Solid Mechanics, Thermodynamics, and Engineering Design. He left the admin building and headed straight to the dorm where he dropped off his class schedule and changed his clothes. Fred insisted that Gus wear the uniform of the day with the Bay City Air logo across the back of his jumpsuit.

Turning his bicycle toward Embarcadero Road, he headed for the airport. Over the last several weeks Gus had familiarized himself with his duties and accomplished every task asked of him with energy and attention to detail. Very early on, Gus had earned trust and respect from his employer. More than that, Gus had proven himself a quick and capable novice pilot, having demonstrated a degree of mastery of all the YPT-9's basic performance characteristics. He hopped off his bicycle and parked it inside the hangar.

Gus' first task of the day was to sweep out the hangar, pick up any stray parts that may have dropped on the floor, and arrange any and all tools that may have been used during the day in their proper storage place. He was heading for the metal janitor's closet to return a broom when Fred called out his name.

CHAPTER 2

"Hey, Gus. Come over here a sec, will you?"

Gus leaned the broom against the wall and trotted across the hangar floor toward Fred's office.

"What's up, boss" Gus asked as he closed the door behind him.

"Gus, by my count, you have eighteen hours at the controls of the Stearman. Our conversations have included the Stearman's limitations, aerodynamics, systems, engine and propeller operation, tail wheel flying procedures, and preflight and engine starting checklists. Do you feel up to one more lesson?"

"Heck yes … any time." He and Fred walked outside onto the tarmac where the Stearman was parked.

"Climb up to the back seat, Gus. I want you to check the battery and mags to make sure they're in the off position. I'm going to pull the prop through a few times to check for hydraulic lock and prime the engine."

Gus began to climb into his usual front seat.

"What are you doing, Gus? I told you to get into the back seat."

"Ah, … you mean …?" Gus began to ask. His heart went from beating to pounding under the sudden rush of adrenaline. He felt as though it would burst from his chest.

"That's right, pal. This is your solo flight. I want you to keep it in the pattern, and give me four landings and takeoffs. After you land, I want you to taxi to the hangar, and then turn around and do another. Keep going until you have completed four landings to a full stop. Understood?"

Gus was thrilled and more than a little nervous. He looked into his instructor's eyes.

"Understood. Uh … Fred, what's hydraulic lock?"

"It has to do with oil and fuel and pressure in the lines. Sometimes, especially in hot weather, a fuel line or oil line can lock up due to a vacuum developing in the system. Pulling the prop through forces fuel and oil into the lines. Now that you've primed the engine and turned the battery and mags off, I'll crank the inertia starter. When I call out 'Switch on,' that's your signal to switch on the battery and both mags after you set the throttle. Remember? We've been through the engine starting sequence before. The only difference is you're going to be on your own."

Fred climbed down and walked around the wing to the front of the plane. He pulled the prop through four times, and checked for any fuel or oil drips. Satisfied, he inserted a hand crank through a hole in the side of the engine faring and started cranking. Each turn of the crank caused the flywheel inside the Aeromarine Inertia Starter to cycle up with a whine that increased in pitch and volume with every rotation of the crank. After 20 rotations or so, he pulled out the hand crank and walked briskly around the wing. "Switch on!" he shouted.

"Switch on! Contact!" Gus grabbed hold of the starter lever and pulled it upward. The clutch engaged the starter, and he pressed the "Booster" button to feed additional spark into the ignition system. The high-pitched whine lowered dramatically, and the propeller began turning slowly. First one propeller blade then another and another crossed Gus' field of vision. The engine coughed a brief cloud of white smoke and then fired up. He set the throttle so the rpm needle settled on 1,100 rpm.

Gus pressed on the right rudder pedal and added enough power to start the biplane moving. Turning right and lining up on the taxi way, he began his roll to runway 31. He had to look first left, then right, over the fuselage to see the taxi way underneath him. Finally, he reached the runway.

He lifted the mic from its hook, pushed the transmit button and announced:

Palo Alto traffic, Bay City Air Charlie One Niner Six. Requesting departure runway three-one. Remaining in the pattern. The sound of his own voice was clear and confident. "I can do this" he said aloud and grinned.

Roger, Bay City Air. The pattern is clear.

With a final quick scan of the engine instruments: oil pressure and temperature, fuel quantity, altimeter and RPM needle, as soon as he got the aircraft rolling he added a little rudder. With an assist from the steerable tailwheel, he turned the plane, and brought the biplane's nose in line with the white centerline of the runway.

The YPT-9 began its takeoff roll as Gus added more power. He kept the stick centered and leaned over the side of the fuselage, so he could see the centerline passing beneath him. Applying rudder as needed to keep the little biplane tracking the center of the runway, as the airspeed indicator reached 40 mph, the tail lifted, and then the mains rose from the ground. At 2100 rpm, Gus pulled the control stick back a tiny bit, and the climb rate jumped to 500 ft/min. He held the climb angle and runway course until he reached 500 ft AGL (Above Ground Level). His racing heart began to slow. *I can't wait to tell Addie, and mom and dad!* he thought.. A smile crept across his face when he realized he was flying … solo!

Gus leveled out and entered a 45° left turn to a heading of 220°. As he started his turn, the nose of the aircraft dropped below the horizon, and his rate of climb became a rate of descent. His elation changed to a feeling of near panic—caused, no doubt, by the sudden surge of adrenalin coursing through his veins. Panic can do one of two things to a person: make you freeze up, or sharpen the mind in a fight-or-flight response. Fortunately for Gus, the latter prevailed, and he immediately corrected by adding power and pulling back on the control stick. *Whew! Just fly the plane, Gus!* he said to himself.

When it was time to position for his downwind leg, he made another turn to the left. Fred's words from their first flight together flashed into his mind, "The best landings are made on the downwind leg. Precise application of altitude, airspeed, and rate of descent is essential. Nail those three things, and you'll enter your final approach spot-on the proper glide slope."

The end of the runway appeared below his left wing. When the runway numbers moved to approximately 45° below and behind him, Gus pulled back the power to begin his descent to land. He descended at 500 ft/min and entered his base leg at 200 ft above the ground. He banked the biplane to the runway heading of 310°. With the airspeed indicator reading 60 mph, Gus was lined up with the runway. He brought the power back and slowed to 45 mph until he was over the apron. He pulled the throttle back the rest of the way, and the biplane settled into a nice flare. The wheels touched down, followed a fraction of a second later by the tail wheel, causing the mains to lift off the runway before settling back down. The one bounce "crow hop" was not a huge concern. The goal to a good landing in a tail dragger like the YPT-9 is to have the tailwheel touchdown simultaneously with the main gear. Gus' first landing as a solo pilot was passable. He repeated the process, and after the fourth and final flight around the Palo Alto airport, taxied over to the Bay

City Air hangar and shut down the engine. Five minutes later he sat down with Fred in the office.

"You did about as well as I thought you would do, Gus. Your fourth landing was an excellent three-point touchdown. The next step is your first solo cross-country flight. I want you to map it out. Put in compass headings, distance between waypoints, airspeed, altitude, fuel consumption and estimated time of arrival at each stop. You will fly from Palo Alto to San Francisco to Oakland and back to Palo Alto. The whole trip will be a tad over eighty-two miles total. You won't need to refuel, but I want you to practice full stop landings all the way. Got it?"

Watching Gus piloting the biplane reminded Fred of his own youth, and how the winds of war shaped his desire to fly. Now, the world was again sinking into global conflict. It was inevitable that the United States would have a need for pilots to fly its fighters and bombers.

AUGUST 12, 1941 / A WEEK LATER

Gus pulled a shop rag from his work coveralls and wiped a smear of oil from the cowling behind the bottom of the engine. He was anxiously looking forward to the flight. The solo cross-country would be his final requirement for unlimited VFR solo flight.

"Climb on in there. I'll do the cranking, and you do the flying. By the way, good job on the flight plan, Gus. I don't think I need to tell you how excited I am for you. You're going to make one heck of a pilot." The veteran pilot wanted to give his young protege all the praise he deserved. What he didn't tell him was that the Stanford undergrad could very well be flying for the United States Army Air Force in another year or so. "I'd be doing the same thing if I were young enough," he mumbled to himself.

Fred pulled the crank through a few more times and removed it from out of the Aeromarine Inertia Starter and then stepped clear of the engine.

"Contact!" Gus yelled from the rear cockpit. He toggled up the two magneto switches and pulled up on the starter handle. After two complete rotations of the propeller, the engine started with a belch of white smoke. With a salute, Gus began his taxi to runway three-one. He keyed his mic.

Palo Alto traffic, Bay City Air Charlie One Niner Six is ready for northwest departure.

Roger, One Niner Six. The pattern is clear. You are cleared for departure on runway three-one.

When the Stearman's landing gear lifted from the runway, Gus did not feel the nervousness that caused no small amount of angst and butterflies when he took off—alone for the first time—from the same runway a week earlier. At this particular moment, angst was replaced by the sheer excitement and pleasure of flying.

"I'm flying! I'm flying! Yahoo!" he shouted into the prop wash. At 3000 ft AGL, Gus turned toward his first stop.

San Francisco Airport, Charlie One Niner Six is six miles south at three thousand feet. Inbound to land full stop.

Roger, One Niner Six. Make straight-in runway five.

Cleared to land runway five. One Niner Six. Over.

On final approach to runway five, Gus felt the Stearman buffet in a right-quartering headwind. He kicked in a little right rudder with enough left aileron to keep himself in line with the center of the runway. He decided to hold his airspeed just above "stall," in anticipation of any turbulence. The additional power made for a wheel landing rather than the desirable three-point landing, but it couldn't be helped. As he was about to touchdown, he centered the rudder, which brought the Stearman's nose in line with the runway as the wheels kissed the pavement. He pulled the throttle all the way back and let the tail wheel lower to the ground. *Good job, so far.*

That was the "touch" part of the landing. Now, he had to exit the runway, taxi back to the run-up area, and radio the tower to take off. Upon receiving departure permission, Gus pushed the throttle all the way forward, and the tailwheel lifted from the surface followed by the main gear. Wheels up completed the "go" part. He was airborne and climbing at 700 ft/min practically before he knew it. Gus turned northwest, flying above the Golden Gate Bridge toward Oakland, on the second leg of his cross-country flight.

His landing at Oakland airport's runway 19 was textbook. On

approach he held his airspeed at 70 mph. By the time his wheels passed over the threshold, his speed was a hair under 55 mph and his wheels were 10 ft above the surface. He pulled the throttle all the way back, and the Stearman settled into a cushy flare with a "squeak" of the tires as they straddled the runway centerline. With a smile on his face, Gus simulated another full-stop landing and taxied back to the active runway. In his mind, he was patting himself on his back, as the Stearman took to the sky for the return home.

Flying southwest, Gus had a beautiful view of the Golden gate Bridge about 20° off the port side. The blur of the propeller combined with the steady drone of the 7-cylinder engine, lulled him into a state of relaxed well-being as he headed for the Palo Alto airport.

Palo Alto traffic, Bay City Air Charlie One Niner Six is ten miles north. Altitude two thousand four hundred, descending to land.

One Niner Six, you are cleared straight in approach runway one-three. The pattern is clear.

As the daylight began to fade, Gus noted the upper rim of the sun settling on the western horizon of the Pacific Ocean. In a split-second flash of emerald-green, the glowing orb sank beneath the surface leaving behind a brilliant panorama of yellow, gold, and red clouds on a back-lit maroon sky. Beautiful!

Gus' few minutes of serenity were ended by a loud metallic "clang!" followed by a spray of black oil on the windscreen. A trail of black smoke traced the biplane's path. A scan of his instruments confirmed he was in trouble. Engine RPM dropped alarmingly, and the oil temperature needle rose into the red zone. There was nothing he could do but shut down the engine. He feathered the engine and leaned the mixture all the way back. The engine coughed and stopped. Suddenly there was no sound. Only the humming of the wire struts bore witness that the Stearman was still in level flight.

Gus' first realization was that he never had a chance of reaching the airport. He needed to find any flat surface to land on before he ran out of altitude and airspeed.

Fred had taught him well, "Maintain the best glide angle. Don't let your airspeed drop below 45 mph. Always be aware of your surroundings, because you won't likely have a chance to hunt for a place to land. You should always be aware of an alternate landing location."

Once over land again, Gus found himself above fields of farmland. Off his left side, a narrow dirt road between two large plots of recently plowed land caught his eye. The road was a little wider than the huge wheels of a tractor, or the wheels of the Stearman, he thought … he hoped. Coordinating the control stick with the rudders, Gus turned the biplane toward the farmer's road while at the same time he keyed the mic.

Mayday, Mayday, Mayday! Bay City Air Charlie One Niner Six. Seven miles north of Palo Alto. Engine out emergency. Losing altitude. Landing in a farmer's field. Repeat, Mayday, Mayday, Mayday! Charlie One Niner Six. Power-out landing seven miles north of Palo Alto.

The dirt road was at a right angle to the paved highway running north out of Palo Alto. Gus knew it was going to be close, but he had no choice. He was losing altitude fast and his airspeed was running barely above stall speed. *Lord help me not to hit a car,* he thought.

A family in a sedan traveling south into Palo Alto from San Mateo was looking forward to being home after visiting relatives for the past two days. The movement of something yellow caught the driver's eye. "There, Thelma. Looks like one of those crop dusters flying low." Before Thelma could respond to his comment, her husband hit the brakes and the Buick came to a stop in time to thrill the three children in the backseat with an up-close view of the Stearman YPT-9.

As Gus approached the farmer's road, the wheels hit the southbound lane of the highway. The yellow biplane lifted up, flew a few yards farther, and settled back down onto the dirt road. He let the biplane roll toward the farmer's barn and then kicked in hard left rudder to spin the plane around. By the time he climbed out of the cockpit, the owner of the farm, Pete Ballinger, raced toward the plane with a sloshing bucket of water hurriedly obtained from a nearby stock trough. He tossed it on the smoking engine and hurried back for another bucketful that seemed to do the job of dousing any remaining fire.

"Hey, young man. I saw you coming down. Mother and I were sitting on the porch. It didn't take long to realize you were stopping by our place for a visit. C'mon up to the house. You can use the telephone to call somebody. If anyone's talking on the party line, just shout for Myrtle. She works the switchboard. Neighbor of ours. Anyhow, you tell Myrtle that Pete told you to tell her to ring you right through."

Gus, Pete Belanger and his wife, Phyllis, sat at the kitchen table talking about Belanger's farm. He lamented over the fact that he couldn't afford to hire a crop duster to spray down his crops. He did okay at market, but he couldn't compete with people who are producing half again as much more on the same amount of acreage. "Yep, times they are a-changin'. Outfits like Bay City Air have increased crop production in California by fifty to seventy-five percent due to the fact that big money from the city has co-opted most of the small farmers into giant conglomerates. Hardly any room for the small family farmer anymore."

Phyllis put out a plate of fresh-baked bread all cut into slices and ready to cover with fresh creamery butter and clover honey.

"Now, Pete, you stop bothering Gus here about our farming troubles. Here's some nice homemade bread, warm from the oven, you help yourself. How about a cold glass of our own milk? You won't find anything this delicious come out of the grocery store."

An hour later, Fred pulled up to the farm in his pickup with the Bay City Air logo on the side doors. Gus excused himself and joined Fred, dressed in his shop coveralls, in the task of figuring out what to do with the Stearman.

"You talk while I remove the cowling, Gus. We need to figure out how we're going to get the Stearman back in the hangar. Grab that toolbox out of the back of the pickup, will you?" Gus did what he was told and soon the two of them removed the engine cowling. Gus told Fred the whole story from the moment the oil spray started, up to and including the landing. Fewer than ten minutes later, Fred discovered the problem. He stepped back from the engine, and wiping his hands on an already dirty shop rag, shook his head.

"You had a hydraulic lock resulting in the cylinder freezing up. Likely a bent rod, too. By the way you described it, that loud bang you heard was the cylinder throwing the rod and freezing up. We're going to need to disassemble the Stearman and trailer it back to the hangar."

Gus was beside himself. *Did I cause the engine failure?* he asked himself.

Well, there's only one way to find out … "Fred, did I cause the cylinder failure?" he asked. Gus couldn't hide the tremor in his voice.

"No, of course you didn't. I pulled the prop through. I know that whenever a radial engine is shut down overnight oil can drain into the lower cylinders. The purpose of pulling the prop through is to circulate the oil. This is important. Oil is incompressible. It can lock up one or more cylinders. Trying to start an engine without pulling the prop through can blow a cylinder. I should have been able to feel it when I pulled the prop through. I would have felt some resistance because of the pressure buildup in the cylinder with all the excess oil in it. I'll have to check into it, but I suspect that the damage was done when I had the engine overhauled. What I think happened was that when they did a test run up on the engine at the mechanic's shop, they had a hydraulic lock. They simply overlooked it and signed off on the rebuild. Come on Gus, let's get back to work."

Between the two of them they had the wings mostly off when a large flatbed trailer rig pulled off the highway and drove up the farmer's dirt road to where Fred and Gus were finishing the removal of the struts and wires from the control surfaces of the wings. With the disassembled Stearman secured to the flatbed, Fred wiped his oil-stained hands on a shop rag and stuffed it into his overalls.

Pete was standing on the porch, hand-in-hand with Phyllis, watching the men, when Fred waved to him and called out, "Hey, Pete! C'mon over here, will you?"

The affable farmer stepped off the porch and approached with a broad grin stretched across his weather-worn face.

"Yessir, what can I do for ya?" Pete asked.

"Well, Pete, I was thinking maybe I could do something for *you.* I owe you and Phyllis a debt of gratitude for the things you've done to help Gus and me. Plus, I owe you for the use of your farm as an airfield when Gus had to land the Stearman. So, let me ask you, what do you use to spray your crops this time of year?"

"Over the next couple of weeks, my farming will be more about pest control. Grasshoppers, locusts, even some moths love the mature corn and grains: wheat, oats and the like." Pete's curiosity got the best of him. "Why do you want to know? Are you planning on buying a farm, young fella?"

"Pete, I still have one flyable airplane and a whole lot of lead arsenate ready to mix up and fill the spray tanks. How 'bout I spray your acreage? How much you got?"

"I don't have enough to pay a crop duster."

"No, no," Fred chuckled. "Not how much *money* … how many *acres* do you have, Pete?"

"Oh. Well, let's see … I have 60 acres in corn, and 40 each in wheat and oats. Lead arsenate will do the job just fine, but I can't …"

"Great! I'll be back in a couple of days to inspect the property, and weather permitting, we'll spray on Saturday." Fred held out his hand and the deal was settled.

Gus rode back to the airport with Fred. The flatbed led the way with the fuselage of the Stearman tied down on the trailer, and the wings fit in lengthwise along the fuselage.

"Gus, I don't need to tell you, with only one plane flying, we need to take a break from your lessons until we can get the Stearman flyable again. It will take me a while to gather together enough money to pay for an engine overhaul. You will be starting your third year at Stanford in a week or two. We're looking at probably February or March before the Stearman will be ready. I promise you, though, that when the time comes, we can pick up where we left off if you still want to. I'm sorry, pal, but I don't see another way."

CHAPTER 3

Classes started again in September. Gus immersed himself in his schoolwork. He rode his bike to the airport to visit Fred a few times. Then, one day in November, he found Fred in the hangar working on the newer PT-17 Stearman. He was removing the spray booms from the wings. A half dozen spray tanks sat against the wall of the hangar.

When Fred saw Gus enter the hangar, he dropped a wrench on the workbench, wiped his hands, and walked over to Gus with a big smile on his face.

"Hey, Gus, it's been a while. It's good to see your ugly face." Fred threw his arms around him and lifted him off the floor in a bear hug that nearly cracked one of Gus' ribs.

"Likewise, boss. I've missed the place. How's business?

"A little slow. A charter flight here and there, but the spraying business dropped way off as it usually does this time of year with fall moving into winter. On a happier note, though, I have accepted a new contract with Hope Memorial Hospital in Oakland. They worked out a deal with half a dozen hospitals from Crescent City and Mendocino down to Santa Barbara for Bay City Air to fly doctors, executives, and hospital supplies and medicines up and down the coast on an as-needed basis. It seems there is enough demand to warrant an investment into a larger plane, and I would be their chief pilot."

"Wow! That's great, Fred. Do you know when that'll happen?"

"I signed the contract last week. The hospital conglomerate ordered a new Beechcraft Model 18 from the factory in Wichita, Kansas. It will be a new build so it will take a couple of weeks. They'll fly the plane into Salt Lake City. I'll pick it up there and ferry her the rest of the way to Palo Alto. I should probably tell you that I will be selling our two biplanes and getting out of the crop-dusting business. By next spring, I hope we can get you trained to fly multi-engine airplanes. Your logbook shows 43 hours in the Stearman. You're ready for multi-engine certification. That is, if that's something you would like to do."

"I don't know, boss, All I can see right now is finishing school. Can I think about it?" Fred's generous offer was a curve ball he wasn't expecting. He knew Fred had confidence in him, but to offer him a future flying for a living? ...Well, he didn't see that one coming.

DECEMBER 1941

With Christmas approaching, Addie occupied more and more of Gus' thoughts. He needed to see her and decided to make the long trip home. It would be less expensive and faster to take the train as opposed to driving. Winter snow in the high Sierra's was not uncommon, and the train offered the safer, less stressful alternative. Like all desirable plans though, providence has a way of changing one's course in life.

No classes were scheduled for Sunday, and Gus' time was his own. He showered and dressed and then decided to take a lengthy bicycle ride to clear his head. Conflicting thoughts sparred back and forth in his mind, and they needed to be resolved. There were the matters of continuing school in Oklahoma, the offer from Fred to join him next year as a pilot in his new medical transport business, and the most important matter of all ... what to do about Addie and their future together.

That evening, the first Sunday in December, began with Gus'

weekly letter to Addie. He always wrote of his deep love for her and affirmed his hope that they would be together forever, but this time before closing, he felt the need to share the struggles going on in his mind. First, he would update Addie about Dr. Day's offer of securing a position in the new Aeronautical Engineering program at Spartan Aircraft in Oklahoma and his busy classroom schedule to prepare for that move. Then he felt he should tell her about the new offer from Bay City Air. Above all, though, he needed to reassure Addie that none of his plans would go forward without her support. As he wrote, a tide of emotion rolled over him. His heart and his mind filled with thoughts of how much he missed her and everything about her: the soft warmth of her hand on his cheek, the laughter in her eyes whenever she smiled, her sense of spontaneity that made every day with her a new adventure. They loved their time together: walking in the park, roaring with the fans at the high school football games, and sharing their most intimate thoughts in quiet conversations expressing the content of their hearts and their desire to be a forever family. As his mind came back to the present, he began writing his missive to Addie. Nearing the end of his letter, he became aware of the small table-top radio in the room announcing the next program: a weekly chat with the First Lady of the United States, Eleanor Roosevelt. Gus enjoyed listening to the First Lady's radio broadcasts. Her voice made him feel at home, as if he were there sitting by a cozy fire. He turned up the volume and lay back on his bed. She began:

> *Good evening. This evening's chat will be brief. The importance of what I have to say comes with the heartfelt endorsement of President Roosevelt. This morning, the President's advisor, Harry Hopkins, together with Secretary of the Navy, Frank Knotts, met with the President in the Oval Office to inform him that an attack by the Japanese Empire on the American naval base at Pearl Harbor has been perpetrated with devastating results. It happened at 8 a.m. Honolulu time. The President has spoken to our commanders of the Seventh Fleet in Hawaii, who have confirmed to him what I am about to confirm to you. The final blow has fallen, and we have been attacked. Please, stay by your radios. The President will address the nation tomorrow morning. For now, I ask for your prayers ... for our President and for our nation. May God bless America. Thank you, and good evening.*

Stunned and unable to move, Gus sat motionless on the end of his bed. He felt vulnerable and alone. Fear turned his thoughts to his family and to Addie. Thoughts of school fled from him. He needed to see Addie … but how? *Maybe I'll quit school,* he thought. *No, that would only complicate things further.* He decided to finish Addie's letter with a post script and then write to his parents.

> *P.S. Addie, I was getting this ready to mail when Eleanor Roosevelt started her weekly chat. I'm sure you know by now that we are at war. I don't know what to do. My plans seem unimportant now. I need so very much to hold you in my arms. Together, you and I can handle anything. I hope you know that you are my life.*
>
> *I'm going to stay put until I have a chance to talk to you and my parents. I promise that I won't make a decision without talking to you first.*
>
> *Forever—with love, Gus*

The letter he wrote to Addie that evening, the seventh of December, accompanied a heartfelt letter to his parents. Within eight days he had received a reply from both of them. Addie's letter was everything that he hoped and even more than he dreamed possible. She wrote of her deep love for him and her commitment to their future together … whatever that future held in store for them.

At his father's insistence, Gus decided to complete the school year. For now, the wisest thing would be to continue with their plans for his education. They would talk about his future during the summer break. After some careful consideration, his dad decided to set up a savings account in Gus' name and deposited in it the substantial amount of $6,750 as an early inheritance. When he replied to his son's letter, he included the savings account passbook in the same envelope.

… *Son, I thought it prudent to give you your inheritance now in anticipation of difficult times ahead for our family and for the country. I only ask that you be frugal. With the remaining money you have in the trust fund for your education, you should be able to finish your undergraduate schooling. Additionally, your grandfather has left you his gold pocket watch, and $300 in cash. Your mother and I, and your little sis, look forward to seeing you in May.*

All our love, Dad

MAY 1942

So it was, that Gus left Stanford for home at the end of his junior year. He knew he would not be returning.

His parents expected him home during the summer break. It would be a joyous reunion, but happy as the occasion would be, it was Addie that filled his thoughts. The letters had been wonderful, but the thrill of seeing her would be indescribable!

Still a two-day drive from Provo, Utah, 21-year-old Gus Bodine's 221 cubic inch Ford Flathead V8 cruised effortlessly along Highway 91 out of Carson City, Nevada, toward Ely—a 320 mi drive. He tanked up in Carson City and filled two five-gallon cans of fuel to store in the trunk. A paper bag full of sandwiches, a full canteen, a sleeping bag, and a first aid kit would see him all the way home. He had withdrawn the remaining tuition money and living expenses from his savings account, and his grandfather's timepiece occupied the zippered pocket of the windbreaker he wore. Packed in his suitcase was a letter from Spartan Aircraft Company inviting him to join a select group of young men to be the first students in Spartan's new Aeronautical Engineering Program. He planned to sit down and explain everything to his parents from the time of his first interview with Dr. Day. He was confident … well, at least hopeful … that his parents would be supportive of his decision.

His entire third year in the mechanical engineering program at Stanford was to have been a beginning step toward a postgraduate degree in the new field of aeronautical engineering. He hoped that the new Spartan Aircraft program would put him back on that track, but the daily barrage of war news threatened to overshadow his excitement over the new direction his life was about to take. Spearheaded by the rubber industry, rationing had begun. No new automobile tires would be sold to private citizens until further notice. Sugar was now rationed to one pound per person per month, and many other food items were under the new rationing guidelines. Gasoline was not being rationed, but speculation of it before the end of 1942 ran rampant in every newspaper across the country.

Just outside Ely, Nevada, an exhausted Gus found an inexpensive motor hotel. A bed and shower for four dollars was better than camping out. *Besides, Gus old man, you'll look a lot better to Addie if you're clean shaven and wearing fresh clothes.* He pulled the Ford into the parking lot of Cactus Jack's Inn.

Two weeks prior to leaving California, Gus had written to Addie to inform her that he was on his way home. The three years of separation had been difficult, lonely years for both of them. Many of his regrets paraded through Gus' mind while he drove. He thought of all the pain he had caused for Addie and himself by staying on at Stanford, living in the dorms, and doubling up on summer classes … not making it a priority to see her over the holidays and summer break was a decision he deeply regretted. Despite the crushing load of schoolwork he imposed on himself, his love for her fed a constant ache in his heart. Many times, he would sit down to write to her, but reason held sway over his love, and he would return to his studies. He planned to graduate with his B.S. degree in three years. His love for Addie never faltered, but his letter writing did. Since the new school year started, he sent letters more frequently, but he still feared that he may have caused their relationship to suffer, perhaps even to fade beyond redemption.

Gus couldn't wait to get back to see Addie. His heart had been pounding in his chest at the thought of arriving home for summer break. He checked the time: 9 a.m. *Only two hundred seventy miles to go!*

He had asked his parents to contact Addie, and let her know that he was on his way. He assumed she would be home for her summer break, as well. Gus turned right and drove toward the Russo's house on Cedar Ridge Drive. He had slowed the Ford a block away when he spotted a familiar car parked in front of the house. It looked like her father's green Chevrolet. Another, newer car, was parked in the driveway. He wondered if … maybe she's home! The thought brushed his mind momentarily and caused a flutter of excitement. *Four o'clock, I'm early.* He parked behind the Chevy and waited for the nervousness to subside by taking in a few deep breaths to calm himself. He stepped out of his car and walked toward the Russo's front door. When he heard the faint sound of voices, he hesitated. Summoning all the courage he could muster, he raised his hand to knock on the door … just as it flew open.

"It *is* you!" She held her arms out, hesitantly at first, about to hug him but then dropped her hands to her side, uncertain of how he might respond. She blushed and smiled. "I … I…"

"I know, Addie, me, too." He smiled and stretched his arms out towards her. She fell into his embrace, and they melted into each other's arms.

"Ah hem … Well, now, who do we have here?" Estelle Russo interrupted from the doorway.

Addie whispered to Gus, "I told mom there was a strange car parked in front of the house behind my Chevy."

"Well, don't keep Gus waiting on the porch, Addie. Bring him in so I can give him a big hug."

Not letting go of each other for even a second, Addie and Gus went into the house.

"Well, aren't you a sight for sore eyes, Gus Bodine! I want to hear all about what you've been doing out in California. Dinner will be ready in half an hour as soon as the garlic bread is done." The redolent bouquet of homemade lasagna wafted from the kitchen. "You're invited, so come on in and sit down."

"I'd love to Mrs. Russo, but if I don't check in with mom and dad first, I'll never hear the end of it!"

"Addie, will you walk with me to my car?"

"Oh, yes, I'd love that."

The two of them walked hand-in-hand down the driveway. Addie squeezed his hand, and without looking at him, said in a near whisper,

"I've missed you, Gus. I'm not sure I know quite how to act with us being together so suddenly after such a long time."

"Addie, I've missed you, too. Hey, why don't we pack a picnic lunch and drive up the Alpine Loop tomorrow morning. We can spend the day in the mountains like we used to … remember?" Those outings engraved indelible memories for both of them that would endure a lifetime: hiking the trails above Tibble Fork Reservoir, and picnicking in the grove of quaking aspen trees painted in rivers of gold that filled the mountains with fall colors.

"I'd love to! Those were such happy times! Gus, do you remember the gazebo in Pioneer Park?"

"Do I ever! Our senior prom before graduation … I had been wanting to tell you since the ninth grade that I ..." Gus suddenly found himself at a loss for words. *I should wait. I love her, but does she feel the same?* Feigning a cough to end his sentence, he turned and opened the car door, climbed in and rolled down the window. "How about a movie tonight, Addie? I looked at the marquis at the Paramount on the way over here. *The Maltese Falcon* with Humphrey Bogart is playing. It starts at seven. Can I pick you up at six-thirty?"

"That sounds wonderful. I'll be waiting." Then she did something unexpected. Addie leaned over toward him, reached through the open window, turned his face toward hers, and kissed him. "My dear Gus, in case you may have forgotten, I love you. I never stopped loving you."

Gus sat frozen behind the steering wheel, unable to move. His breath caught in his throat. "I … I love you too, Addie … I have to go, but we can talk more tonight." In the rear view mirror, he could see Addie blow him a kiss. With a grin as broad as the Grand Canyon, he pumped his fist in the air and shouted a resounding, "YES!"

Five minutes later, Gus pulled into the driveway of his parents' home, a two-story colonial. The front door was unlocked. He let himself in, and stepped into the foyer. "Hello! Is anybody home?"

"In the kitchen! Is that my boy?" his mother called out excitedly.

Gus left his suitcase in the foyer and hurried to the kitchen. The savory aroma of roast lamb filled the room.

He walked over to his mom and embraced her in a warm hug. "Yum! Your cooking smells wonderful, mom."

"Oh, my. It's so good to have you home, son."

"Your father is in in the study, and your sister is in her bedroom. Your room is all made up. Why don't you go upstairs? Dinner will be ready in fifteen minutes. Oh, and tell Catherine to come down to help me in the kitchen."

His mother patted his cheek and returned to the task of dinner preparation: roasted lamb, potatoes au gratin, and fresh asparagus sautéed in garlic butter. A loaf of her egg bread, already sliced, was on the table—Gus couldn't resist it. He grabbed a piece and hurried to the stairs. His mother looked at him with a twinkle in her eye. She loved having at least one of her boys back home. A corner of her heart lamented over the absence of Gus' older brother, Russell, who was serving in the Navy.

"Dinner's ready." Anna Bodine didn't have to ask twice. Soon, the four of them sat down to a sumptuous meal. After a few minutes of exchanging the latest news, Gus tapped his water glass with his butter knife. "Pop, mom, I need to tell you something. I'm quitting Stanford, and ..."

"Excuse me?" Gus' father choked, took a sip of water, then fixed his eyes on his son with a stern expression of concern for the boys' mental state. "Uh … leaving school? May we ask why?"

"Please, let me finish. It's the war, Pop. Most of the guys I know are off fighting the Germans or the Japanese. They're doing something other than sitting on their butts in a boring classroom."

Gerry looked across the table at Anna. His wife's expression of desperation and concern stabbed painfully at his heart. "Yes, and most of those young men were facing the draft. Many of them enlisted to have a better shot at getting into the service of their choice. They didn't have the opportunity that you have of getting into one of the best universities in the country and building a decent future for yourself."

Gus wiped his mouth with the linen napkin "I figure I can finish my education AND do my share for the war effort."

"How, may I ask, can you do that if you've dropped out of Stanford?" his father asked in a sharper tone than intended. He had always maintained that a solid education was the very foundation of success.

"Pop, a wise man once said, 'A man can never know the cost of patriotism until he has worn the armor of God in defense of his family, his religion, his liberty, and his country.'"

Gus' mother had said nothing since they sat down to dinner, but now she found it necessary to mention the concern weighing most heavily on her mind. "We know that, son, but the price may be too much to pay for those, like us, who are waiting behind the lines for their sons to return."

Gus saw the discussion heading in the wrong direction. He waved his hand in the air, looking like he was back in the classroom in the fifth-grade volunteering to answer an important question.

"Wait, wait, wait! We're getting way ahead of ourselves here. I'm not enlisting in the Armed Forces—at least not yet. My academic advisor at Stanford has recommended me for a new degree program in aeronautical engineering. A Mr. J Paul Getty is beginning the program near Tulsa, Oklahoma, to support the development and sales of a new line of airplanes he wants his company, Spartan Aircraft, to build. Here, I have my letter of acceptance from Spartan." He handed the document to his father.

Gus' father read the letter and handed it to his wife. As she read the document, the earlier countenance of concern disappeared from her face, her brow softened, and her perennial smile began to return. She handed the official letter of acceptance back to Gus.

"Well, son, if your mind is made up, your mother and I give you our blessing with one caveat: you must promise us that you will complete your degree at Spartan before you make any decisions that will put you at risk. I assume you know what I'm talking about."

"Yes, sir. I understand. Thank you, pop." He looked at his mother and smiled. "Thank you, mom." The lamb and potatoes had cooled a bit, but they tasted wonderful.

The Paramount Theater on Center Street in Provo was the finest of the four theaters in the city. The Uintah and the Strand, also on Center

Street, and the Academy on University Avenue were filled to capacity every Friday and Saturday night. When the war came along, that changed. Attendance dropped off. The Strand closed its doors.

As Gus and Addie arrived, the Movietone newsreel had already begun with the latest war news. Gus' thoughts centered on his brother. *Oh, Lord. Please keep Russell safe.*

The Maltese Falcon, starring Humphrey Bogart and Peter Lorre, had been playing at the Paramount for almost two weeks. The theater was only about twenty percent full offering Gus and Addie their choice of seats. They climbed to the top of the steps and sat in the center of the back row. The movie theater provided a discrete opportunity to be alone together and whisper quietly. The customers nearest to them sat four rows down at the end of the aisle.

After the news featuring the latest events of the war, a Disney cartoon starring Donald Duck in "Tire Trouble" occupied the screen. Then, the main feature began.

Gus and Addie shared a large bag of popcorn. Two bottles of soda and a package of M&Ms rounded out the treats. All were eaten in the first 20 minutes. Neither Gus nor Addie paid any attention to the movie.

"I thought we could talk here without disturbing other people," Gus whispered, "but that usher keeps walking up and down the aisles with his flashlight looking like he thinks he's a police officer or something. Do you want to get out of here?" Gus asked.

Addie's smile suggested she shared his concern. "Absolutely. I know the perfect place." They left the theater holding hands. To Gus it was like being back in high school.

Pioneer Park held special memories for both of them.

"Addie, do you remember asking me to pick you up and carry you over to the gazebo the night of our junior prom … just like we did in seventh grade at our very first dance?"

"Can I tell you a secret, Gus?" Addie squeezed his hand and looked up into his eyes. "I come down here quite often. I like to sit in the gazebo and think back to that very night. You held me in your arms, and I wrapped my arms around your neck. It felt like my heart might burst with my love for you. I remember thinking that I want to be with you forever, not only in this world but in whatever is to come. The Lord says we can be together for time and all eternity, and I believe Him." The urgency in her voice reflected the depth of her conviction.

Gus lowered his head. He was ashamed for having caused Addie so much sadness—his heart ached for the healing of their relationship. Addie had poured out her deep love for Gus. He felt as much for her. He wanted to tell her, but decided to show her, instead.

They reached the gazebo and stood at the bottom of the steps leading to the covered platform. Gus put his left arm around Addie's waist, reached his right arm behind her knees, and lifted her just as he did back in their school days. Addie giggled and threw her arms around his neck. They kissed in a long and warm embrace.

"Oh, Gus." Her voice trembled and broke. "I still love you—even more that when we were in school. Do I dare ask if your feelings are the same?"

They reached the platform and Gus gently lowered her to a bench. Strangely, he didn't sit next to her. Instead, he bent low on one knee and reached into his jacket pocket.

"What ...?" she started to say.

"Shhh, Addie. …I'm going to answer your question." He produced a small black velvet box and opened it. Inside was a ¼ carat diamond solitaire set in a gold band. "I've had this with me ever since I started school at Stanford. You asked me if I still feel that you and I should be together forever … Adelle Russo, will you do me the great honor of marrying me?"

Addie's eyes opened wide, and her hands flew to her mouth to soften her screech of joy. She took the box and held it in her lap, gazing down at the engagement ring until her emotions settled down. After a moment, with tears rolling down her rosy cheeks, she looked into Gus' eyes and smiled. "Yes! Yes, I will marry you. Oh, Gus!" She threw her arms around his neck and accidentally released the ring box which flew over the railing and into the thick grass.

"Uh, oh," Gus exclaimed. They both scurried down the steps of the gazebo and started looking through the freshly mowed grass for the ring and the box. They found the box but endured a feeling of panic when they saw that it was empty. They crawled around on the grass like a pair of grazing farm animals, noses to the ground looking for the engagement ring.

"I found it! I found it!" Addie cried out. "Whew! Would you hurry and put it on my finger, Gus?"

Gus and Addie lay back on the grass. "I thought I might have to go buy another ring and propose all over again." Gus sighed with relief.

"Oh no you wouldn't. I don't care if I had to search until morning. I might have even called the Provo City Police to help me find it. This is *my ring*," she said with a pouty, coquettish smile."

They walked, holding hands, around the perimeter of the park until 10:00 p.m. Addie's father had asked her to be home by 10:30 p.m. She agreed, stressing to her father that she was a grown woman now, but realized that her parents' love and old traditions never grow too old.

Gus pulled up to the curb in front of the Russo's house, stepped out of the car, and walked around to open Addie's door. As they walked up the steps, suddenly the porch light came on.

"It looks like mom and dad are still up. I can't wait to tell them the news. I want you to come in with me, Gus."

"This should be fun." Gus chuckled.

It would be well past midnight before Gus returned to his car. The smile on his face, if anyone was there to see it, would testify to the fact that Addie's parents were very happy.

MAY 24, 1942

Gus arose at 7:30 a.m. He quickly showered and dressed and then headed downstairs to the kitchen. His mother was busily bouncing from cabinets to stove to the dining room table, all the while humming a pleasant tune as breakfast was carefully cooked and assembled. The small kitchen table seated four, but with Gus home, his mother set the dining room table and used their best china and linens.

"Good morning mom. What's put you in such a happy mood?" Gus pulled a chair out from the table and sat down. He helped himself to a glass of orange juice and a slice of toast which received a generous lathering of butter and strawberry preserves.

"Oh, nothing in particular. It's just nice to have one of my sons home to cook for. By the way, how did your 'date' go last night?"

"Nice. ...Great, as a matter of fact. Uh … mom, when do you think dad and Catherine will come down to breakfast? I have something to tell you all, something I hope will put you into an even more cheerful mood." Gus laughed nervously.

"My, my, what's all this? … And eating in the dining room?" Gus' dad sat down at the end of the table and released a hearty chuckle. "Are we expecting royalty?"

"This is a special breakfast. Gus is home, and he has something to tell us. But, not to worry, he assured me that it would put me in an even better mood than I am at this moment. Mind you, I don't know for a certainty what that news might be, but if it brings happiness to this table, I'm all for it." Anna Bodine brought in platters of scrambled eggs, link sausages, and blueberry French toast with hot blueberry syrup. Orange juice and milk served in crystal pitchers rounded out the sumptuous fare.

"Catherine, will you please offer a blessing on the food?" Dad Bodine asked.

After Gus' sister thanked the Lord and asked him to bless the food, everybody filled their plates. When the clattering noises of glass and china abated, Gus tapped his orange juice glass with his fork.

"All right, everyone. You all get one chance to guess what I'm about to tell you. Let's begin with Cathy."

"Let me think. ...Could it be? ...Hmmm, yes, I think I have it." Catherine stroked her chin as though she were an aged professor emeritus from Harvard. "… They threw you out of Stanford."

Everyone at the table burst out in laughter. Next Gerry Bodine took his turn. He cleared his throat as if addressing a group of assembled businessmen. "You're broke, and you've decided to move back home." Once more laughter filled the room.

Gus held a straight face, and with a deadpan expression worthy of the best straight man in the comedy business, he shook his head. "Not quite, father. Not at the present time, at any rate. Okay, mom. It's your turn."

Anna Bodine rose from her chair and walked gracefully three paces to Gus' chair and placed both hands on her son's shoulders. "It is my pleasure to announce the engagement of our son to Miss Adelle Russo. Last night, somewhere between ten and eleven, the proposal was made on the stage of the gazebo in Pioneer Park."

Now, it was Gus' turn to be taken by surprise. Everyone arose from their chairs and applauded. "How? ...When? ...Who told you, mom?"

"This morning, before you came down to breakfast, Addie's mother called to tell me about it. I could hardly keep from shouting out in excitement. She gave me *all* the details. I hung up when I heard you coming downstairs. Now you know why I was so happy when you walked into the kitchen. Congratulations, my darling boy."

Bear Lake lies along a portion of the border between Utah and Idaho, surrounded by scenic mountains. During the early spring of 1942, the area displayed some of the most beautiful pristine scenery that can be found anywhere among the towering Rocky Mountains. The lake can be reached by driving from Logan, Utah, northeast up Sardine Canyon toward Montpelier, Idaho. Of course, Gus and Addie didn't want to drive all the way to Montpelier, so Gus slowed the car as the vista of Bear Lake open to their view. When he found the trailhead that they had hiked along during the summer following their junior year of high school, he pulled off the side of the road as far as he could.

"This is the place, Addie. I'll get the things out of the trunk." Gus retrieved the hammock and the canvas bag containing nails and a hammer. Addie followed close behind carrying a large picnic basket.

They walked about 40 yards off the trail and found what they were looking for: a grove of aspen trees adorned with new silver dollar-sized light green leaves.

"I think these two aspen trees will do fine, Addie." Five minutes later Gus joined Addie on the blanket she had spread out. They opened the picnic basket containing ground ham sandwiches, a bowl of potato salad, two bottles of Coca-Cola, and two slices of Mrs. Russo's chocolate cake.

"This is wonderful, Gus. Everything is exactly as I remembered. Isn't the lake beautiful?" Addie smiled and lay back on the blanket. Gus decided to climb into the hammock.

"Come on, Addie, climb up here."

Addie reached across Gus' chest and swung herself up. Fortunately for her, Addie was wearing trousers. He held her as she lifted first one leg then the other off the ground. The effort set the hammock swinging with the two of them comfortably suspended two feet off the ground.

Addie lay with her head on Gus' chest. "I can hear your heart, Gus, strong and regular like a ticking clock. It's so reassuring and peaceful."

"And I love holding you in my arms and feeling your breath on my neck, Addie. I was afraid that I ruined everything by putting my schoolwork and flying lessons ahead of what I love most ... you!" Gus spoke softly as he expressed his deepest feelings to her and of his commitment to their future together. They talked about their education, and they both agreed that it was important for them to finish their bachelor's degree programs. They would need that to provide a good life and security for themselves and for their future children. Gus told her about his plans to attend the new aeronautical school at Spartan Aviation near Tulsa.

Addie lifted her head and looked at Gus. "Okay, but we still haven't talked about the elephant in the forest." Addie giggled at her play on the old saying about avoiding talking about difficult issues—they were not in a room, but the elephant's presence was definitely felt.

"You mean the war? ... That's part of the reason why I want to finish my degree program at Spartan. If I maintain a full schedule of classes I won't be drafted. That said, if the war is not over in another year, I may get drafted when I finish school. We, you and I, are going to have some hard decisions to make if and when that happens. But, please, I would rather talk about something much more fun than going to war."

Gus brushed Addie's raven black hair from her brow revealing her dazzling emerald-green eyes with a hint of light blue shining through. They swung in the hammock, powered by a gentle cool breeze, and talked for another hour. They discussed the timing of fitting a wedding into their busy schedule and agreed they would wait to get married until after they both graduated with their degrees. Gus felt that holding off getting married was the right decision. It would please both his mother and father who were already burdened by concerns about Russell being in the Navy. Gus' older brother was safe for now, but his letters home frequently spoke of deployment into a war zone.

America's Seventh Fleet, which had been decimated by the Japanese attack the previous December, was working nonstop with civilian ship builders to replenish the 21 ships that the Japanese sunk or critically damaged by the attack. Included among those ships were the battleships USS Utah, USS Arizona, and the USS Oklahoma. Russell felt that as soon the Navy was ready to go to war, he would be going with them. The Doolittle raid on the Japanese home islands by 18 of the B-25 Mitchell medium bombers, which took off from the carrier USS Hornet the previous April, was the United States' answer to the Pearl Harbor attack. Only moderate damage was done, but it was a wake-up call to the Japanese Imperial Navy, and their air and ground forces. The sleeping tiger of America's military might had awakened and was ready for a fight.

Gus and Addie spent nearly every day together. On Sundays they feasted on the calming and reassuring words of the Lord's gospel. The members of their church, at home and abroad, had been instructed that, "Hate can have no place in the souls of the righteous. ...If in the course of combat, servicemen shall take the lives of those who fight against them, that will not make of them murderers, nor subject them to the penalty that God has prescribed for those who kill ... for it would be a cruel God that would punish his children as moral sinners for acts done by them as the innocent instrumentalities of a sovereign whom He had told them to obey and whose will they were powerless to resist." Those words reassured Gus that service to one's country in time of war is a righteous act of one's duty to God and nation. It is a commitment to the highest ideals of patriotism. Gus believed that there is no place for cruelty, hate, and murder during a time of war; such thoughts must always be kept out of one's heart even during battle.

June gave way to July and before they knew it the Fourth of July parade down Center Street ushered in the annual Independence Day celebration that filled the whole valley with celebratory glee. Gus and Addie attended a rodeo at the Utah County Fairgrounds following the hour-long parade of a variety of floats, high school bands, baton twirlers, Uncle Sam walking along on stilts, and convertibles of pageant queens waiving to their loyal subjects lining the streets. It was a delightful day of laughter and happiness. Hard times and war were forgotten … for a while.

July came to an end with another celebration. The annual "Pioneer Days" was a repeat of the Fourth of July festivities. Truth be told, the celebrating never really stopped. Most of the month of July came loaded with baseball games (Reams Market won the little league championship that year), and there was the annual Elks Purple Day where families of members of the Benevolent Protective Order of the Elks got together in Pioneer Park with sack races, three-legged races, a Ferris wheel, the penny arcade, cotton candy, hot dogs; plus all manner of activities and food to upset the most resilient stomachs. Gus remembered those events with a nostalgic twinge in his heart. He was proud of his Provo heritage: he grew up here, he went through school here, he hiked the Wasatch Mountains, and fished at Lost Creek in the Uintas.

"I have missed this." Gus said quietly. They sat in the porch swing on the back deck of the Russo house.

Addie squeezed Gus' hand. "*What* do you miss, Gus?"

"All of it. I miss everything about the last three weeks with the parades and fireworks and all the festivities. Where else in the world can you find such a celebration of heritage and freedom? We're truly living the greatest experiment a nation can devise, a government based on freedom: the agency to choose our own destiny as a country and as individuals." Gus shook his head vigorously and smiled over at Addie. "Wow! Not sure where all that come from. …What do you say we go grab a movie?"

"Oh, yes! Do you remember the Saturday matinees at the Academy theater? We used to walk to the Zesto ice cream shop after the movie. Either your parents or mine would take us downtown and then pick us up later at the drive-in. Then, finally, when you got your driver's license, your dad would let you borrow the car. That's when dating you became the most fun!"

"Yes, as long as I didn't wreck the car or get a speeding ticket. Dad always said, 'Son, this is our family's car. I depend on it to take me to work which keeps a roof over our head and puts food on the table. If you get so much as a parking ticket or put a dent in a door, your driving privileges will disappear.'" Gus did a pretty fair job of mimicking his father's voice, and he and Addie laughed at his performance. "Thank heaven they let me have the Ford to fix up later that summer."

"Oh, Gus. Will we ever be that happy again? … Wait! … What am I saying?" Addie grinned and laughed. "I am happier *now* than I have ever been in my life!" They snuggled together and swung lazily for a few more minutes until it was time to leave for the matinee.

The night before he headed out for Oklahoma, Gus and Addie discussed their plans for after the coming year of separation. Addie would be done with her bachelor's degree in teaching, and Gus would have his B.S. degree in Aeronautical Engineering *and* a pilot's license. Gus told Addie about Fred Wick and Bay City Air, and of flying the old Stearman, and how he had been forced to land on Pete and Phyllis Belanger's farm when the engine failed. When Gus described the power-out glide and landing, Addie's eyes grew wide with fear as if she had been in the cockpit with him.

"Stop!" she exclaimed – holding up her hand in reflex to her emotions. "Oh, Gussy, that must have been so frightening. Is that sort of thing going to be a part of our life together?"

"No, of course not. I was never in any real danger up there," Gus reassured her. "Flying is actually safer than driving on the highway."

"And you tell me that just as you're about to drive to Oklahoma!"

They both had a good laugh at the irony.

But now, they needed to talk about "the elephant in the forest," as Addie had put it—the war. Gus felt certain, well *fairly* certain, that he would be exempt from the draft if he was working on the development of new military airplanes for Spartan. Addie had her own concerns, of course, but she decided not to voice them to Gus.. She wanted to send him on his way comforted and supported by the knowledge of her deep and unbounded love for him. They promised to write often and committed to at least one or more letters per week. "I like the more part," she said. Gus agreed and upped the ante to twice-weekly letters.

Monday morning, the last day of August, Gus had his car packed and was ready to leave for Tulsa. The 1170 miles would mean putting in two grueling days of driving. He planned to sleep in his car, or at worst he could find a soft patch of grass to sleep on. So it was that it 6:50 a.m., he said "so long" to his family.

After a tearful goodbye the night before and a fitful night's sleep, Gus' fiancée was sitting on her bed writing her first letter of this school year to him. She paused only to wipe away her tears and blow her nose. Weeping and nose-blowing would happen more often than she would like and for different reasons until … and if … the love of her life returned in one year.

CHAPTER 4

AUGUST 31, 1942 / ROAD TRIP

Gus figured he could make the 230 miles to Grand Junction on a tank of gas. His '36 Ford Model 68 Coupe was equipped with a 14-gal tank and drank a stingy one gallon of gasoline for every 17 mi traveled. He carried with him an extra five gallons in a gas can as a hedge against running empty out on the prairie before he could find a gas station. The little "3-window coupe" drove south out of Provo on US 89 until he reached the intersection with US 6/50 just a few miles down the road at the mouth of Spanish Fork Canyon. The winding canyon roads paralleled the railroad tracks that shuttled trainloads of coal out of the canyon to provide heat for Utah's homes and industries. He drove past small coal-mining communities with names like Castle Gate, Spring Glen, Price, and Wellington. US 6/50 took him southeast in the direction of Grand Junction.

Nearing the town limits, he passed state highway signs reading: "Grand Junction 5," and "Slow to 40." He turned off the highway and drove down Main Street looking for a likely place to stop. Needing fuel and food, Gus spotted a gasoline station about two blocks further on the right. He pulled in and stopped next to the pump. To his surprise, a young woman walked out of the garage dressed in work coveralls with

"Sam's Sinclair" stitched across the back. "Jenna" was the name sewn above her left breast pocket. She appeared to be in her twenties. Her hair was done up and tucked underneath a work hat, but there was enough of it showing for Gus to see it was the color of ebony. Blue-green eyes shone from beneath her neatly groomed eyebrows as she smiled broadly at him. Gus imagined for a brief moment that the woman was Addie. …The trick of his mind left him longing for his love back home.

"Hi there. What can I do for you?" She spoke in a lyrical soprano voice which fell pleasantly on Gus' ears.

"Fill it up, please, and check the water and oil levels. They should be fine, but I have about nine hundred miles to drive, and I don't want any surprises." He nodded toward a building across the street. "The café across the street … how's their food? I'd like to grab a bite while I'm here." Then, giving way to his curiosity, he added, "I'm surprised to see a young, attractive woman doing grease monkey work."

Jenna showed her disapproval of the question with a slight downturn of her brow.

"I'm sorry. I didn't mean to offend you. I guess I wasn't expecting to see ..."

"...A woman doing a man's work. Right? I'm also the chief mechanic and part owner. My husband, Sam, inherited the place from his grandfather. He's off fighting the war in Europe in the One Hundred First Airborne. We don't have any kids, so the draft got him. Most of the men around here between eighteen and thirty are doing the same thing." Jenna paused, then changed the subject. Pointing down the street toward the diner, she continued, "The food is wonderful. Shirley's a friend of mine. She'll treat you fine. You want to try her banana cream pie. Go ahead. I'll park your car when I'm done. It'll be waiting for you."

Forty minutes later, Gus left Shirley's diner and walked across the street. His car was parked off to the side of the garage. He opened the glass paneled front door of the gas station and walked over to the counter. Jenna entered through the side door to the garage where she had been working on a '39 Chrysler four-door sedan.

Gus turned to look at her. His earlier comment caused a flush of embarrassment to color his cheeks, and he needed to apologize.

"Miss … um …"

"'Jenna' will do. That'll be three bucks: two sixty for the gas and forty cents for popping the hood. Oil and water are fine, so is the brake fluid, though your brakes are little slushy. You might want to check those shoes. They'll get you to where you're going, but if you start hearing them squeal, you'll need to change them out pronto."

"Jenna, I need to apologize for earlier. You caught me by surprise. I guess a lot of the work that men did before the war is being done now by wives, daughters—wherever women can be found—who answer the call with service like yours. It's a different world than it was a year ago, isn't It?"

Jenna's lips turned up in a half-smile. "I guess it is. …Be safe," she said over her shoulder as she returned to the garage. Then, unexpectedly, she turned back to Gus. "Don't drive tired, now, ya hear?"

Gus waved back at her. "I won't."

From Grand Junction he headed northeast to Pueblo on US 50 via Montrose and then through the Gunnison National Forest to Cañon City.

Gus had been driving for over 12 hrs covering 515 mi. After filling up in Pueblo, he decided to drive on for a couple more hours. First, though, he needed to call Addie. He was alone and driving ever farther from her. He thought of Jenna back in Grand Junction. Her husband was half-a-world away fighting. He admired what she was doing at Sam's Sinclair, but the thought made him lonely … he missed Addie terribly.

He walked into the lobby of the Hotel Vail and was greeted by a uniformed concierge attired in a wine-colored suit with black satin stripes (on the legs and sleeve cuffs), white shirt and black tie.

"Good evening, sir. Are we checking in?"

"No, sir. I'm driving through. May I use one of your house telephones?" Gus asked politely.

The concierge let his eyes scan Gus from head to toe. He pursed his lips in an expression bordering on disgust. "I am so sorry, but the house telephones are for hotel patrons only. There is a perfectly lovely motor hotel on the south end of town," he said as he skillfully walked Gus to the door.

Not wanting to force the issue, Gus thanked the man and left. After all, he wasn't dressed in a suit and tie … only blue jeans, a plaid Pendleton western-cut shirt and his red Stanford ball cap.

He found the right place. The "Belmont Motor Lodge" was newer, albeit a spartan appearing facility. Spread out on one level, the Belmont provided 60 rooms for weary travelers desiring a shower and a bed. *No room service and no snooty concierge here.* Gus smiled at the thought.

The desk clerk was an elderly man. The weathered face and greying hair suggested he might be more comfortable running a farm than herding carloads of families around the lodge. Gus put him at early-to-mid sixties.

"Hello there, young man. Looking to stay with us for a day or two?" the old gentleman asked.

"No, I'm on my way to Tulsa. I wonder if I might use your telephone to place a call to my fiancée in Utah. I will reverse the charges, of course." Gus hoped for a better response than he got from the Hotel Vail concierge.

"Sure thing, to your left, down that short hallway. There are two telephone booths. Help yourself. You need some change?"

Gus traded a crumpled dollar bill for two quarters and five dimes before sliding into the first narrow phone booth. He dropped a dime into the slot and was rewarded with an audible "ding" and a dial tone. He put his finger into the "0" in the rotary dial and spun it to the stop.

"Operator."

"Long distance, please," Gus directed. There was another brief pause.

"Long distance operator. What city and state are you calling, please?"

"Provo, Utah. Academy seven-zero-two-two."

"Thank you. One moment, p-l-e-e-z-z," the operator replied. Gus heard a couple more "clicks" followed by the sound of a telephone ringing.

"Hello," answered Addie's sweet voice.

"Addie? It's me, Gus."

"Gus? Oh! I was hoping you might call. Where are you calling from, darling?"

"Pueblo, Colorado. I needed to talk to you, Addie. I had to hear your voice. The more I drive the more my heart aches to be with you. I *really* miss you." Then, Gus lowered his voice and spoke softly the words his heart alone could not constrain. "I love you more than I can describe, sweetheart. I keep thinking about the night at the gazebo, asking you to marry me and then *almost* losing the engagement ring, and the next morning at breakfast when I told my family that we got engaged. ...Well, I have never seen my parents so happy!"

"Gussy, I miss you too. You need to write to me as soon as you get settled so I'll have your address. I already started my first letter to you. I'm so happy we're engaged. We're not married yet, but I don't think I could feel more bonded to you that I am now.

"...Please deposit twenty-five cents for another three minutes," the operator interrupted.

"Addie, I have to hang up. I'll call you from Tulsa in a couple of days. I love you darling. Bye."

HIGHWAY

With his heart calmed, Gus returned to the car and drove out to the main highway. Turning left, he took US 50 east toward the Kansas state line. The drive became much smoother and faster now. The highway stretched out in front of him and disappeared into the night as Gus descended down the east slope of the Rocky Mountains and into the beginnings of the Great Plains. He was cruising at about sixty miles per hour with the setting sun behind him, but there was enough daylight remaining to see a couple of miles ahead. When he snapped on his headlights, the beams revealed a dark image of what appeared to be some sort of animal lumbering down the road in his lane. "What the ...," he said out loud as he slowed the car. He eased up behind the animal which looked to be suffering, with his head hanging low, walking unsteadily and at a slow pace.

"My gosh, it's a dog!" Gus stopped the car and put the transmission in neutral. He pulled the handle on the parking brake and reached behind him to fetch a canteen of water and a ham sandwich (one of the two that he bought at a diner in Pueblo). He eased out of the driver-side door, and while whistling a happy tune, worked his way around to the front and sat on the edge of the bumper.

"Come here, boy. I'm not going to hurt you. Look here, I have food and water for you." Gus whistled softly again. The dog's tail began to wave back and forth, and he emitted a soft "whuff." Gus took a chance and rose to his feet. The dog didn't run away, so Gus took a couple of tentative steps forward. When the dog was only about ten feet away, Gus lowered himself to his knees, opened the wrapper, and then placed the sandwich and wrapper on the ground in front of him. "Come on. It's all right. Come on, boy."

The scent of the sandwich was too much to resist. Deciding Gus was harmless, the scraggly animal moved toward the stranger who had removed the cap of his canteen and poured some of the water into his cupped hand. The dog moved forward faster and began lapping at the water. Gus poured more, and the dog drank it as well. Licking his jowls, the dog turned and attacked the sandwich.

"What am I going to do with you, fella?" Gus said while checking over the dog for any sign of identification. "No collar ... hmmm. Your coat is all matted. You've been out here for a long time, haven't you?" Gus examined the dog thoroughly, noting, despite the volume of matted fur, the poor thing's ribs practically poked through his skin.

"All right. This is what we're going to do. I'm going to camp here for the night. If you're still here in the morning I'll take you into La Junta. Maybe, we can find out if someone's looking for you."

Gus spotted a nearby dirt side-road and drove over behind a rocky knoll. He gathered some wood and put together a serviceable fire pit. By the light of the fire, he set up his pup tent and laid out his sleeping bag. It was after 11 p.m. when he stretched out on the sleeping bag. His new "friend" didn't have to be invited. The highway dog waited for Gus to lie down and then strolled up next to his rescuer, laid his head across Gus' chest, and closed his eyes.

Gus slept through the night. At daybreak, he opened his eyes. The dog was gone. Gus began to stir and was about to roll over and get up, but he froze instantly. A rattlesnake was coiled on his chest—staring directly at him. Unable to move, Gus' heart rate accelerated, and his breath was locked in his chest. At that moment, the highway dog poked his head into the pup tent, flattened his ears, and a deep rumbling growl emanated from his throat. The dog slowly and stealthily eased his way forward never taking his eyes off the snake. With his upper lip curled into a snarl, the big unkempt mutt was geared up for battle. Hearing the sound of impending danger, the snake whirled around, coiled its body and prepared to strike. Occupied by focusing its attention on the dog, the snake didn't sense the movement of a human's hand. In a single, smooth motion Gus' right fist locked around the snake's body behind its head. He scrambled out of the tent and threw the snake as far as he could. With the threat now gone, the dog's ears relaxed and his tail began a happy swing. Gus lowered himself to his knees and wrapped his arms around the dog.

"You saved my life, highway dog." He wrapped his arms around the haggard mutt and was rewarded with much tail-wagging and face-licking.

Gus packed up the car. He opened the passenger side door, and the highway dog jumped in as though he had done it a hundred times before. US 50 took them east toward La Junta, Colorado. He figured he had a 150 miles remaining in his gas tank, but thought it wise to fill up anyway and buy some food items for himself and the highway dog. That, plus he wanted to give the dog a thorough bath.

He had been thinking of the animal. He was glad to have something other than his loneliness to occupy his mind. "I've got to find something else to call you besides 'highway dog.' Let me think ... got it. You have the red coat of a golden retriever, but your face is almost black like you're wearing a mask, and there's a slightly darker saddle of red around your body. How about 'Bandit'?" The highway dog lowered his chin to the ground and looked up at Gus with sad, soulful eyes. "No? Hmmm, what, then?"

After thinking about it for another minute or so, Gus threw up his arms in resignation. "Well, then, I guess 'Highway' will have to do." His bedraggled companion raised his head and started wagging his tail again. "'Highway' it is then."

Gus thumbed through the business section of the telephone directory inside a Mobil Oil service station while the attendant topped off his gas and checked his oil and radiator. The radiator was down a bit, and he topped that off as well. Inside the phone book, Gus found what he was looking for, *Dr. Vernon's Grooming and Veterinary*.

The service station attendant directed Gus to Dr. 'Vern.' "It ain't far. Down two streets and take a right. In about a block you'll see the sign sticking up on a pole in the front yard."

Dr. Vernon's wife answered the doorbell. She was a matronly lady with a ready smile and a most pleasant demeanor. "Come in, come in. Vern keeps his clinic in the small buildout that he attached to the back of the house." Her eyes fell on Highway, and she took an immediate liking to him. "Well, who do we have here? Why, you look like you just walked in off the prairie."

While Dr. Vern checked Highway over for tics and fleas, Gus told the story of how he came upon the dog and how the shaggy stray saved Gus from a nasty snake bite.

"I was meaning to check around for anyone who might be missing their pet dog. You haven't heard of such a person, have you, Doc?"

"Nope. Scuttlebutt travels fast around here; I'd know if a stranger was asking around about a missing dog. By the looks of the poor critter, he's been out there on the prairie more than a few days."

Gus helped with Highway's bath and grooming. When they were done, Highway had changed from a scruffy bedraggled mutt into a beautiful golden retriever-shepherd mix.

Dr. Vern scratched Highway behind his ears. "You never did say where you were headed, Gus."

"I'm driving to Tulsa. I'm going to finish my engineering degree there and go into designing and flying airplanes."

"Looks to me like you have a decision to make. Are you going to take Highway with you, or leave him here? I reckon he could stay with us until I find a decent place for him. That is, if that's what you want."

"No, that's all right. Highway can stay with me if *he* wants to. What do you say, boy? Do you want to come with me?"

Dr. Vern and his wife had a good laugh as they watched Highway bolt out of the room, run over to the front door of the house, and sit staring at the doorknob.

There was no question that Highway's loyalty had become firmly affixed to Gus.

"I guess I've found myself a traveling companion. Thank you, Doc. Thank you both. How much do I owe you?"

"One dollar." The good doctor smiled at Gus. "Oh yes. I almost forgot ... here. The collar and leash are on the house. You have a kind heart, Gus, my boy. I think Highway there knows that. You drive safely, now, young man."

Gus accepted the gift with a heartfelt, "Thank You." He latched the wide leather collar around Highway's neck, checking it to make sure it wasn't too tight and then attached the leash. With Highway sitting beside him, Gus pulled away from "Dr. Vernon's Grooming and Veterinary." He had fully expected to pay at least five dollars for Highway's do-over. He was touched. People were struggling to make ends meet. The nation had been in a depression for almost 15 yrs. Now, the war was causing even more sacrifice. Yet, there were people like Dr. Vern and his wife for whom service and kindness were the best medicine to heal a wounded nation.

DODGE CITY

Four hours after leaving La Junta, the taller buildings of Dodge City, Kansas appeared in the distance. As he drove closer to Dodge, passing cultivated farmland with neat, maintained barns, houses and silos dotting the plains. Gus thought of Fred and his Stearman. "I'll bet a pilot with a little initiative could make a killing out here," he said to no one in particular. Highway acknowledged with a "whuff" and laid his head back down on Gus' lap.

"What do you say, Highway, ready for some food and a little walk around?" With an approving tail-wag from his companion, Gus soon spotted a Mobil Oil sign in front of a small service station. It was one of many such businesses dotting the highways. He pulled the Ford up to the pump and stepped out of the car. He walked around to open Highway's door when the service station attendant walked up behind him.

"Howdy, Mister. Fill 'er up?"

Gus turned around to face the source of the voice. At first, he thought he would be looking into the eyes of a young woman like the one that helped him in Pueblo, but a boy (no more than ten years old) was standing before him.

"Yes, and do you know a place I might grab a bite that wouldn't mind allowing my dog to tag along?"

"Sure do. My grandma runs a diner with my mom on down the road a piece. Tell her Wyatt back at the station recommended it." The boy started the pump and wiped the windows.

"Hey, I own a dog. Her name is Dixie. What's your dog's name?"

"Highway…. Hey, Wyatt, what's the name of the diner?" Gus needed to settle up and find a place to bed down for the night.

"Oh, yeah. I forgot. It's Mattie's Diner." He checked the pump. "That's two dollars and ten cents for the gas, mister."

Gus and Highway drove about another mile. A large sign sporting the name *Mattie's Diner* in red cursive letters on a gold background, and "Rooms for Rent" in smaller black letters across the bottom of the sign, told Gus he had arrived. He pulled onto the gravel driveway and stopped near the door to the diner.

"Come on Highway. I don't know about you, but I could eat a rattlesnake about now." Highway surprised Gus by demonstrating a perfect heal: walking close to Gus and allowing the leash to hang loose. They entered the diner and walked over to one of four booths lining the wall. Across from them and to the left, was an old-west style bar.

A woman, seeming to be in her late thirties, appeared beside the booth with an order pad in her hand.

"Would you like a menu? We have chicken fried steak on special. Coffee is free. We have three kinds of pie and chocolate layer cake, all fresh made today."

"The young boy up at the Mobil station told me to tell you 'Wyatt' sent me here. I assume that's because I brought my dog with me. He said you wouldn't mind. I'll take you up on the chicken fried steak with coffee and a piece of that layer cake. You wouldn't by chance have any 'throw-away' food I can feed my dog here, would you?" Gus asked.

"Wyatt's my boy. And I'll do you one better. Give me a sec." The woman disappeared through a door at the end of the bar and less than a minute later returned with a shiny metal bowl. She filled it three quarters of the way full of Ken-L Ration dog food, and handed two more cans of the popular dog food to Gus.

"The dog food's on the house. I'll need to charge you a buck and a quarter for yours, though."

Gus and Highway ate hungrily and silently … well, less silently in Highway's case. He licked the empty bowl clean as a whistle sending it spinning across the floor toward the bar. Wyatt's mother picked up the bowl and filled it with water, then brought it back over to Gus.

"I thought your dog might like some water to wash down that food. Are you two driving on or planning to stay the night? I got the impression you might be passing through."

"Well, that depends. Highway and I were thinking of setting up camp somewhere between here and Wichita. We are on what you might call a low-budget road trip." Gus chuckled nervously, a trifle embarrassed by his situation.

The kind waitress reached down and scratched Highway behind the ears. His tongue lolled out of his mouth, and his tail increased its rhythmic pendulum swing.

"I'll ask Grandma Mattie to watch the front. Wait here." She returned with a key in her hand. "Follow me. We have a couple rental cabins. You can stay in one of those for the night. Sheets are clean and there's hot water and a shower. Four dollars okay with you?" They stopped at the first cabin. She unlocked the door, and they stepped inside.

Gus removed the leash from Highway's leather collar, and the dog set about inspecting every corner, nook and cranny of the room. Satisfied, he jumped up on the bed and fixed his eyes on Gus as if asking for his approval.

Gus took note of one particular photograph framed in what appeared to be hand sawn barn wood. It was an old photograph of three men and two women standing side-by-side. There was something familiar about one of the men. Gus couldn't quite make the connection.

"Excuse me for asking, but are the people in that photograph related to you in some way? That first fellow on the left seems vaguely familiar somehow."

"You can call me Sarah." The woman took the photograph off the wall and sat on the end of the bed. "The one on the right that you see standing in front of my great-grandfather is his wife, Nellie 'Bessie' Ketchum Earp. Her husband is James Cooksey Earp. Standing next to James in the middle there is Virgil, and on the end is another brother, Wyatt. We named my boy, Wyatt, after his great-great uncle. You have likely seen a picture of Wyatt Earp somewhere - perhaps a library. Mattie is James' granddaughter."

Gus felt like he had been taken back in time. To meet direct descendants of the iconic Earp family right here in Dodge City where Wyatt had once been a deputy marshal was ... an unforgettable moment. He was speechless.

They talked a while about life in Dodge and about Sarah and her son. Her husband, David Masterson, was a Naval reserve officer and full-time farmer, innkeeper, and handyman whose services could be had with a handshake and a smile. The Masterson family was both respected and loved by the residents of Dodge City. David had been called up to active duty and was stationed at Pensacola awaiting assignment with the U.S. Navy's Atlantic Fleet.

Sarah and Gus finished their conversation, and Sarah excused herself. "I reckon I should get back to the diner. Mattie will be needing some help. It was nice to meet you, Gus."

With a hot shower and a full stomach, Gus crawled under the sheets for a well-earned rest. Highway silently crept his way up close to Gus and rested his head on his new master's chest. There they slept until daybreak.

CHAPTER 5

SCHOOL OF AERONAUTICS

Gus and Highway stayed on US 50 south for a few miles until he saw the turn for US 54 which would take him to Wichita, Kansas. From Wichita, Highway 54 turned south into Oklahoma to a town called Liberal and the 54/64 interchange. He checked the roadmap and turned east toward Enid, Oklahoma, stopping only once to fill up the gas tank in Wellington, Kansas and to take Highway for a run in the local park. They continued southeast, generally paralleling the course of the Arkansas River through Cleveland, Manford, and on into Tulsa.

Gus had no trouble finding the airport. Once there, he simply aimed the Ford at the "Spartan Aircraft Company" hangar. Underneath the banner in smaller letters, the words "School of Aeronautics" told him he had arrived.

He entered the hangar with Highway at his side on a loose leash. The structure was large enough to hold three of the company's Spartan 7W Executive aircraft. Gus could not resist walking over to the nearest one and running his fingertips along the leading edge of the all-metal monocoque low-winged design. He released an appreciative whistle.

"Beautiful, isn't she?" A tallish slender man wearing a pair of polished brown loafers, dark brown pressed slacks, and a white open-collar shirt beneath a saddle tan sport jacket approached Gus. "Is there something I can help you with?"

"I hope so. My name is Gus Bodine. I drove here from Stanford University. I have a letter of introduction from my academic advisor at Stanford, Dr. Prescott Day. It's addressed to Dr. C. Franklin Harrison. It's here in my valise." Gus unbuckled the two leather straps which secured the flap, removed the envelope from Dr. Day, and handed it to the man. "I would be grateful if you could direct me to Dr. Harrison's office."

"He's teaching a class right now, but he should be done in about half an hour. His office is right next to mine. Follow me. Bring your dog. There's a small courtyard behind the hangar. It's enclosed, so I think you'll be safe just letting him run around for a few minutes while we talk." They turned toward a red brick one level building beyond the back of the hangar. The man extended his hand. "I should introduce myself. I'm Paul Getty, and I'm pleased to meet you, Mr. Bodine."

Gus had carried his transcripts from Stanford in his valise along with Dr. Day's letter of introduction. He anticipated the need to carry books and other documents as well, but for now it was quite enough to have added to his valise two cans of dog food, a can opener, and a shiny aluminum bowl. He took Highway to the courtyard and opened one can of Ken-L Ration. "Here ya go, Highway." His furry companion started right in on the food. He was a happy dog. Satisfied, Gus returned to Mr. Getty's office.

"Gus, you are one of seventeen candidates who will be attending the College of Aeronautics program here at Spartan in the fall semester starting this coming week. You may be wondering why Spartan is involved in education and training at all, given the company's history of aircraft design, manufacturing, and testing its own livery of airplanes.

"I bought this company from Bill Skelly in 1930 when I saw an opportunity to turn it into a major player in the aviation industry. We are expanding our manufacturing facilities to provide various aircraft and power plant components with their subsystems for the training of Air Force mechanics on such aircraft as the B-24, B-17, the B-29

Superfortress, and Lockheed's P-38 Lightning. We have entered into a contract with the U.S. Army Air Force to provide basic and primary flight instruction to help fill the ranks of qualified pilots and flight mechanics. We are expecting the first group of students as well as a detachment of the Thirty-First Flying Training Wing within the next few weeks. The successful military candidates who complete the program here at Spartan will then go on to Avenger Field in Texas for Advanced Pilot Training. That's the military side of the coin. As a civilian company, Spartan Aircraft is contracting for the aforementioned needs of the military, but our primary mission is to advance our commercial interests in civilian aviation. That's where you come in, Gus.

"There are currently seventeen non-military students including yourself who will form the nucleus of a new innovative team of design engineers here at Spartan. You will be earning your Bachelor of Science degree in Aeronautical Engineering while working and studying with teams including the Air Force pilot and mechanic candidates. When they move on to Advanced Pilot Training before being assigned permanent duty stations overseas, you and the other civilian students will be continuing your classroom studies as part of your employment. I intend to bring Spartan aircraft up to the level of a leading manufacturer of a new line of executive airplanes by developing a world class design team. We will be competing with such giants as Lockheed, Martin, Douglas, and other companies in the industry. It all begins with education and a shared vision. A lot is involved in this venture that we don't have time to discuss here, Gus. So, are you still interested in a career in the design of exciting new airplanes?" Mr. J Paul Getty waited for Gus' response.

Gus' mind was reeling with the information. The ramifications of his decision would, to a large extent, determine his future career. Like most decisions, though, unforeseen consequences can never be removed from the equation.

"Yes. ...Yes, sir. Now I'm even more interested than when I walked in here this afternoon," Gus answered.

"Good. Of course, your school transcripts from Stanford will be reviewed as well as your resume including any experience you might have with the aviation industry. I'm pretty good at reading people though, and I think we'll be seeing a lot of each other over the next year or so."

Gus walked out into the courtyard and Highway was right there. The big mutt rose up on his hind legs and placed his paws on Gus' chest. Gus rolled over in the grass and wrestled with the dog for minute or two, a respite they both enjoyed! Afterward, he filled Highway's bowl with water from a garden hose, then walked back over to the administration building and down the hall to Dr. Harrison's office.

A too tall and far too slender of a man approached Gus. He was carrying an arm full of books and his briefcase. He reached the door and looked at Gus. "Here, hold these while I unlock the door, will you?"

The ungainly looking Dr. Harrison reminded Gus of Ray Bolger, the scarecrow in *The Wizard of Oz* film.

After reading Gus' transcripts and letter of introduction from Stanford, Dr. Harrison took the time to scan the resume and Gus' pilot logbook. Gus sat nervously listening to "hmmm" and "aha" repeated several times. Finally Dr. Harrison removed his glasses and placed the documents on his desk.

"Impressive for an undergraduate. You seem to have grasped a vision of the future of Aeronautical Engineering in the world of aviation in your "Warbirds" paper. Your resume from Bay City Air presents certain possibilities for you. None of our other students have a pilot's license. Earning one is a requirement for the degree program. I'm sure Mr. Getty will be speaking with you further on that subject. He spoke favorably of you. I take it you had a pleasant discussion with him while you were waiting for me, yes?"

"Yes, sir but I still don't quite understand about *my* work here if you accept me. Mr. Getty spoke of a U.S. Army Air Force training detachment."

"There are two separate organizations here. I don't know how much Mr. Getty told you, so, forgive me if some of what I tell you is redundant. Paul Getty bought out Skelly Oil in 1930 and acquired Spartan Aircraft as well as the associated airplane manufacturing facilities previously owned by William Skelly. The war came around, and the Army Air Force called for an aircraft manufacturing facility to build bombers for the war effort. Additionally, the Air Force needed to expand its training facilities to meet the increasing demand for trained pilots and mechanics. Many training facilities around the country were activated at small airports such as Tulsa Municipal. Mr. Getty committed Spartan Aircraft's School of Aeronautics to becoming one of those satellite training facilities for the Army Air Force.

"The city of Tulsa passed a bond initiative for seven hundred and fifty thousand dollars for the contract. The money was used to build two runways. Construction was begun on Plant Three in that long row of what looks like a bunch of hangars put together end to end on the other side of the runways across from the civilian terminal. Douglas Aircraft is assembling B-24s, A-26s, B-29s and parts for a variety of other military aircraft. Spartan Aircraft is still building its line of small executive aircraft on our side of the airport.

"The second organization is an offspring of Mr. Getty's vision of training you young men to become the future designers of Spartan's new executive airplanes. The Spartan School of Aeronautics and the Army Air Force Training Detachment share the Spartan facilities. Their training airplanes will be hangared at Spartan. Their maintenance facilities will be shared by Spartan's students and Air Force enlisted aircraft mechanic candidates.

"We're still expanding by building student housing, additional classroom space, lab facilities, and three new hangars to meet the training needs for both the military and Spartan Aircraft are under construction. Spartan students will have an opportunity to work with the Air Force mechanics on military airplanes such as the P-38 Lightning, the P-40 Warhawks, and military trainers including the PT-17 Stearman, PT-19, BT-9. Those planes are parked on the tarmac on the Plant Three side.

"Come with me for a short drive, and I'll show you where you'll bunk in, that is, if you still want in the program."

Gus answered with a controlled, "Yes, sir. I do," belying his extreme exuberance.

Dr. Harrison drove south past the new art deco civilian terminal and turned into a parking lot behind a row of three two-story buildings. They looked like military barracks, but the *Spartan School of Aeronautics Student Housing* sign painted on the side of the first building told Gus he had arrived at his new home. Dr. Harrison pulled his car into one of the slots and turned off the ignition.

"They don't look like much, but I think you'll be pleased with what you see inside." Dr. Harrison escorted Gus into "Bldg. 1."

"There are six apartments on each level. Each apartment houses two students. A common bathroom facility is shared by two apartments. Your apartment is Number Four." Dr. Harrison pulled a keychain from his pocket and unlocked the door with a black "4" painted on it.

Gus looked around the room. Two single beds, one on each side of the room, were strategically placed next to closets that had been built into the wall. A medium-sized desk with enough drawers for office supplies and books was placed next to each bed.

"We have twenty-seven students on campus at present. We can facilitate nine more. Any number of students beyond that will be placed off-campus. Those students will have to share the cost of housing with Spartan. Of course, anyone is welcome to live off campus if they have the means to pay for their housing. We have contracted for reduced rates with some of our motor hotels for rooms to handle our overflow students. We hope to have additional on-campus housing completed by the end of the first semester.

"I'll take you back to the admin building to collect your car."

"I have my dog with me, too, sir."

"Dog?" Dr. Harrison's eyebrows elevated slightly.

"Yes, sir. He's in the courtyard behind the hangar. Am I allowed to keep him in my room?" Gus asked, hesitantly, fearing that he may have overstepped his boundaries.

"You will need to find a place for him. We don't have kennel facilities here. Keep the dog with you for now, but keep him on a tight leash. We can't have him running freely, now, can we?"

Dr. Harrison left to return to his office, and Gus began transferring his few belongings from the Ford to his room. When he was done, he walked over to the courtyard to collect Highway, and they walked back to student housing together.

Highway was stretched out on a small woven rug on the floor next to the bed in Gus' room. The dog snorted softly and his ears twitched. *He's probably chasing a rabbit in his dreams*, Gus mused.

The drawers in his room were empty except for the one to the left of his chair. There he found a composition pad of lined paper and a fountain pen with the words *Getty Oil* printed in gold on the barrel of the pen. Gus suspected this was Mr. Getty's subtle message that he expected his students to write home. Likewise, it was a subtle reminder to Gus, himself, that he would not repeat the same mistake he made while at Stanford. Now that he had his Tulsa address, he started his first of many letters to Addie.

> *Dear Addie,*
>
> *I'm here at last. It was a crazy long drive. I picked up a new friend on the way. His name is Highway. You may have guessed that it's a stray dog, and you would be right. He saved me from a dangerous snakebite the first night I camped out on the road. He was half-starved and looked like he had been wandering through the desert for several days at least. I got him cleaned up, and he turned out looking quite handsome.*
>
> *I start classes tomorrow, and I expect I'll be busy. I'm ahead of most of the guys with my work, so I'll be spending quite a bit of time flying. Yes, that's right, all the candidates are expected to obtain their pilot's license. I'm really looking forward to it.*
>
> *Mostly, though, my thoughts turn to you … sometimes when I'm not even expecting it. I can be sitting in a diner eating a sandwich or be studying a manual, and a picture of you will fill my mind and cause my heart to leap in my chest for the want of you and the love I have for you. I can't wait to finish my training and come home to you, Addie. I miss you, my love.*
>
> *I need to go now and take Highway out for a walk. The sun is setting and I have to be back at student housing before dark. I'll see you in my dreams. Oh, yes, here's my address:*

Gus Bodine
Spartan Aeronautical School
Bldg.1, Room 4
2771 Apache Way
Tulsa, Oklahoma

Love always and forever,
Gus

Gus never took his eyes off the books through all of September and October of 1942. He immersed himself in his studies, but, initially, he felt more than a little frustrated by the fact that he had already completed most of the syllabus for Unified Engineering back at Stanford. Surprisingly, he found himself learning even more about materials and structures, fluids and aerodynamics, thermodynamics, physics and dynamics, electronic signals, systems, circuits, propulsion, control systems, probability and statistics. Those courses alone constituted the core curriculum under UE and were organized into two 12-unit subjects to be completed over two semesters. During the final semester, students working in teams of four, would apply their undergraduate knowledge to the design of an aircraft. The completed designs would be reviewed by the Spartan Aircraft design engineers and Spartan Aeronautics School faculty.

CHAPTER 6

NOVEMBER 1942 / PROVO, UTAH

We have all experienced those occasions in life that leave behind indelible memories of enduring joy. Just as likely, though, what remains is sadness instead of joy, the heartache of loss instead of a happy reunion with a returned son and brother.

It happened during the dinner hour with Gerry, Anna, and Catherine sitting at the kitchen table for their evening meal. It was an opportunity to share the events of the day, and, whenever the opportunity arose, to read the latest news from Russell His last letter from Pearl Harbor spoke of departing Pearl aboard his ship and advised his family that they may not be hearing from him for the next several weeks or longer. He assured them that all was well, and he was looking forward to his deployment.

Previous letters had mentioned ongoing flight training while he was waiting to be assigned to a ship. At that time his training involved piloting a Grumman F4F Wildcat carrier-based fighter. The assumption was that his deployment aboard a nondescript "ship" meant that he had gone into battle somewhere in the Pacific theater of operations aboard an aircraft carrier. That letter arrived in the mail six weeks earlier.

"The chicken dumplings were delicious, Anna. I don't think I could eat another bite. It's a treat when fresh meat appears in the grocery store these days." Gerry dabbed at his mouth with his napkin.

"I love that you love my cooking, my darling." Anna Bodine kissed her husband on the forehead and patted the bald spot on the crown of his head.

"Daddy, when do you think the war will end? It feels to me like the worst of it is yet to come. You should hear how the other kids at school talk about it. It seems like almost everyone has a brother or a cousin that is fighting either in Europe or in the Pacific. I don't like to hear the rude comments from many of the kids about Germans and Japanese. Yanni Matsuda stopped coming to school after being bullied so much by a few girls. I don't even know if Yanni will be coming back. I just want things to return to normal." Catherine's eyes glistened with tears at the mention of her friend.

"I don't know, sweetheart. I expect things will not be getting back to normal for some time. It's in the Lord's hands."

Just as Anna began to serve a delicious apple crumble dessert, the doorbell rang.

"I'll get it." Gerry said.

Gerry opened the front door, and his heart leapt in his chest. His breath caught in his throat. It took him a moment before he could speak. "Please, come in. ...I think I should call in the rest of my family."

The two United States Navy officers, a lieutenant commander and a lieutenant junior grade removed their white dress caps and took a seat in the living room.

As Gerry Bodine stood huddled together with his wife and daughter, he nodded for the senior officer to begin.

"On behalf of the Secretary of the Navy, we regret to inform you that Lieutenant Junior Grade Russell Theodore Bodine has been reported missing in action. His ship was on station near the Santa Cruz Islands for the purpose of providing ground support to the U.S. Marines on the island of Guadalcanal. Japanese forces, possessing superior numbers and ships, staged a powerful defense. Their purpose was to destroy American forces on the island and to drive back U.S. forces from the region. Marines of the First Division held their ground, and with the brave help of Navy warships and naval aviator's such as Russell, they were able to preserve the airstrip on the island. That airstrip will serve as a primary staging base as our forces continue the difficult task of pushing the Japanese Imperial Navy and air forces back to their own home islands. Russell never returned to his ship.

"We don't know the precise fate of your son, but you will be our first call when we find out. Naval investigators are still gathering information. You are among many—too many—families who have endured similar losses, and the Navy will keep you informed as the situation progresses. We have brought with us a packet of information describing the resources at your disposal to assist your family. We wish to answer your questions at this time, but please forgive us if we cannot provide specific answers which may compromise national security."

They chatted for a few minutes more, but the family soon realized that the officers were strictly limited in what they could say. Neither of them knew Russell personally. In the end the only thing the two Navy officers could say with any degree of sincerity was, "We're very sorry for your loss."

It was agreed that Gus should be told only that Russell had been unaccounted for, and further information was pending. Anna and Gerry would urge Gus to remain in school for the time being ... he was too close to completing his degree. Russell would have wanted that.

A WEEK LATER / TULSA

Every day since the end of the first week following his arrival at the Spartan school of Aeronautical Engineering, Gus would stop by the admin building and walk to the mailroom. On this day, he removed two letters. One from Addie and one from his father. It was the letter from his father that caught his eye and his attention. Most often it was his mother who wrote about the events going on with the family. This was from *Gerry* Bodine, and it struck Gus with an immediate sense of apprehension. He removed the letter from the envelope and began to read.

Son,

I hope this finds you well. Your letters home are much appreciated. We miss you terribly, Gus, but I must say how very proud we are that you're making such remarkable progress. I assume that flying will occupy as much or even more of your time than your studies.

You may be wondering why it is that I am writing to you, and not your mother. It is a very difficult thing for me to have to tell you that Russell has been listed as missing in action. He was flying a mission to defend the Marine Corps First Division on Guadalcanal. Many planes were lost in the battle. Russell's plane never returned to his ship. We are afraid that the worst has happened. Your mother, sister and I maintain hope that he yet is still alive—perhaps as a prisoner of war in the custody of Japanese forces.

Now, my son, I must say to you from the bottom of my heart that your mother and I wish for you to stay where you are. Stand fast in your studies and prepare yourself for the future with your beautiful Addie.

We are all well here, and it is our prayer that you are also. We will keep you informed if the situation changes regarding Russell. Again, please know that your mother and I are very, very proud of you.

On a final note, Gus, it is my strong desire that we will all stand firm as disciples of our Lord Jesus Christ in this time of need. Our prayers are with you, Gus.

Sincerely and with love,

Dad

Gus slowly folded the letter and put it back in the envelope. He stood there, in the mailroom, feeling the impact of his father's words. A painful sense of loss washed over him. He brushed the sleeve of his shirt over his eyes and sighed deeply. Beset with the recurring thought, *SERVE YOUR COUNTRY,* he left the mailroom. He wasn't sure if the thought was just an expression of his sorrow over the loss of his brother, or if it was truly some sort of spiritual message. He was raised in a family whose ideals were rooted in service to God, country, community, and family. Patriotism was a hallmark of that belief system. The fact that the United States was entrenched in a global war did not escape Gus' growing need to do his share—his duty—but he accepted his father's counsel about staying in school. It wouldn't do him, or anyone else, any good at all if he were to quit school and go home in self-pity and defeat.

Oftentimes, staying awake long into the night cramming for exams, studying, writing semester papers, was the only way he could cope with the loss of his brother, although writing to Addie about Russell helped ease his heartache. Truth be known, now Gus had no problem writing at least two letters per week to Addie and one letter per week to his family. He loved reading Addie's letters. He wrote home to tell his parents that he would indeed be staying in school. He had even called them to assure the family that he would stay the course both at school and with his faith.

The long-distance telephone calls to Addie filled him with such complete joy as to cause a perpetual smile on his face. She was the balm that soothed his aching heart and allowed him to find joy once more. One of his classmates, Steve Anderson, even asked the question, "Why do you smile all the time?" Gus answered simply, "Because I'm in love with the woman I plan to spend the rest of eternity with. What's not to smile about?"

The Army Air Force supplied all the airplanes needed for the Thirty-First Training Detachment. Spartan Aviation would provide the instruction for the military candidates under the supervision of the "31st TD." Two P-40 Warhawks, three PT-17 Stearman biplanes, and three BT-9 Monoplane trainers, powered by the 7-cylinder, 250 hp, Wright Whirlwind R-760 radial engine, had been brought in. A year earlier it was the Wright Whirlwind engine that Gus became the most familiar with during the last half of his final semester at Stanford. Of course, the curriculum would not be complete without the students learning to fly the very planes they were studying in the classroom. Gus was an excellent student, and a not-so-surprisingly adept pilot.

The level of flying experience varied from none to 12 hours logged, or, as in Gus' case, 43 hours! Students had to complete the requirement for a civilian pilot's license prior to graduation. Gus already had his license but had not yet received his night-flying and multi-engine certification by the Civil Aeronautics Administration.

The Civilian Pilot Training Program (CPTP) was created in 1938 with the goal of increasing the civilian pilot population in the U.S. at the rate of 20,000 new pilots per year. To meet the demand, colleges and flight schools such as Spartan Aviation were funded by the federal government and overseen by the new National Aviation Training Association, (NATA) to provide the necessary instruction.

Gus presented his pilot logbook to the school's Flight Training Office. The chief pilot, Harold Croxton, reviewed Gus' credentials and determined that a check ride and a cross-country night flight in one of the Army's PT-17s was all that was needed to award him his CPTP endorsement and updated pilot license. His multi-engine training would begin upon completion of the check ride.

Impressed by his accomplishments and his affable personality, Harold offered Gus a job in the Spartan hangar. The time spent with Fred Wick at Bay City Air was paying off—he was the only student that was hired on specifically as a paid employee of Spartan Aircraft. Gus would join the ground crew that kept Spartan's training airplanes ready to fly. Technically, his boss would be J. Paul Getty, and he was pleased that Getty supported Croxton's hiring decision.

Gus was able to acquire enough chain-link fencing and cement to build a dog run abutting Bldg. 1. At dusk he would take Highway for a run around the school's grounds.

September and October passed, and November came with a drop of temperature and late fall colors. The remaining leaves of autumn were fading to brown and a greyish pallor of muted yellow, orange, umber, and red.

One afternoon in early December, Harold Croxton called Gus aside for a quiet chat. He handed Gus an envelope. "Gus, at this time of year, Mr. Getty likes to give his employees a Christmas bonus. I know you've been hoping to go home for Christmas … I hope this will help. Spartan's school is going to close down for the holiday break. The semester ends on Wednesday, December 23."

"Whew! I was afraid that envelope might contain a pink slip. Thank you, Harry. This means a lot."

"No pink slip—you're too valuable to us, son," Harry said with a wide grin. "School starts back up on the fifth of January. I would expect you back in the hangar on the third. I assume you're going home for the break?"

"No, sir. I was thinking about it, but there are too many things working against the idea. Provo is twelve hundred miles from here, and with the "Victory" law that mandates reducing highway speeds to thirty-five miles per hour, I'd spend almost all my time driving."

Gus opened the envelope. Harold clapped a hand firmly on Gus' shoulder. "Quite the opposite of a pink slip, my young friend. You don't know this but Dr. Harrison, Mr. Getty, me, and the Board of Trustees of Spartan Air have met to discuss the future of Spartan in filling the express needs of the Army Air Force, specifically, to provide pilots with Basic Flight Training. Additionally, we need to train civilian pilots and mechanics for the purpose of growing an air-shuttle service for dignitaries to travel to various military installations and flight schools in Oklahoma and Texas. We can provide the planes, but the Army has also asked us and other civilian flight schools to provide the pilots. Air Force pilots are trained and shipped to theaters of war as fast as they can be acquired. That leaves Spartan Aircraft the rather challenging task of identifying and training new pilots for the 7W Executive. Between now and next week, I will be training you myself. You are the most qualified civilian pilot candidate we have. Once trained, you will be on-call to fly for the United States Army Air Force as a civilian contract pilot. Mr. Getty is depending on you to step up, Gus. The size of your bonus check should help you understand not only Mr. Getty's generosity, but the urgency of his request to bring us online ASAP."

"Wow! I'm honored, but that's a lot of information to deal with, Harry. A question, though: what about my schoolwork and my degree? I don't want to miss graduation next spring because I've been flying too much.

"That's where Dr. Harrison comes in. He has been communicating with your Dr. Day at Stanford. On review of your accomplishments there, combined with your outstanding academic performance here at Spartan during your first semester, they feel that your piloting duties can translate into the remaining academic credits needed for graduation. I'm happy to be the one to tell you that your classroom studies are over. Your piloting practicum is just beginning. If all goes well, you'll graduate at the end of May with your class. Are you up for the challenge?"

Gus paused. During a time of global conflict in which the aviation industry is … and would continue to be … a major player that could well mean the difference between victory and defeat, accepting this newest challenge could thrust him into the middle of a world war. He was reminded of Capt. Moroni, the ancient warrior leader of the Nephite nation. His forces were struggling during a major battle with the opposing forces of the Lamanites. To rally his men, he removed his cloak and wrote upon it, "In memory of our God, our religion, and freedom, and our peace, our wives, and our children." Gus felt that he should fight for no lesser cause … his duty now was here. Gus delayed his response, but only for a moment, as he considered the full weight of the challenge awaiting him.

"Yes, I am. When do we start?"

"Is now too soon for you?" Harold Croxton smiled at his newly appointed protégé. I think it's time you started calling me Harry. You're family now, Gus.

Gus offered what he hoped Harry would read as a self-assured grin of acceptance and replied, "I need to feed my dog first."

SAME DAY / EXECUTIVE FIRST FLIGHT

Gus ran his fingers lightly along the leading edge of the glistening aluminum wing. The monocoque design of the 7W Executive and the sweeping curved lines of the design set his imagination into high gear.

"She's a beauty, Harry. The only thing about this aircraft that I'm familiar with is the radial engine, but even that screams power to me. The old Stearman that I trained in back at Bay City Air was powered by a Jacob R-755, a seven cylinder radial engine. That old Stearman didn't need much power to get off the ground. This engine is a Pratt & Whitney Wasp Junior, isn't it?"

Harry smiled at Gus approvingly. "You know your engines, Gus.

You're right about the Wasp Junior. This engine will generate four hundred and fifty horsepower at two hundred twenty-five miles per hour and twelve thousand feet. The Executive is the fastest single engine airplane in existence built for civilian use. Climb in."

With Gus sitting in the left seat, Harry began explaining the instrument panel and the flight controls.

Gus began to feel more relaxed as Harry continued, "Straightforward and visible, a pilot's eyes need only trace a circle from bottom left, up and across to the right, down, and back to acquire an almost instantaneous awareness of the aircraft's air speed, altitude, attitude, direction of flight, and engine parameters: cylinder head temperature, oil pressure and temperature, and RPMs."

The rudder pedals consisted of wide paddles rather than bars of steel. Throttle, mixture, propeller pitch, and elevator trim were mounted on a pedestal to the right of Gus' right hand. With a steerable tail wheel, the 7W Executive was a piece of cake to control on the ground. The cockpit orientation lasted about 30 minutes including answering Gus' flood of questions.

"The next part will test your recall of what you have just learned. I'm going to call out the names of the instruments on the panel. I want you to point to and touch each instrument, switch, or gauge that I mention. Ready?"

One by one, Harry called out each instrument, switch, lever, and knob. Gus responded without hesitation pointing to and touching each item. Harry ran him through the exercise three more times mixing up the order each time.

"Well done, Gus. You're a quick learner. Now comes the fun part: the engine start sequence."

Harry called out each step of the engine start checklist, and Gus started flipping switches, setting controls, and confirming.

"Set the parking brake," said Harry.

"Parking brake is set," replied Gus.

"Confirm fuel capacity."

"Main fuel tank reading eighty percent."

"Master switch ON."

"Master switch is ON."

"Fuel boost ON."

"Fuel boost ON." The fuel boost pump produced a growling sound as it primed the fuel lines with aviation fuel.

"Set throttle of one-quarter inch."

"Throttle is set at one-quarter inch."

"Magneto's ON."

"Both magneto switches are ON."

"Fuel boost OFF."

"Fuel boost is OFF," replied Gus.

"Clear the prop," announced Harry.

Gus opened the small Plexiglas window next to his head and called out in a loud voice, "Clear prop."

At last, Harry called out, "Engine start."

With his left hand, Gus toggled up the engine start switch, and with his right hand he eased the mixture lever up to "full rich."

The propeller began to turn with a whine, and after three rotations, coughed a white blast of smoke and almost died. Gus adjusted the throttle forward and back a couple times. The engine coughed another blast of smoke, and the propeller settled into a smooth rhythm. The sound of the powerful radial engine brought a grin to Gus' face. "She sounds beautiful, ... just beautiful, doesn't she?"

"Indeed, she does. You handle the controls, and I'll handle the radios." Harry tuned to the tower frequency.

Tulsa control, Spartan One Four Four Two is at Spartan Aircraft hangar. Request taxi for straight-out departure. One Four Four Two: Over.

One Four Four Two, you are clear to taxi to runway three-four via taxiway Alpha, Bravo to Bravo One and hold short.

Harry confirmed the taxi instructions.

Gus kicked in left rudder and added a little power, and the Spartan Executive started its taxi roll.

There were no other aircraft in line ahead or behind them, so Harry had Gus pull off into the run-up area and turn the plane around to face the runway. They performed an engine run-up by bringing the radial engine up to 2400 rpm. Harry guided Gus through the run-up protocol: cylinder head temperature, oil pressure, oil temperature, electrical power, adjusting the mixture for maximum performance, and checking the control surfaces for full and smooth operation.

Tulsa, control. Spartan One Four Four Two requesting departure straight-out, runway three-four.

One Four Four Two. You are cleared for departure runway three-four.

Gus eased the throttle slowly forward, giving himself a chance to center the plane's nose in the middle of the runway. With the engine cowling blocking his view of the white center line, he had to look out the side screen at a point somewhat left of the centerline. He used rudder pedals to work the nose of the Executive back and forth just enough to see the runway centerline appear and disappear. At full throttle, the tail wheel lifted off the ground, and Gus could see the runway stretching out ahead of him. At 80 mph the airplane took flight.

"Positive rate. Gear up." Gus narrated as he toggled the landing gear switch to the "Up" position. "Flaps up." He set his climb rate at 1000 ft/min at 110 mph. By reciting the after-takeoff checklist, he hoped to impress Harry with his piloting skill, but first he needed to affirm to himself the proper and complete process of each phase of flight: pre-flight check, engine run-up, takeoff, climb to altitude, etc.

"Wow! This is way quieter than that open cockpit Stearman I first learned to fly. You can carry on a conversation without being distracted by the engine noise or the wind rushing past the control surfaces."

At Harry's directive, Gus turned the plane southeast to a heading of 145° at an altitude of 10,000 ft.

"Nice. Now, I need you to practice turns to a heading. This will simulate your approach to land. First, turn to three-four degrees and hold your altitude at ten thousand feet. Anytime I ask you to turn the plane, you have to make sure that you set the power and the attitude of the aircraft so as not to lose more than a hundred feet. Remember, when turning, the aircraft's tendency is to lose altitude because the lifting surface of the wings relative to your directional flight is less than when you are flying straight and level."

"Roger that. Turning to heading three-four degrees, maintaining one-zero thousand."

For the next 20 minutes, Gus practiced S-turns and simulating entry into the traffic pattern. Just as he was beginning to feel at ease at the controls of the Executive, he was hit by a shocking adrenaline rush: the engine shut down. He dropped the nose of the airplane just enough to hold his glide at 75 mph. His eyes scanned instruments and switches when he noticed the fuel lever was in the wrong position. It should be pointing straight up to use the main tanks, but it was pointing to the left. He turned the knob, and the engine responded settling into a heart-calming drone.

"Nicely done, Gus. You never know when something like that is going to happen. Loss of engine power can occur for any number of reasons. You responded and had the engine running in about ten seconds. You knew exactly what to check for." He smiled and reached over and patted Gus on the shoulder.

Harry took Gus through several stall scenarios: power-off stalls, power-on stalls, recovery from rolls. They had been flying for two hours; only a trifle less than half their fuel remained on board.

"That's enough for today. You did better than I expected, Gus. I do believe your training at Bay City Air has stuck with you. Your instructor must be an outstanding pilot."

"He is. Fred was one of the American volunteer pilots for the Lafayette Escadrille during World War I. He flew both the British Sopwith Camel and the Spad Pursuit. He later joined the Hat-in-the-Ring squadron commanded by Eddie Rickenbacker."

Gus' time in the air with Harry came to an end when school closed for Christmas on December 23. Most of the students lived within 50 to 100 miles of Tulsa and were able to make arrangements to spend the holidays at home with family. In Gus' case, his family's home in in Provo, Utah, was just too far to travel for the short break.

Harry needed him back and ready to fly by Monday, December 28. He convinced Gus that he needed to fill his logbook with as many hours in the Executive as he could manage, so he could start earning his pay as a pilot-employee of Spartan Aircraft.

Why not start now? Gus thought. He walked to the hangar where he found Harry in his office. "Can I talk to you about flying, boss?"

"Sure, Gus. What's on your mind?"

"Well, I was just thinking. Since I'm not going to Utah for the break, I have five days of free time on my hands. So, why wait until the until next Monday to start getting in my flight time. I figure we can log ten more hours between now and then."

Harry held up both hands and started laughing. "Whoa, slow down their partner. I may have plans for the Christmas break. I'll tell you what. My wife roasts a wicked ham every Christmas—I want you to come and share dinner with us. Evelyn will be delighted, and so will Stevie, Marcia, and Bradley, and Connie. What do you say?"

Gus grinned. "I say that maybe I need to focus less on the flying and more on the people around me. Thanks, Harry. I'm looking forward to it." As he turned to leave, Harry stopped him.

"Hang on, Gus. I'm not done yet. For the next five days, I think it would be a wonderful idea to do some homework. You see those mechanic's manuals on the shelves off to the right? They contain everything you need to know about the systems of the Spartan Executive. I want you to study them until you can repeat the performance specifications from the camber of the wings to drag coefficients and flight characteristics under every imaginable situation. I want you to know the Pratt & Whitney Wasp Junior inside and out … darn near as much as a certified mechanic knows about that engine. The next time you climb in the cockpit, I want you to feel like you're sitting with a good friend. While you're at it, I want you and Highway to keep an eye on the hangar and the planes. I don't want any curious snoopers nosing around where they don't belong."

"You've got it, boss. Thanks again for that dinner invitation. I'm looking forward to meeting your wife and kids."

Gus returned to his room in student housing, such as it was, and spread the aircraft maintenance manuals out on his bed. He began looking through them for the best place to start. The Pratt & Whitney Engine Parts Manual was the logical choice. Any good pilot knows that the power plant is the heart and soul of an airplane. He needs to know how his aircraft will perform in a variety of circumstances including emergencies both common and rare: engine failure scenarios, throttle settings, stresses due to excessive demands during emergency descent and climb, evasive maneuvers requiring rapid and fluctuating engine settings. Countless situations requiring a pilot's immediate response without hesitation could mean the difference between disaster and a safe outcome.

CHAPTER 7

Gus was sitting at his desk in student housing, reading Addie's latest letter, when he heard a loud knock on his door.

"Mr. Croxton, er, Harry. What's up?" Gus asked.

"You are." Remember that PT-17 check ride we talked about the other day? Well, I have a free hour, so grab your flight gear, and let's go. Meet me in the hangar right away." Harry shut the door behind him as he left.

TEN MINUTES LATER

"Good! You're here. I'll take the forward cockpit. You are the pilot in command, so you take the back seat. Climb on up. Time's a wasting," Harry chuckled as he maneuvered himself into the forward cockpit.

"Get yourself settled back there. You'll find a leather helmet with a facemask and pilots' goggles. It's the type A-12 flying helmet with an ANB H-1 radio receiver of the type used by Army Air Force flight crews. The microphone in the facemask is plugged in and ready to go. Just flip the switch marked 'MIC' and we'll do a comm check. Your radio has been reset to the tower frequency. Just press the button on your control stick to talk to air traffic control. You already know all that, I'm sure, but it never hurts to go over the details."

Gus found everything in order in the cockpit. He put on the leather helmet and earphones followed by the goggles and mask.

"Can you hear me all right, Harry?" Gus' voice sounded muffled to himself.

"I read you loud and clear, Gus. I had the engine running earlier, so it's ready for you to start up. I want you to handle the radios and do the flying. I'm going to sit back here and enjoy the flight. Unless you need to ask me for something, I'm not going to say anything. I want you to stay in the pattern and complete four touch-and-go landings. On the fifth landing bring us back to the hangar and shut it down," Harry directed.

Gus radioed the tower for permission to taxi to the active runway while Harry sat back to listen and observe.

Gus scanned the instruments. Satisfied that they were all operating in the green (normal operating range), he announced he was in position and requested permission to depart. After informing the tower that he would be staying in the pattern, he lined up the Stearman on the white centerline of runway 16L. He found a visual reference point to help him keep centered on the runway, then added power. There was a low mountain peak straight in front of them in the distance no more than eight or nine miles away. Gus applied throttle. The plane yawed toward the left, and he corrected with the rudder pedal. He rotated into the air at 55 mph and set his climb rate to 500 ft/min.

While completing his four touch-and-go landings and takeoffs, Gus bounced twice on the first landing, once on the second, and squeaked the tires softly for a perfect three-point landing on attempts three and four. All the flying skills from Bay City Air were back. His final landing was as good as he had ever done! He taxied the plane back to Spartan's hangar and shut down the engine.

Hank and Gus walked into the hangar, while a Spartan mechanic chalked the tires and started his after-flight inspection.

"Not bad for a rookie." Harry chuckled. "You've passed your check ride in the Stearman. Next comes your cross-country … a nighttime flight under visual flight rules. Here's your route with the waypoints listed. I want you to map your flight on the aeronautical chart. Include your heading, altitude, estimated airspeed, time of arrival at each waypoint, fuel consumption, and estimated total flight time. Plan your time of departure for 9:30 p.m. tomorrow night. I know it will be Christmas Eve, so keep an eye out for Santa's sleigh." Harry winked and grinned.

"Your flight plan is thorough: waypoints, fuel consumption plus reserves, headings and altitude, departure and arrival times, and comms' frequencies. I see you have alternate airports identified in case you can't make it to a primary waypoint. What about the weather?" Harry asked.

"Clear to partly cloudy with no rain. A full moon on tap, so I should be able to find some of the prominent landmarks. I plotted the course with my flight calculator, and allowing for magnetic declination, I've set it as indicated on the map. I'll be following Highway Sixty-Six from Tulsa southwest to Sapulpa, Bristow, Chandler, and on into Oklahoma City. Turning north-northeast toward Ponca City, my primary reference will be Highway Seventy-Seven. I'll be crossing the point where the Seventy-Seven intersects the Cimmaron River. From there I'll fly the map heading into Ponca City where I'll stop for fuel. I plan to depart Ponca City at twenty-three fifty-five hours local time, arriving back at Tulsa at zero two hundred hours. I feel like I'm good to go, boss. Ponca City to Tulsa should be a snap. I'll follow the Arkansas River southeast all the way home. I estimate four hours and thirty minutes enroute including refueling time in Ponca City." Gus eyed his friend and mentor, trying to read a response.

Harry acknowledged the flight plan with an affirmative nod. "Looks good. Come on out to the plane, and I'll pull the prop through for you."

Standing by the prop, Harry waited for Gus to buckle into the rear cockpit of the Stearman.

"Switch off," Harry called from the ground.

"Switch off!" Gus affirmed.

Harry pulled the prop through three complete rotations and stepped away.

"Contact!" Gus shouted. He set the throttle and mixture and toggled up the starter. The propeller started turning with a whine, then coughed once. A familiar plume of white smoke belched from the exhaust manifold, and the engine settled into a smooth idle.

Tulsa control, Army One Four Three Bravo requests taxi to runway two-six, straight-out departure.

Roger, One Four Three Bravo. You are clear to taxi. Notify Tulsa control when ready for departure.

Gus taxied the Stearman away from the Spartan ramp toward the taxiway. He stopped short of the runway and called the tower for clearance to depart. There was no traffic in the pattern, and he was given permission to take the active runway.

At 500 ft AGL, Gus turned to a heading of 240° magnetic and continued his climb to 4000 ft. He could see the lights of Highway 66 stretching out in front of him below his left wingtip. He reached his designated altitude, and adjusted the mixture and throttle to hold his airspeed at 97 mph.

Flying at night under clear skies over relatively flat terrain, a pilot's most dependable visual references are highway lights, or clusters of lights indicating populated areas such as incorporated towns. In Gus' case those markers were Sapulpa, Bristow, and Chandler. By following the lights of Highway 66, Gus had no problem identifying each of those towns as he flew over them. He radioed Bethany control at about six miles out.

Bethany control, Army One Four Three Bravo inbound to land runway three-four, touch-and-go.

Roger, One Four Three Bravo. The pattern is clear for your straight in approach, runway three-four.

Gus had flown the Stearman at night many times with Harry in the forward cockpit. He centered the plane between the two rows of runway lights, reduced his air speed to 70 mph and began a gradual descent of 500 ft/min. At 50 mph, he passed over the runway threshold. Gus reduced his throttle to idle and allowed the Stearman to settle into a flare. He let the plane settle to the pavement and then eased the throttle forward all the way. The Stearman leapt into the air, and Gus turned toward his next stop, Ponca City airport. He located the long string of lights headed north northeast out of Ponca City. "There you are, Highway Seventy-Seven," he said out loud.

A shiver ran through him. The open cockpit Stearman was an icebox on Christmas Eve. Anticipating the cold, he followed Harry's advice and dressed in winter long underwear, woolen socks, heavy denim pants, and calf-length leather flying boots. His jacket was Army Air Corps issue consisting of a heavy leather outer shell with a thick, plush, sheepskin inner lining. He wore insulated leather flying gloves. His leather helmet provided some warmth to his ears and face, yet despite his cold weather gear, his body temperature, though not hypothermic at the moment, felt like it was headed in that direction. He wore a white four-foot-long scarf around his neck which was presently tucked inside his jacket. While squeezing his knees around the flight control stick, he untucked the scarf and looped it over his head to cover his ears and much of his lower face.

The lights of Ponca City popped into view about 25 miles in front of him. "Light a fire, folks, I'm in need of heat!" It felt good to hear his own voice. "If anyone could hear me hooting and hollering up here, they'd think I was nuts. Atta boy, Gus. Russell would be proud. You found your waypoint." The runway lights appeared off his right wing.

Ponca City Control, Army One Four Three Bravo is six miles south, at three thousand and descending to land. Receiving your radio range signal. Turning right traffic for runway one-two.

Gus' landing was perfect. After taxiing up to the only hangar at the airport, he felt like a human popsicle. He couldn't wait to warm himself. While he chalked his tires, a pair of headlights flashed on from the right side of the hangar. A tanker truck pulled up in front of the Stearman's left wing.

"You the fella called from Tulsa for eighty-seven octane?" A fortyish, slender man walked over to Gus with his hand extended. "Name's Wagstaff … Paul Wagstaff."

"Gus Bodine. Ten to fifteen gallons ought to do it, Mr. Wagstaff. I appreciate you coming out in such cold weather at this time of night."

"No problem. What in blazes are you doing flying in an open cockpit Stearman at twenty-five degrees if you don't mind me asking? Don't you know that this is Christmas Eve?" Paul Wagstaff inserted the avgas nozzle. After pumping in five gallons, he moved over to the other wing and completed the refueling.

"Trying to catch up with Santa's sleigh. I hoped to spot him before I got all the way back to Tulsa," Gus quipped. Not seeing so much as a smile on Paul Wagstaff's face, Gus figured he would pay the man and head for the hangar to warm himself before climbing back into the cockpit.

As he entered, Gus saw only one tiny light shining inside the hangar. A desk and chair stood unoccupied over in one corner. Another desk and workbench stood against the wall on the other side. A small stove at the end of the workbench provided some warmth, and the aroma of coffee from the pot sitting on the stove filled the work area. Gus found a chair and picked up a newspaper someone had left on the desk.

A few moments later, Paul Wagstaff, came in rubbing his cold hands together. He made his way to the hot brew where he filled two cups.

"Boy, you look half frozen. Here, this will warm us both right up." Wagstaff extended one of the cups to Gus.

Gus was not a coffee drinker, but he needed something hot inside him. He thanked Paul and forced down a cup full of the bitter brew.

"Thanks, Mr. Wagstaff. Now I need to be back on my way. Only one hour to go, and I'll be back home." He smiled inwardly for calling Spartan his home. *I guess it is my home for now … at least until I finish school.* The thought only made him long for Addie. Christmas was no time to be away from the one person he loved the most. *I can't wait to call her tomorrow morning.*

The engine was still warm and did not require the propeller to be pulled through to prevent hydraulic lock. Gus hunkered down in the rear cockpit behind the windscreen. After starting the engine, he checked the instruments. Cylinder head temperature, manifold pressure, oil temperature. All were in the green. He throttled up and taxied out to the end of runway 21. He knew no one was listening for him at Ponca City, but he announced his departure according to protocol.

Ponca City control, Army One Four Three Bravo departing straight-out runway two-one for Tulsa.

Once airborne, Gus turned slightly farther east than his calculated course. He was looking for the lights of US Highway 77. When they appeared, he adjusted his course south southeast to a heading of 145°.

About 20 minutes into the flight, he found himself passing through a few light wisps of clouds. The lights of the highway disappeared for a few seconds and then reappeared. *Uh oh, this isn't looking good.* He backed his throttle off a tad and dropped his nose. He hoped the skies might clear up if he were closer to the highway, so he reduced altitude to 3500 ft. The elevation of the ground along this part of the route was between 2,100 and 2,150 ft. Within seconds what little visibility he had disappeared. Snow pelted his windscreen, and the world around him went black.

Gus had been airborne for over 40 minutes. He was more than halfway home with only about 30 minutes of flight time remaining.

When he charted his flight, Gus marked his alternate waypoints just in case he had another emergency like he did back in Stanford in Bay City Air's old biplane. One of the waypoints was a small dirt strip at the juncture where US 77 crossed the Cimmaron River. *If I can spot the bridge, I should be able to find the dirt strip,* he thought. The plane's magnetic compass was the only means of estimating his directional flight. He knew, when he got closer to the airport, he would pick up Tulsa's four-course low-frequency radio range signal (the main navigation system used by aircraft for instrument flying in the 1930s and 1940s). He made sure he had the radio tuned for the signal before he left Ponca City.

The clouds broke sporadically revealing the ground a mere 500 ft below him. He could not see the highway, however, he got a faint glimpse of water. "Is that the Arkansas or the Cimmaron?" he asked himself out loud. The control stick started to shake slightly and the plane was visibly descending. Gus pushed the throttle all the way forward. The engine answered with a higher pitch sound as the RPMs increased. He eased the stick toward him expecting the nose to raise … but it didn't.

"Darn! Ice! I've got to put this plane on the ground!" He knew he had less than one minute before the plane stalled and crashed.

The Highway 77 bridge jumped into view a mere three seconds before he passed over it. He banked the Stearman left, knowing that the dirt strip was only 100 yds or so north of his present location.

Poking his head over the left side of the fuselage and then the right side, he squinted his eyes and wiped the ice from his goggles in hopes of spotting something that would indicate level ground. Just at that moment he passed beneath a break in the clouds and a beautiful white full moon lit up the ground.

"There!" He leveled his wings, pulled the throttle all the way back, and kicked in hard right rudder. He hoped he was over the runway. The Stearman had lost altitude with Gus' maneuvering and was a mere 20 ft or so above the surface, still at 60 mph, when the landing gear slammed into the dirt. The plane skewed to the left when his wheel struck a rut, but, thankfully, he was able to bring the plane to a stop before it ground looped. He pulled the mixture back and the engine stopped. Slightly shaken, Gus climbed out of the cockpit. Fearing the worst, he walked up to the left wheel. It had rolled clear of the rut and appeared to be undamaged. The leading edges of both wings were caked with a thick layer of ice that could have caused a high-speed stall. Gus breathed a sigh of relief. ...He was definitely down for the night.

He checked the time. His grandfather's old pocket watch read 1:20 a.m. *Nobody is going to be driving out here tonight. I better rig some sort of a shelter.*

Gus and Harry had discussed some of the problems with flying at night in the middle of winter. Since Harry was not going along on this ride, they decided to throw a few extra things into the forward hold: a tarpaulin, a sleeping bag, a box of wood matches, and a flare signal pistol with three flares ... just in case.

Gus climbed back into the cockpit and unfolded the tarpaulin. There was no wind, so there was no need to tie down the tarp. He hunkered low into the cockpit and pulled the tarp over the top to cover the windscreen and himself completely. He kept his scarf snugly tied over his ears and wrapped around his face. He folded his arms tightly around himself. After about an hour, his chills had stopped and his body heat, trapped beneath the tarp, raised the ambient temperature in his confined quarters to a tolerable level. He had been awake for over 20 hours, and his eyes grew heavy. At last, he allowed himself to drift off.

CHAPTER 7

"Gussy. ...Gussy, wake up. Come on, sleepyhead. You need to get the plane back to the airport." The voice belonged to Addie.

"What plane? It's Christmas morning, sweetheart. Can't I just sleep in for a minute longer?"

"No, 'darling,' you can't. Pry your butt out of that cockpit. You need to fly the Stearman back to Spartan." The voice was no longer Addie's, but that of a very grumpy Harry.

"Man, you had me scared half to death, Gus. When the snow hit Tulsa, and you had not checked in, I thought you must've gone down somewhere. I'm glad you filed a good flight plan. I've been searching for you for a couple of hours now. I found the bridge you marked as a waypoint on your chart right there." Harry pointed behind them, and there in the distance, they could see the bridge where Highway 77 crossed over the Cimmaron River.

It was beginning to get light, but the sun had not yet appeared over the eastern horizon. Gus checked his pocket watch, 6:40 am. Between the two of them, Harry and Gus pushed the Stearman back toward the center of the still empty highway. "Climb on up there, Gus. You have a cross-country flight to finish."

Gus checked his rudder, elevators, and ailerons for free movement. He and Harry had knocked the ice off the wings, and everything appeared to be ready for an engine start.

"Pull the prop through will you, Harry? Switch off!"

Harry pulled the prop through five rotations.

"Clear prop!" Gus toggled up the magnetos followed by the starter. He eased forward the mixture, but the cold engine chugged once and quit.

"Switch off! One more time," he announced, and Harry pulled the prop through three more rotations.

"Clear prop!" Gus advanced the mixture gradually, and when the engine didn't catch, he pushed the throttle in and pulled it back a couple of times. The extra prime of the fuel line did the trick, and the radial engine came to life.

1942 / CHRISTMAS DINNER

Later that day, Gus—warmed and rested—and Highway joined Harry and his family for Christmas dinner. Ham, sweet potatoes, string bean casserole and home canned peaches with cream made for a sumptuous meal. A generous bowl of Ken-L Ration with a couple of strips of jerky was served to Highway.

Harry tapped his glass with his fork. When he had everyone's attention he produced a folder containing two documents.

"Gus, I am holding two documents that I hope will provide you the best darned Christmas present you can hope for. Merry Christmas!"

Gus took the envelope and removed the contents. In about two seconds, an ear to ear grin spread across Gus' face. "Holy mackerel! It's my CPTD endorsement and CAA pilot license. I can carry passengers now!"

Gus spent the next couple of hours talking flying with Harry and playing board games with the Croxton family. He couldn't have felt happier if he had been home celebrating with his own family. In fact, Harry was becoming a brother to him, and his children were as nephews and nieces in his heart. Evelyn, Harry's wife, hugged Gus affectionately as he was about to leave. "Gus, you must promise to let us meet Addie this coming summer."

"She will love you, Evelyn. Thank you. Dinner was delicious."

Harry Croxton was on the floor of the hangar pre-flighting the Executive when Gus arrived for work on December 26. Normally, Gus would've had a couple of days off, but except for Christmas day, he and Harry worked six days a week getting flight time in toward his multi-engine rating. Increasing his hours flying the Executive in addition to the Army PT-17 Stearman, Gus became type certified in both of those aircraft and was set to begin training for his multi-engine certification in Spartan's Cessna T-50 "Bobcat."

Additionally, Harry and the rest of Spartan's flying instructors were training the other student pilots, while Gus, with a few Spartan mechanics, worked on setting up the lab for the engineering practicum involving the mechanical engineering aspects of the radial engine. With graduation less than four weeks away, the practicum would represent the collective work of all the undergrad students of the first graduating class of the Spartan Aircraft School of Aeronautical Engineering. Of course, they would be receiving a certificate of completion only for their work at Spartan. The Baccalaureate Degree itself would be presented by each student's resident university or college.

"Hey, boss. Are you getting ready to take the Executive up?"

"Yes I am, and I'm going to need you to fly right seat. We'll be heading down to Wichita Falls to pick up an Army Air Force VIP at Sheppard Field, then we'll fly back here for an important meeting with some of the Air Force Training Detachment brass.

"Suit up, Gus."

Harry got back to work, while Gus, trying not to show *too* much excitement, headed for his quarters to change into his flight gear.

CONTRACT FLIGHT TO SHEPPARD FIELD

Sheppard Field, Texas, was a major U.S. Army Air Force training base for non-pilot crews during WWII. The demand placed on the USAAF Training Command to place the numbers of trained personnel needed around the globe was staggering. To fill the increasing need, civilian technical schools and flight schools were being contracted to use their facilities to augment the military production of qualified mechanics and technology specialists such as aircraft repair and mechanics, and radio operators; as well as communications specialists in air traffic control, radar, cryptographic encoding and decoding of classified messaging, and a variety of other MOS specialties.

The Spartan Executive descended on final approach to runway 15R at Sheppard Field at 10 a.m. They were directed to the VIP parking area adjacent to the control tower. A plane handler guided the aircraft the last several yards to the tiedown area.

Gus unlatched the side passenger door, as an Air Force enlisted man placed some portable stairs beneath the opening. A pair of 1940 Chevrolet Army staff cars approached from the direction of the small passenger terminal. The lead car flew two fender flags, each bearing three stars signifying that a Lieutenant General was on board.

The three-star approached Gus. Behind him was a bird colonel and a major.

"Bart Yount." The General extended his hand which Gus shook enthusiastically.

"Gus Bodine, sir. I'll be your pilot today. Welcome aboard. We'll get underway just as soon as everyone is buckled in. Plan on about an hour and forty-five minutes, so if anyone needs to use the bathroom first, we'll wait for you."

Gus climbed in and worked his way up to the cockpit. Harry had moved to the right seat. Heart pounding and proud as a peacock, Gus would be the PIC (pilot in control) for the flight back to Tulsa as well as the return flight to Sheppard the following day.

Enid Army Airfield and Hatbox Army Airfield, both in Oklahoma were civilian airports. Like Tulsa Municipal Airport, they were U.S. Army Air Force contract training sites. Both Enid and Hatbox were sending their representatives to Tulsa to meet with Lieutenant General Barton Yount, commanding officer of the Army Air Force Central Flying Training Command, to discuss the technical manpower demands of the U. S. Army. Spartan Aircraft was chosen for the meeting due to its central location, its programs of Aeronautical Engineering and pilot training for the civilian sector, and because it was a contractor for the training of United States Army Air Force flight mechanics. Thus, J. Paul Getty and the Dean of the School of Aeronautical Engineering, Dr. C. Franklin Harrison, would be key players in the expansion and role of Spartan Aircraft and other civilian contractors dotting the map across the nation.

The flight from Wichita Falls, Texas, was smooth and uneventful. They touched down at Tulsa at 12:10 p.m. Gen. Yount and his entourage deplaned and headed straight for the Spartan Aircraft administration building.

Gus stood outside on the tarmac supervising the refueling of the Executive. He completed a walk-around inspection of the plane.

Satisfied, he turned to head back toward the hangar when he was approached by Gen. Yount's aide. Gus noticed the major wore the wings of pilot over three rows of campaign ribbons above the left breast pocket of his uniform.

"Mr. Bodine, I'm Major Pete Crossfield. Do you have a minute to chat with me? I'd like to ask you a couple of questions."

"Sure thing, Major. I have to tell you, though, I don't know a whole lot about what goes on around here with the Army Air Force training."

"I just want your perspective, Gus. You're the senior upper classman in this school. I figure you might have some insight as to the morale among the men in your class."

"Sure. I worked with a few of them in the shop where we learned all about radial engines, specifically the Pratt & Whitney Wasp Junior. As for morale, I'd have to say they were all business. For a bunch of young guys like me, they are serious about their work: focused, and curious to learn. The few guys I've met personally are anxious to complete their training successfully and get to work on the real thing." Gus waited for the next question.

"What would you say about the quality of instruction?"

"It's excellent, sir. Professional, thorough ..." Gus paused, wondering where the conversation was headed. He thought he had a handle on it, but now he wasn't sure. "If there is anything lacking, sir, I'd have to say that there isn't enough one-on-one teaching being done. Especially in the hands-on practicum portion of most courses involving Air Force trainees. The ratio of students to instructors is too high. There should be more qualified instructors to mentor individual students. Those students will soon be sent into a war zone to work on the airplanes that are flying missions every day. I value the mentoring of my instructor, Harry Croxton. I believe the other students will benefit from similar one-on-one instruction."

Pete Crossfield smiled and nodded his approval of Gus' assessment. "Your observations are concise and informative, Mr. Bodine. Have you considered putting on a uniform yourself?"

The question was a departure from the subject of the USAAF Training Command detachment.

"Gus. Please, call me Gus. I'm happy to help, sir. To answer your question, yes … I've thought about it a lot. More so since my brother was shot down in the Pacific a few weeks ago. He's listed as MIA, but I doubt he's still alive."

"I'm sorry to hear that. I'm sure you know that the United States Army Air Force is in need—desperately in need—of qualified pilots, like yourself, to take the battle to the enemy and end this war. We can certainly use men of your caliber to make that happen. Well, I better get back inside. Nice talking to you, Gus." The major smiled, turned, and walked back in the direction of the "admin" building.

As Gus stood there a moment pondering their conversation, he had a stronger prompting than he had ever experienced … one word: *SERVE!*

At 6:00 p.m., General Yount's meeting with the civilian contractors and USAAF Training Detachments ended. Dinner was provided in the school's mess hall. Of course, Gus and Harry were invited as well.

Gus caught Maj. Crossfield's attention from two tables over and nodded his head. The officer raised the first two fingers of his right hand to his brow in a saluting gesture.

When Gen. Yount and the others rose from their table, Gus stood and excused himself, leaving Harry alone with a confused expression. He looked at Gus and shrugged his shoulders in a "What are you doing?" gesture. Gus simply grinned and headed in the direction of the major.

"Major Crossfield, I've been thinking about what you said. I'm ready, sir. Can you help?"

"Yes, I can. Don't do anything for a few days. You will be receiving a letter, the contents of which should plow the bureaucratic field, so to speak. That letter will explain itself to you. Good luck, Mr. Bodine. Oh, by the way, I need your home mailing address in Utah."

By the time the Executive landed at Sheppard Field the sun was setting, and the muted light of dusk was settling over their flight path. After dropping off the passengers, Gus and Harry pointed the nose of the Executive at the white centerline of runway 33L and departed for Tulsa.

———

CHAPTER 7

THE DECISION

"What was all that with you and that major?" Harry asked.

"Something that's been on my mind a lot for the last couple of months, Harry. Ever since my brother Russell got shot down, I have had a nagging thought ... no … more of a prompting, really, to serve my country, my family, the cause of freedom. I asked Major Crossfield if he could help me become an Air Force pilot. He agreed to do what he can, and he'll let me know in a few days what I need to do." Gus needed Harry's endorsement and anxiously awaited his response.

"Well, Gus old man, now that you're graduating, I can't say that I'm surprised. I guess I would probably be doing the same thing if I were in your shoes. Have you told Addie, yet?"

"No, not yet. I know I have to tell her. I'm just afraid she will call off the wedding. Frankly, I wouldn't blame her, but I'm going to do this, Harry. I can't justify avoiding my duty any longer."

The next day, Gus decided to make the calls to Addie and his family. Graduation was scheduled for the following week, and two weeks from then, on May 23, he would enter the United States Army Air Force Aviation Cadet Training Program. Three months later, in August, he would receive the rank of second lieutenant and wear the wings of a pilot.

Gus sat at the desk in his room, took a deep breath, scratched Highway behind the ears, and picked up the phone. He dialed "0" for the operator. His first call would be to his fiancée.

"Hello …?"

"Addie, it's me."

"Gus, darling! I wasn't expecting you to call today. You usually let me know ahead of time. How are you? When are you coming home? Everybody is so excited about the wedding. We have a lot of planning to do before then."

"I know. ...I know, sweetheart. There's something I need to tell you first. It's important."

"Okay. You sound serious. Has something happened?" Addie voice started to quiver.

"I ... I ...," Gus paused, searching for words.

"Gus, darling, you're scaring me. Something has happened. What is it? Whatever it is, we'll handle it ... we'll handle it together."

"I have decided to enlist in the United States Army Air Force. I'm going to be a pilot, Addie." Gus' heart pounded in his chest. He held his breath waiting for Addie's reaction. When he got it, it took him completely off guard. What he heard over the telephone was laughter ... Addie was laughing.

"Addie, did you hear what I said?" Gus couldn't understand why she was laughing.

"I'm fine, Gus. (Giggling sounds.) ...Oh, my. You had me worried there for a minute."

"Addie, I don't understand..."

"Oh, Gus. I knew in my heart something like this was going to happen. You love flying. I know how you admired Russell for doing what you are doing now. It was just a question of 'when', not 'if.' So, now, when are you going to be home? We have wedding arrangements to make."

Gus knew he was a lucky man, indeed! "Graduation isn't until next week, but I don't have to wait. Dr. Harrison will award me my diploma tomorrow. Highway and I will hit the road the next day, on Tuesday, and we'll expect to be home by Thursday.

"... I love you so much, Addie!"

CHAPTER 8

MAY 6, 1943 / HOME

When Gus drove from Stanford to Provo a year earlier, he had his belongings packed in the back seat of his 1936 Ford coupe. For his trip from Tulsa to Provo, he removed the back rumble seat (it was more of a trunk than a seat) which enabled him to pack all his belongings into the empty compartment. Much to Highway's satisfaction, he rode "shotgun" with Gus.

They drove to Dodge City where they spent the first night. The Shamrock Motor Hotel was not exactly a five-star resort, but the price was reasonable, and the bed was comfortable. The "C" gasoline ration card on the car window authorized all the fuel he needed to make the trip. He was glad for his status as a United States government employee at Spartan Aircraft which qualified him for the card.

He arrived home before 1 p.m. on May 6. He didn't bother unloading his things from the car. He and Highway entered the side door leading into the Bodine's kitchen.

"Anybody home?" Gus waited for an answer and walked into the kitchen which was oddly unoccupied. "Hello … Mom? Dad? Anybody!" Still, no answer.

As Highway followed Gus into the living room, they were swamped by family. Even Catherine had taken the day off from school to welcome her brother home. Addie stood back and waited her turn. When Gus' mother finally stepped back to make room for her son's fiancée, Addie rushed into his arms and buried her face in his neck. She whispered quietly in his ear, "I love you, Gus. Welcome home, darling."

"Right back at you, kiddo," he exclaimed as he swept her off her feet. He brought her to his lips and kissed her, albeit a brief brush of his lips against hers. As he set her gently back down, he whispered "I can't wait until we can be alone together." There would be plenty of time for more intimate expressions, but not in the living room full of family.

Highway had been ever so patiently sitting at Gus' feet, wagging his tail, and moving his head rapidly to eye each unknown individual in the room. Finally, he got the attention he needed.

"This must be Highway." Addie knelt and put her arms around the big friendly mutt. "Thank you for saving my Gus, and welcome to our family, Highway." To his sheer delight, she gave him a good scratch behind his ears before rising to her feet.

Highway didn't need a leash. Unless Gus was moving, he was perfectly satisfied with just sitting by his human's feet and watching the world through excited doggy eyes. So, when Gus said something to Addie and started walking, it mattered not to Highway where he was going - only that he was going somewhere with Gus.

"Come with me into the kitchen, Addie. I need to feed Highway."

The family knew Gus was bringing Highway home. Gus had asked his mother to buy a few cans of dog food and a bag of kibble for his dog.

Addie watched as Gus spooned out a generous portion of Ken-L Ration and filled another bowl with water. He carried the bowl of dog food while Addie carried the water into the mud room off the kitchen. Highway, who had been excitedly watching … and smelling … the process, followed closely behind them.

"We haven't had a chance to talk about Highway, Addie. Things have been happening so fast."

"We haven't had a chance to talk about a lot of things that need to be settled, Gus." Addie said in a near whisper. "We need to find someplace quiet where we can be alone and talk. Let's take Highway with us so the family won't have to worry about him. Can we leave after the welcome home party? Is an hour okay with you, Gus?"

"Yes, and do you mind taking your Chevy? I've done enough driving to last me for the rest of the year," Gus sighed. Then they both had a good laugh.

THE GAZEBO

By 3:00 p.m. the welcome home party was over, and the house was empty of the gaiety of happy gatherings once more. Addie's parents had returned home as had the few of Gerry and Anna's closest friends that had been invited.

Gus, Addie, and Highway drove to the park. Fortuitously, the gazebo was absent any visitors at the moment. This spot had been their favorite venue for talking about their budding emotions that eventually grew into the abiding love they now felt toward each other. They ascended the three steps to the deck of the gazebo and sat on one of the white benches.

Highway looked up at Gus with tail wagging and eyes pleading for Gus to remove his collar. "Here ya go … it's okay, boy. Go play."

At that precise moment a group of children walked across the park past the gazebo. With them were two medium-sized dogs. Highway leaped off the deck in one bound and ran over to the other dogs. Gus and Addie gasped, but he didn't charge, instead he pulled up short and barked once, again with the tail wagging. Apparently the other two dogs, and the children as well, understood the absence of any threat. They walked over to Highway to pet him, and the dogs and kids all joined in the fun of running around the park.

Gus took Addie's hand in his and looked into her eyes. "Thank you, Addie," his eyes nearly teared over, "for ... for everything." He brushed the heel of his left hand over his cheek.

Addie placed the palm of her hand on Gus' face. "If you only knew how committed I am. When you put that ring on my finger the last time we were here, in my heart I became your wife. Well, in matters only having to do with the heart, not any other part of our bodies." Gus was somewhat surprised by her naughty reference, until they looked into each other's eyes and started laughing … both wore mischievous grins on their faces.

They turned to matters of the wedding. Invitations had been mailed out by Addie and her mom. There would be just a few family friends and nearby relatives attending the reception following the ceremony which would take place in the Bodine's backyard. A floral archway, festooned with a variety of garden flowers lovingly grown and nurtured by Gus' mother, marked the spot where Gus and Addie would exchange their vows. The exact date was yet to be determined, but time was short.

"Gussy, we need to be married before you go off to war. Knowing that we will be together for eternity means everything to me … to us, I mean." Addie's voice trembled. She was filled with love for Gus and terrified that she might lose him, but she still couldn't bring herself to talk to him about her fears. He had enough to worry about as it was.

"Addie, I will return … safe and sound. I promise! Now, I'm ready to start having fun. No more talk about me not coming back to you. Agreed?"

"You're right. We're not planning a funeral; we're planning a wedding! By the way, Gus, I don't see Highway anywhere."

Gus stood. He couldn't see any dogs or children playing anywhere in the park within his field of vision. *Oh, no. Where are you, Highway?* Gus put two fingers to his lips and whistled loudly enough to set Addie's ears ringing.

They heard a distant bark off to the right and saw a flash of golden fur. Highway was at a full run and headed right for them. He jumped to the deck of the gazebo and tackled Gus. Had Gus not been ready for the impact of the 80-lb animal, he would've been knocked on his keester, but he instinctively planted one foot behind himself as a brace. Gus kept his balance and allowed Highway to give his face a thorough tongue washing. Addie joined in the lovefest, and Highway reaped the benefit of a tummy rub and much scratching behind the ears.

Still laughing and enjoying the moment, Gus took Addie's hand, and the three of them headed back to the car.

CHAPTER 8

On May 14, 1943, five days before the wedding, Gus received a telephone call from Kearns Army Airfield. Major Bartholomew Baxter of the U.S. Army Air Force Training Command Detachment informed Gus that he was in receipt of a priority stamped envelope from the office of "Lieutenant General Barton Yount, Commander USAAF Training Command." The document, according to Maj. Baxter, contained all the necessary papers for Gus' enlistment and assignment to the USAAF Aviation Cadet Training Program commencing May 27 at Randolph Field near San Antonio, Texas. Maj. Baxter asked to see Gus ASAP to sign his enlistment papers and be sworn in. His final comment to Gus was, "Son, I don't know how you are connected to the Commanding General of the United States Army Air Force Training Command, but I for one do not want to mess this up. I will expect to see you tomorrow at exactly thirteen-hundred hours. A VIP Visitor's Pass will be waiting for you at the main gate. I will see you there. Understood?"

Gus was driving north on State Road 89 to Kearns Army airfield. Highway was navigating from the right seat. Gus' watch read 12:15 p.m. *I'm early, but better early than late.* Things were happening fast for Gus. On his return trip home, he would be Cadet Gus Bodine.

"From civilian to G.I. today, married in four days, leaving Provo for Randolph Field on the twenty-fifth of this month. I figure I'll get a very close haircut and be marching with my training unit on the twenty-seventh. What do you think about that, Highway?" Of course, Highway did not understand a word of what Gus said, but he had an uncanny ability to read human emotion. He placed his chin on Gus' lap, raised his eyebrows and fixed on Gus' eyes with a forlorn and sympathetic expression that would've melted the hardest of hearts.

Gus reached over and scratched Highway behind the ears. "Everything's okay, boy. Everything is good, and you are going to be one happy dog. Not only do I love you, but so does Addie. You are going to be staying with her until I get my first leave, which will be around the end of June. You and I have traveled a lot of road together, 'Highway dog.' I wish you could understand how much you have come to mean to me."

Gus stepped up to the door marked "Pass and ID" and entered.

"Can I help you, mister?" an Army Air Force corporal asked from behind his desk.

"Yes, I have an appointment with Major Baxter."

"Second door on your right." The corporal nodded his head in the direction of Maj. Baxter's office. When he got to the right door, Gus didn't know if he should knock first or just open the door and walk in, so he did the latter. He walked into what could only have been an outer office. Two female enlisted personnel, one a three striped sergeant and the other a private first class, were sitting at desks busily typing. The staff sergeant stopped what she was doing and smiled up at Gus.

"You must be Mr. Bodine. I'll tell the major you're here." She knocked on the major's door and stepped inside. After a moment, the staff sergeant waved Gus into Maj. Baxter's office.

Ten minutes later, with a new military countenance and a slight grin, Gus walked out carrying a manila envelope containing his orders to report to Randolph Field in Texas for the beginning of his first phase of training.

THE WEDDING

At 2 p.m., on May 19, in the Bodine's backyard, a nervous Gus stood beneath a colorful floral archway, courtesy of his mother's flower garden. Addie, escorted by her father, walked across the neatly trimmed grass, between two rows of seated guests, to the scratchy sounds of Mendelssohn's *Wedding March* played on an old Victrola record player. Addie was radiant in her mother's wedding dress from 23 years earlier. Gus was attired in his dark suit, a brand-new white shirt, and a black bow tie … feeling a little like a penguin on parade.

The ceremony to seal their love brought tears to the eyes of nearly every woman and even some of the men who attended. Fortunately, most of the men carried white handkerchiefs for just such an occasion.

After the nuptials, the bride and groom and the rest of the wedding party relocated to the reception that was held at the Russo's backyard patio and garden. The women in the two families had decorated the patio with colored crêpe paper streamers and balloons. The wedding cake came from the ovens of both mothers, who, when the cake was ready to be iced, joined in the Russo kitchen and labored together for the better part of three hours to create their multi-layered masterpiece. The inscription read:

Gus & Addie
Together Forever
May 19, 1943

The next three days, the couple spent their honeymoon camping at Lost Creek reservoir in the Uintah Mountains northeast of Provo. Of course, the beginning of their new life together would not be complete without the third member of the family, Highway.

The days were spent hiking along trails, fishing, lying together in the hammock and talking about the deepest and most intimate desires of their hearts, some of which were realized sooner than later. Highway was experiencing the whole camping adventure from his K-9 perspective chasing rabbits and squirrels interspersed with generous episodes of splashing in the reservoir. Whenever Gus or Addie snagged a trout, he showed his approval by leaping into the water and displaying the retriever part of his mixed breed. The thrashing fish were too much to resist.

The morning of May 25, 1943, began with a family gathering and somber farewells. Anna Bodine came up with the idea of preparing a breakfast for themselves and the Russos. The invitation was delivered to Addie's parents the day prior to Gus' departure.

At 6 a.m. the doorbell rang. The dining room table had been set, and the house was redolent with the aroma of blueberry pancakes, spicy sausage patties, hash brown potatoes, scrambled eggs, croissants with honey-butter, and hot cocoa. The sumptuous breakfast cheered the spirits of all in attendance. After the kitchen and dining room were put back in order, Addie's parents wished Gus success and safe travels and then returned home.

Gus walked out the back door and across the backyard to the dog run. As he opened the chain-link gate, he was greeted instantly by an excited ball of fur, tail wagging, and a pink tongue lapping at his cheeks. He rolled around in the grass with Highway, laughing and enjoying every minute until it was time to leave. Gus rose slowly, brushing some grass from his trousers and shirt. "Well, fella, I'm off to Randolf Field to train in the big planes. I'm going to miss you, Highway. I know my leaving is as hard on you as it is on me. I need you to love Addie and take good care of her for me, will you? I may be gone for quite a while, but I promise you, I'll be back, and we'll be playing together in the park again before you know it."

Highway reluctantly allowed Gus to put him back inside the dog run and latch the gate.

"So long, boy."

CHAPTER 9

FORTRESS TRAINING

Addie drove Gus to the bus station in Provo. Tearfully, they kissed and embraced and said their farewells. Gus climbed the steps of the bus. Before the door closed, he turned to Addie and extended his arm and hand in a farewell wave and called out, "Together forever, my love!"

The Continental Trailways bus took Gus to Gallup, New Mexico, where he transferred to one that took him to San Antonio, Texas. A military bus would pick him up at the terminal and take him, and presumably other civilian-attired cadets, to Randolph Field.

Because the demand for new pilots was at its peak, modifications had to be made to manage the large number of pilot candidates. A staged program had been put in place consisting of On-line Training, Classification, and Preflight Training. On-line Training was the term for busy work given to cadets when there were no open spaces in the next level. In the Classification stage, cadets were processed through physical and mental testing, and it would be determined whether they would be trained as a bombardier, navigator, pilot, or assigned to other non-flying technical fields. Thanks to Gen. Yount's letter, Gus was able to forgo those first two stages and entered the third which was known as "boot camp." With Gus' civilian certification as a pilot, he was allowed to demonstrate his flying skills with an instructor who was authorized to award Gus his cadet flying wings and direct him to report to Flight School and Basic Pilot Training. There, he acquired the skill of formation flying, aerial navigation, night flying, and long-distance flying.

Gus was able to acquire 70 flight hours in a Vultee BT-13 Valient trainer aircraft. Similar in flight characteristics to the Spartan Executive, the Vultee was powered by a Pratt and Whitney R-985, 9-cylinder, air cooled radial engine. Similar in horsepower at 450 hp, the Vultee enabled Gus to pass through Basic Pilot Training at the top of his class—a ranking which rewarded him with an assignment to Advanced Pilot Training in multi-engine aircraft. Transferring to the Replacement Training detachment at Kelly Field, also near San Antonio Texas, he was introduced to the Beechcraft Model 18 (U.S. AAF designation AT-11) twin engine trainer. Gus accrued an additional 75 hours of multi-engine flight time.

On completion of Advanced Pilot Training, he was able to replace his cadet wings with the wings of a U.S. Army Air Force pilot and received his commission of Second Lieutenant. *I wish Addie could pin these wings on me. How I miss my sweetheart!* A warm smile crossed his face as he headed for the flightline to board the C-47 that would take him to Smyrna Army Airfield in Tennessee and the Forty-Sixth Pilot Transition Training Detachment on October 2, 1943.

OCTOBER 1943 / SMYRNA ARMY AIRFIELD

Transitioning to the B-17 was an entirely different animal from piloting a Cessna Bobcat or Beechcraft D-18. Climbing into the cockpit of a B-17 Flying Fortress could be likened to learning fifth grade math then advancing straight to calculus. Two pairs of throttles, twice the number of instruments with a few more thrown in to further boggle the mind. The pilot manual read like the San Francisco phonebook … it was a post graduate course in Aeronautical Engineering in and of itself.

CHAPTER 9

WORDS OF WISDOM

Gus and the other 13 pilot candidates in his group formed up in a three-column formation of five men, with the exception of one column of four men. They stood before a line-abreast group of four officers. One of them, a major, step forward to address the group.

"I'm glad to see that none of you seem to have forgotten your basic training of military courtesy and regulation of standing at attention. We will continue to follow proper military protocol throughout transition training.

"You are officers in the United States Army Air Force. You are here to be trained to prepare yourself for battle. Like any soldier, your weapon of choice, together with the skills and discipline you will develop in the wielding of that weapon, will in large part see you home to your families when the hostilities cease. There is a bus parked on the street to my left. We will board that bus which will take us to the flight line where you will meet that weapon of choice … the B-17 Flying Fortress."

Gus found a window seat. His classmates settled in, some sitting by themselves and others together. One man, a redheaded, freckle-faced, lanky fellow of nearly six-feet tall plopped down next to Gus.

"Howdy. Name's Plunkett, Sandy Plunkett. Sandy is short for Sanford, but my mother is the only one that calls me that and only when she's upset with me."

"Gus Bodine, Sandy. You sound like you're from the Midwest. I'm guessing the Dakotas, maybe Montana. I'm from Utah, myself. I'm pleased to meet you." Gus extended his hand. Sandy Plunkett grabbed it and gave it a firm shake.

"Cascade, Montana. Cattle country. You're from Utah. Are you a Mormon?"

"Yes I am, dyed in the wool, true blue, through and through," Gus offered with a grin.

Sandy nodded approvingly. "There are some folks down the street from my family's house who are Mormons. Nicest folks you would ever want to meet. The Bridger clan runs the Rocking Double-B. It's one of the biggest ranches in the state, and my dad is the ranch foreman for them."

Gus was tempted to talk more with Sandy, but the conversation came to an end when the bus stopped and the doors opened.

"Everybody out. Form up on the tarmac," the major commanded.

Major Enrique Rivera stood in front of the small group of trainees who were standing at attention awaiting his instruction.

"Stand at ease. What you see behind me is a B-17 Model 'E' Flying Fortress. Over the next six weeks you will each have many opportunities to be at the controls of this aircraft. There is much to learn before that happens, beginning with familiarization of the operational specifications of the Fortress. To that end, you will hit the books for the first two weeks of Transition Training. The 'E' model that you're looking at has a few interesting modifications from her predecessors the 'C' and 'D' models, most of which have to do with armament. Would anyone like to enlighten us as what some of those modifications are?" Having no volunteers, the major moved closer to the nearest line of five men. Gus, was the first man in line.

"Lieutenant Bodine."

"Sir, the modifications in armament are as follows: a dorsal gun turret, located behind the radioman is an add-on to the 'C' and 'D' models. Also a tail gunner position has been added. Both stations are equipped with two AN-M2 fifty-caliber machine guns each capable of firing eight hundred to one thousand rounds per minute. Other modifications include widening the teardrop shaped waste bubbles of the 'C' and 'D' models to a square, flat opening, allowing for a wider range of fire and improved visibility for both waist gunners, sir."

"That is correct. Now, raise your hand if you already knew everything Mr. Bodine just described." None of the other candidates raised their hand.

Maj. Rivera shook his head almost imperceptibly. "There are fourteen of you. I would expect that three or four of you will wash out of B-17 qualification and will be assigned to fly C-47 and C-54 aircraft with the Air Transport Command. Initiative, gentlemen—that quality which allows you to see ahead and to approach a challenge from an oblique perspective—is what will see you through this transition phase and prepare you for combat. You must train your minds to anticipate the unintended consequences of combat as well as those consequences that are before your eyes at any given time. Your eyes, ears, hands, and feet are constantly working to maintain a stable and controlled environment within your aircraft. As a pilot you can easily be so focused on the instrument panel, throttle settings, altitude, direction of flight, and your position within the formation that you may not be as sharply aware of a situation developing outside of your aircraft. At any given time, the enemy may attack, or your wingman might stray away from the formation enough to make him vulnerable to an attack, from an Me 109. Or, perhaps you note an increase in the concentration of flat bursts near your position in the formation, or experience a subtle change in the feel of the performance of your aircraft. That 'seat-of-your-pants' feel is as much intuition as it is a physical sensation. Mr. Bodine's knowledge is the result of planning ahead for something he *knew* was coming, but not *when* it was coming. You all knew that you would be training in the B-17. If you were waiting to learn only when it came time to study it in the classroom, then you lack the vision to see an unintended consequence of your choice to be here in this place and at this moment in time. Knowledge alone will not see you through the battles you will face. You have to learn to think outside the bubble that is your Fortress."

Ground school for transition pilot such as Gus, consisted of 90 hours of classroom instruction intertwined with logging one hundred hours of flight time at the controls of a B-17E. For the next two weeks the new pilots attacked the manuals learning the layout of the Boeing B-17E/F model's various systems and performance specifications. In short, in addition to learning how to fly a four-engine bomber in every conceivable situation that he might be exposed to when flying combat sorties, he was expected to know enough about every crew member's job that he would have some understanding of every man's role in the crew and be able to perform some of their duties should the situation arise. The first opportunity to be at the controls would come in two weeks later.

OCTOBER 17, 1943 / FIRST FLIGHT

The candidates were paired up to allow each of them to take their turn at the controls. Their instructor, Captain Nick Bayless would be in the right seat co-pilot's position to critique and assist the candidate. For all intents and purposes, Gus would be the PIC of the mightiest heavy bomber to ever take to the skies. He was delighted when he found himself paired with Sandy Plunkett. As past study partners and roommates they were good friends.

"Lieutenant Bodine, you are the PIC. I am here to assess your knowledge and piloting skills. I may be asking you some questions along the way, but unless you ask for my direct intervention, the aircraft is yours. I'll handle the radio, while you concentrate on flying the aircraft. Today we're going to be practicing takeoff, climbing to cruise altitude, flying inside the traffic pattern, and practicing approach to landing. For now, Plunkett, you will observe until it's your turn to be at the controls. Do not say anything ... just imagine yourself in the left seat, and let your mind take you through the motions. You'll get your opportunity to switch places with Lieutenant Bodine shortly."

"Copy that, sir," Sandy Plunkett acknowledged.

"We have already gone through the walkaround, so talk me through the engine start checklist, Lieutenant Bodine. This brings up an important subject. Always put the checklist card in front of you and follow it to the letter. Even after you have gone through the process a hundred times. One simple mistake could result in catastrophic damage that would prevent you and your crew from participating in a critical mission."

"Emergency ignition switch ON." Gus voiced as he turned on the emergency ignition switch. "Master battery switches ON. …Inverters ON. …Checking for proper voltage output of 26 volts. …Check landing gear control switch in neutral … flap control switch in neutral. …Set parking brake.

"Checking free movement of all control surfaces." Gus moved the control yoke and rudder pedals to ascertain free movement of the ailerons, elevators, and flaps.

Lt. Bodine opened the side windscreen and put both hands out the window. With his right hand clenched in a fist, he slammed it down striking the open palm of his left hand.

The action told the ground crew to connect the portable power unit preparatory to starting the number one engine.

Gus continued, "Opening all fuel shutoff valves. …Co-pilot, open all carburetor air filters. …Setting propeller controls for high RPM. … Turning on number one magneto switch …"

For each step that Gus completed of the engine start checklist, he commanded the co-pilot, Capt. Bayless, to complete the corresponding item such as opening the cowl flaps, checking hydraulic pressure, checking that the fuel transfer valves were in the OFF position, starting each engine's fuel booster pump, in order, prior to starting the engine.

"Starting number one," Gus commanded.

As Capt. Bayless held the start switch in the ON position for the number one engine, the propeller began to turn. When it coughed out a blast of white smoke, Gus moved the mixture control to AUTOMATIC RICH.

Gus checked the oil pressure indicator. The needle began to rise, and as the engine warmed up, the needle stopped at "50" (pounds per square inch). He opened the throttle to 1100 rpm.

Gus and Capt. Bayless repeated the process until all four engines were purring.

Capt. Bayless radioed the control tower and requested permission to taxi for departure straight-out and runway 29.

Gus ordered the tail wheel lock to be released and completed the final instrument check. Confirming that all engine instruments were operating in the green normal range, Gus was ready to taxi the bomber to the runway. He used the throttle controls to the outboard engines to turn the plane, and the Fortress began a slow rolling turn toward the taxiway.

"Now you know why it is critical to follow every item on the engine start checklist, the engine run-up checklist, the takeoff and climbing to altitude checklist, and the cruise checklist. Sounds like a lot to do sitting there in the left seat, doesn't it, Lieutenant …?" Capt. Bayless stated more than asked.

"It sure does," Lt. Bodine agreed.

With a single smooth motion, Gus opened all four throttles to FULL THROTTLE. The pitch of the engines rose until the roar of the Wright R-1820 Cyclone engines vibrated throughout the bomber. Were it not for the earphones that every crew member wore, the noise would've made talking to each other impossible.

The Fortress lifted from the concrete runway at 100 mph indicated. Gus ordered the gear brought up and flaps raised when the bomber reached a positive climb rate of 125 mph.

Beginning his climb to an altitude of 12,000 ft, Gus set the engine RPM to 2300 and checked to ensure that each engine's manifold pressure gauge read just a tad over 38 inches of mercury (Hg). He leaned the fuel mixture for "best performance" and maintained 135 mph indicated during his climb out. At 8,000 ft he ordered the air intake filter turned off, a safety precaution to prevent turbo overspeed. When he reached cruising altitude, Gus leveled off and pulled the throttles back to 2,000 rpm. He checked to affirm the manifold pressure on all four engines was holding steady at 34.7in.

"You have a fire in your number two engine. What do you do?" Capt. Bayless queried.

Without hesitating, Gus rattled off the protocol for an engine fire. "Close the fuel shutoff valve to the affected engine. Feather the prop which will prevent oil from being pumped into the flames. Next, reduce the airspeed, but maintain altitude. Close the cowl flaps and pull the CO_2 charge to the affected engine."

"Quite right, Lieutenant, but what if the fire is in the exhaust and not in the engine itself?"

"Usually, a fire in the exhaust is caused by a mixture of air and fuel that's too rich. The first thing to do is move the mixture control to 'lean.' Then, attempt to blow out the fire by running the engine up but not to exceed 2300 rpm. Close the cowl flaps, and close the fuel shut-off valve to the affected engine. Pull the CO_2 charge to the affected engine if the fire continues."

For two hours, Gus was grilled on one emergency procedure after the other. The lieutenant answered all the questions succinctly and without hesitation. All the while, Capt. Bayless was taking notes on his clipboard. There were no "atta boys." Every pilot candidate was expected to know the information.

"Take us down, Lieutenant Bodine." Capt. Bayless smiled. The smile was all Gus needed.

Capt. Bayless called the tower for landing instructions. Gus settled the bomber into a 145 mph, 700 ft/m descent for landing.

The cockpit of a B-17 is a complex piece of machinery, making it more than any one man can accomplish to make sure that all switches, levers, buttons, and instruments are in their proper position and functioning correctly while at the same time operating the flight controls. The co-pilot is instructed by the pilot to perform many of those required functions.

"Check load adjuster for center of gravity," Gus ordered.

"Load adjuster's checked," came the reply from Capt. Bayless.

"Set altimeter."

"Altimeter set."

Gus called for each item on the checklist. At 145 mph indicated, and with the Fort descending at a smooth 700 ft/min, Gus called out the last few items:

"Flaps set one half."

"Flaps set at one-half, Skipper."

The term "Skipper" brought a grin to Gus' face.

"Gear down."

"Gear down and locked," Capt. Bayless responded when the green signal light flashed on indicating the landing gear were in position for landing.

Gus trimmed the elevators. The resulting drag on the airframe slowed the plane even further. Adjusting the trim tabs made it easier for him to keep the nose up without having to apply excessive back pressure on the control yoke.

"Full flaps. Call out airspeed, please, Captain Bayless."

"140 ... 135 ... 130 ... 125."

Gus held the bomber's nose on the white line of the runway. The runway threshold was in view. At his current rate of descent his wheels would be at about 10 ft above the surface when he passed over the apron of runway 29.

"120 ... 115 ... 110, 105, 100."

The B-17's main landing gear touched down with a "squeak" on the concrete followed by the tailwheel lowering gently to the runway.

"Flaps up."

"Flaps are up."

"Unlock the tail wheel."

"Tail wheel unlocked. Well done, Lieutenant Bodine."

Sandy Plunkett was next in the driver seat. Gus' job was to watch and learn as Capt. Bayless took Sandy through the same routine. Sandy was a quick study, performing every task with confidence and knowledge. At the end of the day, Gus and Sandy recapped the flight in the debriefing session, going over every item in detail from the engine start sequence to engine shutdown. Both pilots paused several times in the debriefing to point out shortcomings in their performance … simple things like forgetting to close the cowl flaps, and hesitations in applying emergency procedures during simulated engine-out scenarios.

"Gentlemen, your knowledge is not in question. Additionally, you each demonstrated an acceptable command of the functions and operational protocols of the B-17. The reason why you will acquire one hundred hours at the controls of the Fortress is to commit that knowledge to a level that becomes more instinct than deliberate memory recall. If you were still in high school, I would score you both with a solid B+ ... well, make that an A-, but I don't want you to get big heads. I will provide both of you with a written critique of today's flight pointing out the highs and lows of your performance. Nothing short of a solid "A" should be acceptable to you. Overall, I would say you are both off to a good start."

CHAPTER 10

DECEMBER 3, 1943

Throughout the remainder of October and the month of November, during his continuing training at Smyrna Air Force Base in Tennessee, Gus felt as though he spent less time on the ground than in the air. Fifteen hours per week found Gus at the controls of a B-17 practicing visual and instrument navigation, night flying, formation flying at various altitudes and formation configurations: line abreast formation, diamond formation, three-plane V formation, and staggered line formation. Neither he nor Sandy Plunkett knew which, of the many bombardment groups operating all around the world, they would be assigned until they got to MacDill.

The 12 remaining pilots of the original 14 who entered the program at Smyrna, were called to a meeting in the briefing room for reassignment to the newly formed Air Force School of Applied Tactics at MacDill Army AFB, Florida. While there, Gus would meet the rest of his crew. At this stage he didn't know whether he would be the PIC of the B-17 Flying Fortress, or a co-pilot. He would know as soon as he opened the manila envelope containing his orders.

Well, here it is, he thought as he opened and read his orders. He wasn't aware of holding his breath until he released it with a loud sigh of relief. *Pilot*!

At 8 p.m. Tennessee time, it was only 6 p.m. in Provo, Utah. He stepped into one of the four telephone kiosks in the mailroom and dialed "0" for the base operator at Smyrna.

For security reasons all outgoing telephone calls had to be monitored by the communication center specialist with a security clearance. That individual was responsible for ensuring no compromising information was discussed during an unsecured phone call.

"Connecting to the long-distance operator now, sir. You are reminded that any information regarding your current duty assignment or future deployment is prohibited. Any violation will be reported, and you may be subject to disciplinary action under the Articles of War."

Gus heard a few clicks followed by a distant ring tone.

"Hello …?"

Gus recognized Addie's voice in an instant. "Hi, sweetheart."

"Oh, Gus! Hello, darling. How are you? At last, I get to hear your voice. I miss you so much. Have you been flying a lot? When do you finish your training? When can you come home?"

"Whoa! Slow down. I miss you too, my love. When I come back home, you can bet I'll never want to let you out of my sight. I keep thinking of our honeymoon. I want to be back there with you with my arms around you."

"Oh, Gussy, I love you so much."

"Addie, I can't say much about what I'm doing or where I'm going from here, but I can tell you that I'll be leaving for another assignment soon. I'll write to you when I find out where and when. We don't even know which unit we will be assigned to, yet. Things seem frustrating at times, partly because I'm restricted from talking over the telephone about my work (audible sigh). …So, how are you doing, my beautiful bride? I worry about you working at Geneva Steel. That can be dangerous work."

"Darned hard work for sure, but the other girls and I are watched closely to make sure we're safe. Our supervisor, Bud Grimes, tells me I'm a quick learner and a hard worker … it was good to hear. I have a whole new appreciation for the term 'hard labor.' My friends used to tell me stories about their fathers coming home from work and falling asleep in their easy chairs. …When the phone rang just now, guess what I was doing?"

"(Chuckling) Well, let me think ... sleeping in your chair? I wish I could be home to take that burden off your shoulders. I've talked to a few fellows whose wives or girlfriends are doing the same thing. For the most part, those women are working in the factories. They're welding and riveting the steel sheets and armor plating you're producing at Geneva Steel, into ships, tanks, airplanes and countless other machines and products. I'm so proud of you, Addie.

"Are you still walking in the park with Highway when you can?"

"I try to do that twice a week. He's such a blessing to me. I can't look at him without thinking about you, darling. I let him stay in the house now that the weather is getting so cold outside. He sleeps on the floor. ...Well, he starts there, but when I wake up in the morning he's always lying on top of my bed. I love that big furry mutt. He kind of grows on a person."

"This is the base operator. You have one minute remaining on your call."

"Sweetheart, I have to hang up. Other guys are waiting to make calls. You should get the letter I wrote soon. It will tell you more. I love you, darling, more than I can possibly put into words. Your love fills my heart, Addie. When I finally return to you after my job is done, I want to start a family with you."

"Me, too, Gussy." Addie's voice was subdued, almost to a whisper. "Bye-bye, sweetheart."

"Bye."

Ten days passed by without a letter or a call from Gus, so when she saw the Air Mail stamp on a letter sitting atop the table in the foyer one afternoon after work, Addie dashed upstairs. Highway barked once and was hot on her heels. She was exhausted from a day of hard work at Geneva, but nothing else mattered, not even her aching feet, arms, and shoulders. How she loved Gus' letters. Every time the postman delivered a letter, she felt the growing commitment to their future together. She was about to close her bedroom door when her mother's voice called out from the kitchen.

"Addie, dear, is that you? Dinner's almost ready. "

"I'll be right down, mother. I want to freshen up a bit first. Can you give me fifteen minutes?"

"Fifteen it is, darling."

She closed the bedroom door and walk over to her bed. Carefully running the letter opener under the flap of the envelope, Addie withdrew the letter. She sat down, kicked off her shoes and lay back on her pillow. She closed her eyes for a moment and imagined Gus sitting beside her … speaking the words which he wrote:

> *My darling Addie,*
>
> *The inevitable day that we knew was coming is closer than I thought. Rumors abound, but it looks like the air group will deploy sometime in the next few weeks. I can't tell you the precise date of our departure, or our destination. I can say there is a big meeting coming up in a few days to brief us on the details, but I wanted to share the scuttlebutt with you. The sad news is, there's likely to be no telephone service where I'll be going. I will not be able to call you, but we can still write. It will take many days for a letter to reach you.*
>
> *One of two things will determine how long I will be gone. After fifty missions, I can come home, or, if the war ends sooner than that I'll be in your arms faster than Highway can reach his food bowl at dinner time (ha, ha). Speaking of, is he still sleeping with you? He better plan on making room for me when I get back. Maybe we should buy a bigger bed.*
>
> *I'd better get this letter to the mail room, my love. I'll try to call you sometime soon. You'll probably get another letter before then, though.*
>
> *I love you, Addie … "Only forever, if you care to know."*
>
> *Yours, Gus*

After dinner, Addie and her parents chatted for a few minutes. Addie felt her eyes growing heavy, and her thoughts wandered from the conversation. She excused herself and went upstairs. After relaxing in a hot bath, she went to bed and slept straight through until her alarm awakened her at 5:00 a.m.

That workday at Geneva Steel began with Addie being given the responsibility of verifying the manifest of 48 tons of steel plating destined for Norfolk Naval shipyards in Virginia. The plating was loaded onto a flatbed rail car in six pallets by a huge "Whirley" crane that had a lifting capacity of 60 tons. The control cabin was 90 ft above ground affording the operator a 360° view while he communicated via telephone with the riggers on the ground.

The weight of the steel plating required the use of steel pallets rather than the wooden pallets used for lighter shipments. After the pallets were loaded, the crane lifted them to the flatbed rail cars. Each pallet was attached to the crane's hook by a system of chains and turn buckles.

Addie gave the go-ahead to the rigger boss. His crew attached one of the pallets to the crane's eye hook and began the orchestration of lifting an eight-ton pallet to the rail car.

Addie took her mind off the loading process while she double-checked her manifest. Had she looked up she would have seen the pallet swinging overhead directly above her. A turn buckle that secured one of the four chains to the pallet was rusted, and the strain of the weight caused the eye bolt to pop out of the buckle. When the resulting shift of eight tons of steel plating reached a critical angle, the whole assemblage tipped.

Bud Grimes heard the initial snap of the turnbuckle when it gave way. He reacted instinctively sprinting toward Addie, tackling her, lifting her feet off the ground and propelling her away from the impact point. She landed hard against some crates of armor plating used in heavy bombers to protect the cockpit crews. Not a second later, dazed but safe, Addie watched as the eight-ton load reached the end of its brief journey—falling on the ground exactly where she had been standing.

Addie's mother was near the telephone when it rang.

"Hello," she said pleasantly.

"Is this Mrs. Estelle Russo?" a somber sounding male voice inquired. The tone of his voice quickened Estelle's heartbeat. She instinctively knew something was wrong. She didn't know what, but she braced herself.

"Yes, this is she. Who's calling, please?"

"This is Allen Case, Mrs. Russo. Your daughter, Addie, has been injured at work and …"

"Hurt? My Addie? How … what?"

"She's at Provo hospital, Mrs. Russo, in the emergency room. I'm here in the waiting room. She's conscious and talking, but … hello? …Hello?"

Addie's mother had hung up after Mr. Case said her daughter was in the emergency room!

Fred, Addie's dad, worked across town, but before Mrs. Russo could call him, she needed to call her neighbor Izzy Sharple whose phone number she knew by heart. Not only was Izzy a neighbor, but a close friend and weekly Bridge partner as well. Estelle dialed Izzy's number and got an answer after the first ring.

"Hi Izzy, this is Stel. Addie has been hurt at work. I need a ride to the hospital. Can you help?"

"Stay put, Stel, and catch your breath. You sound like you are positively going to explode. I'm coming straight over, kiddo." She didn't wait for Estelle's thanks. Izzy Sharple ran to her car parked in the driveway and 'laid rubber' for the Russo house a block-and-a-half up the street.

Addie's mother called her husband, and agreed to meet him at the hospital. She had no more than hung up the phone than she heard a screech of tires and a staccato blare of a car's horn coming from in front of her house. The cavalry had arrived in the form of Izzy Sharple's maroon 1940 Chrysler Windsor 4-door sedan. Ten minutes later they arrived at the hospital.

Addie's mother checked in with the nurse's station and was told that the doctor was still with Addie. She pressed the nurse for more information.

"Is she going to be alright? How badly was she hurt?"

"I'm not at liberty to say, Mrs. Russo. If you will take a seat in the waiting room, I'll tell the doctor you are here.

Estelle Russo and her friend Izzy Sharple had barely sat down when Addie's father entered the emergency room waiting area, and Estelle rushed to the comfort of his arms.

"Oh, Fred! What are we going to do? What am I going to tell Gus? What if we lose our sweet Addie?"

Fred lowered his wife to one of three sofas in the room and looked at her squarely eye-to-eye.

"Now, sweetheart, let's not borrow trouble before it knocks on the door. Have you talked to the doctor yet?"

As if on cue, a doctor entered the waiting room. He glanced at the dozen people either sitting or pacing nervously.

"Addie Russo's family?" he queried.

"Yes. That's us. Is Addie … is she …?" Addie's mother fought for control and reached for the handkerchief that Fred offered her.

"I'm Doctor Riley, one of the ER physicians. Your daughter is going to be fine. She suffered a concussion and cracked two ribs that are causing her some pain, but she should be fine."

"Oh, what a relief. How did it happen? Can we see her, Doctor Riley?" Fred asked.

"Yes, of course, but she's still a bit groggy from the concussion. We'll need to keep an eye on her for a couple of days, but she should be able to go home then, barring any unforeseen complications of her injuries. I understand she was pushed out of the way of a falling pallet of steel."

Addie was awake when her parents entered the draped off space around her bed.

"Oh, Addie, my darling daughter. How are you feeling, sweetheart?" Her mother's eyes began to tear up again.

"I'll be alright, mom. Please, don't cry."

Addie's father bent low and kissed his daughter's cheek. "Do you know what happened, honey?"

"All I remember was that I was in the railyard checking the manifest for a load of steel plating, when I was hit from behind and knocked off my feet."

Fred told her what Doctor Riley had told him of the incident.

"Someone pushed me out of the way of a falling pallet of steel? I didn't see who it was. I woke up here. Whoever it was, saved my life,"

Addie said. Her voice was growing weak. "I need … I need to know who."

"Shhh, sweetheart. You rest, now. Your mother will stay with you, and I'll see you tomorrow. I have some calls to make."

At 8:00 a.m. on December 9, Fred Russo pulled up to the patient loading door in front of the ER entrance. Addie's mother accompanied the nurse who was pushing Addie along in a wheelchair. With Fred's help, Addie gingerly eased into the front passenger seat.

Addie was quiet on the ride home. She appeared despondent to her mother; enough so to prompt Estelle to ask, "What are you thinking about, sweetheart?"

"Everything. I think about Gus, mostly, wondering when … or if … I'll ever see him again."

"Of course you will, honey. You mustn't think of such things."

"I know, mom, but I can't help thinking how close I came to being crushed in that accident. Poor Gus is … or will be, putting himself in harm's way every day. If it hadn't been for someone risking his own neck, I would have …" Addie became silent again. A tear ran down her cheek.

"Daddy, can we go over to Geneva? I need to let Bud Grimes know that I'll be going back to work in a couple of weeks, and I need to know who it was that saved my life."

"Not today, Addie. You need to stay off your feet. Anyway, there's something I need to show you when we get home."

After the short drive to the Russo house, Addie was helped over to the sofa where she stretched out comfortably against a pair of overstuffed pillows her mother had brought in from Addie's bedroom. On the coffee table lay a copy of the previous day's edition of The Daily Herald. Addie decided to catch up on the local news and work the crossword puzzle.

Suddenly, she cried out, "Oh, dear God, … NO!" She dropped the paper on the floor exposing the front page headline: "Local Hero Crushed While Saving Co-Worker's Life."

Bud Grimes' wife and four children, together with extended family and many friends and acquaintances, gathered at the cemetery on a cold tenth of December to honor him. Addie Russo was in attendance and took the opportunity to speak to Bud's wife. She thanked her for her husband's bravery and talked about her friendship with him. Betty Grimes turned the conversation to Addie, inquiring after Addie's health and if she was coping alright. Addie's spirits were lifted by Betty's genuine concern and best wishes.

CHAPTER 11

MACDILL ARMY AIR FORCE BASE, FLORIDA

While Gus was in Tennessee, training in B-17 operations, enlisted crewmembers received their training at technical schools in locations across the southeastern United States. After the Japanese attack on Pearl Harbor, the demand for technical training grew exponentially with a flood of new enlistees. Because technical schools did not require pilot training, the Army Air Forces needed alternative training locations to fill the burgeoning demand. Four hundred and fifty-two hotels, countless warehouses, theaters, convention halls, even athletic fields and parking lots from Mississippi to Texas, Oklahoma, Georgia, and Florida were equipped for service as technical training schools.

The integration into a cohesive combat ready unit of enlisted nonflying technical personnel with aircrew members including pilots, navigators, bombardiers, and co-pilots, was the job of the Army Air Force School of Applied Tactics, headquartered at MacDill Army Air Base.

DECEMBER 4, 1943 / 483RD BOMBARDMENT GROUP

The first order of business was the assignment and gathering of individual crews to begin training in one of the four new B-17G heavy bombers. Gus knew he had a one in three chance of being selected for one of the Fortresses parked on the tarmac—a fact that spiked his anxiety level. More of the "G" types were expected over the next few days. The 12 pilots in his group from Smyrna AAF base were not the only pilots in attendance. A dozen others from various training bases arrived the previous day. In all, the two new bomb groups - the 483rd and 463rd, would each be 16 planes strong before being deployed to Italy. The commanding officer of the newly created 483rd Bombardment Group, Fifth Bombardment Wing, Fifteenth Air Force, was Colonel Paul Barton. Col. Barton's second in command was Lieutenant Colonel Edward J. York.

The two senior officers entered the hangar, and Master Sergeant Gene Halvorson called the group to attention.

"Group, ahh-ten-HUT!" Everyone snapped briskly to attention.

Gus estimated there were in excess of 600 men sitting in folding chairs on the floor of the huge hangar. Almost one-third of them were officers like Gus, and the rest were enlisted NCOs.

Gus nudged Sandy Plunkett. "Nine of those guys are going to be our crewmates, Sandy. I guess we'll find out soon enough who they are."

"True that, but I'm more anxious about whether our new assignments here will be as pilots or co-pilots," Sandy said quietly as he looked around at the other men.

Col. Barton greeted the combined complement of the fledgling unit.

"Good afternoon, gentlemen. We are the 483rd Bombardment Group Heavy ("Heavy" being a designation for 4-engine bombers) organized this past October following the creation of the new Fifteenth Air Force in September. The four squadrons of the 483rd Bombardment Group are as follows: the 815th, 816th, 817th, and 818th - formerly the 840th bomb squadron. They began their training at Ephrata Army Air Base in Washington. Most of you have been with us from the beginning. We moved to MacDill five weeks ago when staffing was still underway. To you new arrivals, welcome! Other aircrew personnel are forthcoming, and we anticipate a full complement by the thirteenth of December.

"As you've seen outside, parked on the tarmac, are four brand spanking new B-17G models. Four of you newly assigned officers will be in command of those aircraft. All four of the new crews are assigned to the 816th Bomb Squadron. More Fortresses are in route as we speak. Some are the newer models. Others are the earlier 'G' and 'F' models. Over the next four or five days there will be sufficient numbers of them flown in from various locations to bring to full strength two new bomb groups: the 468th and 483rd. Before we move to the business of announcing the assignment of crews by their pilots, Lieutenant Colonel York will conduct the remainder of this meeting. Colonel York."

"Gentlemen, sitting on the dais in front of me, are four envelopes. Each of these contains a list of names chosen for each position on the crews of the four Fortresses parked outside on the tarmac. I will now announce the names of each pilot: Lieutenant Gus Bodine, Second Lieutenant Brent Stanley, Second Lieutenant Andrew Garrison, and Second Lieutenant Sanford Plunkett. You four officers will step forward and read off the names of your crews. As your names are read, you will assemble at your assigned space on the floor here in the hangar. You will then be given an opportunity to greet each other and exchange names. In one hour, you will adjourn to the parking ramp for your assigned aircraft. Pilots, you will board your men who will take their assigned position as crew chief, radioman, bombardier, navigator, co-pilot, and gunners. There will be no flying today. By sixteen-hundred hours, you will dismiss your crews to return to their billets. At sixteen thirty hours, everyone here will report to the mess hall for chow.

"Pilots, you will also find your mission assignments for tomorrow morning contained inside the larger envelope. Read them over, share them with your crews, and be ready to assemble back here, in this hangar, at zero five hundred hours for your mission briefing. Wheels up will be at zero six forty-five. Everything you need to know is contained in your mission packets. Enlisted personnel will report to the flight line at zero six hundred."

Gus was the first to announce the names of his crew. Each name was read and matched with his assigned specialty. Each NCO then walked to the assigned area in the hangar, identified by the tail number of the aircraft to which he was assigned.

CREW BRIEFING AND INTRODUCTIONS

"I'm Lieutenant Gus Bodine, the new aircraft commander for 43-37594, one of the new 'G' model Fortresses parked on the tarmac outside this hangar. We all share something in common, fellas. That is the simple fact that none of us have been inside that particular aircraft. Getting to know her, and getting to know each other, will be the focus of our efforts beginning right here and now. With that in mind, as I call out your name, please stand. You have exactly thirty seconds to tell us the most important things you want us to know about you. I'll begin with myself. I'm a Utah boy, raised as a Mormon. I'm married to the most wonderful woman in the world, Addie. She is my greatest love. My second great love is flying airplanes. What you should know about me, fellas, is that I don't take lightly the things upon which my life depends. I expect everyone here to take the attitude that survival in this business depends on how well we do our jobs both as individuals and as a team. The hardware is the tool of our trade. Our passions: family, faith, country, and crewmates, will combine to see us through the hardships ahead. We will push the hardware to its maximum potential. We will push ourselves to survive the night of our darkest fears. We will win the day to see the light of our greatest desires emerge victorious.

"Lieutenant Barenz, you're up." Gus sat down on the army issue steel folding chair. Second Lt. Henry "Hank" Barenz, co-pilot, stood before the crew.

"Name's Hank Barenz. Born and raised in D.C. and Virginia. I graduated from Virginia Tech. I'm third of five siblings, and the only boy. My dad owns and operates a gasoline station and car repair garage. I never knew I wanted to be a pilot until I enlisted and said, 'Yes' when the recruiter asked, 'You want to learn how to fly planes?' They put me in Basic Flight Training, and since then, as my flying skills have grown, so has my realization that I was born to fly. I have come to love being lifted above the clouds … where somehow, I feel closer to heaven. And, I'm a newlywed to the prettiest gal in the Blue Ridge Mountains."

One by one each man told his story. Their faces, unfamiliar and strange at first, began to take on life. Navigator, Lieutenant Philip Day, eldest son of a university professor and a schoolteacher mother. Phil made it through Basic and Primary Flight School only to wash out due to a freak accident that left him with a broken ankle. After the ankle healed, Phil was given the choice of navigator school or cross training as a cargo pilot.

Lieutenant Alvin Wendelford, elementary school teacher and the only member of his family to attend college, answered the call to duty by enlisting. He liked the idea of serving his country from the sky rather than slogging through the mud from France to Germany. There was a slot open for bombardier school, and he snapped up the opportunity.

The rest of the crew took their turn, each story differing in detail, but following a similar pattern of leaving the familiarity of family, community, freedom, and peace to fight for their country. The war, as frightening and as horrific as the fires of hades, was an ocean away; but for men like Gus' crew, the flames of patriotism that drove them to take up arms, were lit by the thought that their actions would insure that such oppression would never come to America's shores. Men like Tech. Sergeant, flight engineer, Billy "Dink" Dinkleman; waist gunner, Tech. Sergeant Robert Sykes; radioman, Staff Sergeant Martin Gonzalez; tail gunner, Staff Sergeant John "Woody" Carpenter; ball turret gunner, Staff Sergeant James "Clay" Clayton; and waist gunner, Staff Sergeant Stan Wagner rounded out the crew.

"On a final note, gentlemen, we need to name this beautiful lady." Gus ran his hand over affectionately over the nosewheel.

Woody Carpenter spoke up, "Skipper, I think we all agree that you should have the honor as our commanding officer. Right fellas?"

The men voiced their approval with a resounding "Hear, hear!"

"Thank you, fellas." Gus didn't take long to announce the name this beauty would be known by. It came to him when he was made her pilot in command. If it's okay with you, let's call her *Addie's Armor* - after my wife, to commemorate the work that she and the other women back home are doing for the war effort. Our plane could well have armor on her right out of the Geneva Steel plant where my wife worked."

Another cheer by the crew settled the issue—*Addie's Armor* was *their* B-17!

DECEMBER 13, 1943 / MISSION BRIEFING

With the arrival of the remaining aircrews, the 483rd Bombardment Group (Heavy), was at its full complement.

There— on the floor of a hangar with its new organizational logo of a winged sword suspended point down to a colorful blue, red and yellow banner declaring "AB NUBLIBUS VINCEREMUS" (Victory From the Clouds) mounted over the door—the 483rd Bombardment Group, Fifth Wing, Fifteenth Air Force, took on life.

The final stage of combat training began on December 13, 1943. In nine weeks the 483rd would leave the United States.

Thirty-six crews sat in gray steel folding chairs chatting quietly about the upcoming training mission. Speculation about where they were headed and the specifics of target selection, ordinance loadout, and a dozen other details would be explained.

Master Sgt. Gene Halvorson, the 483rd First Sergeant, approached the dais and called the room to attention. Five hundred men rose to their feet, and silence fell over the hangar.

Commander Col. Paul Barton and his Executive Officer, Lt. Col. Edward J. York, entered.

"Be seated." Col. Barton waited while the assemblage of B-17 bomber crews settled in for the mission briefing. He turned toward the map behind him depicting the areas of Sarasota, Manatee county, and MacDill Army Air Force Base. Highlighted within a red circle was the bombing range at Avon Park Army Airfield about one hundred miles south-southeast of MacDill Army Air Force Base.

"Tomorrow morning, the fourteenth of December, the 483rd will commence bombing and gunnery practice over the Avon Park Army Airfield bombing range. This will be your first and only practice mission as crews. You have all been trained individually at various bases around the southwest United States. You have mastered your skills and prepared for this day. What you have not done and will do tomorrow, is work as a cohesive team. You will be brothers linked by a common two-fold purpose: complete your mission and return to base … alive.

"We will depart MacDill in four flights of nine aircraft in squadron formations. We will then form four single squadron combat boxes separated vertically and horizontally. Martial at one-five-thousand feet. Proper separation is essential. We wouldn't want to drop bombs onto one another, now would we?" Col. Barton paused a moment for the bit of nervous laughter to settle.

"Loadout will consist of twelve each, 100 M38 A2, practice bombs which will be fitted with M1A1 spotting charges. Gun positions will be furnished with one hundred fifty-caliber rounds each. Following the bombing practice, four target drones will be deployed strategically to draw fire from the waste gunners, tail gunners, and turret gunners. Your instructions are to hold formation and not be drawn off into a one-on-one situation. The strength of the Fortress is the defense we offer one another by maintaining a tight formation. Ground crews are completing the loadout and fueling operations as we speak. You will report to the flight line promptly at zero five-thirty hours. Wheels up at zero six fifteen hours. Questions?"

"Yes, sir. Will there be spotters on the ground to measure mean points of impact (Mean Points of Impact)?" The question came from Sandy Plunkett, Gus' new friend.

"Yes, Lieutenant. Those personnel will be placed at expedient distances armed with their spotting equipment. Please reserve your best MPIs for the designated targets, and avoid direct hits on the spotters." Again, the Colonel's effort toward levity was met with a few appreciated lukewarm chuckles … a reminder that this was a serious business, but one's psyche needed its lighter moments as well.

"Your mission packets will explain the order of attack in line formation once you reach the IP (Initial Point).

"As for you pilots, Lieutenant Colonel York and I have observed each of you in the air and on the ground. Your success as commanding officers depends on more than piloting skills. We have also assessed your military decorum, command abilities, and rapport with your crews with regard to mutual respect and trust. You have all demonstrated a high level of excellence both as commanding officers and pilots. That having been said, I will announce the flight leaders for tomorrow's mission. The officer commanding Blue Flight, which will lead the group on this exercise, will be Lieutenant Gus Bodine …"

Blue Leader? Wow! I did not see that coming. With his heart pounding heavily in his chest, Gus was glad the others had their eyes on Col. Barton. He felt certain that if they saw him … the way he saw himself at that moment … they would see the face of a man on the verge of panic.

"Colonel York and I will be orbiting the drop zone in a twin D-18. We will be silent observers only, monitoring you on the plane-to planc-frequency. As far as you're concerned, radio silence between you and me is the order of the day. You are on your own, gentlemen. This is the only opportunity you will have to practice your skills in a simulated combat scenario.

"The second flight, labeled Red Flight, will be led by Lieutenant Sandy Plunkett. The third flight, Green Flight will be led by Lieutenant Stephen Miller and the fourth flight will be led by Lieutenant Alonso Juarez, designation Yellow Flight. Your attack order will be Blue Flight followed by Red Flight, then Green Flight, and finally Yellow Flight. Again, attack will be in staggered line formation for each flight. This will allow the MPIs to be quickly assessed for your individual crews by the ground spotters. All bombs will be dropped from an altitude of twelve thousand feet.

"Once completed, the Group will re-form at fifteen thousand feet and return to base. Debriefing will commence at sixteen hundred hours following chow. Wheels up at zero six fifteen. Any questions?"

"Yes, sir, I'm … uh … Lieutenant Juarez, sir. At what point will the gunnery practice follow the bombing sortie, sir?"

"Lieutenant, the Luftwaffe doesn't wait for us to finish dropping our ordinance before hitting our Forts. They have a habit of gunning for us whenever it's to their advantage. You may expect the drones to be on you at any point. And remember, gunners, those P-40s towing the target banners are not armed with live ammo, but you are. Try not to shoot any of them down. You will be credited only for the holes you put into those streamers, understood?"

"Yes, sir!" came the unanimous reply.

"You'll learn to know each other to the extent that you will anticipate what the man next to you will do even as he does it. To that end, I have scheduled classroom time in Hangar Two for the pilots and bombardiers to discuss the interface of the new bombsight technology with the autopilot. Mister Abel Fischer of the Sperry Corporation will be there to explain the new equipment and answer questions."

CHAPTER 12

HANGAR #2

"Gentlemen, my name is Abel Fischer. I'm part of the design team that has been working on a method to improve on the current SBAE (Stabilizing Bombing Approach Equipment). You bombardiers are aware of the lengthy time needed to level and stabilize the platform for the Norden bomb site. By adding a third Gyro, spinning at thirty thousand rpm, we are able to level the bombsight platform much more quickly and accurately. Stated simply, the new Sperry bombsight, when paired with the A-5 autopilot will stabilize the aircraft along all three axis: yaw, pitch, and roll. It will do it more quickly and with more accuracy than the Norden 'M' series bomb sights. Your 'G' model Fortresses are equipped with the new A-5s mounted on a Norden M-XV sight. When paired with the Norden M-class bombsight or the Sperry S-1 bombsight, heading adjustments will be automatically accomplished. Pilots, your role will be to oversee the actual progress of your aircraft, but once turned over to the bombardier, a practice of 'hands off' the flight controls would be the most prudent."

The following four hours were spent with pilots and bombardiers putting their heads together to discuss the new protocol for the acquisition of targets.

"Well, it looks like you will be guiding us all the way to the target, Al. How do you feel about the equipment?" Gus queried his new bombardier.

Lt. Wendelford pushed his service cap back and scratched his head. "I understand the technology, Skipper. The old 'F' model Forts I trained in used the Norden Mk-XV bombsight. On those older models, the pilot had to handle heading adjustments due to turbulence, and it always took a lot of time to level the gyros on the platform well before reaching the target. We've gone over the manual for the new equipment and had opportunities to bench test the new A-5/S-1 interface in mock scenarios. This new system should speed up the whole process. As long as I do my job, we'll be fine."

DECEMBER 14 / 0545 HRS (THE NEXT DAY)

Lieutenants Bodine and Barenz completed the preflight walk around on *Addie's Armor* and then climbed up the crew letter into the cockpit.

Hank's expression when he looked at Gus was one of curiosity and concern.

Gus returned the look with a steady gaze.

"Something on your mind, Hank?"

"No, no. It's just that you've got a look on your face like you're about to get a butt-spanking from your papa. Something's got you rattled."

"I have to admit, I wasn't expecting to lead the whole group into our first and only bombing practice. New plane, new crew jitters. I'll get over it, partner. We'll be fine." Gus forced a smile and released a lungful of air with a "whoosh." "Things have settled down back there, and I think it's time to check in with them."

He keyed his mic to Sgt. Gonzalez, the radioman. "Sergeant, put me through to the crew."

"Pilot to crew: Status check. Call it in:

"Mic check. Navigator?"

"Navigator: Roger."

"Bombardier?"

"Bombardier: You are loud and clear, Skipper."

"Engineer?"

"Engineer: Copy."

"Radioman?"

"Acknowledged. You are five-by-five, sir."

"Dorsal gunner."

"Dorsal gunner: Copy."

"Waist gunners."

"Left waist: Copy.

"Right waist: Copy, sir."

"Tail gunner?"

"Tail gunner: Copy, sir."

"Belly turret?"

"Turret: Copy."

"Let's start em' up, Hank."

Gus held the Engine Start Checklist on his lap and opened the windscreen next to his head. He signaled the ground crew to attach the power generator.

"Master switches ON," Gus commanded.

Lt. Barenz pushed the switches up. "Master switches ON."

"Inverters ON."

"Inverters are ON, Skipper," the co-pilot responded.

"Check voltage."

"Gauge reads twenty-six volts."

"Check parking brake ON."

"Parking brake is engaged."

With each command, the clicking of switches, the hum of electrical equipment, and whine of various servos told the story of a Fortress coming to life.

"Booster pumps and pressure ON."

"Booster pumps ON. Pressure reading normal."

"Set throttle for number one (engine) and prime the engine," Gus ordered, glancing over to watch Hank set the throttle for the inside engine on the port (left) side.

"Start number one."

"Starting one."

All three of the five-and-one-half foot Hamilton blades on the number one engine began to claw at the sky with the "whine" of the turbines ... slow at first, like the talon of some giant awakening raptor. After three rotations, the engine caught and belched out a cloud of white smoke. With the throttle set at 1000 rpm, Gus ordered the outboard number two engine started. The process was repeated until all four engines were rumbling at a smooth idle.

Pilot Lt. Bodine was ready to taxi the Fortress to the runway. His heart rate settled into a cool 61 beats per minute. The exacting routine of preparing the bomber for departure settled his nerves. He released the brakes and began a slow taxi toward the end of the runway.

"How are the engines looking back there, Sergeant Dinkleman?" Gus asked the flight engineer over the interplane crew frequency. Sitting behind the co-pilot in front of a panel of gauges, Sgt. Dinkleman scanned oil pressure and temperature, manifold pressure, cylinder head temperature, mixture setting, and RPM indicator for all four of the radial engines. Those gauges were duplicated four times so that each engine gave the engineer its own reading.

"All gauges are in the green, Lieutenant."

Gus turned to his co-pilot. "I have the controls, Hank. Radio the tower for departure,"

MacDill tower, Army Three Seven Five Niner Four ready to taxi. Departing straight-out. Over.

Army Three Seven Five Niner Four, you are cleared to taxi runway two-seven. Please expedite departure. Over.

Addie's Armor was the first plane to go wheels up at exactly 0616 hrs. With all four Wright "Cyclone" turbo-supercharged engines flexing a combined 4,800 hp, she took to the sky in a 900 ft/min climb with a grace that belied her total weight and payload of over 21,500 lbs.

As Blue Flight Leader, it was Gus' job to arrive at the marshalling point at 15,000 ft where he would orbit in a broad circular pattern until all of the flights had formed the assigned squadron box of four flights of four aircraft each. When accomplished, Gus would lead the squadron box from the martialing area to a point just short of the IP, 20 miles north of the target area, at the Avon Park Army Airfield Bomb and Gunnery Range.

As the Lead pilot of Blue Flight, Gus was the acting Group Leader for the exercise. Col. Blount would be watching how Gus handled his unexpected leadership responsibilities and would no doubt include his observations in Gus' after-mission debriefing.

Group Leader to all flights: Blue Flight will lead out and re-form in staggered line formation. Bombing altitude will be twelve thousand feet. Upon completion of the bombing portion of the exercise, Blue Flight will proceed to the next marshalling area awaiting the group to re-form. We will remain in squadron box formation for the gunnery practice. Your briefing packets describe your aircraft distances for both vertical and horizontal separation and airspeed. Flight Leaders please make sure the protocols are followed precisely. Group Leader: Out.

Blue Leader to Blue Flight: We have reached the IP and are turning toward the target. Assume staggered line formation. Watch your separation. Turning toward target now.

"Pilot to bombardier and gunners, arm your weapons."

Blue Leader to flight: Hold airspeed at two hundred miles per hour indicated. Keep your horizontal separation at one to one-and-a-half miles from the aircraft in front of you to give the spotters time to mark the MPIs of each plane's pattern. After bomb release, proceed to the marshalling point. Acknowledge.

Blue Two, roger!

Blue Three, roger!

Blue Four, roger!

The four B-17Gs, all Blue Flight, slipped out of the four plane diamond formation into staggered line formation.

"Target zone dead ahead. Lieutenant Wendelford, are you about ready to take us to the drop zone?"

"The platform is leveled and ready, Skipper. You can release the controls. I have the aircraft." ...*Now, this is scary. It's worse than driving a speeding car down the turnpike without touching the steering wheel or the brakes or accelerator. I feel like I'm tied to the front end of a runaway locomotive*, Al mused.

"Have you ever driven a speeding car down the turnpike without touching the steering wheel or breaks, Skipper?"

"Nope ... have not, and I hope I never will. Not being a drinking man, I should have no problem avoiding that particular scenario."

Lt. Barenz offered a lighthearted chuckle.

"I think I would have to be a little drunk myself to do this very many times," the lieutenant quipped.

There was no noticeable change in the sound of the engines, the occasional buffeting of the airframe, or the needles on the gauges showing airspeed direction of flight and altitude. Everything thing seemed to be humming along nicely at 200 mph.

Gus and Hank had a ringside seat as the Avon Park Army Airfield Bomb and Gunnery Range approached their 12 o'clock low position.

"We are on target. …Bomb release in five … four … three … two … one. Bombs away!"

With the clanking, metallic crash like that of a stack of baking racks being dropped to the floor, 12 of the 100 lb M38 M-2 practice bombs dropped into the sky from the plane's belly.

Addie's Armor flew to the marshalling coordinates where she orbited, awaiting the remainder of the 483rd to join-up. No sooner had Blue Flight completed its nine-plane formation, a frantic call came over the plane-to-plane radio frequency:

Bogies, six o'clock high! Coming out of the sun!

The announcement came from the tail-gunner of *Virgil's Virgin (#42-102382).*

Gus keyed his mic:

Blue Leader to all planes: Maintain formation and choose your targets. Pilots, fire on your command.

For the next eight minutes the sky was full of banner-towing P-40 Warhawks darting and weaving their fighters through the formation of B-17s, trying to entice the Forts to break formation for a better shot at the "enemy."

Soon after the last of the B-17s joined the formation, the fighters disappeared leaving the bombers in peace.

Debriefing was scheduled for 1600 hrs giving the crew of *Addie's Armor* the opportunity to gather together at the enlisted mess to compare notes on the practice sortie. Normally, the Officer's Mess accommodations were more nicely appointed: linens, table service, no waiting in line. However, the food was equally palatable at the enlisted dining hall, and Gus was pleased when TSgt "Dink" Dinkleman asked the officers to join them for chow.

Navigator Phil Day, bombardier Lt. Wendelford, co-pilot Lt. Berenz, and Gus entered the chow hall and immediately spotted the enlisted crew. SSgt Gonzalez raised his hand and motioned the officers over to the three rectangular tables which they had moved together for the occasion.

The six enlisted men stood as one but were immediately waved down by Gus.

"Sit, fellas, no need to stand for us. We're all family here, aren't we?" The "family" comment did not fall on deaf ears. The enlisted men glanced at each other, approving of the suspension of protocol, and as a gesture of unity, all of the NCOs broke out in broad grins of approval and sat down.

"What about it, fellas? Shall we all load up some trays before we get too involved in the events of the day?" ball turret gunner, "Clay" Clayton, invited. The smallest man on the crew, Sgt. Clayton also had the largest appetite.

"My favorite time of day—chow time!" Clay was the first out of his seat and first at the chow line.

The meal served that day was Salisbury steak, mashed potatoes and gravy, corn, peas, bread and something called "margarine" that passed for butter. Milk, coffee, and water were to be had from stainless steel dispensers at the end of the chow line. Soon, everyone at the table got down to the business of filling the empty hole in their gut. No one had bothered with breakfast since full stomachs and bladders did not mix well with a mission loaded with stress and apprehension. With the pressure off, they were all glad to sit down to a generous hot meal. The mess hall folks, the guys that put together three-square meals a day for over 1,000 men, always offered a little extra to the flight crews. They understood that many of the men wearing the flight jackets with the squadron emblems emblazoned over their hearts would not live to see another Christmas or New Year's Eve celebration.

Everyone was looking Gus' way to lead the discussion, so he tapped his tin cup with a fork and cleared his throat.

"Fellas, from where I was sitting, *Addie's Armor* performed without so much as a hiccup. Tech. Sergeant Dinkleman's engines purred like kittens. Comms were orchestrated by our radioman, Staff Sergeant Gonzalez. Whether I had to talk plane-to-plane, or to the whole group, he spun the dials on the radio like he was born to it. And you gunners … well, I don't know if you put any holes in those target drones, but you were all business. It sounded like each of you got plenty of shots off. How do you men think you did?"

Sgt. Carpenter didn't hesitate. "When I spotted a P-40 coming in at our three o'clock and banking hard right, that beautiful yellow streamer gave me a sweet broadside view in my sights. I know I must have put a few holes into it. I prayed to God I wouldn't hit the fighter. Those pilots really know their business."

"I'll say. Those fighter jockeys set us up just fine. All I had to do was lead the P-40, wait for him to make the right turn and … pow-pow-pow!" Sgt. Stan Wagner mimed a convincing dorsal turret gunner at work by holding his arms outstretched and shaking them the way they would recoil from twin fifty-cals being fired. A gunner is shaken down to his boots. His hands, arms, shoulders and back grow numb with the pounding of two jackhammers spitting out 850 armor-piercing rounds per minute each.

"How about you, Lieutenant Wendelford. Any problem with the new bomb sight?" Gus asked.

"None at all. The accuracy of the Sperry A-5 autopilot paired with the Norden bomb sight depends on the calibration of the three gyros. They have to be leveled on the platform perfectly. How was it in the cockpit, Skipper?" Lt. Wendelford asked.

"Piloting a Fort with a crew of ten men and a full load of bombs and being told to take my feet off the rudders and hands off the controls was a little unnerving at first. Then the expected didn't happen … the plane didn't flinch. She just kept on cruising. I could have taken a lunch break, and no one would have noticed."

The crew of *Addie's Armor* chatted while they ate. Gus could feel them growing together as brothers, and Hank noticed, too. He smiled at Gus, nodding his head with approval. These were more than ten men, trained in the duties of their trade. They had become family—brothers—united by the fires of war, choosing to fly and fight for peace for their families back home and for their country … *and* for their freedoms and their God.

DEBRIEFING

Col. Barton stepped to the podium and waited for the chatter to settle down. Behind him was a large map depicting the target area. Circles of white, yellow, and green overlay the clearly marked targets of concentric red circles within circles.

"Good afternoon, 483rd."

"Good afternoon, sir!" came the unanimous response.

"As you can see by the chart behind me, we've marked the areas of the most concentrated points of impact for each of the four flights. From an altitude of twelve thousand feet and during daylight hours with clear visibility, we would expect to see eighty-five percent of your ordinance hitting within a one thousand foot radius of the target center.

"Gentlemen, as you know, our two heavy bomber commands in the European and Mediterranean theaters of operation, the Eighth and Fifteenth, have not had the technology needed for precision bombing. The Brits have practiced saturation bombing covering German industrial centers, with heavy urban civilian populations, reporting in excess of eighty-six percent effectiveness with their Lancasters and Mosquitoes. Our 'heavies' of the Eighth and the Fifteenth have been focusing on industrial complexes in less densely populated areas, and bombing during daylight hours. Effectiveness on the target has been about eighty percent, but with less collateral damage on the civilian population. That is until now.

"The people from the Sperry Corporation have asked to share with you the data of the bomb run. ...Mr. Fischer."

Abel Fischer, the rep from Sperry who conducted the familiarization training of the new Sperry autopilot, stepped to the pulpit.

"When we measure bombing accuracy, we apply an algorithm to define the Mean Points of Impact, or MPIs. The result can be defined in terms of a percentage of overall effectiveness. You heard Colonel Barton describe the high degree of effectiveness by the Royal Air Force. Their MPIs were expanded to include the most damage done to a target including surrounding concentrations of civilian housing. Thus, the eighty-nine percent MPIs claimed by the Royal Air Force appears impressive, but when weighed against the civilian losses, the cost seems extreme. Engineers at Sperry have developed a new, more precise autopilot. When paired with the Norden MK-XV bomb sight, it produces a more accurate precision bombing platform. You are among the first pilots to apply the new technology in a large concentration of heavy bombers under wartime conditions. Here are the results:

"Blue Squadron, ninety-three percent of your bombs struck the target with an MPI of less than a one thousand foot radius of target center. Red Squadron, ninety-one percent. Green Squadron also at ninety-one percent, and Yellow Squadron, eighty-nine percent. Gentlemen, these outstanding numbers are made even more remarkable by the fact that none of you have previously used the new technology. I might add that Blue Squadron was the only box of B-17s who used the S-1 Sperry bomb sight paired with the A-5 autopilot.

"I'll turn the podium over to Colonel Barton. Thank you."

"Men, I know you have all been wondering and ... well, I must admit to a degree of speculation myself ... as to what our next assignment will be and when we will deploy. Command is keeping a tight lid on things, so I can't give you the specifics, only that it will happen sometime in late February or early March. I can give you some good news, however. Our training will continue over the next few weeks here at MacDill until the 483rd is assigned its next PCS (Permanent Change of Station) assignment. Your training mission here at the Army Air Force School of Applied Tactics will continue. Honing your skills in the air and in the classroom will continue." With that bit of news, a wave of grumbling washed over the group. Col. Barton chuckled and held up his hand. The assembled crews quieted down.

"I know, I know. At times it must seem like we'll never get a chance to use those skills you have all worked so hard to acquire.

"I have been authorized by Command to grant limited leave to a few of you. Starting with air crews, married personnel will be granted 20 days. Unmarried crew members will be given fourteen days leave. Ground personnel assigned to the 483rd, and those scheduled to deploy, will be given fourteen days leave as well. There are a large number of support personnel who are billeted here at MacDill, not assigned to the 483rd, who will remain on base, subject to their parent PCS commands. Leave time will be on a rotation basis beginning with the first group starting on December 20 and ending on January 9. The second group will begin their leave January 10 and end January 30. February 1 through 21 will be for the third group. Authorization and travel vouchers are available for officers at Base Operations. Enlisted men will pick up their papers at Base Personnel. The base switchboard will be open for calls to families from zero seven hundred to eleven-hundred daily. Your calls are limited to two minutes each. Make the best of it, gentlemen. And, Merry Christmas to everyone."

Gus and Hank exited Hangar #2 following the briefing and headed towards the Group Headquarters building behind and across the street from the hangar to check the leave roster. The list of names was posted on a cork board outside the main personnel office that handled all of the in-and-out processing of Army Air Force officers and enlisted men.

Gus scanned the page. He found his name, and Hank's as well, on the list of names slated for the first 20 days, December 20 thru January 9.

"Yes! I can't wait to call Addie and give her the terrific news. What about you, Hank?"

"For sure. Virginia is only about eight hundred miles north of here. I can probably catch a bus, or maybe a stand-by flight, from MacDill to Langley. I need to get right on it, though."

Hank started to walk away, then stopped and turned toward Gus. He extended his hand. "Good luck, Skipper. I hope you find a ride." The two friends shook hands and Hank was gone quicker than Gus could say "Merry Christmas."

Gus decided it would be best to arrange his travel itinerary before calling Addie. She might need to drive up to Salt Lake City to pick him up.

By 1930 hrs (7:30 p.m.), Gus fell into his bunk exhausted. His day started at 0400 hrs, followed by the mission briefing, the practice bombing and gunnery mission, the debriefing, and finally the frantic and fruitless search for a ride to Utah. *I need to just rest for a minute.* The thought barely entered his mind before the lights went out. He awakened over two hours later with an epiphany blaring out three letters in his mind, "A - T - C." *Why didn't I think of that before!* he thought. The Army Air Transport Command's chief mission was transporting supplies, military personnel, and replacement airplanes to overseas locations. It was primarily operated by former civilian airline executives and pilots who were "drafted" to create and staff a military version of the largest airlift organization in the world. Although there was not a parent ATC command presence at MacDill, there was a detachment assigned to process incoming flights of AAF personnel and equipment. Gus headed for building 13C, the office of the ATC detachment, and one Captain Phineas "Fin" O'Hanlon.

"So, you're looking for any ride to Utah on the twentieth. Hmmm … now, let me see." Capt. O'Hanlon thumbed through a stack of manifests of flights coming into and out of ATC bases such as the Thirty-Sixth Street AAF Station in Miami, Morrison Field near West Palm Beach, and Miami Army Airfield.

"Ah, here we go. A Ferry Flight of nine B-25 Mitchells is coming in tomorrow at Morrison Beach AAF Station in West Palm Beach. The 25s will go through a final inspection before departing for Lagens Field in the Azores and then on to their combat assignment." Capt. O'Hanlon waited for the obvious question, which came immediately.

"So, what's that got to do with me?" Gus asked anxiously.

"Everything, Lieutenant, Everything! The 25s are coming in from a repair depot at Hill Field in Ogden, Utah."

"Yes, but …" Gus began.

The captain raised his hand in a silencing gesture. "Hold on, I'm getting there. The Ferry pilots will be dead-heading back to Utah on your day, the twentieth, on a C-46 Commando loaded with engines. Estimated departure time of zero six hundred local. They'll refuel at Barksdale (AAF Base) in Louisiana and fly on to Hill Field. ETA at Hill is twenty fifteen hours. What do you think? I'm sure they'll have a space-available seat open. Do you want me to get you on that plane?"

"Done and done, Captain. And many thanks."

"No problem at all Lieutenant Bodine. Truth is, Morrison Field has traffic moving in and out all day every day. It's like they're a major airline over there. Many of our pilots are former airline jockeys. Consider yourself added to the manifest, my friend, and Merry Christmas." Capt. O'Hanlon offered a hand, which Gus happily shook.

On December 16, Gus stopped by the mail room following one of many familiarization flights in *Addie's Armor.*

One of the pieces of mail was a letter from Addie, dated four days earlier.

CHAPTER 12

My Love,

You're probably wondering why you haven't heard from me in the last several days. A lot has been going on here.

It's been almost two weeks since I had a little accident at Geneva. I will be alright, but I was slightly injured when a load of steel plating broke loose from a lifting crane.

Gus let out an audible gasp and rapidly read on …

My boss, Bud Grimes, pushed me away from the falling pallet. I sustained two cracked ribs and a concussion. The head injury is doing much better, but I'm still feeling a little tender if I bend or turn suddenly. So, that brings me to a decision I made, and I hope you will agree.

I quit my job at Geneva. You know I'm not one to quit anything once I decide to do it, but the very sad news is the unintended consequence of the pallet of steel breaking free from its moorings—it took a life. Mr. Grimes was crushed beneath the pallet of steel plates. He died instantly after pushing me free of the falling load.

I feel blessed that I was healed enough to attend his funeral.

Oh, Gus! I am so sorry that I did not listen to you and to mom and dad. You all told me that it was dangerous work. I went into that job with my eyes wide open, hoping to do my part for the war effort, yet I was blind to the risks that were right in front of my face all the time. I truly believe that those people who work in such dangerous professions are heroes in their own right.

As far as my immediate future is concerned, I have signed up for classes for the spring semester starting after the holidays. I want to continue with my degree. I would like to be finished by the end of fall semester about this time next year.

Gus, I'm sorry. I'm sorry that Bud Grimes' family will be without a husband and father because I hastily took a job I had no business doing. I think I wanted to be your hero as you are mine. I hope I can get over this horrible thing that I caused in a moment of carelessness. I should have looked up instead of checking off items on a stupid clipboard. I honestly don't know if I can forgive myself. I wish you were here even for a day or a minute, to hold me … even a phone call. I will just have to pretend that I'm talking to you instead of writing. I think then the void of darkness I find myself in, might lift so I can see the light again. Oh, darling, if only I could hear your voice.

On a positive note, Highway knows something is going on. Whenever I'm sitting down or lying-in bed at night, he is always there with his big, furry head on my tummy and those beautiful brown eyes begging me for a scratch behind the ears. Highway has a special angel spirit that makes me feel more at peace when he's with me. I don't know what I would do without him!

Gussy, keep promising me you will come home to me. Despite all of the horrors of what could happen to you that plague my thoughts every day, I need for you to come back to me.

On a final note, I know you are unable to tell me when your group is going to deploy. I only know that it will be soon. Perhaps you are already gone and waiting to arrive at your destination before you can write to me. Wherever you are, my love, know that I love you with all of my being, with all my heart, and with all of my soul.

Yours always,
Addie

Gus checked the time on his grandfather's pocket watch that he always carried with him. It was 9:15 a.m. *Still plenty of time to call Addie,* he thought to himself. He walked over to the officers' club and stepped inside of a telephone kiosk in the lobby.

The switchboard at the Base Communication Office was busy with holiday telephone traffic, but one of the amber 'O club' lights flashed on and the E-4 enlisted man operating the switchboard adjusted his mic and jacked in.

"Base operator," a pleasant baritone voice announced.

"I'm First Lieutenant Gus Bodine with the 483rd Bomb Group. I have …"

"Good morning, sir. I'm aware of the protocol setup for pilots and crews of the 483rd. Would you like an outside line, sir? I can reach your number from here."

"Yes, please. It's the Provo, Utah exchange, Academy four, one-seven-seven-nine."

Gus heard a couple of clicks and then a ring tone. He waited for an answer, and after several rings, decided no one was out of bed for the day. It was only 7:30 a.m. Provo time. Just then, a click and a groggy voice came over the line.

Addie had a fitful night's sleep, and at 4:00 a.m. had turned off her alarm clock hoping to sleep through until at least eight o'clock. A very wet tongue and audible, "Woof!" brought her to instant wakefulness. The telephone at her bedside was into its final ring when she snatched the receiver off its cradle.

"Hello," Addie announced in her lower-than-normal sleepy voice.

Gus decided to play a little game by altering his voice.

"You called?" Gus said in a fair impression of radio newsman, Walter Winchell.

"What! ...Who is this?"

"Has the darkness begun to lift, yet?" Gus asked in his normal voice.

"Gus! Oh, my. Oh ... Highway, what are you ..."

Highway was all over the place. His tail was slapping at Addie's face one second, and the next, he was licking and barking at the phone.

"Gus, talk to your dog ... PLEASE!" Addie held the phone to Highway's ear with one hand while she held the dog's head still with the other.

"Highway! High ya boy. I love you, Highway. Lie down now. There's my good boy."

"What did you say to him, Gus. He's finally laying down. I know, I'll give him a treat."

"Not right now, Addie. I'm short on time. I have news to tell you."

"Oh no, Gus. Are you shipping out?" Addie suddenly felt apprehensive.

"I'm leaving on an airplane on the twentieth." Gus said in a pretend somber voice.

"In four days? Oh, darling, we won't get to talk again, will we? ... Before you leave, I mean."

"I'm afraid not. I guess you'll have to make do with an early Christmas present. If you could have any gift, what would it be?" Gus asked in a light-hearted voice.

"Oh, sweetheart, it would be for Santa to drop you down our chimney." Addie giggled.

The operator interrupted the Santa Claus wishing game. "I'm sorry, sir. Your allotted time has expired. Please, end your call."

"I have to go, Addie. I love you, baby."

"Me too, you, my husband." ...*Click.*

After Addie hung up she lay in bed staring up at the ceiling. She was struck by Gus' comments about wishing for her favorite Christmas present. "What was it he said … 'I guess you'll have to make do with an early Christmas present?' Hmmm …," she said to Highway. She pictured Gus sitting in the hearth of the fireplace all covered with soot … and then she laughed.

Addie's mother knocked on the door. "Addie, dear, eggs and toast are on the table. I'm going to need your help wrapping some gifts this morning. Who were you talking to on the phone?"

"Mother, if we're going to have a conversation, you may as well come in."

Addie's mother opened the bedroom door and entered. Addie had a smile on her face.

"Well, whoever that was on the phone, it sure put a smile on your face," she said with an all-knowing grin. "I've missed seeing that."

Addie swung her legs over the side of the bed and stretched her arms over her head. "Mom, I feel like going outside with Highway and throwing snowballs. Maybe we'll take a nice walk down to the park."

Her mother stood before her and clasped both hands to her breast. "Adelle Russo … er, Bodine, that phone call worked a miracle."

"It was Gus, Mom! I think he's coming home for Christmas!" Addie squealed in delight.

Gus checked into the small passenger terminal adjacent to the control tower at Morrison Army Air Force Field at 0500 the morning of December 20, 1943. The passenger services attendant, a WAF tech. sergeant, greeted him.

"Good morning, sir. Are you Lieutenant Bodine?" the sergeant asked.

"I am. I'm booked on a standby flight to Hill Field in Utah. Am I still good to go?" Gus knew "standby" meant that he didn't have a guaranteed seat. Any higher-ranking officer or additional cargo being added to the manifest at the last minute could bump him off the plane.

The female tech. sergeant pulled a clipboard from a hook on the wall behind her. The manifest, which had been updated late in the afternoon of the previous day, showed 1st Lt Gus Bodine among a list of nine other names of Army Air Force personnel scheduled to depart on a C-46 Commando at 0600 hrs. "You arrived just in time, sir. I was just ready to announce boarding for you and the nine WASPS (Women's Airforce Service Pilots)."

Gus climbed the portable stairs to the side door of the twin-engine transport. He found his "seat" and stuffed his duffel bag underneath. He pulled a shoulder harness down across his body and buckled himself into the nylon webbing that pulled down from the bulkhead along the inside of the fuselage. The other passengers, all WASP shuttle pilots, found unoccupied "seats" and made themselves at home. No doubt they had been through the same routine countless times.

HILL AFB, OGDEN, UTAH

At 9:10 p.m. local time, the Commando touched down at Hill Field. When the access door was opened, Gus descended the stairs into a 36° F foggy night. He pulled up the collar of his woolen, double-breasted trench coat to warm his ears. The cold breeze sent swirls of powdery snow playing tag across the tarmac beneath the incandescent lights lining the flightline.

He quickly closed the door behind him and approached the "PASSENGER SERVICES" counter against the far wall of the spacious airport terminal.

"Can you help me, please?" Gus asked the attractive brunette attendant behind the counter. "I need to arrange transportation to Provo."

"Certainly, sir. There is a shuttle service to Provo four times per day. There's one leaving in about three hours, at twelve-thirty, then tomorrow morning at seven-thirty, and eleven-thirty, and four-thirty tomorrow afternoon. It's for Hill Field civilian workers, but I'm sure you can find a seat on the twelve-thirty a.m. bus. The pickup point is behind this building."

"Thanks, but is there any other service? … Maybe a civilian bus terminal nearby?" Gus inquired with a clearly excited and impatient expression on his face and in his voice.

"Yes, sir. There's a Greyhound bus station in Clearfield. Let's see … I have a schedule here some place," she said as she rummaged through a drawer behind the counter. "Oh, yes, here it is." She smiled and jabbed her finger at the brochure. "Leaves at ten-thirty. I can call Base Transportation for you. Clearfield is only five minutes from the main gate."

Gus thanked the young woman who dialed the number she had apparently memorized.

"Hello, Allan? How are you, honey? …Oh, I'm fine, thanks. Say, I have a pilot out of MacDill who is in need of a ride to the Clearfield bus terminal … Greyhound. That's right. Thanks, darlin'. He'll be waiting right here for you. What? ...Oh, I'd love to, sweetie. Dinner and a movie would be a treat. Tomorrow night is perfect."

Gus was pleasantly surprised by the woman's resourcefulness. "Your boyfriend?"

"Yes, indeed. He's a civilian contractor. They handle most of the routine military taxi service on base. Allan is working a swing shift. He hasn't had a run all night, so he's glad for the break."

An olive-green 1940 Chevrolet, with a white star emblazoned on each of the doors, pulled up to the bus terminal. "Here we are, Lieutenant. Merry Christmas. You're lucky Eileen was working tonight. I'm not supposed to drive one of the staff cars off base without specific orders, so I'll be hustling back to the motor pool as soon as I drop you."

"I really appreciate this, Allan. Thank you, and Merry Christmas." Gus climbed out of the car, and Allan sped off with his tires throwing a flurry of snow behind him.

The Greyhound bus made good time driving straight through to Provo in just over an hour. He slung his duffel bag over his shoulder and stepped into a clear night sky lighted only by a few incandescent streetlights and a brilliant blue-white full moon. It was apparent that it had only started snowing here shortly before the bus pulled into the depot The snow itself was crystalline and pristine, a sparkling carpet of a billion tiny diamonds shimmering in the moonlight.

A single taxi occupied one of the "Passenger Loading Only" spaces in front of the building. There was no driver in the car, but the engine was still pumping clouds of condensate into the air. Gus stepped into the small terminal building and approached the ticket counter.

"Excuse me, sir," Gus said to an elderly gentleman who had his back turned to Gus and his face buried in the early morning edition of The Daily Herald.

"Eh?" The old man turned to face Gus. "Oh, howdy, young man. What can I do for you?"

"Who's driving the cab outside?" Gus asked.

"Oh, well … that would be Elliot … Elliot Denny. He's in the John, er, Men's Room."

"Thanks, I'll wait for him right here if you don't mind."

"Army Air Force Pilot?" the old fellow asked, struggling to make conversation.

"Yes, sir. Right on both counts."

"Uh … Elliot should be right out. …Oh there he is now." His duty done, the ticket agent picked up his newspaper and continued where he left off.

"Are you mister Denny?" Gus asked. "I'm in need of a ride if you don't mind, sir."

"Well, sure thing. Let's get you outside. The car is nice and warm. …I left the heater on."

"Home on leave, young man?"

"Yes, sir. It's a surprise gift from command. Our deployment date was set back, and command decided to let a few of us go home for Christmas. I can't wait to see my wife and dog."

Elliot Denny released a spontaneous burst of laughter. "Wife *and* dog! …Must be some dog, Lieutenant."

"It's a long story. Addie and I are newlyweds, and we didn't even have time for a real honeymoon before I had to report for duty." Gus felt uneasy about talking to strangers about such personal things. He changed the subject. "Two-seventy-four North, First West, Mr. Denny, if you please."

Elliot Denny never lifted the flag on the taxi's meter and bade Gus a "Merry Christmas" before driving away from the Russo house.

Gus was thankful to the people who had gone out of their way to help him get home - from Capt. O'Hanlon back at MacDill, to the young woman and her boyfriend at the motor pool at Hill Field, and now Mr. Elliot Denny. It may have been a cold winter's night, but the thought truly warmed his heart.

At 12:20 a.m., Gus started up the walk to the front door. All of the lights were off. As he was about to ring the doorbell, he heard a dog barking. A few second later, the porch light came on, and Fred Russo opened the door. "Sorry, mister, it's a little late in the day for the Fuller Brush man. Come back tomorrow," he grumbled. He shut the door in Gus' face, then opened it again with a broad grin, and welcomed Gus inside. "Well, what are you standing there for, son? Get in here out of the cold." Fred slapped him on the back while pulling him inside. "I had you there for a second, didn't I, Gus, my boy?"

"You're right. There for a moment, I thought you might have gone senile!"

They both had a good laugh, but Highway was determined to get the attention he wanted, so he did what he did best and leapt into Gus' arms throwing him to the floor. Gus got thoroughly licked, and Highway got plenty of scratching. "There's my good boy. There's my Highway dog." Gus was in tears … overjoyed at being home.

"Hey there, flyboy, save some of that for me!" Addie was standing at the top of the stairs. Dressed in her PJs and a plush bathrobe. Her brunette hair was in a tousled disarray that nearly covered one side of her face. She brushed the locks from her eyes and held out her arms. "Come up here, husband, and let me give you a proper 'welcome home.'"

Gus complied … happily. He ascended the stairs, two at a time, having left his duffle bag in the foyer. He swept Addie off her feet into his arms. "Addie, oh Addie, my love. My heart has ached for this moment, especially when I heard that the guys were being given an unexpected holiday leave." He dropped Addie on the bed, and she yelped when a jab of pain shot through her side.

"Oh! …I'm so sorry, sweetheart. Did I hurt you?" Gus sat on the side of the bed. A look of sincere concern and worry was etched on his brow.

"It's okay. …I'm alright. My ribs are still a little tender from the accident. The doctor said it would be a couple of weeks yet before I would healed enough to run a marathon … as if I ever did (chuckle)."

Gus didn't know quite how to handle the subject of intimacy. He was suddenly struck with two realities that were not on his radar. First and foremost, Addie may still be processing Bud Grimes' last act of heroism, the price of which cost him his life. Survivor's guilt could deepen her depression if she tried to set aside her grief by having 'fun' with Gus and feeling all the more guilty for it. The second of Gus' concerns was Addie's sore ribs. He didn't want to cause further injury and pain. Despite every fiber of his being yearning for her, he decided to not press the issue. Rather, he would follow her lead.

"I'm going to take a shower and freshen up, then I'm all yours, my love.

———

Addie turned to face Gus and rested her hand on his shoulder. "Gus, honey, are you awake?"

"Hm? … yes, I'm awake. Are you okay?" He yawned and turned to face his wife.

"I think so. I don't know."

"What's on your mind, lover?" Gus asked.

For a moment Addie fell silent, pondering how to bring up the subject of intimacy. Always one for telling the unvarnished truth without mincing words, she decided that a straight-forward approach was best.

"Well … I guess I thought we would be falling all over each other by now, but here we are like a couple of oldie-weds in our fifties who think of bedtime as a time for sleep. I hoped you would be ready for some serious cuddling after being away such a long time."

"Oh, Addie, my love, I've thought about nothing else … but I was thinking you'd rather not rush into things, you know, because of the accident and Mr. Grimes … and your cracked ribs."

"Gus, I admit, I had a few really bad days. But, since Mister

Grimes' funeral and the talk I had with his wife, Betty—oh, Gus, she's such a compassionate and spiritual lady. She told me she knew that her husband was on that loading dock for a reason: to look after *me*! She misses him terribly, but her spirits are lifted by knowing that they'll be together again in heaven. She told me that the best way I can honor him is to live my life to the fullest and to help others do the same.

"Now, husband …," she whispered as she reached her hand underneath the sheet. "I'll give you one guess as to what you think will make me a happy woman right now."

"Why, Adele Russo-Bodine, if I didn't know better, I'd say you're trying to seduce me."

Highway snorted once and jumped off the bed. He curled up on his blanket in the corner of the room, snorted again, got up, circled once, laid down and closed his eyes.

At 7:00 a.m., as Gus and Addie were dressing for the day, Gus asked if she would mind driving him over to his parents' house first thing.

"Of course, darling. As a matter of fact, I have an idea that should make it a lot more fun. What do you say to making it an even bigger surprise for your family?" They finished dressing, and before they left the Russo's, Addie set up the surprise with a phone call to Gus' parents.

Gus' mother was busy doing what she always did first thing in the morning—preparing breakfast for Gerry, Catherine, and herself. She was humming "Away in a Manger." To say Christmas was her favorite time of the year, would definitely be an understatement. Starting the day after Thanksgiving, she insisted that Gerry put up all of the outside lights and help her with the indoor decorations and the Christmas tree. The decorations wouldn't be taken down until after New Year's Day.

The telephone, which sat on a small cutout in the wall separating the living room from the kitchen, began ringing.

"Now who could that be?" She wiped her hands on a kitchen towel and picked up the receiver.

"Hello, Bodine residence," she announced.

"Mother Bodine, this is Addie calling."

"Addie, sweetie. It's so very nice to hear from you. How are you doing?" Anna Bodine hadn't heard from her daughter-in-law since the accident.

"I'm doing much better, thank you. As a matter of fact, I would like very much to bring over a little Christmas surprise. I've really missed you. Maybe we can compare notes and catch up with each other on news about Gus." Addie suppressed a giggle. Gus sat ear-to-ear with Addie, hearing every word his mother said.

"Can you come over right away? I can set another place at the table for breakfast," Gus' mother offered.

"That would be wonderful. I can be there in fifteen minutes. Oh, may I bring Highway?" Addie asked.

"Of course, dear. I always have dog food on hand for that loveable creature."

Addie, Gus, and Highway piled into Addie's Chevy and drove to the Bodine's. When they pulled into the driveway, Addie and Highway approached the front door. As soon as Gus' mother greeted them and closed the door, Gus waited for five minutes before getting out of the car.

"Hi, mom. Thank you for inviting me over." Addie hugged her mother-in-law.

"You are most welcome, dear. We have all missed you, sorely. Speaking of 'we'…" Anna Russo walked over to the foot of the stairs and called out, "Alright you two slowpokes, breakfast is already on the table, and Addie is here, so get a move on!"

Gerry, dressed in his workaday suit and tie, and Catherine in a below-the-knee plaid skirt, sweater and penny loafers, sat down at the kitchen table after exchanging hugs with Addie. Gerry was about to bless the food when the doorbell rang. "I'll get it."

"No, dad Bodine, could you let mom do it? I've been meaning to ask you something." Addie spoke with an urgency that brought a curious look to Gerry Bodine's face. Anna got up to answer the door. Suddenly a very shrill cry of utter joy, of a decibel range high enough to shatter crystal, filled the house.

"What the …" Dad Bodine rose to his feet just as Gus entered the kitchen. Catherine virtually flew out of her seat and ran to her brother. The ensuing hug-fest was garnished with tears of gladness, laughter, and kisses.

"Catherine, set another place at the table. Your brother is joining us," Gus' mom gleefully announced.

The morning was spent sharing the joy of Gus' return. Gerry and Anna Bodine shared stories of his childhood with Addie and brought out two large family photo albums. Several of the photos taken during their later school years at Dixon Junior High and Provo High School were of Gus and Addie together. Even though Addie had heard most of the stories and was familiar with the contents of photo albums, she and Gus enjoyed every minute of this impromptu family gathering.

"I have an idea, Addie. Let's spend the next few days before Christmas visiting all of the places and doing the things we did back when we first met. We can go to a couple of movies like we did when we were in school. We can have a 'do-over' and pretend we're just kids without a care in the world."

"Oh, Gus, I think that's a great idea!" Addie said. "I wonder if the Zesto is open."

Gus and Addie made the best of their time together. Addie's parents decided to make Christmas eve a gala celebration by inviting a few of their very best friends and including Gus' parents and Catherine. In all, 32 friends and neighbors got together, some of whom had sons in various branches of the Armed Forces serving in both Europe and the South Pacific. Of course, Gus' sister, Catherine, had to have a couple of her favorite friends invited to the party as well. For one evening, no one talked about the war. It wasn't planned to be that way, but it seemed that everyone had enough … enough grief over lost sons and brothers, enough fear of losing more lives to a cause that testified more of madness than nobility.

On January 7, Gus knotted the tie on his freshly ironed shirt and pulled on his olive drab woolen #51 coat. He fastened the campaign belt and donned his officer's dress cap with the distinctive eagle emblem. Thus attired in his "pinks and greens," Gus and Addie walked downstairs where Gerry and Anna Bodine, Estelle and Fred Russo, and Highway waited to say their goodbyes. The mood was somber and the hugs were long.

After Gus hugged everyone, he and Addie left for the bus station. He couldn't risk flying back on standby status for fear of having a cancellation. The Greyhound bus route to MacDill AAF Base would take two days but guaranteed an on-time arrival.

Addie pulled into the parking lot of the bus terminal and shut off the engine. She turned to look at Gus. She was determined to remain stoic, but when her chin began to quiver, and her eyes filled with tears, she could no longer keep up the pretense.

"Come here, my love." Gus pulled Addie over to him and held her firmly. "Let it out. …Let it all out."

"Oh, Gussy. You *have* to return to me," she cried into his shoulder. "I don't think I could stand living another day if you were to die. … Promise? …Please promise me.

"I promise, Addie, with all my heart and soul. I will return to you." They kissed long and hard. Both wiped away tears.

Gus opened the rear passenger door and pulled out his duffel bag. He walked away from Addie's car and then turned around. Waving a final goodbye, he called out to her, "I will come home to you!" He watched her Chevy pull out from the bus station and recede in the distance.

CHAPTER 13

FEBRUARY 23, 1944 / MACDILL ARMY AIR BASE, FLORIDA

Warning orders were received on the twentieth of February. Word went out that the 483rd was deploying … destination: Italy. A group briefing involving all members of the 483rd Bombardment Group (H) was scheduled for February 26 at 0700 hrs.

Gus and Hank Barenz shared a room in one of the B.O.Q. barracks. Anticipating the scheduled briefing time, Gus set his alarm clock for 0545 hrs. Hank's reaction to the early wakeup was to throw his pillow at the clock. Gus beat him to it and turned off the blaring alarm.

"C'mon, Hank, rise and shine. It's a quarter 'till six. You can't sleep all day. The crew will meet us at the hangar for the briefing, and I want to grab some chow before we head over there."

The two men walked into the officer's dining hall and sat down to some S.O.S. (hamburger gravy over toast) underneath eggs with a side of link sausages, toast and coffee. Gus passed on the coffee, opting for a glass of cold milk instead.

"What do you think, Hank? England or the Med? I hear the Fifteenth Air Force is going to boost the air war and take some of the load off the Eighth and Twelfth. There's even some scuttlebutt about using a few of the Russian airfields as refueling bases for our Forts so we can hit targets deeper into Germany."

"If I had a choice, I'd take England," replied Hank. "I think mail service is faster there. I guess when it comes right down to it, the 'Krauts' can shoot us down just as easily any place we go. Gus, all I can think about is getting home to my gal. I miss Linda so much I just want to end this insanity and go home."

"I hear that, pal. Leaving Addie after New Year's Day ripped my heart out. To make things worse, my brother, Russel, got shot down over Guadalcanal. But ya know what? We are the best doggone Fort drivers in the Group. You and I are going to make it back home. Being shot down just isn't in the plan." Gus' thoughts drifted back to Addie and the Christmas surprise of his unexpected 20 days of leave. His imagination placed him there, with Addie, on their last night together of those precious days. And then, knowing that in a very few days he would be half-a-world away and knee deep in the rages of war, he wondered what she was doing at this very hour. He smiled then, as an image of Addie, sitting in the gazebo with Highway at her side, came to his mind's eye as clear as if it were a photograph.

NEXT DAY / PROVO

Addie lay in bed enjoying a pleasant calm that had settled over her. She had been feeling the sadness which accompanied the end of Gus' unexpected leave over Christmas and New Year's. Now, three days after he left to return to duty, the sadness had been overtaken by the blessings of calm and peace. It seemed as though the Lord understood her loneliness.

She dressed and headed downstairs where her mother was preparing a breakfast of eggs, bacon, and toast with marmalade.

"Good morning, dear. Did you have a nice sleep?"

"Yes, thank you. Actually, it was quite ..." Addie stopped in mid-sentence, as her stomach suddenly decided to perform acrobatics, leaving her in need of a bathroom ... fast. Highway, who was dozing lazily on the floor of the warm kitchen, jumped to his feet, tail wagging, and followed Addie. He sensed her urgency, but not its source. Maybe Addie's sudden rush might mean that a treat for him was somehow in the offing—to Highway, the world was all about him.

"Are you feeling all right, Addie?" her mother asked.

"I'm not sure, mom, but I've felt like this nearly every morning now lately. It's probably nothing. I'm usually back to normal around noon or so."

Estelle Russo's eyes teared up a little bit, and her lips curled upward into a curious smile. "Or maybe it's not 'nothing.' Maybe it's 'something' … something very nice. How do you feel about a little drive to the doctor's office?"

"Why?" Addie didn't understand at first. Then it hit her. "Oh, oh my goodness. Yes … can we get an appointment right away? Oh, mom, please let it be so."

Four days later the phone rang. Addie picked up on the second ring. "Hello. This is Addie Russ … I mean *Bodine.* This is Addie Bodine. Who's calling, please?"

"Mrs. Bodine, this is Doctor Liddle. Do you have a moment to talk with me about the examination you had earlier this week?"

"Yes, Doctor."

Estelle Russo came down from the upstairs bedroom and caught the look on Addie's face. Addie waved her over, close to her, where she could hear Addie's side of the conversation.

"Do you have the results of the pregnancy test? Uh huh … yes, I understand. So, am I …? I am. YES! YES! YES! Oh, thank you, Doctor Liddle. THANK YOU SO VERY MUCH! Uh … yes. Tuesday morning next week will be fine. I think nine o'clock will be wonderful. I will. Yes … no hard work. Thanks, bye-bye.

"I'm going to have a baby! Oh, I have to write to Gus and tell him."

Addie's mother suggested inviting Gus' parents over for a celebration dinner to share the good news. And so it was that the Bodines and Russos shared the joy of their first grandchild's forthcoming birth sometime in November.

MISSION BRIEFING

Col. Barton (483rd BG Commander), Lt. Col. York (Deputy Commander), Lieutenant Colonel Cyril Carmichael (Executive Officer), Lieutenant Colonel Wallace Linn (Operations Officer), were seated behind the dais.

At 0700 hrs precisely, the group's 1st Sgt, Master Sgt. Gene Halvorson, called the 483rd BG compliment of over five-hundred men to attention. Col. Barton stepped to the dais.

"Good morning, FOUR EIGHTY-THIRD!"

"Good morning, sir!" came the unanimous reply.

"Be seated, gentlemen. Before we begin, I would like to introduce you to a welcome addition to our command. Some of you may recall his exploits as a pilot of the Dolittle Raid back in forty-two. Colonel York and his crew made it all the way to Russia before his B-25 ran out of fuel and forced him down. After a year spent interred in a Russian camp, Ed York and his crew 'liberated' themselves by escaping. I have asked him to brief you on the coming deployment of the 483rd to Italy. Please welcome Lieutenant Colonel Edward J. York."

"Italy, eh? Well, I guess that answers the 'where' question. Now we get to the 'how' and 'why,'" Hank whispered to Gus.

Col. York stood and approached the podium. "Gentlemen, we will say farewell to MacDill and depart on the second of March. The plan calls for the ground echelon to travel by rail to Camp Patrick Henry, Virginia. Duffels only, men. Storage space aboard ship will be minimal. Very likely you'll be hot bunking. On the twelfth of March, you will board a three-ship convoy of 'Liberty Ships' under the command of Lieutenant Colonel Carmichael. Your destination is Brindisi, Italy, via the Strait of Gibraltar."

Col. York stepped in front of a large map depicting the Atlantic seaboard, the Atlantic Ocean and key islands, the Strait of Gibraltar, and the Mediterranean Theatre of Operations. He used his pointer to indicate waypoints terminating at Foggia, Italy.

"The air crews will fly the 'seventeens' to Hunter Field in Georgia for refueling, then over the Mid-Atlantic Route via Bermuda, here, then across the Atlantic Ocean to Lagens Field in the Azores; into the Med. to Tunis, in North Africa; then north across the Mediterranean to one of the many bases in or near Foggia, Italy. As of now, that will be either Sterparone or Tortorella. Pilots, co-pilots, and navigators will attend an updated briefing on March 1, at zero six hundred hours, where you will receive information on headings, altitude, airspeed, formation, marshalling coordinates, and the most current weather conditions. Briefly, though, from Hunter Field, squadrons will fly in standard flights of three in 'V' formation with fifty yards of separation between flights. The 815th will lead out, followed by the 816th, 817th, and 818th in fifteen-minute intervals. Colonel Barton will command the group from the lead plane of the 815th. I will fly as his co-pilot. When we enter the Straits of Gibraltar, we will re-form into a combat box formation. Enemy encounter is not expected, but the Germans are known to test our defenses by flying surprise incursions. There will be no air cover. The Ground crews are readying your Forts as we speak. On a final note, the Forts will take on ammo at Lagens Field as a precautionary measure."

FEBRUARY 27, 1944

The Commanding Officer of the 816th Bombardment Squadron, *Avenging Angels*, Major Willard Sperry stood before the nine pilots and co-pilots of his command.

"Gentlemen, the 816th will be designated Blue Squadron for the purposes of communication between and among the four squadrons and the Group Leader. The 815th will be designated Green Squadron, the 817th is Red Squadron, and the 818th is Yellow Squadron. Our Forts will take the form of three flights of three planes each in standard 'V' formation with separation between planes of fifty feet. Flight Leaders are as follows: I will lead the squadron in the first flight, designation Blue One Leader; First Lieutenant Diedrich Fein, designation Blue Two Leader; and First Lieutenant Gus Bodine as Blue Three Leader. Remember, maintain fifty feet of horizontal separation between planes. Vertical separation between flights will be fifty feet as well."

The meeting went on for 20 more minutes as Maj. Sperry

responded to all of the "ifs" "ands" and "buts" before closing the meeting.

"I'm sure you will want to meet with your crews. The officers' club will be off-limits to the 816th at twenty-two hundred hours on Tuesday the twenty-nineth. I don't need to tell you that the base switchboard is closed to all outgoing calls to families. As of now, each of you needs to take into yourself the attitude and mindset that we are at war. From this point forward we have but one purpose … to defeat our enemies and restore peace. You are dismissed."

"What do you say we check the mail room and then head over to the O club, boss?" Hank suggested.

"Good idea, I need to drop a letter in the box." Gus had written a letter to Addie updating her on the group's deployment. As usual, the body of the letter was rich in words of deep love and absolute devotion. He knew that he might not be able to receive mail for many days or even weeks. He was hoping that a letter from Addie was waiting for him in the mail room.

There was.

My darling Gus,

I'm writing this on February 20. I hope you get it before you are deployed. I hope I will get your letter in the next day or two giving me that news. Speaking of news … are you sitting down? Do you remember telling me, just before you left, that you wanted to start a family? Well, I hope you really meant it, because I'm pregnant, complete with morning sickness and strange food cravings!

Oh, Gus, I could not be happier. I will keep you informed of how things are going with our baby. Are you happy? Are you as thrilled as I am? I know you are. I thought we had reached the height and the breath of love between a man and a woman, but I love you now even more than I thought I ever could.

I'm planning to start back at BYU until the baby comes. I'm hoping I can finish my degree. When you come home to me, I want us to have a home of our own to raise our little boy, or girl, and celebrate together the beginning of the rest of our lives.

For now through eternity, darling, I remain…

Forever yours,

Addie

"Yes!" he shouted, pumping his fist in the air. Gus folded the letter back into the envelope and placed it in his left shirt pocket closest to his heart. He thought he might never stop smiling.

"Wow. Must be *some* letter. Good news?" asked Hank.

"The best. I'm having a baby … I mean, Addie's pregnant. I'm going to be a father, Hank!"

Gus tightened his harness and looked over at his co-pilot. "You ready, pal?"

"Yep. Let's get this show on the road," Hank replied, then added, "On your command, Skipper."

Gus began reading off the engine start checklist. Hank's job was to confirm that each item was within its proper position and setting preparatory to the engine start sequence.

"Fuel transfer valves OFF."

"Transfer valves OFF."

"Open fuel shutoff valves."

"Fuel shutoff valves open, Skipper."

Gus read through each of the 17 items as Hank verified settings and switch positions from cowl flaps to generators. "Before-start checklist complete, Skipper."

"Master Switch ON," Gus directed.

"Master Switch is ON."

Gus ordered battery switches and inverters switched to the "ON" position, followed by the booster pumps (ON).

"Turning one." After four full rotations of the three-bladed Hamilton propellor, the turbocharged Wright R-1820 Cyclone caught hold with a belch of black smoke before settling into a smooth idle. Minutes later, with all four engines warmed up, *Addie's Armor* was ready to begin her taxi roll to the runway.

"Pilot to engineer: How do the engines look, Sergeant Dinkleman?"

"All gauges in the green, and she's runnin' sweet, sir."

Addie's Armor taxied to the runway. When the Fort in front of Gus started its takeoff roll, Gus brought his bomber into position. Thirty seconds after the preceding aircraft lifted off, Gus began his takeoff roll.

"Lieutenant Barenz, add power for takeoff."

Hank moved the mixture controls to "Full-Rich," and advanced all four throttles gradually, being sure to lead the engine RPM, until full throttle was reached. It was Hank's job to keep an eye on manifold and oil pressures to be certain that manifold pressure never rose above 35 inches Hg.

The nose wheel lifted from the ground, and at 115 mph the main wheels lifted from the runway. Gus watched the airspeed climb, and when the Fort's wheels were approximately 10 ft above the surface, he ordered the wheels raised.

"Left main is up," Gus called out.

"Right main up," Hank Barenz affirmed. "Gear up and locked, Skipper.

At 130 mph, Gus ordered the flaps to be raised and set his climb rate at 700 ft/m. When *Addie's Armor* passed over the far end of the runway, he banked the bomber to the left toward the other Forts which were in various stages of forming up for the flight to Hunter Field, Georgia, a distance of 320 miles, or a little less than two hours flight time.

"Pilot to engineer: Report status," Gus requested.

"All gauges are operating within normal range. Temperatures and pressures are spot on. We are good to go, sir." TSgt Dinkleman responded.

"Copy that. Pilot: Out."

"Hank, take us to the marshalling area and put us in position with the rest of the squadron. I'll handle the radios and make sure the other guys in our flight are in position."

CHAPTER 14

MARCH 8, 1944 / 0600 HRS / LONG HOP TO KINLEY FIELD, BERMUDA

Descending by flights from the marshalling area above Hunter Field, the B-17s of the 483rd Bombardment Group descended into a left traffic pattern, and in 30-second intervals, entered on final approach to land at Hunter Field to take on fuel. The planes' tanks were filled with 100-octane gasoline. Fueling and aircraft maintenance inspections lasted the remainder of the day and through the night until wheels-up the morning of March 3.

When the last fuel truck left the flightline, the bombers' propellers began to turn. One by one the Forts taxied to the runway and departed the United States for Castle Island, Bermuda, and Kindley Field—a distance of 938 miles across the Atlantic Ocean.

"Pilot to crew: We'll be in the air for about five and a half hours. Find a comfortable spot at your stations and settle in. We'll all get a chance to stretch our legs when we land in Bermuda. My understanding is that the chow hall will be open for us at Kindley Field."

Gus did a visual check of his two wingmen. First Lieutenant J. R. Holladay's *Sweet Adeline* was in excellent formation position off his right wing, but Sandy Plunket's *Montana Cowgirl* had drifted back slightly from Gus' left wing, and his number three engine was blowing a faint trail of white smoke.

Gus switched his radio to the plane-to-plane frequency.

Flight Leader to Bravo-three-Lima: Sandy, bring it in a little closer, pal. You're too far out. You're trailing some smoke from your number three. Over.

Copy, Leader. Increasing power to the other engines. Oil temp gauge on number three is still in the green but is reading a tad high. Adjusting mixture. Over.

Gus watched as Sandy corrected his position.

Good formation position. When we land, have your engineer check out that oil temp problem.

Roger that, Flight Leader. Bravo-three-Lima: Out.

Addie's Armor droned on across cloudless skies at 12,000 ft. The azure waters below reflected a million dazzling diamonds dancing across the ocean surface. The east coast of the United States had dropped below the horizon line, and the island of Bermuda had yet to appear in front of them. One's imagination could picture them flying over a different world, one whose geography was that of a water world devoid of the sounds and activity of life other than that which thrived below the endless confines of the global sea.

"Beautiful, isn't it, Hank?"

"Huh? …oh, uh, sorry Gus." Hank pulled the brim of his service cap back from over his eyes. "I guess I nodded off."

"Sorry to wake you. I was just saying how beautiful the ocean is."

"Yes, it sure is. Say, why don't I take the controls, and *you* get some shut eye?" Hank offered.

"Thanks. I think I'll do just that. The controls are yours." Gus watched Hank as the co-pilot's hands gripped the yoke. He unlatched his harness, leaned back and pulled the bill of his service cap down to shade his eyes from the sun which had risen high in the clear sky ahead.

Finally, a little less than five hours after leaving Hunter Field, a thin line of land appeared on the horizon ahead.

Blue Leader to Blue Squadron: Flight Leaders, form up in Trail position by flight to land Kindley field.

In order to accommodate the heavy bombers' demand for a longer runway on the big island of St. David's, the U.S. Army Corps of Engineers, in cooperation with the U.S. Navy and Britain's Royal Air Force Transport Command, set to work levelling Long Bird Island at the north end of St. David's Island and a few other small islands in Castle Harbor. Using the soil and rock gained from that process, they backfilled the north end of the island, adding 750 acres to Bermuda's land area. The new runway, 12/30, of 9,898 ft in length, plus the additional infrastructure required to house and maintain a large force of USAAF support personnel, became Kindley Field (named after U.S. Ace pilot Field E. Kindley who flew with the RAF in WWI).

Maj. Sperry, led the squadron into Kindley Field. Lt. Fein and his three Forts were next following Maj. Sperry.

Blue Three Flight Leader to flight: On my command, we will change to trail formation preparatory to landing. Blue Three Lima will follow me, and Blue Three Romeo will bring up the rear. Acknowledge.

Blue Three Lima: Copy, Lt. Holladay confirmed.

Blue Three Romeo: Copy, Lt. Plunkett confirmed.

Thirty-six B-17s of the 483rd Bombardment Group (H) filled the tarmac in front of three hangars. Ground crews immediately set themselves to the task of refueling the bombers. Cowlings were removed from the engines which underwent a thorough inspection and cowlings were replaced.

With an extra 216 mouths to feed, preparation for the evening meal in the chow hall had to start early and meant calling in extra people from cooks to servers. The food had to be hot and ready on the serving line for the hungry crews. The 145 officers of the 483rd would dine at the officers' club mess, relieving the enlisted mess hall of at least some of the burden.

Gus and the officers of Blue Three Flight sat together and shared their observations of the flight thus far. Gus looked across the table at Sandy Plunket.

"Sandy, did your number three engine give you any more trouble?"

"Nope, but I told Sergeant Conover to stay with the ground crew until they find the problem. I don't like the idea of making the long jump to Lagens with a questionable engine. I'm going to head back to the plane after I finish chow. Maybe I can hurry things along." Lt. Plunket took another bite of what almost passed for chicken-fried steak, downed the rest of his coffee, slid his chair back, and tucked a small white box under his arm. "Want to walk along with me, Gus?"

"Sure. I know a little about radial engines. Maybe I can be some help."

Montana Cowgirl, tail number 43-01036, appeared to be in no shape to fly. The cowlings were laying on the tarmac, and two men were standing on rolling stairs working on the number three starboard inboard engine. TSgt Christopher Conover saw the two approaching officers.

"Hey, Lieutenant!" The flight engineer descended the stairs and saluted both Sandy and Gus. "We need to get those cowlings back on, sir, and do a run-up on the engine, but I think we fixed the problem … a cracked seal on the oil filler cap. It was spraying oil onto the exhaust stack."

"That's good news, Sergeant Conover. Here, I hope you like bologna and cheese." Sandy handed his flight engineer the boxed in-flight meal. "You should get back to it, then. I'll climb up to the cockpit and assist you with the run-up if that'll be of any help."

"I'll join you, sir. I need to check the instruments on my board while you handle the controls. It'll take the ground crew a couple of minutes to re-install the cowlings and police (cleanup) the area while I polish off the sandwich. Much obliged, by the way, sir." Sgt. Conover shot a grin to his commanding officer then sat down on the B-17s left main wheel and attacked his impromptu lunch.

MARCH 10, 1944 / 0700 HRS (TWO DAYS LATER)

At sunup, 300 men were scrambling aboard the 36 Forts of the 483rd Bomb Group. Kindley Field was abuzz with activity. The roar of 144 Wright-Cyclone engines could be heard by everyone on St. David's Island.

Every pilot knew precisely where his airplane needed to be positioned within the coalescing group formation. Situational awareness was critical starting with each flight leader who mothered his two wingmen into position: heading 078° east-northeast, altitude 15,000 ft, wind 258° at 4 mph, airspeed 160 mph indicated, and 50 ft horizontal separation from wingtip to wingtip.

Ten minutes after the last bomber went wheels up, the group turned eastward for Lagens Field, the Azores, a distance of 2,138 miles. With the advent of "Tokyo" tanks (self-sealing fuel cells) installed in later models of the B-17F, and all B-17Gs, the range of the Forts was extended by 40 % … an improvement that made the long jump to Lagens well within the bombers' range.

MARCH 10 – 16 / LAGENS FIELD, THE AZORES

While the bombers were taking on ammunition and receiving their final maintenance once-over to ensure combat readiness before departing for North Africa, the crews of the 483rd Bomb Group were housed in tents for the eight days needed for the refit.

After Gus positioned his cot and rolled out the thin mattress provided for their stay, he removed his shaving kit and a clean change of underwear from his duffel bag. He was about to head for the outdoor shower, when his eyes caught Lt. J. R. Holladay sitting motionless on his cot. Holladay's mattress had yet to be unrolled, and his duffel bag remained closed and latched by his side.

"Well, J. R., we made it to Lagens without any problems. How was your crew's performance?"

"It's not my crew that concerns me, Lieutenant."

"What, then? Is it the plane?"

"No. *Sweet Adeline* is perfect. It's me." J. R. became quiet, and he lowered his head slightly.

"Go on," Gus prompted as he took a seat next to J. R.

"Up 'till now the flying has been relatively stress free. Apart from the mechanics of managing the plane and crew, it's not much different from Advanced Pilot Training. But now, with the planes taking on ammo …" With an almost imperceptible shake of his head, J. R. continued, "…I don't know if I'll be up to the task of combat and being responsible for nine other lives."

Gus nodded his understanding. "J. R., none of us is ready for that. A WWI pilot who taught me how to fly back in California, told me that, 'The shock of combat is like walking through the gates of hell when you expected to be passing through the pearly gates of heaven.' He survived that experience and did so gallantly with seven confirmed shoot-downs to his credit." Gus was struck with an idea. …"I feel uncertainty creeping in, too, J. R. I also worry about my new wife and family back home. I think you and I need to keep an eye on each other. You know … to help each of us get through the hard patches. What do you think?"

"Yes, I think that might help. You know, you and I met only a few days ago, but I think we're a lot alike. Family is everything. I'm a newlywed, too, … well, almost. My fiancée and I are planning to get hitched when I get back home. But, I come from a large family. We're farmers in Colorado … mostly beets and barley. J. R. was clearly proud of his rural upbringing. Gus found himself wanting to know more about Lt. Holladay, "farmer."

MARCH 17, 1944 / 0700 HRS / 483RD DEPARTS LAGENS FIELD

The Forts of the 483rd BG were ready for combat. In addition to 10,000 rounds of ammo, additional protective armor was installed around the flight deck, radio station, and flight engineer station. All totaled, just over two tons of weight had been added to each aircraft.

On the morning of March 17, the crews of all 36 combat-ready bombers boarded their Forts in preparation for departure to Tunis in North Africa via Gibraltar. Allied war ships were on constant patrol on both the Atlantic and the Mediterranean sides of this important passage into the Mediterranean Sea from the Atlantic Ocean. At 15,000 ft altitude, the air crews spotted the bow waves of a few large ships passing through the Straits of Gibraltar. The "Rock" was plainly visible. Tail gunner, Woody Carpenter, caught a glint of light from a plane below and behind *Addie's Armor* and the 816th Bomb Squadron. Woody liked to carry a pair of binoculars with him, so he reached inside the leather case and removed the lens caps to catch the glint of reflected light in the form of a B-17.

"Tail gunner to pilot: Sir, I spotted a Fort flying way below us at our six o'clock low. Looks like he's dropping out of formation."

"Copy, tail. Good eyes, Sergeant Carpenter. I'll call Group Lead. Pilot: Out." Gus switched his comm to the Group Leader.

Blue Three Leader to Group Leader: Over.

Group Leader to Blue Three Leader: Go. Col. Barton's voice sounded loud and clear over Gus' headset.

Sir, my tail gunner said he spotted a Fort dropping out of formation.

Copy, Blue Three Leader. The situation is in hand. Group Leader: Out.

FORT DOWN

Sometimes a series of seemingly unconnected events can become the instruments in a concerto of catastrophe and unintended consequence. Such was the case with one 818th Bombardment Squadron B-17G that was the last unit to takeoff from Lagen Field. Aircraft #43-37460, *Thor's Hammer*, commanded by First Lieutenant William Garrison Bendix was the unwilling recipient of 146 gallons of AVGAS of a lower octane than is prescribed for the Wright 1820-97, 9-cylinder engine. The results of which could have ranged from a rise in cylinder head temperature and oil temperature, to decreased power and rough engine performance. However, when an engine is run for an extended time, the problems can be much more serious. Overheating in the cylinders can cause detonation, torching of the edges of the cylinders, and engine failure.

Still 200 miles out from Gibraltar, Lt. Bendix reported rough engine performance and higher than normal temperature readings on two of his four engines. Within minutes, he was experiencing detonation in the cylinders, and the flight engineer recommended feathering the suspect inboard starboard engine. It was then that a cascade of events spread to the other engines. Lt. Bendix ordered the crew to prepare for ditching. He notified the flight leader, Captain F. Willing, that he needed to drop out of formation, which he did. His wingman in Yellow One Flight dropped back and stayed on Lt. Bendix's wing. With wheels up and 50% flaps, *Thor's Hammer's* airspeed dropped to 115 mph. The plane's tail struck the water, followed less than a second later, by the fuselage. The plane cleared the next swell of ocean, but struck harder this time and buried her nose. All electrical systems had been shut down as had the fuel lines. The crew followed ditching protocol and quickly had the two five-man dinghies and their Mae West life vests inflated. An American destroyer retrieved the men 36 hours later There were no deaths, and the entire crew were cleared to return to duty.

TUNIS

The 483rd remained in Tunis for two weeks, mostly for some much needed "R&R." Instead, what they got was the tail end of the rainy season that runs from late January thru mid-April.

It was on such a rainy day that Gus found himself with some time to spare. It was a "down" time for him, meaning no practice sorties. Hank was at the officers' club, which, two months before the 483rd arrived, was a bombed out civilian office used by Tunis airport administration personnel.

Gus always had a pad of writing paper and a couple of pencils stashed in the drawer of what passed as a nightstand next to his bunk. He was about to begin a letter to Addie. He couldn't say too much about where he was and where he was going, but he could let her know that he had arrived safely at a nondescript location. Just before he started writing, an NCO stepped into the tent and called out.

"Lieutenant Gus Bodine. The group executive officer requires your presence ASAP." The young man stood at attention and waited for a response.

"Over here, Sergeant.

Following the sound of the voice, the sergeant walked briskly over to Gus' bunk. "I'll tell Colonel York you will be along momentarily, sir."

"Do you have any idea what this is all about, Sergeant?"

"No, sir. Probably a shakeup in personnel. There's been a lot of that going on. If there's nothing else, sir, I'll be on my way. Oh, I almost forgot. He wants you in 'pinks and greens.'"

"Headquarters, 483rd Bombardment Group (H)" was printed in bold black letters beneath the group's insignia of a shield depicting a winged sword dominating the center. The sword penetrated a black sphere at the bottom representing the triumph of Allied Arms piercing the darkness and bringing light to the victim people of Axis oppression. Beneath the shield was inscribed AB NUBLIBUS VINCEREMUS, meaning, "Victory from the Clouds."

Gus knocked on the door labeled "Lieutenant Colonel Edward J. York, 483rd Executive Officer."

The same NCO that appeared in Gus' tent, opened the door and waved Gus into the small office. Col. York was flipping the pages of a file folder that clearly had the executive officer's rapt attention.

Holding a salute, Gus formally announced, "Sir, First Lieutenant Gus Bodine, reporting as ordered, sir."

"Take a seat, Lieutenant. You know what this is?" Lt. Col. York gestured toward the folder he had been reading.

"It looks like a personnel file, sir." Gus recognized what it was, and it made his gut do flip-flops until the conversation continued.

"Your personnel file, to be precise, Lieutenant. I've been reading it. You're probably the most experienced pilot in the group that's still a first lieutenant. You have quite a story to tell, Bodine. Your squadron commander thinks so as well. I'll cut to the chase.

"Major Sperry has been called back to the states. He will lead a development team to fabricate a new gunnery sight using reflective lenses. The sight is his own creation and could increase the gunnery effectiveness of our bombers. His departure means that his executive officer, Major Fred Ashworth, is moving into the Command position and our operations officer, Captain Keates, will fill the executive officer slot. We need someone with demonstrated leadership and organizational skills with a good eye for serving the mission of the 483rd to replace Captain Keates. Before Major Sperry left for the states, Colonel Barton, and Major Sperry, met with me, and we decided his replacement should be you, … Captain." Col. York fixed Gus with a steady gaze. The corners of the Colonel's lips almost turned up into a smile. The man was clearly enjoying the moment.

"Captain? … Me, sir?" Gus was a child again, remembering be awarded for Outstanding Pitcher in the Western Boys Baseball Association. He played for Hayward's Market that year. His coach and the store manager, Brig Mitchell, always brought an occasional éclair and day old doughnuts to practice. …Gus had an epiphany: *captain's bars are much sweeter than doughnuts!*

"Yes, you. Come to attention, Lieutenant." Col. York opened a black velvet box containing a pair of captain's bars. Removing the single bars of a first lieutenant, he handed them to Gus, then pinned the two shiny silver railroad tracks on Gus' shoulder epaulets. "You'll want to meet with Captain Keates and pick his brain. He's all business, and he'll give you the straight 'poop.' You will continue on as command pilot of *Addie's Armor*."

Stifling his immense pride in the moment, Gus replied, "Yes, sir."

"We'll need to brief all squadron personnel regarding the change of command, but you may consider yourself to be on the job as of now. You are dismissed … Captain."

Tunis Airport and the surrounding community were mostly a bombed-out mess made worse by the relentless sand that turned into a quagmire, off and on, in the winter months. The 483rd landed on one of the "on" days and the crews were welcomed by rain and mud. The battle for Tunis was pretty much over by the end of November 1943. When the British RAF and the U.S. Fifteenth Air Force moved onto the airport at Tunis, the first order of business was the repair of the runway and operations facilities. The numbers of military personnel far exceeded the growth of housing, mess, medical, and latrine facilities. Most of the enlisted G.I.s had their share of trench digging and honey dipping. Tent cities were hastily thrown together. The tents provided shade from the sun's glare, but the tent flaps did nothing to prevent the ever-present grit from blowing inside through the cracks. When it rained, water seeped in and mud was dragged in on boots. A cot was provided to rest one's head, but there was no mistaking these quarters for the Ritz Carlton. Life at Tunis was far from R&R.

Col. Barton never allowed grass to grow under the feet of his flight crews. In spite of overcast skies and the periodic heavy rain, bombing practice sorties continued daily. There were many small islands off the coast of Tunis. One unnamed and uninhabited island was used for target practice. Squadrons rotated, taking turns at dusting the island. The bombs were 100 lb demolition bombs. The explosives were removed and replaced with 12-gauge shotgun shells which exploded a white powdery substance that showed up very well in photos. The crews would be debriefed (interrogated) after every practice mission: what was the weather at altitude? … winds aloft? … formation? … indicated airspeed? …visibility? And, bombing was critiqued on "mean points of impact." The pilots, bombardiers, and navigators had to present their own assessment of each plane's performance. Gus' 816th bomb squadron got in three sorties before the group left Tunis.

Spring brought the opportunity for relaxing on the beaches on the south shore of the Mediterranean Sea. Swimming, volleyball and gorgeous views were a balm even for the hardest to please. Stretches of white, pristine beaches; lush pastures; and rolling pine-clad hills almost made one want to forget about the ongoing destruction of centuries-old architecture and the countless lives turned upside-down by the ravages of war. By early April, when warm spring weather began to dry things out, and the mud returned to sand, it would be time for the 483rd to depart for their next temporary base of assignment, Tortorella, Italy.

Meanwhile, the ground echelon—scheduled to arrive at the port at Brendisi, on the coast of the Adriatic sea about half-way up the boot of Italy—would travel from there by rail to their permanent base of assignment about 225 kilometers north of Tortorella, at Sterparone USAAF Base. Their job was to prepare Sterparone for the B-17 Flying Fortresses ... including the building of a new 6,000-ft runway.

Rather than wait the two weeks or so for Sterparone to be upgraded, the decision was made to put the 483rd to work flying combat missions with the 99th Bombardment Group, the only American tenant organization at Tortorella.

MARCH 29, 1944 / DEPARTING TUNIS

The 483rd departed in squadron "V" formation of nine planes each. The order of departure was based on the positions of the squadrons on the parking ramp: 815th, 840th, 817th, and 816th.

Col. Barton led out with the 815th in *Legal Tender,* aircraft #42-18491. The assigned pilot, Lt. Zefron Overbridge, sat in the tail gunner's position where he could keep an eye on any air traffic behind and within his 180° field of vision and report back to Col. Barton periodically about the 483rd's progress.

Col. Barton knew it was not the best idea to spread out the group, but with the crowded conditions of having so many squadrons, time was needed to park each arriving squadrons and prepare for the next. The two tenant organizations, the USAAF 99th Bombardment Group (H) and the RAF 231 Wing, had split the base along national lines. The American 99th BG (H) used the west side of the Field for its B-17s and B-24s. The British RAF used the east side for its Wellingtons, Vickers, Avro Lancasters and Consolidated LB-30 Liberators. Tortorella was so heavily occupied that base personnel lived in a complex of tents organized by units. The headquarters building of the 99th, was located off-base in the village of Tavemola. Hangar space was at a premium, and most mechanical work was done in the 150 concrete hardstands (paved areas where heavy vehicles can be parked without sinking into the otherwise unpaved surface).

The 816th Bomb Squadron was the last to land at Tortorella, trailing behind the 815th by 30 minutes. Looking at the base from the sky, Gus could easily identify the 6,700-ft runway that marked the dividing line between the USAAF and the RAF.

"Pilot to crew: We're about an hour-and-a-half out from Tortorella now. Before we get too busy with preparations for landing, I just want to extend my gratitude to all of you. Col. Barton told me recently that *Addie's Armor* has distinguished herself by the discipline and professionalism of her crew. I agree. I'm proud to call you all my friends … my brothers … in the righteous cause of defending the liberties of all freedom-loving people. We are about to leap into the fray. We must do so with one purpose—to destroy the Nazi regime so it can never again threaten the people we have sworn to defend." He paused waiting for any response but got only silence and little background "white noise."

"Hey, Skipper?" the voice of SSgt "Clay" Clayton, tail gunner, pierced the silent radio waves.

"Sergeant Clayton? Do you have something to add?"

"Oh, no, sir. All I wanted to ask was, well … um … are you going to be doing more 'speechifying' whenever we go up? …Sir?"

Gus knew very well that he was being set up by the jokester turret gunner. Clay was a quick-witted improvisationist as good as any comic on the stage. He was always ready with a quip of some kind. Whenever he was engaged in a conversation with another person, or preferably a large group of friends, one could plan on being the butt of one of his signature punchlines. Gus decided to play into Clay's trickery.

"Well, I don't know, Sergeant Clayton. I thought a nice 'l-o-n-g' motivational speech before each mission might be inspiring to everybody. What do you think?"

"Oh, say it ain't so, Joe! Lord, have mercy!" About five seconds of merciful silence later, Sgt. Clayton continued with a melodramatic plea, "Sir, I respectfully request a transfer. I hear that *The Grim Reaper's* tail gunner is in the hospital, and they are looking for a replacement."

Addie's Armor radio operator, SSgt Marty Gonzalez, patched the entire conversation between Gus and Clay over the plane's intercom so that every man had a good laugh at the humorous exchange.

Hank Barenz looked over at Gus, who returned a likewise ebullient gaze at the co-pilot. Both men broke out laughing.

"Tail gunner to pilot: Sir, I see what looks like three bogies at our six o'clock. Too far out to read their markings. …'V' formation. …Two fighters and one multi-engine."

"Clay, this had better not be a joke.

"Gunners, charge your weapons. Radio, put me on to Group Leader," Gus ordered.

"Tail gunner to pilot: Skipper, the heavy looks like a Fort … it's a B-17, sir!"

One glance at Hank told Gus his co-pilot considered it no joke. Hanks eyes were ablaze with concentration, scanning instruments, checking the sky for signs of other intruding aircraft.

Blue One Flight Leader to Blue Leader: Three bogies coming in at six o'clock high, Gus announced to the 816th Squadron Leader, Maj. Ashworth. *Two fighters and one possible friendly. Stand by. …Over.*

Copy, Blue One. Blue Leader to all planes: Re-form in combat box formation. All planes prepare for combat. I will request air support and alert Group Leader. Blue Leader: Out.

The Forts of the 816th formed a nine-plane "box" formation where equal distancing from nose-to-tail and wingtip to wingtip was no more than 50 ft of separation.

Blue One Leader to Blue Leader: The heavy is a Fort … repeat, the bomber is a Bravo One-Seven. He's dropping to our altitude. Landing lights just flashed on. Over.

Blue Leader to Blue One Leader: We need to I.D. the heavy. You're taking point on this one. Acknowledge.

Copy, Blue Leader.

"Pilot to radio: Sergeant Gonzalez, scan all known frequencies. See if you can establish a comm link. Over," Gus ordered.

"Roger. …Stand by."

Blue One Leader to Blue Leader: Request permission to drop out of formation to establish the intruder's intent. Over.

Gus waited for Maj. Ashworth's response.

Risky move, Gus, but permission granted. Keep your guns trained on the bogies. I will request a fighter escort from the 325th Fighter Group at Foggia. Over.

Copy, Blue Leader.

"Radio to pilot: Skipper I've got him … patching you in, now."

…Wir sind freundlich und unbewaffnet. Wiederholen Sie, das ist Oberst

Werner Baumbach vom Referat II/KG2000 der Reichsabwehr. Ich beantrage Asyl. Über.

This is Captain Gus Bodine of the United States Army Air Force. Do you speak English? Over.

I do indeed, captain. I am Colonel Werner Baumbach of the Reich Abwehr KG/2000. I have vital information regarding the Reich Abwehr actives and war plans. I am requesting asylum for myself and for my companions. We are at your command, Captain. Over.

Colonel, please form up behind my aircraft. Order your escort fighters to follow behind in line formation. Be advised, that failure to comply with any of my orders will be taken as a hostile act, and you will be fired upon. Acknowledge.

Acknowledged, Captain.

Gus hadn't realized he was holding his breath throughout the exchange with Col. Baumbach. He forced himself to relax releasing a pent-up exhalation, and then continued …

Reduce your airspeed to one-eight-zero miles per hour. Maintain five-zero feet of separation off my tail. We will be joined by American fighters who will escort your flight of three to your destination. Acknowledge.

Acknowledged. Moving into position now, Col. Baumbach replied. *Thank you.*

An hour later, the 816th Bomb Squadron was vectored in for final approach to land at Tortorella, Italy. A flight of three P-40s from the 325th Fighter Group orbited the runway to insure that the German Fort and her two escorts were down, and the crews were in the hands of the MPs.

"After-landing checklist, Hank." Gus called out to his co-pilot who responded by manually completing each item and calling out their condition:

"Hydraulic pressure, seven hundred pounds."

"Cowl flaps, open and locked."

"Turbos OFF."

"Booster pumps OFF."

"Flaps are up."

"Generator switches OFF."

Gus followed the ground handler's directions and brought *Addie's Armor* to a full stop.

He set the engines to 1200 rpm and allowed them to run for 30 seconds.

"Okay. …Shut down two and three, Hank."

Hank pulled back the mixture controls to the OFF position on the two inboard engines.

"Shut down three and four."

The propellors of the two outboard engines slowed to a stop. Gus locked the tail wheel. He turned off all electrical switches after insuring that all engine instruments had settled to the bottom of their neutral positions. Finally, he turned off the main line and battery switches. He set and locked all controls. "We are home at last, Hank. Welcome to Italy."

"Home, sweet 'crowded' home. That was some trip, Gus, my friend. I thought for sure we were going to get into a fight with the bogies."

"For sure. I wonder if we'll get to meet those fellas face-to-face. I'd like to meet the men who fought for their freedom against Hitler and the Reich. That took some hutzpah," Gus added enthusiastically.

A jeep approached the two pilots. Hank blew a shrill whistle between his fingers as if he were hailing a cab in Manhattan, and the driver swerved in their direction.

"Hop in, sirs. Where ya headin'?" the Army corporal asked.

"We don't know. Can you direct us to where the crews of the 483rd Bomb Group, 816th Bomb Squadron are billeted? I'm Captain Gus Bodine, and the officer next to me is First Lieutenant Barenz."

"I'm headed in that direction. All you new guys are in 'Tent City' over there behind Hangar Three. That's the one with the 99th Bomb Group 'Diamond Backs' insignia. That whole area used to be where the base theatre and officers' club were located. The theatre's behind the operations office next to Hangar One now, but the O club is still in the same place. You'll see a Quonset hut when you walk through the gate into the compound."

The jeep driver dropped Gus and Hank off at the guard shack which served as the entrance to the expansive compound. A sign made of scrap wood marked "Officers' Quarters," scrawled in white paint, directed them toward their tent. Someone had been considerate enough to put signage on each tent with the group and squadron designation clearly displayed. Gus entered their assigned tent.

The U.S. Army tents were designed to accommodate 16 men. Officers, ranked O3, O2, and O1, (captain, first lieutenant, and second lieutenant) were assigned 12 per tent. Currently there were eight bunks and eight steel double-door lockers arranged in groups of four. Five of the bunks were occupied. The two men nearest where Gus and Hank stood, looked up at the newcomers.

"Gus Bodine and Hank Barenz. Well, bless my soul. You two are the last to arrive." First Lieutenant Eric "Goober" Trapp stood and offered the new arrivals a welcoming handshake. "You remember John Walton, here, don't you?"

"Of course, we do. Good to see you both. Where's everybody else?' Hank asked.

"Either at chow or the O club most likely. Say, why don't you two get yourselves squared away in here, then we can scout out some chow together." Lt. Walton offered. "Here, I'll lend a hand." Grinning, Walton opened his locker and withdrew a wrench and a Philips-head screwdriver and tossed it to Gus. He pointed to the far end of the tent where several large cardboard boxes were neatly stacked. "Courtesy of the 505th Supply Company. Help yourself, gents."

Gus hefted the tools and smiled at Hank. "I guess if we intend to get any rest tonight, we'd better get started, eh partner?" The pair pulled locker and bunkbed hardware from the boxes and began the assembly process.

CHAPTER 15

APRIL 1, 1944 / HEADQUARTERS, 483RD BOMBARDMENT GROUP

TORTORELLA, ITALY

Col. Paul Barton, Commanding Officer, 483rd Bombardment Group (H), sat at his desk in the Group Operation's Office. He had been told by the Fifth Wing Operations Office that a new mission was coming down the chain of command—a mission that would amount to a baptism of fire for the 483rd. He wasn't surprised when the phone on his desk, with a dedicated "scrambler" line, came to life with a loud jangle.

"Colonel Barton," he answered. The voice on the other end was that of the Watch Officer, Fifth Wing, Fifteenth Air Force Operations. Col. Barton listened attentively. He knew the drill and was organizing his mental checklist as he listened. The 483rd was being put on pre-mission alert status. The forthcoming information would arrive in one lump sum. He and the group operations officer would forward the mission details to all relevant lower echelon departments including ordinance, aircraft maintenance, ground operations, as well as squadron commanders and operations officers.

The trickle-down flow of information coming to the group commander followed the chain of command starting with the numbered (e.g., Fifteenth) Air Force Chief of Operations who selected the targets, the size of the force needed to accomplish the mission, and a coordinated plan for the participating divisions. This information, which included all supporting details, became the Field Order (F/O). Since certain key departments needed more time than others to get their preparation done, it wasn't unusual for those departments to get the mission details well ahead of the air group's receipt of the formal F/O.

"Yes, uh huh. Set for when? Yes … yes. That's not much time, but we'll make it work, sir."

Col. Barton's initial alert notification also included the target code and mission date. Within the hour, every pilot, navigator, bombardier, radioman, and ordinance officer in the air group had received the alert via each squadron's operations officer. Every man … officer and enlisted, alike … would attend a mission briefing for his specific function.

There was so much brass in the room that one almost had to wear sunglasses to withstand the glare. Shining the brightest were the three stars of Lieutenant General Ira Eaker, Commanding General of U.S. Army Air Forces in the Mediterranean. Gen. Eaker was senior to General Carl Spaatz, Commander of the new Fifteenth Air Force. Other notable officers present were Col. Paul Barton, Commander, 483rd Bomb Group; and Colonel Ford J. Lauer, Commander, 99th Bomb Group.

Gen. Eaker opened the meeting with an explanation of the mediocre performance of precision daylight bombing.

> *"'Project Point Blank' opened in October last year with a series of maximum effort missions aimed at destroying, or at least critically reducing, German domination of the skies over Europe. The largest of those air battles took place on the fourteenth of October, when the bombers of the Eighth Air Force attacked the ball bearing plant at Schweinfurt. On that day the Eighth*

Air Force lost eighty-eight heavy bombers and six hundred forty-two American lives. That single battle reduced America's strategic bombing forces by eighteen percent. To this date, since the activation of Project Point Blank, the Eighth and Twelfth Air Forces have lost over one-third of their heavy bombers and crews, while the overall goal of reducing the capability of German production of large numbers of aircraft has been only partially successful. That is mostly the result of the limited range of our fighter escorts. To reach our most distant targets, fighter escorts have had to withdraw from the battle area leaving our Forts and B-24s defenseless against overwhelming numbers of German fighters. Such losses are unacceptable. Worse, they are unsustainable.

"Gentlemen, Point Blank must be completed successfully over the next few weeks to prepare for the Allied invasion and liberation of Europe. This is how we're going to do it ..."

Gen. Eaker went on to describe the important changes in battle strategy for the USAAF, which included:

- Increased range of existing P-38 Lightning and P-47 Thunderbolts with added external drop tanks, and new models of the P-51 Mustang using the Rolls-Royce 12-cylinder engines, will enable escorts to remain on station until the bombers complete their bomb runs.
- The new combat "box" formation that will allow better and more efficient gunnery results for the defense of the bombers themselves.
- The introduction of shuttle bombing.

"Although this final item has not yet been implemented, we fully expect to have at least three Soviet airbases near the Prussian border that will be equipped to receive our heavy bombers for purposes of refueling and rearming. This new availability will allow our bombers to attack the most distant targets, then they will refuel at the Soviet bases and be able to bomb German targets on the return leg of each sortie.

"Vital to the Luftwaffe aircraft reproduction facilities are the ball bearing factories in Steyr, Austria, and the marshalling yards and aerodromes in various locations within Hungary and Romania.

"We, meaning the Allied forces, must achieve total dominance in the skies

within the next few weeks. General Carl Spaatz, General James Doolittle, General Curtis LeMay and I, are directing all bombardment groups under our command to plow the road in preparation for the Allied invasion and liberation of the whole of Europe. This will bring an end, once and for all, to Adolf Hitler and his Third Reich.

"Now, I will turn the time over to Colonels York and Lauer."

Col. York stepped to the lectern. Behind him was a large map of the target. A curtain was currently covering the map. Every pilot and crew member in the room tensed … sitting forward on the edge of their chairs. For some it was the first chapter in a waking nightmare that had no foreseeable end. In a moment, they would learn all of the details of what would mean the last day of many of their lives.

As the curtain was moved slowly to the side, bombing altitude, weather, course changes, waypoints, air cover, expected enemy resistance in the air and from the ground, and bomb and ammo loadout became evident. On Col. York's signal, a tech. sergeant aide pulled the curtain aside the rest of the way, revealing a visual of the entire mission strategy. The attack plan would take them over known concentrations of anti-aircraft batteries. Primary and secondary targets were revealed with accompanying explanations of their importance. The realization of the enormity of the mission brought an uneasy silence to the room, until just as quickly, the stoic, expressionless faces began to reflect a collective spirit burning with a fire of resignation and determination to complete the largest single bombing mission to date in the war … and for some, the *first bombing mission of the war!*

Col. York continued, "On April 3, two days from today, elements of the 99th Bombardment Group and the 483rd Bombardment Group will join together in a combined attack on the industrial and ball bearing plants in Steyr, Austria. Two squadrons each from both groups, thirty-six Forts strong, will launch the strike at zero six hundred hours. Air cover will be provided by P-51s of the 301st and 302nd fighter squadrons. The 301st will precede the Forts and are assigned to aggressively seek out and destroy any aircraft in the area of the attack route. By the time our Forts reach the IP, enemy fighter resistance should be significantly reduced. After our bombers have dropped their ordinance and are ready to turn for home, the 302nd fighter squadron will escort the bombers back to friendly skies. Flying this first combined mission will be the 348th and 416th squadrons from the 99th Bombardment Group, and the 816th and 817th squadrons from the 483rd Bombardment Group. Participating squadron commanders, your orders are waiting for you at Base Operations. A briefing update for all crews will be held at zero four hundred hours, on April 3, in this hangar. Wheels up at zero six hundred on that day.

"On a closing note, attacks on enemy industrial and ball bearing plants, marshalling yards, and aerodromes will occur on a daily basis. Squadrons of the 483rd Bombardment Group and the 99th Bombardment Group will alternate, allowing each crew to stand down one day for every day they're in the air. Hopefully, this new strategy will give the ground crews sufficient time to keep our planes airworthy and flight crews freshly rested.

"Command has determined that the number of missions flown to qualify for return to the states is set at thirty. Of course, this figure is subject to change based on the overall needs of the military."

Word spread fast about the mission. The tents were buzzing with the news. Mostly, members of the participating squadrons for whom the Steyr mission would be their first, picked the brains of the men who were veterans.

Gus pulled open the drawer to his small writing table at the head of his bunk. He removed a pencil and lined essay pad. It had been two days short of a month since leaving MacDill Army Air Force Base, and this would be his first letter to Addie from Tortorella.

My Darling Addie,

How I miss you! With all of the travel from base to base over the past few weeks, I haven't been able to write at all. I wish I could tell you where I am, but I'm only allowed to say it's somewhere in Italy.

Oh, how happy I am, Addie. The news of your pregnancy arrived at MacDill Air Force Base just before we left for Italy.

Sweetheart, I want us to have our own home and to start our lives together just as you said in your last letter to me. I carry that letter with me every day. I don't know if it's my imagination, but I believe I can still smell the aroma of your perfume on it (since none of the other guys have said anything, I suspect it's more my own imagination), just know that you are with me every minute of every day.

We begin the "real thing" in a couple of days. We'll be doing our thing pretty much three to four days per week from now until this war is over, hopefully by sometime next year. I'm fine, and I'm enjoying the warm spring Italian climate, although I haven't had the opportunity to see the sights of Italy yet.

I wish I could be more specific about the "how, when, and where" of things, but the censors would redact it anyway. There's no law preventing me from telling you that I love you more than life itself. I promise you, sweetheart, there's no power on earth that can prevent me from coming home to you.

Okay, change of subject. How are you getting along, my love? I guess by now you are back in the swing of things at school.

How's Highway doing? I miss that big furry critter.

Oh, I almost forgot to tell you. I have been promoted to captain, so I'll be sending you a few more dollars each month. I hope it helps some. I know money is pretty tight what with the rationing and all.

I'll write again when I can. When you write, send your letters to:

Captain Gus Bodine
483rd Bombardment Group, 816th B.S.
APO 410 C/O Postmaster, NY, New York

Love Always,
Gus

Gus sealed the envelope and carried it to the mail room, the thought running through his mind that, *This might be my last letter to Addie*, repeated itself. *What reason do I have to believe that I can survive this war? Over thirty percent of our seventeens go down, and their crews are dead or captured!* It seemed to him as if he might be carrying his own epitaph.

He entered his quarters (tent) and found Hank Barenz lying on his bunk with his service cap pulled down over his eyes.

"Pssst. Hank, are you awake?" Gus whispered.

"Yeah. I don't think I'll be able to sleep until after the mission. I'm wound so tight that … well, I want to get smashed … cross-eyed drunk! If I were a drinking man, I'd probably do it, too." He sat up on the side of his bunk. "How do you keep so cool headed, Gus. It's like you have ice water in your veins."

"You'd be surprised, Hank. I just mailed a letter to Addie, and I can't help thinking it may be the last one I'll ever write. I'm scared half to death. Uh … that's just between us, okay?"

"Absolutely, Gus. Let's get out of here and grab some chow; what do you say?" Hank stood and tucked in his shirt.

"Sounds good. After chow, though, I want to check on *Addie's Armor* and make sure everything's buttoned down for the mission. Maybe we should get the crew together, and we can all go over to the flightline together."

Addie's Armor's bombardier, Phil Day, and navigator, Al Wendelford, were at the O club finishing up their breakfast when Gus and Hank entered. Al waved and shouted, "Hey, Skipper, over here!"

Gus and Hank strolled over to the table and joined the two officers.

"I'm glad to see both of you" Gus said. "Hank and I were just talking and thought it might be a good thing to get the guys together and give the plane a once over, you know, to make sure everything is ship-shape."

They chatted a while, then Phil and Al headed for the enlisted men's quarters in search of the rest of the crew. After finding Dink, and Bob Sykes in their tent, the four of them spread out to find the rest of the guys.

An hour later, Gus and Hank arrived at the flightline. Their bomber looked ready to go. An MP staff sergeant stood by with his M1 Garand rifle at "sling arms" (hanging off his shoulder) position.

"Good afternoon, Sergeant. I'm Captain Gus Bodine, the operations officer of the 816th Bomb Squadron. I've asked my crew to meet us here to give our ship a quick once over before the mission tomorrow." Gus presented the sentry with his I.D. The NCO looked them over and handed the documents back to Gus.

"Sir, I've been ordered to not allow anyone but maintenance personnel on the flightline."

"Hold on there, Sarge." TSgt Dinkleman approached. "Name's Dinkleman. I'm the flight engineer of this Fort. Do I qualify as 'maintenance personnel'?"

"I reckon you do." A slight grin came over the officer's face. "I take it these officers are here to supervise your inspection of this aircraft. Am I right?"

"Right as rain, Sergeant. Won't take more than about fifteen minutes." Dink smiled at the man as if they were very best friends."

"Make it fast, gents. I don't want to be tested on how far I can stretch the rules if the O.D. (officer of the day) should happen by."

When the rest of the crew showed up, Gus had them assemble together. "Fellas, what do you say to taking a quick crew photo? I, for one, would like to able to dust off a family album twenty years from now just to remind myself what a sad and unattractive bunch of chumps you guys were." The remark was received with much booing and laughter.

"I'm in, Skipper, as long as you include yourself among the 'unattractive chumps.'" With the whole crew whistling and clapping their approval, Gus took out his Kodak Brownie—that he just happened to bring along for the occasion.

"Hey, Sergeant," Gus called to the MP non-com. "Would you mind doing the honors?"

The MP agreed to handle the camera work, and the crew of *Addie's Armor* was immortalized on film.

"Okay, guys, we have fifteen minutes to check everything out: bombs fused and tagged with arming wires properly installed, weapons are clean and ready for use, and the ammo load-out is correct. I'll want a comm check, so everyone needs to be at their station. Let's do it. Everyone climb aboard while Lieutenant Barenz and I do a walk around."

A few minutes into the equipment check, TSgt Sykes was inspecting the .50 caliber guns on both waist positions. He pulled the slide bolt back on the starboard weapon and immediately discovered that the locking slide was not operational. Further checking showed that the locking slide spring was missing.

"Waist gunner to pilot: There's a problem with one of the waist guns, Skipper. There's a broken locking-slide spring. All of the other guns are good to go. I'll take care of it ASAP, but it's a stupid mistake."

"Copy that, Bob. Check back with me as soon as the problem is fixed. Pilot: Out."

Sgt. Sykes walked over to the ordinance shop and told the NCO I/C (in command) on the morning shift about the problem. One very angry master sergeant had a conversation with the corporal assigned to *Addie's Armor*. The AN-M2 machine gun in question was restored to operational condition before noon. Corporal Evan Manning spent the rest of his shift on the floor with a machine gun of the same type, disassembling and re-assembling it while naming each part and its function.

CHAPTER 16

ON TARGET

At 3:00 a.m., the air raid siren sounded a long steady blaring scream lasting 10 seconds. Sixty seconds later, the military version of a very annoying alarm clock sounded again. In an instant, thousands of incandescent light bulbs flashed in "tent city." A frantic scurry of activity with a scramble to the flightline ensued. To the men of the 483rd Bombardment Group, the alert siren was a jab of adrenaline.

Those pilots and co-pilots assigned to the day's mission quickly dressed and assembled on the floor of Hangar #2 for the mission briefing. No history lessons were taught regarding past operations and strategies, no patriotic call to arms came from the brass, and there was no saber rattling to insight the call to duty in the hearts of the men who chose to fly and fight. The mission briefing was all about business: formation of the "combat box," horizontal and vertical separation of aircraft, marshalling coordinates and altitude, order of attack by squadron and flight, bombing altitude, communication protocol and a dozen other procedural issues related to delivering 108,000 tons of destructive ordinance on target.

The mission briefing ended with Col. Lauer giving a "time hack" (every man in the room synchronized his wristwatch to that of the officer in command). The officers had chow waiting for them in the mess. Most of them knew that drinking a lot of fluids before a mission was counterproductive, so a light breakfast of scrambled eggs, sausage, and toast - and no more than a glass of water or a cup of coffee - satisfied the majority. The simple breakfast ended, and it was time to head for the flightline.

Gus, Hank, Phil, and Al piled out of the GMC CCKW "Jimmy" two and one-half ton troop-carrying truck and walked over to *Addie's Armor*. The enlisted crew were assembled and were ordered into the plane.

Gus caught sight of Sgt. Sykes. "Sykes, over here."

The waist gunner trotted over to Gus. "Yes, sir." Sykes threw Gus a salute.

"Make sure your guns are ready to lock and load. I would appreciate it if you would pass the order to the other gunners. Check the ammo belts, too."

"Yes, sir." Sykes disappeared into the belly of the aircraft.

Five minutes later, the outside walk around was completed. Gus signed off on the Form 1-A and handed it to the crew chief.

Gus and Hank buckled themselves in and began the task of bringing aircraft #43-37594 to life. The auxiliary power unit was disconnected, and the pre-flight routine began.

"Read the list, Lieutenant Barenz"

"Fire Guard." Hank recited from the pre-start checklist.

"Clear left … Clear right." Gus answered back after checking the switch's position.

"Master Switch."

"Switch ON."

Hank called out each item on the engine start checklist, in its proper sequence, down to, "… Start number one."

"Turning one!" Gus called out the open, side, wind screen. He toggled up the starter switch on the left inboard engine, and did the same to the magneto switches. The engine caught hold after Gus counted six blades passing by his view. First a belch of white smoke then all nine cylinders lit up. He set the throttle to 1200 rpm. It would take about 45 seconds for the oil temperature to warm up.

The process was repeated three more times, until all four Wright Cyclone engines were idling at 1200 rpm.

Gus ordered the radio turned on. "Pilot to crew: Ready to taxi. Call in."

"Navigator: All set."

"Bombardier: Ready to go, Skipper."

"Radio: Check."

"Tail gunner: Check."

"Ball turret: Ready, Skipper."

"'Waist' is good to go. All guns are charged."

"Engineer: All temps and pressures are green to go, Captain."

Gus performed the engine run-up, and *Addie's Armor* was ready to start her taxi roll to the runway. Using only the engines and rudder to turn the 65,500-pound bomber, Gus turned behind the aircraft in front of him and followed it to the active runway. There was no need to ask the control tower for permission to depart—a bomber was prepared to go wheels up every 30 seconds.

"Here we go!" Gus' right hand grasped all four throttles using the palm-up technique which allowed him to operate all four throttles and "walk" them up to full power. Lt. Barenz' job was to watch the engine instruments to insure proper function of rpm, manifold pressure, oil and hydraulic pressure, and temperature gauges.

At 115 mph, Gus applied slight back pressure on the yoke, and the bomber lifted off. "Wheels up," he called.

Hank toggled up the landing gear and glanced out the right wind screen to confirm the wheels up condition. "Right wheel is up."

"Left wheel is up," Gus affirmed.

Addie's Armor headed for the marshalling area north of Tortorella at 15,000 ft AGL (above ground level). Within ten minutes, the 36-plane formation turned north on a heading of 349° N at an altitude of 15,000 ft at 160 mph, IAS (indicated airspeed). Their course would take them approximately 675 miles to the target in Steyr, Austria, while making several course changes designed to confuse the enemy as to the location of the primary target.

If the 301st Fighter Group did its job, the Luftwaffe would think twice about hitting the bombers after tangling with the "Tuskegee Airmen" in their P-51s. The "Mustangs" were outfitted with the new

Merlin-Rolls Royce 12-cylinder supercharged 1,490 hp engine (compared to the old Allison 1,125 hp) giving them superiority over the German fighters in power and performance.

Each squadron and flight had an assigned communication call sign for the purpose of inter-plane communication. The 816th Bomb Squadron leader's call sign was "Blue Leader." The three flights of three-planes each were Blue One, Blue Two, and Blue Three. Gus was the flight leader for Blue One and was given the call name of Blue One Leader. So, it was with each of the two squadrons of the 483rd Bombardment Group. Using the colors of blue and red, they were distinguished from the "Alpha" and "Bravo" designation of the 817th squadron. The same pattern of communication was used for the 99th Bombardment Group.

Nineteen B-17s of the 99th Bombardment Group were the lead element of the 37 bomber "combat box" formation— a staggered diamond formation where planes had to maintain 50 ft of vertical and horizontal separation from the nearest planes above, below, left, and right. The 483rd BG (Gus' group) took up the rear of the formation. For them it was the first combat mission. The 99th had been flying missions for Twelfth Air Force since March of 1943. They were re-assigned to the Fifteenth Air Force in March of '44 as part of the buildup of the USAAF bomber forces in the Mediterranean under Lt. General Ira Eaker who commanded both the Twelfth and Fifteenth Air Forces. The men of the 483rd were the "new guys on the block" who cut their teeth flying training and combat mission s with the 99th BG since their arrival in Italy back in March.

THE BLACK CURTAIN

Group Leader to all planes: We're ten minutes out from the IP. Gunners, charge your weapons. Bombardiers, make your ordinance ready. Our escort is at our three o'clock high. Looks like a squadron strength of 15 P-51s. If there's any resistance, we should be seeing the Luftwaffe anytime. You amateurs of the 483rd stay tucked in, stay alert, and keep your heads on a swivel.

"Pathfinder" was a B-17 equipped with a radar guided bombsight.

The crew of that B-17 was chosen from the best crews with the best on-target accuracy record in the group. Major Mitt Cliburn of the 99th BG had flown #42-3552, *Shady Lady*, on 22 missions, the last four as a Pathfinder PIC (pilot in command). His bombardier, Captain Clyde Weiskopf, had a dedicated radio frequency assigned to him to coordinate the release of the group's ordinance. When the time came for Pathfinder to order "bombs away!" all B-17s would release their bombs simultaneously. Flying in the combat box formation allowed them to achieve the tightest mean points of impact (MPI) possible. The purpose of this strategy was two-fold: to maximize the destruction of the target with a compact concentration of 108 tons of demolition bombs, and to minimize collateral damage to the civilian population. To Gus, the later purpose weighed on his mind far more than a good score on an MPI report.

Gus toggled up his microphone.

"Pilot to crew: Lock and load, gunners. The enemy will hit us before the eighty-eights open up. The 301st fighters plowed the field, but those Messerschmidt and Focke-Wulf drivers don't turn and ..."

"Tail gunner, sir. ...At our six o'clock, coming in hot! ...At least a dozen ... vectoring for attack!"

The peaceful drone of the four Wright-Cyclone engines, relaxing as they were, gave way to the chattering roar of the tail gunner's twin AN-M2 .50 caliber guns spitting out 850 rounds per minute of armor piercing bullets, dueling the lead element of three Fw 190 Luftwaffe Fighters with their two 20 mm Mauser cannons in the wings and two 13 mm cannons over the engine.

SSgt Carpenter placed his gunsight ahead of the German fighter that had targeted *Addie's Armor* for the kill. Woody released half a lungful of air and held his breath. He willed his mind and body to focus on the enemy plane. With another burst of fire, his guns found the target. A flash of debris exploded from the fighter, and the plane went into an immediate spin, trailing smoke behind. All the planes of the 483rd were firing freely at the attacking targets.

The rookies of the 816th and 817th Bomb Squadrons, including *Addie's Armor*, bore the brunt of the assault from the rear. One bomber from the 817th was trailing smoke from the outside port engine and was dropping out of formation with all of its guns firing.

Flashes of sunlight reflecting off the aluminum fuselages of a squadron of the P-51D "Red Tail" Tuskegee fighters arrowed into the surprised Fw 190 fighters. The German pilots had seen the planes of the 301st Fighter Squadron turn back toward their base but had not anticipated another American fighter group entering the fray. The 302nd Fighter Squadron swarmed on them—driving them away from the B-17s. The Fort gunners silenced their weapons. As fast as the attack had come, the threat from the sky was gone. The threat from the ground was about to begin.

"Pathfinder to all planes, reaching IP coordinates in ten, nine, eight, seven, six, five, four, three, two, one. IP acquired, turning to target."

———

It began as a few bursts of black smoke in the distance. When the amorphous puffs drew closer and increased in number and frequency, the crews could hear the "crump … crump-crump-crump!" of the exploding German 88 mm cannon fire. Finally, Gus and the crew of *Addie's Armor* could feel the plane buffeting under the force of the ack-ack barrage of exploding artillery. Close calls often shook the plane so severely that men would be knocked off balance.

"Hold on, Hank!" Gus called out in an outburst of near panic as the bomber yawed and almost entered a flat spin after a near hit by a flak burst. "Oh no! … Oh no …" he cried as he tried to maintain control of the bomber. He had a flash of an image of a giant child's hand waving a toy B-17 to and fro … up and down. *Look Mommy, I'm flying, I'm flying!* the giant three-year-old shouted gleefully in Gus' head.

"Pilot to crew: If you're not strapped in, DO IT NOW!" At that same moment a loud "whang!" was heard, and the steel armored plate, between the bomb bay and the radio operator's table, shifted. A gaping hole appeared in the fuselage beneath SSgt Marty Gonzalez. He felt himself being jerked out of his seat, but thanks to his harness, he remained at his radio console.

"Radio to pilot: Do you read me? Over!"

"Pilot to radio: Roger, you're five-by-five, Sergeant. What happened back there?"

"The ack-ack blew a hole in the floor under my butt. Shook me up some, but I'm okay," Marty said. He reached down to his throbbing derriere and brought up a hand stained red with a small patch of his own blood.

"Copy that, Marty. Radio seems fine. How does the panel look?"

"Everything's operational, sir. You may want to do a comm check from the cockpit, though ... just to be sure."

The formation continued through the black wall of flak for over a minute, then, as the ack-ack subsided, Pathfinder came online.

Pathfinder to group. Target in one minute. Hold altitude at two-zero thousand, airspeed one-six-zero indicated (244 mph), heading zero-eight-seven degrees.

"Bombardier to pilot: Hold position ... opening bomb bay doors. Engaging autopilot now. On target ... holding steady ... steady ... bombs away!" called out Lt. Wendelford while toggling up the bomb release levers. The dozen 500 lb bombs fell in the sequence predetermined by the Intervalometer which the bombardier set prior to the launch of the mission.

Blue Leader to Flight Leaders: We are on target. Repeat, we are on target! Turning to rally point, maintain formation.

Without the weight of the bombs pressing on them, the B-17s of the 483rd were able to increase their airspeed to 260 mph. When the 302nd Fighter Squadron escort fighters reappeared, the Forts assembled into a diamond formation for the return to base.

For Gus, the welcomed silence from the exploding ground fire was interrupted by the urgent voice of TSgt Sykes, "Waist gunner to pilot: Skipper, we have a problem back here."

"What is it, Sergeant Sykes?" Gus asked anxiously.

"It's Marty Gonzalez, sir. He's been hit. It must have happened with that last burst of ack-ack just before we released our bombs. I shot him up with some morphine and applied a pressure bandage on the wound. Looks like the bleeding has slowed down."

"Copy that. I'm on my way. Pilot: Out."

"Hank, take the controls. I'll be right back."

Gus unbuckled his harness and worked his way back toward the bomb bay. Marty was stretched out on the catwalk next to the now empty bomb racks. Sgt. Sykes was seated in the radio operators position in front of the radio panel. Gus didn't expect to see the amount of blood that Marty had lost, and his concern for his radioman ratcheted upward. He bent as low as possible to get a closer look.

"Hey, Marty. How are you feeling, fella?"

"I feel tired … sleepy. Morphine helps. I guess I'll be okay, Skipper. Sykes is helping me. It's cold, though."

"We'll get you on the ground ASAP, Marty. Are you comfortable enough? I don't want to move you."

"I'm fine, sir. I'll be okay." Sgt. Gonzalez closed his eyes. Gus turned to Sgt. Sykes and spoke in a whisper.

"You've examined the wound, Sykes. What's your assessment?"

"I wish we didn't have so far to go. He's lost a lot of blood. When I found him he was slumped down in his seat bleeding badly."

"Okay. Good work, Sykes. We'll divert to Ramitelli. Can you operate the radio board?"

"I think so, sir. Give me a minute to find the frequency for Ramitelli. I'll let you know."

"Copy that. I need the tower frequency to get vectors." Gus worked his way back to the flight deck.

"Lieutenant Day. I need a heading to Ramitelli."

"Yes, sir." The navigator flipped thru his navigation charts, then crunched a few numbers. "Turn to heading one-niner-five degrees, Captain. The new heading will take you down the coast of the Adriatic. Ramitelli Army Air Force base should be about one hundred twenty-five miles. You should have no problem getting a visual."

Blue One Leader to Blue Leader: Over.

Blue Leader: Read you. Go ahead.

Blue One Leader: Reporting one injured crewman. Request permission to leave the formation for Ramitelli Army Air Force Base.

Roger, Blue One Leader. Keep an eye out for enemy aircraft. You should pass beyond enemy airspace in about twenty minutes. Good luck, Captain.

Gus switched over to the inter-phone so he could talk to the crew.

"Pilot to crew: Sergeant Gonzalez has been wounded by ack-ack shrapnel. We are diverting to Ramitelli. Gunners man your stations and lock and load your weapons. Test one burst each. Keep your eye out for enemy fighters. We will pass into friendly skies and about ten minutes. Until then, stay sharp. If we're spotted, some hot dog German pilot may think he has come on a defenseless B-17. We may have to give him an education, so be ready. All stations report status."

"Engineer: All instruments are in the green, and the aircraft is good to go."

"Navigator is good to go, Skipper."

"Turret gunner: Operational."

"Waist gunner: Guns ready."

"Tail gunner: Locked and loaded."

"Ball turret: Check."

"Bombardier: Ready, Skipper."

Addie's Armor flew on toward the border of Italy and Austria. The American bomber had to cross nearly 80 mi of enemy airspace without any air cover. Tension in the plane mounted as they drew closer to San Candido on the Italian side.

"Tail gunner to pilot: Two bogeys coming in at five o'clock!"

The two "enemy" planes drew closer. Oddly, they did not separate to set up a double-pronged attack. Rather, they approached on a parallel course.

"Hold your fire, gunners," Gus called through the inter-phone. "They're friendly!"

Seconds later, two Red Tail P-51D fighters, from the American 302nd Fighter Squadron, eased up on the right side of the bomber.

Gus switched to the plane-to-plane standard frequency. *"Brother, are we happy to see the two of you."*

"Happy to be of service, sir. Lieutenant Samuel Washington Rice at your service.

We were told by your Group Leader that you have wounded on board and that you are headed for Ramitelli."

"That is affirmative. Our ship picked up some flak from the eighty-eights. I need to get my radioman to the medics ASAP."

"Follow us, sir. We'll lead the way."

Addie's Armor flew on with no further sign of German interference. They crossed into Italy and flew down the west coast of the Adriatic Sea.

Gus radioed Ramitelli:

Ramitelli tower, Army Three Seven Five Niner Four is a Bravo One-Seven declaring medical emergency. We have one wounded crewman down from shrapnel to his lower body. He is alive, but actively bleeding. Over.

Three Seven Five Niner Four, you are cleared straight-in approach, runway one-six. Emergency vehicles standing by. Watch for tall trees on approach. Our runway is only forty-five hundred feet long. Over.

Roger. Clear to land runway one-six.

An ambulance was standing by at the end of the runway. Gus and Hank taxied the bomber to the far end of the strip. The ambulance pulled up to the crew ladder. Bob Sykes and "Dink" Dinkleman lowered the wounded Marty Gonzalez into the waiting arms of the medics.

None of the crew wanted to leave the Mobile Army Surgical Hospital. Instead, they all waited outside and paced while they re-hashed the enemy attack.

"I should have checked on Marty after that last hit. The blast cut through the fuselage like it was cardboard. It left a hole bigger than my fist," TSgt Robert Sykes commented.

"Nothing you could have done about it, Sykes. We were all too busy trying to survive," TSgt Dinkleman said in a somber voice. He buried his head in his hands. "I just hope we got him to the medics in time." Dink and Marty had become good friends, and it was he who was affected most by Sgt. Gonzalez' situation.

Two hours later, a tired, blood-spattered doctor stepped out of the "surgery and recovery" tent. He pulled down his surgical mask and looked at the nine men who had been waiting.

"He took three units of blood while we stitched him up. The shrapnel nicked his femoral artery. You were right to keep him immobilized. If you had tried to move him, he likely would have bled out. As it is, he'll need to stand down from duty for three to four weeks."

"When can we see him, Doc?" Gus asked the surgeon.

"Give him an hour to come out of the ether, then he'll be able to talk for a few minutes, but ONLY a few minutes, and … I'm sorry, but only the two of you officers will be able to visit with Sergeant Gonzalez."

Gus and Hank stood by until Marty was awake enough to talk, then a nurse escorted them to his bed.

"Hi ya, Sergeant. How are you feeling?" Gus asked.

"Just dandy, sir," replied the always ebullient jokester … even fresh out of surgery! "This place is really a pain in the butt, though." Gonzalez grinned, then winced and groaned for effect.

"What did they tell you about returning to duty, Marty?" Hank asked.

"It'll probably be a few weeks, sir. I think they'll send me to a big hospital up-country in Rome to rehab. I don't think I'll be sitting around much, though." They all had a good laugh at Marty Gonzalez' ability to make light of his situation. "I guess you'll be getting a replacement for me. I'll sure miss you guys."

Gus rested his hand on Sgt. Gonzalez' shoulder and patted it lightly. "You just get well, Marty. The doc wouldn't let them see you, but the guys will be glad to hear you're going to be okay."

Gus and Hank returned to the Fortress and the crew, who were all standing by, anxiously awaiting the news of their friend. Gus told them of Marty's surprisingly good condition and relayed the surgeon's prognosis for his recovery.

"That's about it, fellas. We'll be assigned a replacement radioman, but it may take a few days. Sergeant Dinkleman, do you think this lady will get us back to Tortorella without falling to pieces?"

"We counted seventeen bullet holes in her … and three ack-ack penetrations. Miraculously, though, all of her systems appear to be operational."

"That's good news. Let's climb aboard. Chow is waiting back at base."

CHAPTER 17

PROVINCE OF FOGGIA, ITALY / STERPARONE USAAF BASE

For the next two-and-a-half weeks, the B-17s of the 483rd conducted bombing missions against industrial ball bearing plants at the Steyr, Austria, marshalling yards; aerodromes at Budapest, Hungary; aerodromes in Bucharest; and marshalling yards at Ploesti, Rumania, and Leskovac, Yugoslavia.

TSgt Sykes pulled double duty as both radioman and waist gunner making *Addie's Armor* eligible for mission status.

Since December 1943, it had become increasingly clear to the allied air forces that the Nazis were moving much of their industrial war machine farther east, too far for the range of the B-24s and B-17s of the United States Army Air Forces. Even with the extended range provided by "Tokyo tanks" (additional fuel cells fitted to the interior of the wingtips), the B-17s would still be unable to make the return trip to their home base. The welcome transfer of the air echelon of the 483rd from Tortorella to Sterparone promised access to targets farther east in the direction of Prussia.

Finally, on April 22, the air element of the 483 Bombardment Group (H) joined the ground element who had already arrived at the new base at Sterparone (located in the province of Foggia about 220 kilometers north from the air echelon's temporary quarters at Tortorella). The 483rd's full complement of air and ground echelons were together again for the first time since leaving MacDill Air Force Base, Florida, six weeks earlier.

On April 23, Gus and the crew of *Addie's Armor* joined the rest of the 816th and the pilots and crews of the 483rd BG in a briefing of their initial mission as an independent Air Group. They would fly their first bombing mission over the German industrial and aircraft assembly plants in Austria at Schwechat, Bad Vöslau, and Wiener Neustadt.

MISSION BRIEFING

Col. Barton sat to the side of the battle map covered by the traditional curtain. Next to him was the Group Operations Officer: Lt. Col. Wallace Linn, and Group Executive Officer: Col. Edward York. Pilots and co-pilots occupied the first couple of rows; navigators and bombardiers sat behind them; enlisted crew men with a need to know, such as radio operators, sat behind the officers. Col. Barton stood and approached the podium.

"Good morning 483rd." Col. Barton flashed a winning smile. "Today marks the briefing of our first independent mission as an air group of the Fifteenth Air Force. You have all been flying "tail-end-Charlie" sorties behind the veterans of the 99th Bomb Group. Well, fellas, we are the veteran crews now, and you own Sterparone United States Army Air Force Base as the sole tenant organization of this facility."

A spontaneous round of "Hip-hip-hooray!" echoed throughout the hangar. Everyone had looked forward to settling into their new "home." It wasn't much, mostly put-together bombed-out farm buildings, a few houses, and a too-short dirt runway.

"Now … to the business at hand." Col. Barton pulled back the first part of the curtain showing the route of their approach to the target … straight up the coast of the Adriatic Sea.

"Our three main targets are German industrial and aircraft

manufacturing plants at Schwechat, about 30 kilometers west from Sopron, Hungary; then south to Bad Vöslau; Austria, and on to Wiener Neustadt and it's aircraft assembly plant. The P-51s of the 332nd Fighter Group will provide air cover. Bombing altitude will be two-zero thousand feet. Colonel York will lead the mission from Pathfinder … call name, Triple Play. The 815th is call name, Red Leader. Aircraft designations will be Red One, Red Two, Red Three, and Red Four." The 816th will be Blue Leader, and Blue One, Blue Two, Blue Three, and Blue Four are your aircraft call signs. The 817th is Green Leader, with Green One, Green Two, Green Three, and Green Four for your aircraft designators.

"Command authority for the bomb run is assigned to the 815th, 816th, and 817th Bombardment Squadrons individually. We found this advisable inasmuch as each squadron has its own assigned target. That strategy is the brainchild of Group Operations Officer Lieutenant Colonel Keith Vincent. Borrowing three Forts each from the 818th our squadron strength will increase from three flights each to four flights. The 815th will strike the farthest north target of Schwechat. The 816th will hit Bad Vöslau, and the 817th will hit the third target at Wiener Neustadt. We'll hit those three facilities simultaneously. We will marshal in group combat box formation, proceed to the Austria-Italy border where we will split into our attack formation of three twelve-plane squadrons, fly to our targets and return home. Loadout will be eight five-hundred-pound demos and twenty one-hundred pound incendiary bombs. Standard one thousand rounds of ammo for each gun have been loaded onto the Forts by the armorers."

Col. York continued the briefing with reports of weather conditions over the target, latest intel on Luftwaffe strength in the area, ack-ack, secondary targets, and a half-dozen other details.

After the briefing, Gus, Hank Barenz, and Phil Day headed over to the new Officers' Mess Hall for some chow. Gus spotted Jeremiah Holladay.

"Lieutenant Holladay! Over here!" Gus called out. J. R turned toward the voice, saw Gus, and trotted over to the three officers.

"Gus, it's good to see you, man." The two men shook hands enthusiastically.

"Lieutenant J. R. Holladay, I'd like for you to meet Hank Barenz, *Addie's Armor* co-pilot and my good friend."

J. R. offered his hand to Hank. "Pleased to meet you, Lieutenant Barenz."

The not-so-uncommon fare of the day, served up by the food service staff, was Salisbury steak, canned corn, and mashed potatoes with a gelatinous gravy that defied description. The men dug in with enthusiasm as they talked about the mission and old times.

Gus wanted to get an idea of how Jeremiah was coping with his anxieties the two of them discussed several days earlier. "So, J. R., how are you feeling about tomorrow's mission?"

J. R. stuffed a forkful of "sawdust" steak into his mouth and chased it with a gulp of coffee.

"Fine, actually. Funniest thing …" he finished off his coffee and continued, "after that last mission with the 99th, with the Luftwaffe firing at us and ack-ack exploding all around, I started feeling pretty darned good about my chances. I think I was more concerned about my ability as a PIC to get my crew safely through the fight. Oh, and I meant to thank you again for the pep talk."

"You're welcome. I think that's something we can all use from time to time."

Addie's Armor rolled down the corrugated steel runway, gaining speed until the thrum of the tires that accompanied the roar of the engines suddenly ceased as the mains lifted the 25,000 lb B-17G from the runway surface.

"Positive rate. Gear up."

"Gear up, Captain," Hank Barenz replied.

Gus watched the airspeed climb past 125 mph indicated and called for the flaps to be raised.

"Flaps up," Hank answered as the green light confirming the flaps-up condition flashed on.

There's a time at the beginning of every mission when an almost peaceful lull falls over the formation after it's assembled, when every Fort becomes part of a single entity … an organism born into the world, whose purpose is to return order and peace to the chaos and destruction imposed by warring nations. It's a time to listen to the voice of order, of justice and humanity.

As *Addie's Armor* grew closer to the first puffs of flak, Gus was moved to talk to his crew.

"Pilot to crew: Fellas, I've had Marty Gonzalez on my mind this morning. I know he misses us as much as we miss him. I can't stop thinking about him. His presence is with us. Let's fly this mission for Marty and pray for his full recovery."

Before anyone could respond, the voice of Col. York ended the period of "the calm before the storm."

Group Leader to all planes: Acquiring the IP now. Bombardiers, arm your bombs.

When the armorers placed the bombs in their "cradles" in the bomb bay, two fuses were screwed into each bomb: one in the nose and one in the tail, and secured by cotter pins. Each pin was tagged, and when the cotter pins were removed, the bombardier checked each pin's corresponding number on a form provided by the armorer. Al Wendelford would return the bag of cotter pins to the armory upon return to base.

"Bombardier to pilot: All bombs are armed and ready, Skipper." Lt. Wendelford reported."

"Pilot to bombardier: Copy."

Approaching the targets from the west, the 483rd "box" formation split into three squadron boxes of 12 planes each. Designated Red, Blue, and Green Squadrons, each squadron set its course for the assigned target. Since the 816th was assigned the aircraft assembly plant at Bad Vöslau, the course change was only a deviation of five degrees west of their present location.

Thirty seconds after the group split, the German Luftwaffe rolled out the welcome mat. Five Fw 190s and two Me 109s dropped out of the sky.

"Tail to pilot: SEVEN BOGIES, SIX O'CLOCK HIGH! They're dropping out of the clouds … and here come the Red Tails after them! Oh, you beautiful Mustangs!"

The pulse rates of the ten crewmen increased dramatically with the sudden adrenaline rush born of equal parts fear and anticipation of the imminent battle. It is, perhaps, a human trait that causes us to take for granted that gift, which is the greatest of all gifts … life itself! Taken for granted, that is, until a force greater than our will to live, threatens to take it from us. The men of *Addie's Armor* charged into a battle for life, bonded as one in the desperate "fight" side of the primal paradigm … "fight or flight."

The German fighters had one pass before the American P-51s would scatter them.

The enemy planes concentrated their fire on the "tail-end-Charlies" of Blue Squadron. The trailing B-17 in Gus' flight was *Sweet Adeline* commanded by 1st Lt Jeremiah Holladay.

With 50 ft of vertical and horizontal separation between airplanes, the gunners in every plane had ample opportunities to release the firepower of their .50 caliber AN-M2 guns, and within seconds the deafening gunfire and smell of cordite filled the bomber. One of the Fw 190s flashed by Gus' wind screen just as a burst of gunfire from the six .50 cal wing guns of a pursuing P-51D struck the German's plane, stitching a line of bullets along the fuselage and into the engine. An ugly belch of flames and smoke burst from the enemy fighter as it rolled over and entered a steep dive. Gus, felt somewhat conflicted by finding himself hoping the pilot was able to bail out.

The enemy attack lasted less than five minutes. The Red Tails of the Tuskegee Airmen, plus the combined fire power of the B-17s, had destroyed four of the seven enemy planes, but that wasn't the reason for the abrupt departure of the remaining three fighters. The curtain was about to go up on act two. A few black popped-corn-shaped bursts appeared in front of the 12 bombers of the 816th,

"They're getting our range. In a few more seconds, we'll fly into a wall of that stuff," Gus said.

"Pilot to crew: The enemy fighters are gone. Lock down your guns and strap in. We're in for a rough ride"

Blue One Delta to Blue One Leader: J. R. Holladay called in from *Sweet Adaline.*

Blue One Leader: Over.

'Sweet Adaline' is losing oil pressure on number four engine. …Reducing RPM and opening cowl flaps. …Reducing airspeed. …I think we'll make it to the target,

sir, but … Uh oh! Number four just blew! … Shutting down and feathering the prop. Increasing power to remaining engines.

Do you need to abort, Blue One Delta? Over.

Negative, Lead. Staying on course. Will keep you advised.

Copy that, J. R. Blue One Leader: Out.

The innocuous puffs of black smoke buffeted the plane feeling much like minor turbulence, but within seconds those harmless balls of cotton in the sky revealed their claws. Shrapnel from the air bursts rapped on the fuselage like a hundred ball-peen hammers hitting a trash can all at once. The noise alone was unsettling, but when the ack-ack came closer to finding its mark, sudden death appeared much closer. Then came the reality of the fear of every bomber crew— vital systems of the Forts were being rendered inoperable from the power of 88 mm anti-aircraft cannons ripping out control cables or hydraulic lines, or tearing out of part of a wing or empennage … or worse. Suddenly, the Flying Fortress seemed much less a fortress than a coffin.

One after another, sometimes several simultaneous near hits bounced *Addie's Armor* every which way. Again, came Gus' vision of a giant child's hand waving a toy B-17 through the air. *Look, mommy! The crew are getting air sick. They don't like being tossed around inside my airplane.*

Pathfinder to all planes: Coming up on the drop zone in 5-4-3-2-1, bombs away!

Lt. Wendelford released a salvo of all eight 500-lb-demolition bombs, followed by all 20 of the 100-pound incendiary bombs. A cloud cover forced the bombing altitude to be lowered to 15,000 ft which was the lowest recommended altitude for a heavy bomber. The upside, of course, was to deliver a tighter pattern of explosive power on the target. The downside meant an increased kill rate from the German eighty-eight ground fire.

"On target! On target! Well done, Al."

Their air cover was waiting for them at the rally point about ten miles south of the target area. Gus could see another squadron-size group of B-17s at his three o'clock flying on the same heading as the 816th.

"Pilot: Group status report … call it in."

"Navigator: Check."

"Nose gunner: Good to go, Skipper."

"Engineer: All instruments in the green."

"Radio: Check."

"Waist gunner is operational, Skipper."

"Ball turret is good to go."

"Tail gunner: Check."

"Bombardier: All packages delivered at the right address, Skipper."

Blue One Leader to Blue One Delta.: How is "Sweet Adeline" doing, J. R.?

Blue One Delta to Blue One Leader: My co-pilot Lieutenant Grotton is down. One other wounded. Pilot is wounded but maintaining control. I've lost all pitot-static instruments: altimeter, airspeed, and attitude indicator. Compass is gone, too. Rudder control is damaged, and tail gunner is down and unresponsive. Over.

Copy, Blue One Delta.

Blue One Leader to Blue Leader: Request Blue One form up on Blue One Delta to escort 'Sweet Adeline's' RTB (Return to Base). Further request three Papa Five Ones to escort us to peaceful skies. Over.

Stand by, Blue One Leader.

A full minute passed before the 816th squadron leader responded to Gus' request, *Blue Leader to Blue One Leader: Your request is cleared. Blue One, form up on Blue One Delta. Your escort is on its way.*

Blue Squadron: Slow airspeed to two-four-zero indicated.

The operations officer of the 483rd, Lt. Col. Keith Vincent, stood on the deck outside of the control tower. His binoculars hung low on his chest suspended by a leather strap. They were a gift from his wife, Helen, on his birthday, in April of '42, following his graduation from the military academy at West Point. He qualified as a B-17 pilot and remained stateside as a pilot instructor until the formation of the 483rd in December 1943.

"Any sign of them, yet?" the operations officer asked.

"No, sir. They should be well inside Italian airspace by now." The radio came alive with white noise—an indication that the frequency for the air group was hot.

Sterparone control, this is Triple Play. How do you copy? Over.

You are five-by-five, Triple Play. Report status. Over.

We have wounded aboard Blue One Delta. 'Sweet Adeline' is damaged. Request medics and crash vehicles be in place. Blue One Delta will be first to land. Over.

Suddenly, Col. Vincent called out, "There they are! One plane has an engine out and another engine trailing smoke … no flaps. She's on a low approach … about two miles out."

LIEUTENANT J. R. HOLLADAY

Blue One Delta: I have no green lights indicating landing gear are down and locked, and I have no flaps control. Elevator is slushy.

Blue One Leader to Delta: Standby. I'm going to do a visible check on your gear.

Gus throttled back and allowed the nose of *Addie's Armor* to drop below the horizon into a shallow descent. Leveling off at *Sweet Adeline's* altitude, Gus could see all the landing gear of J. R.'s Fort extended.

Blue One Leader to Blue One Delta: All your landing gear are extended. I can't tell if they're locked. I recommend a shallow approach. Go easy on the brakes, J. R. You don't want to buckle one of your mains.

Roger that, lead. Meet you in the chow line back at base. Blue One Delta: Out.

"Easy does it, little lady. Line up with the runway." Lt. Col. Vincent coaxed under his breath. If he had squeezed the two-by-four wooden railing any harder, he would have splintered it.

J. R. Holladay's pulse rate was more than doubled. He looked over at his co-pilot. First Lt "Theo" Grotton sat motionless in his seat. His face was turned to the right, away from J.R.'s view. His eyes were open … staring lifeless and unblinking.

The end of the runway approached at breakneck speed. With no flaps and only a minimum of rudder control, Lt. Holladay passed over the apron of the runway at 110 mph. His main landing gear was a scant 10 ft above the surface.

The normal landing speed of a B-17, with an empty bomb bay, is 80 mph. J. R. pulled the throttles back to idle and allowed *Sweet Adeline* to settle on the temporary runway at 100 mph.

He applied either right or left brakes only when the nose of the Fort was drifting off the center line. He was eating up runway at an alarming rate. With only 1400 ft remaining, the bomber thundered forward at 50 mph. He worked the brakes, first left then right. Each time the nose of the airplane veered slightly. His airspeed indicator slowed to 40, then 30 mph.

A rocky, unfarmed patch of boulders and brush awaited the bomber, and when the plane reached a brisk speed of nearly 10 mph, J. R. hit the brakes rather than risk what lie beyond the fence now a mere 60 ft ahead. He waited until the last possible second then applied full right brake to turn the plane onto the ramp. Several ground personnel scampered to avoid being hit by one of the three Hamilton propellers still turning at nearly 1,000 rpm. As it was, the right wingtip passed over a waiting ambulance causing the corpsmen to run for cover. As soon as the plane came to a complete stop, hands trembling uncontrollably and sweat staining his shirt, J. R. shut down the engines and all electrical systems: batteries, inverters, magnetos, radios and generators.

The medics were at the plane almost before the number four propeller stopped turning. Two corpsmen rushed to the open bomb bay and waited to receive Lt. Grotton's body as crew members gathered to lower him into their outstretched arms. The two medics laid the dead co-pilot's body onto a stretcher and into the waiting ambulance. Another corpsman remained behind to check Lt. Holladay's lacerated head. A fragment of debris had struck his face and caused quite a bit of bleeding, but, thankfully, not rendering him incapable of getting the plane down.

Once on the ground, J. R. walked around *Sweet Adeline* taking note of her battered condition. He was surprised at the amount of damage that was done to the vertical stabilizer and rudder … estimating that close to half of their surface area was missing!

"Sir, we're heading over to the hospital with your crewmen, and we need to tend to your head injury. There's an empty a seat in the ambulance for you." The young corpsman, a corporal, walked with J. R. back to the waiting ambulance. A second ambulance, bearing the bodies of the co-pilot and the tail gunner, had already departed.

Two weeks later, at an awards gathering in Hangar #3, 1st Lt

Jeremiah Holladay was awarded the Distinguished Flying Cross (DFC) for flying his severely damaged Fort back to a safe landing at Sterparone USAAF Air Base. Lt. Col. Vincent testified of the superior piloting skills of Lt. Holladay.

"OPERATION FRANTIC"

"Operation Frantic" was the result of a complex political game of one-upmanship. The Big Three allied political leaders: Franklin Roosevelt, Sir Winston Churchill, and Joseph Stalin, met in Tehran in November 1943. Discussions included the progress of the war, post-war rebuilding, and the political future of Germany in a world without the strong-arm bullying of Adolf Hitler and his Third Reich.

Pres. Franklin Roosevelt was enthusiastic about Gen. "Hap" Arnold's proposal of shuttle bombing Germany's most distant industrial complex of aircraft assembly plants, aerodromes, ball bearing plants, and marshalling yards. The B-17s of the USAAF would fly to bases in the Ukraine, land, refuel, and take on more ordnance, then strike at German targets on the way back home to their bases in Italy and England. "Frantic" would open the door to American bombers flying out of Soviet Bases in Siberia to bomb targets of the Imperial Japanese industrial-military complex.

The Russians agreed to the proposal in principle. Three bases in the Ukraine would be used for shuttle bombing. The operation would be run from Poltava in the Ukraine under the command of Lt. Gen. Ira Eaker.

Between December 1943 and March 1944, the United States poured millions of dollars into the project for improvements to the Russian bases: housing for the large cadre of American military personnel, and lengthening and strengthening of existing runways along with all of the itinerant infrastructure that goes into maintaining facilities for 74 of the B-17s. After those improvements were completed, and before any American troops entered the Ukraine, Joseph Stalin hit the United States with his latest demand that no more than 1,200 permanent party personnel would be allowed on any

Russian facility—greatly limiting the size of any Air Group using their base for shuttle flights.

It was feared that the reduction of the number of Allied troops and airplanes could compromise the effectiveness of Operation Frantic. Additionally the advancing of Soviet troops along the Russian front happened faster than the allies expected, and German industrial targets were abandoned or relocated farther into Germany, thus reducing the operational value of the program. Despite these concerns and the waffling of Stalin on the terms of the agreement, USAAF Command felt that there were enough valuable German targets to justify the first mission. The only other option was to abandon the Ukraine bases and leave tens of millions of dollars' worth of equipment and vehicles in Soviet hands. "Operation Frantic I" moved forward.

Lt. Gen. Eaker, then commander of the Mediterranean Allied Air Forces, was tasked with putting together the first shuttle bombing mission, which he unofficially named Operation Frantic "Joe" (aimed at Chairman Joseph Stalin's frantic decisions leading up to the operation). Gen. Eaker decided to command the mission himself from the right seat of *Yankee Doodle Dandy II*, one the B-17s of the 99th Bomb Group.

MAY 28, 1944 / HEADQUARTERS, 483RD BOMBARDMENT GROUP

As the new Operations Officer of the 816th Bombardment Squadron, Capt. Gus Bodine attended a pre-mission briefing for the first shuttle mission. Utilizing elements of the 483rd, 99th, and 97th Bomb Groups (totaling 130 of the B-17s escorted by 70 of the P-51s) the mission of "Operation Frantic I" called for the bombing of marshalling yards at Debrecen, Hungary, and Oradea, Romania. After landing at Poltava and Mirgorod in the Ukraine, the bombers would take on fuel and ordinance, and bomb both targets again on the way back to their bases in Italy.

Mission number 21 for *Addie's Armor* took to the air on June 2, 1944. This would be mission number seven for the new radioman, TSgt William Richardson, raised on an Idaho potato farm. "Spud" Richardson was possessed of an even-tempered engaging personality, and quickly won the friendship of the entire crew. His closest friend among the crew, TSgt Sykes, was instrumental in bringing him up to speed and feeling less like a rookie.

At 0600 hrs, Gus and his band of sky warriors boarded the Fortress and checked their equipment. In the "front office," Gus and Hank went through the lengthy checklist and brought the bomber to life. With all the switches and levers in place, Gus slid open the side windscreen and called out:

"Clear left! Turning one!"

With the whine of the servos, the three Hamilton blades of the number one Wright Cyclone engine began to turn. After two complete rotations the engine coughed out a dark cloud of smoke as the propellor blades sped up briefly … then slowed. Just when Gus figured he'd have to perform a restart, the engine coughed again followed by a rumbling low throaty growl as every cylinder caught hold. He adjusted the throttle and RPM settings and repeated the process with the other three engines.

With all four engines idling at 1200 rpm, Gus called for a crew report.

"Pilot to crew: Status check," he called over the intercom.

One by one, each of eight men called in his status. The bombardier, navigator, engineer, radioman, and gunners had all completed their personal checklists, and *Addie's Armor* was ready to roll.

The marshalling yards at Debrecen in Hungary and Oradea in Romania, were major distribution points of war troops, armament, fuel and supplies needed to sustain the German *Wehrmacht* (the combined armed forces of navy, army, and air force along the eastern front).

When the B-17s reached their marshalling points, 27 of them split off into a three-squadron combat box. The 815th, 816th, and 817th Bomb Squadrons of the 483rd Bombardment Group (H), would leave the main body and fly to the second target: the marshalling yards at Oradea. Gus was in his customary command position as Bravo One

Flight Leader, one of the three flights of Forts comprising the 816th Bomber Squadron. The Forts were escorted by nine P-51 Mustangs.

Group Leader to all planes: Watch for bogies and don't get trigger happy. Remember, we have nine Mustangs covering our six. Intel says that any ack-ack or German fighters should be minimal over Oradea.

"Why is that?" Hank asked.

Gus glanced over at his co-pilot. "Why's what, Hank?"

"Why are ack-ack and Kraut fighters expected to be light over the target?"

"Oh. Well, for one thing, Oradea is closer to the Ukraine and the Russians than Debrecen, and the Krauts are spread out too thin protecting their cities and larger targets in the center of the country where there's more fighting. The other reason is that they simply won't expect American bombers to reach this far east. They don't know about Operation Frantic ... until now that is.

Twenty minutes later, Col. York's voice came into their headsets again:

Group Leader to Flight Leaders: The IP is only a couple of minutes away, fellas. Make ready all demolition and incendiary bombs. Flight Leaders, maintain tight formation. Out.

The 27 planes droned on toward the target. Gus' two wingmen trailed out behind *Addie's Armor,* 50 ft above, below, and off the wing tips of the nearest plane. The adrenaline started, and the inherent fear settled in ... the fear associated with carrying three tons of death to a fated destination of an enemy that wants nothing more than to blast you out of the sky. In times of conflict, every pilot enters a mission with the question in mind, *will my number be up today?* If he wants to keep flying he learns to suppress the thought ... drive it down deep, until it's no more bothersome than the itch of a mosquito bite. For some, the question can lead to depression, drinking too much, tangling in barroom fights, gambling ... anything to vent or quell the fear. For many, like Gus, prayer and nurturing close family ties with letters is the balm that soothes a fearful heart.

Group Leader to Flight Leaders: Entering the IP in five, four, three, two, one, IP acquired. Target acquisition in five minutes. Pathfinder is in place. No more radio communications between planes at this time. Bombardiers, check your calibration between the bombsight and autopilot. York: Out.

"Pilot to Bombardier: How are things in the Bombay, Al?"

"Ready to go, Skipper."

"Copy that. Staff Sergeant Richardson will switch you over to Pathfinder's radio channel."

"Tail gunner to pilot: Three enemy planes, six o'clock high! Line abreast. They're peeling off and diving on us, sir!"

The three Fw 190s gave it their best shot even though they knew they were undermanned and out gunned. No matter which flight of bombers they chose to target, the combined defensive power of the tightly formed group easily fended off the aggressors. After their first run on the bombers, the German fighters were set upon by six American P-51s. The enemy fighters withdrew.

"Pilot to crew: Status report."

"Tail gunner: Check."

"Right waist gunner, locked and loaded, Skipper. I think I nicked one of them."

"Radio: Check. ...Say, don't those guys ever stick around for the party? They bugged out fast."

"Engineer: All instruments in normal range, Skipper."

Just as the last crewmen called in for their status check, *Addie's Armor* was rocked by a near miss from German 88 mm ack-ack fire. The familiar black puffs of anti-aircraft fire were light and sparce. Group reported no hits on any of the Forts.

"It looks like we really caught them by surprise, Hank. This is about as close to a milk run as we've had. They may want a rematch when we leave the target area."

"True that."

Pathfinder to all planes: Slave your autopilot in five, four, three, two, one ... I have your aircraft. Coming up on target ... on my command ... bombs away!

Lt. Wendelford toggled the bomb release to SALVO. The 500 lb bombs dropped first followed by the incendiaries.

Group Leader to all planes: On target! On target! We are RTB.

Unaware that they were being shadowed, the American formation of heavy bombers turned for home and led the Heinkel He 111 straight to their Soviet base in Mirgorod.

After landing safely back at Mirgorod, the flight crews of the 27 Forts from the 483rd that bombed Oradea were called into a briefing that revised the Oradea bombing sortie. Instead of splitting into two groups, the new orders were changed to have the entire one hundred thirty B-17s attack Debrecen only. No explanation was given, but it was clear to the brass at MAAF (Mediterranean Allied Air Forces) that Joseph Stalin was growing increasingly uneasy over the whole "Operation Frantic" idea. Although there were six more "Frantic" missions, none were as successful as the first. In fact, the base at Mirgorod was brutally attacked by the Germans and severely damaged because of the Soviet's weak defense of the base, and more importantly, because of their refusal to allow American fighters to defend the Soviet shuttle bases. The Mirgorod incident set the stage for closing down the operation.

"Well, if that doesn't take the cake, Gus. We help the Russians build up their bases, give them millions of bucks worth of technology and equipment, and they turn up their noses at us. No more protection at the Russian bases means endangering our men and planes. We should shut down Operation Frantic entirely."

"I get where you're coming from, Hank, but, *we're* not wearing the stars. We're stuck with a raw deal, and we'll just have to make the best of it."

CHAPTER 18

MEMMINGEN

By July 1944, Operation Frantic was failing. It was becoming increasingly clear to the Fifteenth Air Force that costs were beginning to override the benefits of the shuttle bombing campaign. The risk of German Luftwaffe attacks on the three Soviet owned shuttle bases was made much greater when Chairman Stalin ordered his Air Forces to be the sole defender against any German attack from the air. The American P-51s stationed at Piryatin, 75 in all, would have been all that was needed to protect the B-17s flying into the other bases at Mirgorod and Poltava in Ukraine. Stalin refused the American Eighth and Fifteenth Army Air Force all command authority where it involved the protection of Soviet military bases, stating that his air force was more than sufficient to protect its own bases. Then, on the June 22, an armada of 150 German bombers attacked Poltava in a blitz that lasted two hours. The Luftwaffe destroyed or severely damaged 69 American B-17s and most of the munitions in the bomb dump. The Soviet defense was lackluster at best and failed miserably, Soviet anti-aircraft gun fire failed to knock down a single German bomber. Because of a shortage of fuel at the shuttle bases, Operation Frantic was suspended throughout July. The Fifteenth Air Force was forced to strike German targets close enough for the Fortresses to reach a target and be able to return to their bases in Italy. One such prime target was located at Memmingen in southeast Germany, 922 km (573 mi) from Foggia, Italy, and the U.S. bases of the Fifteenth Air Force.

JULY 17 / PILOT BRIEFING – MEMMINGEN MISSION

Col. Paul Barton stood in front of the 360 pilots and crews of the 483rd Bombardment Group who were assigned to spearhead the combined Fifth Wing mission to attack the aerodrome and aircraft assembly facility at Memmingen. Located 116 mi southwest of Munich, Germany, the facility was a center for the assembly of single-engine fighter aircraft and twin-engine medium bombers. More alarming was the fact that it was a training center for the elite Luftwaffe pilots selected for the testing and deployment of the Me 262 jet fighter and the prototypes of the newly designed "Arado Ar" class of jet bomber and multi-role aircraft.

"Good morning, gentlemen. Tomorrow, at zero six hundred hours the 483rd Bomb Group, combined with units from the 463rd, 301st, 99th, 97th, and the second group of bombers will assemble in Wing Formation over the Adriatic Sea and proceed east into Germany. Our target is the Memmingen aircraft assembly plants and aerodrome. In addition to assembling Me 109s and Fw 190s, the aerodrome is housing the training and test facilities for the new Me 262 jet. The Fifteenth Air Force considers this a high priority target.

"For this mission we'll be flying in three twelve-plane boxes to enable a tighter spread of our ordinance. Other Air Groups will be similarly organized for a total aggregate of two hundred seventeen Fortresses. A radar equipped Pathfinder Fort will lead the attack. Bomb release will be accomplished simultaneously on Pathfinder's command. To accommodate the formation pattern, the 'Aces & Eights' of the 818th Squadron will assign three of their aircraft to each of the 815th, 816th, and 817th Bombardment Squadrons. Loadout will be a dozen five-hundred-pound demos plus eight thousand rounds of ammo for each gun. Air cover will be provided by the P-38s of the 82nd Fighter Group and the P-51s of the 332nd Fighter Group.

"Recently, the German's have had limited success intercepting our radio communications on the plane-to-plane frequencies and have been able to divert some of our planes into ambush encounters with their fighters. The security code for this mission is 'Marconi.' Radio operators will use the code if there is any doubt of the authenticity of a message.

"Wheels up at zero six hundred hours, gentlemen."

JULY 18, 1944

Two hundred seventeen B-17s of the Fifth Wing, Fifteenth Air Force, circled over the open water of the Adriatic Sea and began the choreography of forming up by flights, squadrons, and groups into the diamond-shaped configuration of a Combat Wing. Beautiful to behold from the ground, the immediate purpose of the airborne armada of American bombers was to avoid any mishaps in the air that might endanger civilians on the ground. The Combat Wing Formation required precision of both horizontal and vertical spacing among the planes of the various organizational units. Any miscalculation on the part of a pilot could result in the collision of two or more bombers as well as the tragic loss of numberless souls on the ground.

As the pilot in command of *Addie's Armor*, flying in only one of the over 200 bombers in the formation, Gus felt isolated and alone. His anxiety from the flood of overwhelming "maybes" with countless unforeseen consequences, the threat of approaching storms, and the weak intel from Command, added to the worry knot growing in his gut. He felt himself on the verge of panic as cold tendrils of fear wormed their way into his mind.

The Luftwaffe had wreaked havoc on the Fortresses during daylight bombing missions despite past efforts to hide Command's intentions to blast the enemy manufacturing of fighters and bombers into submission. Memmingen was one big thorn in the side of the Fifteenth Air Force.

The Fifth Wing turned inland, only to find themselves facing storm clouds along a cold front between the massive assembly of B-17s and their targets: the aerodrome and aircraft assembly facilities at Memmingen, Germany.

The storm clouds were building raising doubts about the 217 bombers' ability to maintain proper separation and visibility.

———

"What do you make of those storm clouds, Skipper?" Lt. Hank Barenz asked.

"Trouble. I'm worried that the Wing might be forced to abandon the primary target if that storm front gets any worse." Tension stiffened the muscles in Gus' shoulder and back. With the 483rd Bomb Group leading the formation, Gus knew that if Col. Barton diverted and went for an alternate target, the bombing at Memmingen would be aborted.

"Pilot to crew: We're twenty minutes from the IP. Check your equipment. Bombardier, arm your bombs. Set for auto release. Gunners, charge your weapons … one burst. Fire when ready."

Gus caught Lt. Barenz' furtive glance. "Something on your mind, Hank?"

"Usual stuff. What is this, number twenty-one for us?" his co-pilot asked.

"Twenty-two, if your counting, Hank. Number eight with our current crew." Gus was quiet for a second, then added: "Hank, I need your head in the cockpit now to concentrate on the mission. Take the controls."

"I have the controls," Lt. Barenz confirmed. He gripped the control yoke a little tighter and took note of the pressure of the rudder pedals on the soles of his feet.

Capt. Gus Bodine was the 816th Bomb Squadron Operations Officer and temporary executive officer. As such, he commanded the squadron from the Bravo Flight Lead position. On the Memmingen mission, his job was to make sure the nine Fortresses in his squadron were in proper formation.

Gus eased himself gingerly past the stations of the flight engineer and radio operator to enter the bomb bay. The bombardier, Lt. Al Wendelford, was checking the racks to confirm the settings for each of the 12 deadly AN-M64 demolition bombs.

"Is everything buttoned down back here, Al?" Gus asked.

"We're ready, Captain. What about the weather? Those clouds look pretty mean."

Before he could answer Al's question, Gus' headset came alive with Hank Barenz' voice, "Skipper, Group Leader is on the horn. ...Sounds urgent!"

"Copy that, Hank. I'm on my way."

The line of cumulus clouds that had started building 100 km south and west of Memmingen had developed into a massive thunderhead that reached from a low ceiling of 6,000 ft to as high as 37,000 ft. With only 12 min before the bombers reached the Intercept Point (IP), the Wing Commander gave the order to divert the main part of the body to alternate targets, thus averting the dangerous storm head growing in front of them. It was decided that the risk of losing aircraft to mid-air collisions was too great.

Gus worked his way back to the cockpit and jacked into the comm in time to hear the voice of Col. Barton, the C.O. of the 483rd, over the plane-to-plane frequency:

...With the absence of Red Two, Blue One and Two, and Green One and Two, that leaves Red One with the remaining four boxes (squadrons of twelve planes each) to strike at the primary target. It's up to us to choose to continue toward the primary target or divert to secondary targets. We can still do a lot of damage with our thirty-seven bombers. Flight Leaders, the choice is yours. Authenticity code is "Marconi." Over.

Bravo Squadron to Group Leader: Let's hit the primary target, Gus replied.

Charlie is in all the way, Lead.

Copy. Our air cover may or may not be with us. Most of them diverted with the majority of the body. Pilots, I have instructed Pathfinder to lower our bombing altitude to one-five thousand feet. All planes descend to one-five thousand feet. This will put us under the clouds and improve our visibility over the target. We need to get ahead of this storm. Increase indicated airspeed to two-two-five mph. Watch for icing in these clouds. IP waypoint in niner minutes. Maintain visual contact with your wingmen at all times. Group Leader: Out.

The lead B-17, Pathfinder, had the responsibility of determining the bomb release point for the entire wing. The radar guided Automatic Flight Control System (AFCS), which links the Norden bomb sight with the B-17's autopilot, would take control of the autopilot with the flip of a switch by the bombardier. The pilot's job would be to maintain speed and altitude, and AFCS would deploy his bombs automatically when the B-17 reached its predetermined release point. The bombardiers in all other planes would release their bombs at the same time.

Gus noticed his right wingman drifting out of position.

Bravo Flight Leader to right wing: Close it up, Sandy, you're too far out. How's your ship doing?

Gus' friend, Sandy Plunkett, the affable son of a Montana cattle ranch foreman, was possessed of an even tempered, kind, and often times humorous personality.

A-okay, Bravo Leader. 'Montana Cowgirl' is hummin' like an angel. Just a routine sortie, eh, boss? 1st Lt Sandy Plunkett replied.

I wish that were true, Sandy. No visual on our air cover, yet. The boys from the Eighty-Second and Three-Thirty-Second Fighter Groups must have gone on with the rest of the wing to the alternate targets.

The steady drone of the four radial engines remained unchanged. At times, one could be lulled to sleep, but the turbulence associated with flying into the storm cell had kept everyone on their toes until they broke into the clear, and the sky became peaceful once more.

A premonitory chill shot down Gus' spine. *Was this the lull before the storm?* The thought caused him to grip the control yoke even tighter.

Blue Leader to Blue Squadron: Be alert, fellas. We're about to fly into hell. Check your chutes and strap on your survival vests. Remain at your stations. Blue Leader: Out.

Gus always wore his C-1 survival vest underneath his leather wool-lined flight jacket. If needed, he only had to fasten the snaps. It was bulky and uncomfortable, but he always felt it was a precautionary measure for "when," not "if," his luck ran out.

Red One Leader to all planes: IP acquisition in three, two, one, check. Breaking out of the clouds now. Pathfinder, Red One is in position.

Bravo, in position, Gus announced.

Charlie is in position, Red Leader.

Lil' Abner, the last plane in Charlie Flight, emerged from the storm cell. The tail gunner's frantic voice broke the silence.

Bogies six o'clock high! There must be a hundred of 'em! Me 109s and Fw 190s!

Red Leader to group: Hold your positions. All gunners, fire when ready! Col. Barton ordered.

Charlie squadron occupied the rear box of 12 of the B-17Gs. The German fighters went for them attacking in six-plane waves. The sky was a hornet's nest of fighters—first one, then another bomber burst into flames from the barrage of 20 mm and 30 mm cannon fire from the German Luftwaffe. Another B-17 broke apart when the entire empennage separated from the rest of the bomber sending ten men and three tons of high explosives into a death spiral. No parachutes were seen.

The remaining B-17Gs of the 483rd Bomb Group fought back valiantly against overwhelming numbers of the enemy shooting at least 35 enemy fighters from the skies at the cost of six of their bombers.

The 24 Fortresses of Alpha and Bravo Flight, and six remaining bombers of Charlie Flight flew on to the primary target while in the midst of the German onslaught.

Nine minutes after the first B-17 was shot out of the sky, another wave of enemy reinforcements entered the fray. Eight P-38 Lightnings of the 82nd Fighter Group scattered the German attack, but not before the last two planes of Charlie Flight were destroyed sending burning bodies tumbling freely to the earth. The Tuskegee P-51s of the 332nd joined the conflict on the tail of the Lightnings. The outnumbered German fighters abandoned their attack on the American bombers to engage the P-38s and P-51s.

The air battle with the enemy fighters abated, but the remaining Fortresses faced another threat: ground artillery opened up on the in-coming American bombers. A wall of black splotches filled the air space between the 483rd bomb Group and the target, courtesy of dozens of long barreled 88 mm anti-aircraft gun emplacements.

Buffeted violently by the cannon bursts, the 483rd flew on, holding their positions. One Fort in the flight on Gus' starboard side took a direct hit on the port wing root. The left wing, unable to handle the wing-load, bent upward then separated from the fuselage.

Bail out! Bail out, you guys! Gus yelled out loud with an urgency born of desperation that he could do nothing to stop. Shaken from the intensity of the battle, Gus brought his trembling hands under control and keyed his mic …

Bravo Leader to all planes: Close up the formation and prepare for bomb release.

Gus checked his right wing. Sandy had *Montana Cowgirl* in perfect position. Zeke Smith and his *Achtung* was positioned off Gus' left wing but was trailing smoke.

Flight Leader to left wing: Zeke, check your number three engine. You're trailing smoke.

Copy, Flight Leader. Oil pressure is still green but dropping. Cylinder head temperature is high. I'll continue on to the target. After the drop, I'll throttle back number three.

In an instant, Gus' focus was diverted from his wingmen to the mission at hand as the lead plane announced:

Pathfinder to all aircraft: Bomb release in five - four - three - two -one. Bombs away!

The remaining 29 Fortresses of the 483rd Bombardment Group released a total of 174 of the 500-lb demolition bombs, which rained down on the primary target.

With the bomb-bay doors closed, Gus put *Addie's Armor* into a 45° right bank.

Bravo Flight: We are RTB.

UNINTENDED CONSEQUENCES

WHANG! The deafening metal-against-metal explosion caused by a nearly direct hit of an exploding 88 mm shell burst behind the co-pilot's seat, stunned Gus briefly. His bomber dropped out of formation and entered a slow-turning spiral, losing altitude at an alarming rate. He attempted to bring up the nose and level the plane, but the yoke and rudder pedals failed to respond. Switching on the autopilot only slightly reduced the rate of descent.

Black smoke was trailing behind the two starboard engines. Gus pulled the fire bottles releasing a blast of retardant into the flaming engines. The cockpit filled with smoke. 1st Lt Hank Barenz, Gus' friend and co-pilot, lay lifeless and crumpled in his seat. The windscreen next to his head was blown in.

Addie's Armor entered a steep spiraling descent.

"PILOT TO CREW: BAIL OUT! BAIL OUT! BAIL OUT!" Gus unbuckled his harness and worked his way out of his seat. Hearing no sign of life, he began groping his way through the smoke for an exit—an escape hatch, an ack-ack hole, … anything.

Catching a glimpse of daylight streaming in from the radioman's station in front of the bomb bay, Gus pulled himself in the direction of the light. Frantically reaching for a handhold, he grabbed the upper arm that was once attached to SSgt "Spud" Richardson. The horror of the moment, the carnage inflicted on his crew, would not hit Gus until later. For now, the instinct of survival gave him the single-minded focus to pull the dead radioman clear of the gaping hole in the fuselage and crawl his way toward the opening. Fighting the G-force of the spiraling bomber, Gus caught a glimpse of the German forests and farmland below spinning crazily before eyes alternating with flashes of clouds and blue sky. Thrown off balance back into the plane by the centrifugal force of the spinning B-17, Gus scrambled desperately toward the outside once more. He was dangerously close to not having enough altitude to deploy his parachute.

"God help me, Addie, I will not die here!" he cried. With one final muscle-wrenching effort, Gus grabbed a jagged shard of steel with his gloved hand and pulled himself through the opening.

Tumbling head-over-heels, he fell clear of *Addie's Armor.* Gus stretched his arms and legs out as far as he could in order to stabilize his body in a face-down position. With fewer than 2000 ft to the ground, he pulled the "D" ring and his chute deployed.

CHAPTER 19

DOWN

The sound of birds chirping and the hollow "rat-a-tat" of a woodpecker boring a hole in a pine tree in search of a morsel, perhaps a grub or ant, echoed through the forest. At first, Gus was disoriented … unaware of how he got there. With closed eyes and a deep breath, his head cleared, and his memory returned. He was hit by the shock of what had happened over the last few minutes … or hours. As he lay there, he began to assess each limb and joint, and felt for any wounds, but, surprisingly, all was well except for a few bumps and scrapes. "What time is it?" he asked no one in particular. He wiped clean the face of his Flying Officer Chronograph with a silent prayer of thanks that it was still ticking. *It's eighteen-thirty hours* (6:30 p.m.). *We were over the target at … Lord in heaven, I've been out for over five hours.*

Considering the formation had turned southwest and was heading for home when the Luftwaffe hit them, Gus figured he couldn't be more than 40 miles from the Italian border.

Daylight was quickly fading to dusk, and the sun hung low in the western sky. Gus decided to hunker down until daybreak. He found a depression on the east slope of a small knoll where grass had grown up around the sides and partially over the top of several large boulders.

He removed his heavy flight jacket and survival vest and went to work scooping out most of the leaves, smaller stones, and dead grass. He gathered several armfuls of pine needles and fallen pine boughs, spread them out evenly inside the hollow he had created, and spread the parachute over the top.

The temperature dropped noticeably with the setting sun. Gus slipped back into his flight jacket, crawled onto his makeshift "bed," and used the excess parachute material as a blanket. By laying on his side and bringing his knees up to his chest in a fetal position within the depression, he found he could conceal his body from view of any enemy eyes ... while keeping warm.

At the first light of day, Gus surveyed his tools of survival. His vest contained enough C-rations for three days if used sparingly, and he confirmed that there were four extra seven-round magazines for his government model .45 caliber ACP semi-automatic pistol still in its leather lined holster. Rounding out his provisions were two small boxes of wooden matches sealed inside cellophane wrappers, two fishhooks, a 50-foot roll of fishing line, a compass, and his potential lifeline to freedom: a topographical map of Germany showing major roads and railways.

He figured if he stretched out his supplies, and could find potable water, he could survive a week to ten days. He was thankful for a sturdy Ka-Bar hunting knife, with a 7-inch blade, given to him on his 16th birthday by his father. It was his only non-issue item. Using his trusty Ka-Bar, he fashion a knapsack out of nylon lines and pieces of panels cut from his parachute. He attached the makeshift pack to the back of his survival vest with more cordage from the parachute. It didn't look pretty, but it was serviceable. It was time to go.

Gus cleaned up the modest campsite, unfolded his map, and began calculating an escape plan that would give him the best hope of survival. He considered taking the shortest and most obvious route southwest to the Swiss border. However, Switzerland, being a neutral government, and not wanting to make waves with the Nazi Wehrmacht, might not take kindly to him showing up at their doorstep.

All that aside, there was the question of the Swiss border being the most heavily guarded border along the southern boundaries of Bavaria. He could be taken prisoner by the Swiss and then turned over to the Germans as a gesture of appeasement. He needed a route to get back into Allied territory, even if it meant adding another week or more onto his trek. So, he headed southeast toward what he hoped would be the Austrian border. There is a narrow strip of Austria that lies along the southwest border between the German state of Bavaria on the north and the Italian border to the south. Austria was a German state and therefore part of the contiguous Nazi territory. By staying in the woods as far away from roads and towns as possible, Gus felt he had a chance of making it through to the Italian border. He set his course for the Inn River, a tributary of the lower Danube River, running west from Salzburg, Austria then southwest to Rosenheim. From Rosenheim it would be a long, treacherous, and very cold trek up and over the Bavarian Alps into Italy. At the earliest, Gus was looking at making it into Italy sometime in late August … maybe four to six weeks … at best.

The going was slow, even treacherous at times. Boulders, uneven terrain, and fallen trees were constantly threatening to trip him. Countless streams and small rivers feeding off the Danube and Elbe rivers forced him to retrace his steps, sometimes several miles, to find a suitable crossing. Fearing they would be well traveled by German soldiers, he stayed well off the roads and used the heavily wooded forests for cover making the going much slower.

By the fourth day, he estimated he had traveled only seven kilometers. He finished off the rest of his C-rations the day before. His energy depleted, the need for food began to occupy his every thought.

A rugged hill lay in the path ahead. He didn't want to skirt around since it was already late afternoon, and pangs of hunger were gnawing at his stomach. *Okay, Gus, let's go see what the view from the top might tell us.* To his dismay, the strenuous hike up the hill soon became a grueling, scrambling climb that took every ounce of his dwindling energy.

After dropping to his knees to catch his breath, he removed his survival vest, and stood tall to get a better view, taking care to stay hidden by the foliage. In the valley below, a little more than a mile distant, a natural pond fed by a tributary of the Elbe river, presented itself as an opportunity to catch a fish and allay impending starvation. Gus noted that a cart path led from the far end of the pond, winding its way through the mountain grasses, and ending at a farmhouse. He couldn't make out much detail, so he began a hike downhill to the pond.

———

Using his Ka-Bar, Gus cut a small branch about an inch-and-a-half in diameter and four feet long. He notched one end of the pole, then looped the end his fishing line from the survival kit, around the notch and tied it tightly to the pole. He attached one of the two fishhooks to the other end of the line. About two feet above the hook he tied a splinter of wood to the fishing line to serve as a weight and a float just like he had done many times as a boy. *Now for the bait.* Gus spotted an abundance of moss at the base of the spruce trees dotting the landscape. *Hmmm, that looks like a possibility.* Uprooting a patch of moss and lichen, he quickly had a store of bait in the form of beetles and insects of several varieties. He dug a little deeper and revealed a bed of suitable earthworms.

After attaching an earthworm to the hook, Gus eased stealthily through the trees. It was only about 20 ft to the water at the edge of a pond that looked to be about 50 yds across by possibly 28 to 30 yds at its narrowest point. He waited for about ten minutes, and seeing no signs of human life, sucked in a breath and stepped through the trees.

He cast the fishing line as far as he could. The wood splinter sailed out, then sunk beneath the surface and bobbed back up. "Yes!" Gus whispered … barely restraining the "Whoopee!" threatening to escape his lips. He wedged the pole between a couple of large rocks and returned to his knapsack beyond the tree line. In just under 15 min, he was rewarded with a jiggle of the pole followed by another. Dashing toward the wooden rod, he reached it just as it popped free of the rocks. He quickly grabbed it and pulled a 12-inch-long trout from the pond. Gus gutted the fish, fileted it, and five minutes later, had 14 bite-sized pieces of fresh-water trout sushi. He didn't want to chance building a fire, so he ate the fish raw, chewing every bite thoroughly before swallowing. It would be twilight before he ventured toward the farmhouse.

Much of the roof and one side of the house was lying in rubble. It appeared to Gus that the house had been destroyed by an explosion. Various grasses and bushes had already encroached upon the property allowing Gus to feel safe from any prying eyes. Near the house was what appeared to be a burned-out barn. He wondered what might have caused the loss of somebody's farm. "Whatever it was, Gus old man, maybe we can find something useful in the rubble."

CHAPTER 20

MISSING

July 24 of each year is a time of celebration in all of Utah and parts of several surrounding states. It was on that day, in 1847, the first wagons and handcarts of the Mormon pioneers, entered the Salt Lake Valley. Having fled from persecution imposed upon them in Ohio, Illinois, and Missouri, the Latter-Day Saints felt they had finally found the place where they could build a great city and a temple to be a House of the Lord.

Addie Russo-Bodine and her sister-in-law Catherine spent the morning until mid-day enjoying the festivities. The annual Twenty-Fourth of July Parade began one mile north of Center Street on University Avenue, proceeding south to Center Street, then west to Geneva Road. The nearly half-mile long procession of brass bands, baton twirlers, lavishly decorated floats, and visiting dignitaries sitting atop shiny convertibles, lifted the hearts of even the most war-weary and troubled citizens of Utah County. The parade itself was barely half the size of its prewar glory, but the joy it brought was beyond measure.

"Let's walk over to liberty Park. There's a carnival, and the Elks

Club is sponsoring some fun family activities. They're even cooking hot dogs and hamburgers," encouraged Addie.

"Sounds fun, but it's a bit of a walk. Are you up to it?" Catherine asked.

Mrs. Gus Russo was in her seventh month of pregnancy. She had been on her feet for the last three hours and wanted to rest, but she didn't want the excitement of the day to come to an early end.

"Absolutely. Besides, it's been too long since Highway and I have enjoyed a walk through the park. What do you say, boy? Shall we see what's happening at the gazebo?"

Highway barked one time, and with tongue and tail wagging, trotted along with the two women.

There was no mail delivery on the 24th of July since it was a state holiday, so it was a surprise when a Western Union courier knocked at the door of the Bodine house. Gus' mother, Anna, answered the door. Her customary smile upon greeting guests changed to an expression of curiosity, and, perhaps, an edge of concern.

"Oh, hello young man." Concerned turned to worry when the messenger, with a now somber expression, reached his hand out to Anna Bodine. An envelope was clasped in his hand. Anna took the message and bade the young man a happy day. She slowly turned and walked into the living room where Gerry Bodine was reading the weekly edition of the "Daily Herald" newspaper.

"Gerry, read this … I can't." Anna handed the telegram to her husband and sat on the edge of the sofa on the verge of tears. She interlaced her fingers and prepared for the worst. Gerry hesitated, then picked up a letter opener from the end table by his chair. He was about to open the envelope when Addie and Catherine entered. Highway walked over to Gerry and lay on the carpet at his feet. The dog's earlier excitement had suddenly given way to a general air of malaise.

"What's wrong?" Catherine asked.

"Something has happened. …What?" Sensing that the tension in the room had something to do with the envelope in her father-in-law's hand, Addie became more insistent. "What is it? …PLEASE!"

"Come, sit by me, dear. You, too, Catherine. Your father is about to read the telegram." Anna Bodine looked over at her husband. "Go ahead, Gerry."

Gerry H. Bodine

274 N. 2 W. Provo, Utah

The secretary of war desires me to express his deep regret that your son Capt. Gus G. Bodine has been reported missing in action since 18 July 1944 while flying a mission over Memmingen, Germany. Details will be forwarded to you as they become known to this office.

Lt. Gen. Ira Eaker, USAAFMC

Silence filled the room. Addie's eyes teared up and her chin quivered. Without saying another word, she quickly arose from the couch and ran upstairs to her bedroom nearly tripping over Highway as he dashed to catch up with her. When they reached her room, she closed the door and fell onto bed. Sensing her despair, her precious furry friend jumped up beside her and nuzzled his head under her chin. All Addie could do was weep … and pray.

…Please, Father in Heaven, let my husband be alive. Please take him in thy loving hands and preserve him. Return him to the family who loves him, and let him know his child….In the name of Jesus Christ. Amen.

Daylight faded. Addie had been pleading with God and begging for his mercy for hours. At last, feeling exhausted but comforted and hopeful, she got up, opened the bedroom door and walked into the bathroom. She splashed warm water on her face and patted it dry with a towel before hanging the towel back onto the rack. Addie was doing the things she had always done, but she was just "going through the motions," while she processed her thoughts and emotions. She left the bathroom and saw Highway sitting patiently waiting for her.

"Come on boy. I'll bet you're starved. I could use a bite to eat myself."

Gus' parents and Catherine were sitting around the console radio listening to an episode of the Jack Benny program with guest stars Barbara Stanwyck and Dennis Day.

"Hello, Mother Anna and Father Gerry. And how are you feeling, Catherine?"

"Better than I felt a few hours ago and after I had a good cry," Catherine replied.

"And how are *you* doing, dear?" Gus' mother asked.

"A bit better. I needed some time to sort things out, you know … to try to make sense of that telegram. I've decided on some things. May I talk with you?" Addie asked.

"Why, of course you can." Gerry turned off the radio. "I think it's a good thing to share our thoughts. We've all been traumatized by … well, the news of losing our boy.

"That's just it, Dad Bodine. We haven't lost him. The telegram said he was "lost" while flying on a mission. He's probably in one of those horrible prison camps where those Nazis have our boys. Maybe he's wandering around, trying to find his way back to friendly lines, or he's in a hospital, injured. He's alive! I've been praying about it, and I feel peace and assurance in knowing that Gus is still alive … somewhere."

"Yes, my dear. We know. We had a family prayer, too. I would have called you down to join us, but I know you needed your alone time.

"You said you decided some things?"

"Yes, I have. I'm going home … to my parents' house. Just for a couple of weeks or maybe longer. I need to spend time with mom and dad. I'm due sometime the last week of September, but I promise I'll be back before then. I hope you understand."

"Absolutely. They're your family … your roots. The memories of your childhood and happier times are there. When we get more news about Gus, we'll call you right away."

CHAPTER 21

ALBERT AND HELGA

Gus saw that there was a path trailing from behind the derelict farmhouse into the woods. He decided to follow the path to its end. The woods thinned out and gave way to what was once a small orchard, now overgrown with various grasses and flora. The trees were still producing apples and pears. There was even a cherry tree. Very few cherries remained, but the apple trees were heavy with fruit at that time of year. The quality of the fruit was poor and mostly riddled with worms, but there was more than enough food here for one man's needs.

The path went on for another quarter of a mile and abruptly ended at a paved road. Gus didn't want to expose his position to any anyone that might be on the road, so counting his blessings, he left the orchard and walked back to the ruins of the old farm. He needed to forage for any useful items he might take with him.

I wish I could stay here, but if they're looking for American survivors of the Memmingen mission, this would be a good place to look. I need to get out of here, he thought.

He put as many apples into his makeshift knapsack as it would hold and struck out once more for the Austrian border. It was agonizingly tough going. For the next five days he battled with nature's obstacle course of dead, fallen branches and logs; sharp rocky inclines; thick brush; and the occasional stream with its slick bottom and mossy rocks. Many times he had to slow his place to avoid a life-threatening fall.

Once more, Gus' body began to fail him. Starving and weak from exertion which sapped the strength from his atrophied muscles, his body caved to the ground and fainted into a delirium of racing images and memories. …He was at the gazebo, and he could see Addie there. She was beckoning for him to stand. …*You can do this, Gus. Remember your promise and my love!* Her voice was so clear.

Every muscle in his body was punished to their extreme and weak from lack of fuel. Overworked joints: knees, shoulders, ankles, even his back—suffered. The weight of the knapsack felt like he was carrying a full grown man. He was simply too exhausted to go on. He prayed constantly for strength to persevere. His food supply was reduced to whatever creatures occupied the bedding of the forest. Inside of deadwood, and underneath the mossy, fern-covered forest floor, resided a world of grubs, beetles, worms, and species of bugs he had never seen in his life. Mushrooms abounded in this climate. Some he didn't dare risk, but he recognized one or two species that his stomach could abide. What little he knew about them was enough to make him avoid accidentally ingesting the poisonous and hallucinogenic varieties.

Two weeks after the fateful bombing of the Memmingen industrial complex and marshalling yards, Gus had traveled only about 40 kilometers. He was scarcely able to carry his own weight and found himself forced to stop more frequently for periods of rest.

Well, Gus old man, you need a different strategy. You'll have to stay on the roads and travel at night.

Late in the afternoon on day 17 of his survival trek, Gus headed northeast, toward a dirt road that he had been skirting for the last hour. He planned to find it, wait in the woods beyond the tree line, and then, under cover of darkness, step onto the road and continue east until he found the one that would take him south to the Austrian border.

A wide stream stood between Gus and the road. If it had not been for the three-quarter moon shining down through a clear night sky, Gus would not have attempted to cross the boulder-strewn creek. Stepping into the cold water, he began to gingerly work his way across to the other side, but the odds were against him. He stepped down on an uneven, slick rock, and his foot shot out from beneath him. Trying to regain his balance, he turned his right ankle inward with an audible "pop!" An excruciating jab of pain traveled from his ankle to his knee taking his leg out from beneath him. He fell headlong into the icy water. The knapsack was more weight than he could bear with his injury, so he worked his way out of the straps and desperately pulled himself to dry ground ... sans his survival vest!

Unable to walk, Gus was left with facing the final reality of the end of his freedom and the beginning of whatever Hitler's Third Reich had in store for him. *I'm sorry, Addie. ...I'm so sorry.* Faint from exhaustion and ravaged by pain, Gus dragged himself to the edge of the road. His last thought disappeared into the black void of unconsciousness.

RESCUE?

Albert and Helga Richter were modest farmers from Rheinsberg (about 40 kilometers northeast of Berlin). They traveled twice each month to Stettin to barter and trade with other farmers and to attend their Protestant church. The services there were carefully monitored by soldiers of the German Reich, but Albert and Helga always left feeling spiritually lifted and thankful for their meager sustenance.

On Sunday evening, while traveling back to their farm, Helga noticed a dark form lying on the side of the dirt road.

"Albert, what is that laying at the side of the road? It looks like someone has fallen."

"Probably just someone who has had too much to drink," Albert responded and urged on his two draft horses.

"No, Albert, we must stop. Look, it is a man." Without waiting for a response from her husband, Helga stepped to the ground even before the wagon wheels came to a complete stop.

Kneeling by the unconscious stranger, she placed her hand gently on his forehead and brushed the hair from his eyes. Gus moaned weakly.

"Albert, come. We must help him. This tattered coat he is wearing is that of an American soldier … yes, a captain," she said on further examination.

Albert knew better than to offer any resistance. He knew his wife well enough to understand her heart … the heart of a ministering angel. With an audible grunt, Albert lowered himself to the ground and helped his wife load the American officer onto the cart.

"We must cover him. Here, help me with the canvas."

The two of them pulled the canvas tarpaulin over their goods and baggage—and Gus. Albert tied down the tarpaulin, and the couple continued their drive to the farm.

The Richters continued along the rural dirt road passing one farmhouse after another with only a few scattered buildings in between. Albert reigned in the two draft horses, set the handbrake, and turned to Helga, "I want to check on the American and see if I can wake him up. We need to prepare to deal with the soldiers guarding the main road." He stepped down, walked to the rear of the wagon, and loosened the tarp. As he pulled it aside, he suddenly found himself staring down the barrel of Gus' .45 caliber semi-automatic pistol.

"Are you German military?" Gus demanded, hoping the fellow standing in front of him understood English. That didn't mean he wouldn't turn in the American pilot to the authorities.

"If I were a German soldier, you wouldn't be lying underneath the canvas among half-empty crates of my personal belongings. My wife and I present no harm to you, American."

Gus didn't have a choice. If the man were a Nazi sympathizer, Gus would find out sooner than later. He returned his weapon to his belt and winced … even that much motion set his lower leg and ankle into a spasm of pain.

"We will be approaching a Wehrmacht guard station soon. We must devise a strategy that will discourage them from looking beneath the canvas. I believe I have the answer, but it may cause additional discomfort for you." Albert told him of his plan and then fastened the tarp tightly over Gus.

Midway into the second day of their journey, Albert set the stage for his ruse. He removed a bottle of schnapps from among their personal belongings. While they were still out of view of the guard station, Albert opened the bottle of schnapps and took a long swallow.

He then poured a good portion of the bottle's contents over his clothing and climbed onto the bed of the small wagon. Helga volunteered the use of a handmade quilt. She had tried to sell it in the town of Eberswalde about 15 km northeast of Berlin. A few small offers were made, but no one had enough cash to buy it. Bartered goods abounded, but the Richters were in need of cash.

With Gus' leg wrapped in the quilt, and braced with several slats from a wooden box that was full of late season turnips, beets, potatoes and apples at the beginning of the trip, Albert lay down on top of the canvas, trying to not put any weight on the American's leg, and started into an old German ballad. His image of an old, harmless, drunk farmer was complete.

Twenty minutes later, on the outskirts of Schwedt, a village on the banks of the Oder River, and only two kilometers from their farm, Helga reined in the horses and put on her best smile.

Guten Tag, Frau Richter. Hatten Sie a profitable Reise? an elderly soldier inquired, asking Helga if she had a profitable trip to market. Helga was glad that Franz Bryner was on duty. He was a local villager and was forced into the position by the Wehrmacht so the younger men could join the fight against the Allies. Of course, Franz and the Richters were on sociable speaking terms. The Richter's were respected by the locals for their many kindnesses to those in need.

Jawohl. Albert hat sich aber zu sehr amüsiert ... schon wieder. She blamed Albert's apparent state of inebriation on the success of their trip.

Dann stören wir ihn nicht weiter Guten Tag bis zum nächsten Mal, Frau Richter. (Then we won't bother him anymore. Good day, see you next time, Mrs. Richter.)

They bade each other farewell, and Helga put the horses into motion with a "click" of her tongue and a slight flip of the reins.

"Sit, captain."

"In that?" Gus doubted the man's sanity until he finally understood.

"We need to place you in the house basement. Come, I will help." Albert Richter had cushioned the tub of the wheelbarrow as best he could with a couple of horse blankets and a generous portion of hay.

Albert took most of Gus' weight while Gus hopped gingerly on his good leg and lined up his fanny with the wheelbarrow. Together, they lowered him into it. Albert stepped out of the barn into sunlight and waved to Helga who was standing at the end of their property. She waved her left hand (the all-clear signal). A raised right hand would have meant traffic was on the road. One could not take too many precautions for fear that a local villager might be overheard by the Germans talking about "the stranger at the farm of Albert and Helga Richter." Albert grabbed the handles and soon was walking at a brisk pace toward the house. Gus had the impression that there was more to Heir Albert and Frau Helga Richter than met the eye.

Gus made it down to the basement with Albert on one side and Helga on the other helping him, literally, one step at a time.

"It occurs to me that I have not told you my name. I know your names are Albert and Helga. My name is Gus … Gus Bodine."

"Ja, ja. We know this. Your identification was still in your purse, er … how you say … 'wallet.'" We must talk about how we will return you to your Air Force, ja? It is too dangerous for you here. You must stay in this room until your strength is good. Then, we hand you to others. You are with us for two to three months for leg to get better. Ja?"

"Ja … yes. I am sorry for the trouble I have brought to your home."

Gus needed time enough to heal from his injuries, and time to regain his strength. The weeks spent without proper nutrition had resulted not only in the loss of considerable weight, but the loss of critical muscle mass as well. His weakened physical condition would work against him if it came down to trying to outrun the Wehrmacht.

As soon as he rested up, he started taking charge of his own rehabilitation. First came free weights: an old milk can caught his eye, and a bucket, and the coal bin that fed a stove to heat the house by convection heat and air exchange. Adding coal to the milk can and bucket would work nicely to provide the weights. A regimen of sit-ups and pushups could be managed while not putting too much pressure on his injured leg. Gus still had his Ka-Bar and along with some of

Albert's tools, he deftly shaped pieces of wood into splints and a crude cane from the branch of a spruce tree. …A long road was ahead.

"Addie, it'll be a while, but I will come back to you … and to our child." His words fell on no ears but his own, but saying them aloud added to his conviction of their truth. His heart beat strong with determination to keep his promise to Addie.

CHAPTER 22

THERE'S HOPE

The telephone on the small table in the hall adjacent to the living room rang out two loud bursts, paused, then two more bursts.

"I'll get it, Mom." Addie braced herself with her right hand on the arm of her father's overstuffed easy chair and pushed herself and her over-sized belly to a standing position. Pressing her left hand on her lower back to ease the constant ache that had taken up residence there for the past month of pregnancy, she waddled over to the black rotary dial telephone and picked up the receiver.

"Hello, this is Addie Bodine."

"Oh, Addie, my dear. I'm so glad that you answered. I have some important news. A Western Union telegram was just now delivered. I haven't read it. I thought you should be here. I could bring it over to you, if you like," Gus' mother offered. Even though it was all she could do to wait for the news, good or bad, she had to wait to read it with Addie.

"No … no, that's okay. I'll come right over. Thank you, Mother Bodine … er, Anna."

"Mom, I'm going to run over to Gus' parents' house for a few minutes," Addie called out on her way to the front door. Without waiting for an answer, she grabbed a sweater from the hall closet and left.

Addie sat in her Chevy and started to insert the key into the ignition when her hand began to tremble uncontrollably. Her eyes teared up, and she lowered her forehead onto the steering wheel. "Stop it, Addie. Just stop it!" she admonished herself. She brushed the tears from her eyes and started the car.

When Anna Bodine saw Addie pull up to the curb, she opened the front door and stepped out onto the porch.

Addie walked up the three steps to porch, put her arms around Gus' mother, and they squeezed each other tightly in a firm … albeit awkward … pregnant hug.

Trying to delay any potential bad news, Mother Bodine said hesitantly, "Come inside, dear. I have some nice cold lemonade, and I think I can find a fresh lemon-drop cookie or two to go with it."

"Maybe after we read the telegram, Anna. I don't feel like lemonade right now, if that's all right with you." Addie was holding a handkerchief. She was wringing it so tightly that it was threatening to tear asunder.

"Yes, of course." Gus' mom reached into her apron pocket and withdrew the Western Union telegram. Almost reluctantly, and with hands shaking slightly, she handed the envelope to Addie.

Dear Mrs. Bodine,

The following information regarding your husband's aircraft which was reported missing on 18 July has reached my desk. A P-51 escort fighter followed your husband's B-17 after it was struck by anti-aircraft artillery. The pilot of the fighter aircraft reported seeing five parachutes from your husband's bomber deploy before the bomber crashed. This office will inform you of future developments.

Sincerely,
N. F. Twining
Major General, USAAF
Fifteenth Air Force, Commanding

"He's alive. I knew it!" Addie shouted.

"It does look hopeful…but don't those airplanes carry more people than that?" Anna asked.

"The telegram said that five parachutes were sighted. That doesn't mean there weren't more, and it doesn't mean that Gus wasn't one of those five men."

"Oh, I do hope you're right, Addie. With all of my heart, I hope you are right." Then, Gus' mother smiled and asked, "How about that lemonade, now. Would you like to stay and we can talk some more?"

"Oh, yes! And a cookie would be lovely, thank you."

SUPRISE

On September 29, 1944, the trees were dressing themselves in their red, gold, and orange festive decorations. The day was made even more spectacular when the sun arose and Addie's world was sheltered beneath the azure canopy of a clear midday sky. Addie and Highway had walked to Pioneer Park. On those days … the ones filled with love and memories of their time with Gus … the gazebo was a repository of memories going back to their first visit to the white bandstand in their seventh grade year at Dixon Junior High School.

"Ouch! What was that?" Addie placed her hand on her tummy. She could feel the baby moving inside of her, but she had not felt any pain … that is, until now. "Highway, I think we should back to the house. I don't know if it's my time, but I think I need to be with mom. C'mon, let's go."

As Highway and Addie walked back to the house, she was hit by another jab of discomfort … still very mild though.

Entering through the side door leading into the kitchen, Addie called out, "Mom, where are you? I'm home."

"Upstairs, dear. I'm just making up the beds. Why don't you heat some water for tea, and I'll be right down."

Holding back her excitement, Addie struck a match and held it near the gas jets on one of the stove burners, then turned the knob on the front of the stove a half turn. After placing the teapot on the burner, she placed four cookies on a saucer and put them, with two napkins, on the table. That's a simple task, done many times, that barely requires mentioning, but this time it was punctuated by more pain … definitely contractions.

Nature decided to teach Addie who was going to be in charge for the next 16 hrs - and that was neither Addie nor Highway. The top dog in this little soirée was definitely mother nature.

At the precise moment of Estelle Russo's entrance into the kitchen, Addie's water broke onto the kitchen floor.

"Uh, oh, it looks like we had better get you to the hospital." Addie's mother turned off the stove burner and walked with Addie to her car.

HAPPY BIRTHDAY

Dr. Harold Riley, M.D., was a family physician who brought both Gus and Addie into the world in 1921. Back then, he shared his office, in a converted cottage-style house, with Dr. C. Bertrand Hayward who was on the fast track to retirement. At age 68, Dr. Hayward did just that, turning his share of the practice over to then 32-year-old Dr. Riley. In 1939, when the new Utah Valley Hospital, on 500 West and 650 North in Provo, opened its doors, Dr. Riley found it to be the perfect venue for his now well-established practice.

When Addie's Chevy pulled up to the main entrance with her mother behind the wheel, honking the horn like a New York City taxicab driver in a traffic jam, an astute orderly practically ran to the car pushing a wheelchair.

"This young lady is about to give birth. Her physician is Dr. Harold Riley. You must notify him immediately."

As luck would have it, Dr. Riley was in his office, voicing updates of a few patient files onto his wax cylinder dictation machine, when the telephone on his desk rang. He picked up and was informed by the receptionist that Addie Bodine was in labor and waiting for him in exam room number one.

After an exhausting 16 hrs of labor, Addie was ready to push. Fully effaced and dilated, Addie gave it everything she had while wondering why any sane woman would ever wish to subject herself to the endless, unimaginable agony that she was enduring. When Gustav Russell Bodine entered the world with a scream, Addie had her answer. "Gus … my sweet baby boy. Oh, how I wish your daddy was here!" *Where was he?* It had been so long—six weeks—since his plane went down. *If he had been taken prisoner of war, wouldn't the Germans have identified him so the Army could notify me?* …

Gus Jr. passed all of his newborn milestones: skull size, muscle reflexes, weight and length. Addie and her baby took to breast feeding with ease.

Dr. Riley removed the stethoscope from his ears and smiled approvingly at Addie. "He's doing fine, Addie, just fine. Would you like to go home today?"

"I would like that very much, thank you."

"Very well, then. I'll write the discharge order into your file, and you can be on your way."

Estelle Russo pulled the car into the drive-through in front of the main hospital entrance. The same orderly that helped Addie out of the car three days earlier, wheeled the new mother and baby to the car. He opened the passenger side car door and helped them into the passenger seat.

"Thank you. You do good work." Addie said. The orderly thanked her and closed the car door. The three headed for home.

Less than ten minutes after leaving the hospital they pulled into the driveway. Addie waited for her mother to come around the car to help. As soon as they entered the kitchen through the side door, Highway could be heard in the backyard barking to be allowed to join the happy event of Addie's return.

"I put the bassinette in the living room and started a nice fire in the fireplace. Why don't you sit down and relax. You want me to let the dog in?"

Addie laid the baby in the bassinette. "No, mother … thank you , though. I'd like to bring Highway into the house myself."

Addie took Highway's leash from off the coat hook and stepped out onto the back porch. Highway trotted over to her and allowed her to attach the leash to his dog collar.

Addie knelt and gave his ears a good scratching. "I have a surprise for you, Highway. He's waiting for us in the living room. Let's go meet baby Gus."

Highway allowed himself to be led into the living room. He sat on the floor next to the bassinette without having to be told. His nose twitched steadily sniffing the air in the room. There was something different here. His brain processed the new scent, and he decided he liked it … clean, new life, non-threatening … a living thing … and familiar. Highway's tail started wagging to a staccato rhythm as he looked up at Addie and "huffed" his approval. From that day forward, Highway was the protector … the ever-faithful sentinel … lying close to the bassinette whenever he had the opportunity.

CHAPTER 23

HELPING HANDS

By early November, ten weeks since he broke his ankle and was taken in by Albert and Helga Richter, Gus was at a point in his rehabilitation where he was able to bear weight. With the aid of a crutch (a gift from Albert's skilled craftsmanship), Gus was able to move around more freely and take on more rigorous physical conditioning.

His two benefactors were kind and selfless people. In a relatively short time, he had learned a great deal about them: they were devout in their faith as protestants, having strong testimonies of the Messiah; they kept a dogeared and well-used Bible printed in German; they believed that the gates of heaven would be opened to the righteous among the children of God; and repentance and baptism were essential to spiritual growth. Gus was convinced it was that testimony that caused them to stop on the side of the road and take a stranger under their care. He would be ever thankful for their kindness and humanity. All the more reason he felt it was time to be on his way. Albert and Helga avoided talking about the risk of discovery in their efforts to be Samaritans to those in need, but there was no doubt of its ever-present danger.

One late afternoon, on the day when storm clouds threatened to bring an early snow storm to the area, Gus offered to help Albert bring in fuel for the fireplace. Accessibility to coal for the furnace downstairs was based on the needs of the military. What little coal was provided for domestic use, came rarely and in small amounts. The furnace, therefore, would be used only during the coldest weather. Albert spent much of his time from September through early December laying in stocks of wood. Fireplace sized cuts of pine and spruce were stacked against the back of the farmhouse … three deep and over five feet tall along the full length of the rear wall.

"Albert, I need to talk with you, if you have a minute after we're done."

When they came in from outside, Albert motioned to Gus to sit at the table in front of the fireplace, and Helga joined them.

"I don't wish to bring danger to you by staying with you any longer. For that reason, I need to leave soon," Gus said. "I am nearly healed, and you can't do anything more for me than what you have already done."

"Yes, and there is danger here for you, too," replied Albert. "The Wehrmacht does not announce their visits, but they do visit. They look for American escapees from the camps, or for airmen, like you, who have parachuted and sought refuge."

Albert smiled and winked. "I will show you something. Come." Albert opened the trap door once more and led Gus down to the cellar. As he did so, he continued, "The German soldiers are most active now. They are withdrawing from the east and the west as the allies are pushing the front farther into Germany. This has caused much movement on the roads and the rail system. Fortunately, the Gestapo has been quiet for many weeks. We believe that is because the war is lost and that it will soon end. Already, there are rumors that the prisoner of war camps are overcrowded, and the Wehrmacht cannot provide enough troops to care for such large numbers. Escapes happen frequently. As part of the resistance, Helga and I provide assistance in arranging for Allied escaped prisoners to regain their freedom."

Gus was curious—and excited.

Albert walked toward a tall object concealed beneath an old moth-eaten wool blanket. He removed the blanket and revealed a lovely, handcrafted walnut wardrobe. The doors of the wardrobe were latched and locked. He removed a small key from his pocket and opened them. The interior of the wardrobe contained items of clothing hung from the single narrow rod extending the width of the wardrobe. What looked like a number of blankets were folded and placed on the floor of the wardrobe. Underneath the blankets were two drawers that Albert pulled open.

Gus could not believe his eyes. "This is telegraphy equipment. Is this how you communicate with others in the resistance?"

"We use it when we have need to inform our contact of allied airmen who require assistance rejoining their units. Our contact has the means to notify the Red Cross that you are alive. They will notify the American OSS (Office of Strategic Service) who will coordinate with the resistance for your removal to neutral territory."

"Are you saying that we can get word to my family that I'm alive?"

"Indirectly, yes. If the contacts inside the Wehrmacht believe it is safe to do so, a coded message will be sent to a high-ranking officer who oversees an independent communication system of the German reserve forces. This officer will use that system to get word to the American OSS that an American aviator is in need of extraction. However this high-ranking officer acts only on information provided by the resistance using the coded communication system. It is then verified by another German officer, a captain who is in direct communications with various resistance organizations including the SPD (Socialist Democratic Party), and the KPD (Communist Party of Germany) and the Polish Home Army (AK). Helga and I were both raised in Poland, and joined the AK in 1940. We are citizens of Germany, but our hearts beat with Polish blood. I'm sure you understand that I cannot tell you the names of the German officers who are involved."

"I understand. When will I know if contact has been made with the OSS?" Gus asked.

"Lines of communication are open to send and receive coded messages two days each week and only within a fifteen-minute window. We must wait until you are strong. Your ankle is almost healed. In two weeks, we will begin the process. Arrangements will be made, and you will be placed in the care of an AK team that will be responsible for getting you to a safe house in Poland."

Their escape plan struck Gus as very dangerous. He knew they were closer to Poland, but it was still under German control. Without other options, he reconciled himself to Albert's plan. "Alright. I'll continue regaining strength. Will we talk again before you send the message?"

"Yes, we will speak once more about it when the operation is in place," Albert affirmed.

For the next two weeks, the Richter's "house guest" was allowed upstairs during the day where he was invited to share meals with them. Gus dedicated himself to putting his body in the best possible physical condition to endure the hardships ahead. He hung onto the hope, at last, that a door was opening … and beyond that door was home.

On the eve of what would be Thanksgiving Day in America, Albert called Gus aside and asked Helga to join them. They seated themselves at the table in front of the fireplace where a cheerful fire warmed the room. Outside, a layer of fresh snow covered the ground. The sky was completely overcast with clouds heavily laden with moisture. Overnight there would be another six to eight inches of snow on the ground. At over 6000 ft above sea level, the winter of 1944-1945 would be the coldest and wettest winter on record in the region … and the most dangerous and challenging time of Gus Bodine's life.

Albert held Helga's hand. "It is time. We will transmit the message of your survival to our contact in Salzburg. When he receives confirmation that your extraction has been approved, we will be notified that the AK team will be dispatched. I will take you to the pickup location using the same method that we used to bring you here. Are you ready to ride in a bumpy wagon underneath the canvas one more time?" They all chuckled.

Albert, Helga, and Gus descended the stairs into the cellar. Albert had already set up the antenna which was attached to the wall of the house by two clamps. He connected the copper wire leads to the mast and threaded the other end down into the coal chute. Helga attached that end of the wire leads to the telegraph key.

Helga would compose and send a message using a code book that was supplied to them by Captain Julius Stryker, the junior officer on General Friedrich Olbright's staff, whose responsibility it was to verify the legitimacy of the extraction operation. Albert's job was to crank the hand-operated generator that would bring the batteries up to the correct voltage. Once accomplished, Helga would then send the coded message to their AK contact in a neighboring village 15 km from the Richter farm.

"When exactly will we leave for the pickup point?" Gus asked.

"I cannot be precise, but we should receive a coded message in the next day or two giving us a time and place for the rendezvous. Dress for the cold, but bring no more than what you wear. The going will be most difficult because of the weather. It is likely that you will be crossing the Bavarian Alps. Your team will provide water and food to see you through to your destination. Ja?" Albert spoke in a somber, quiet tone. Clearly, he had formed an attachment to the young American bomber pilot seated across from him. Gus understood, because he, too, had come to feel friendship and a deep respect for Albert and Helga Richter.

Two days later, on November 25, Gus, Albert, and Helga sat at the table for a dinner of *Chlodnik* (a cold soup made of beets, cucumbers, and dill in a cream base), and *Pierogi* (dumplings stuffed with chicken, potatoes and sauerkraut). The delicious meal must have nearly emptied the Richter's food larder. The thought of such a lavish gift caused Gus' heart to swell with love for them.

After eating, Albert said, "It is almost time to activate the system."

Voltage output on the batteries was brought up to power, and Helga keyed in the phrase indicating their line was clear and that they were awaiting confirmation of the previous message.

"*Was ist das*? Albert, the line is open but there is no answer."

Then the telegraph key started to chatter.

Helga jotted down the reply, "*Gestapo! Laufen!* (Gestapo! Run!)." Her face turned white with fear.

Albert spoke hurriedly, "You must leave, Gus. The Gestapo have found our contact and will be here soon. They cannot know you were here."

Albert and Helga climbed the stairs and closed the trap door. They pulled a handwoven carpet over the door and moved back the table and chairs. Quickly, Helga placed eating utensils on the table as though preparing an evening meal for the two of them.

———

Gus was ready to go. He put on a heavy woolen coat given to him by Albert from the items that were inside the wardrobe. It looked like, at one time, the coat had belonged to a British aviator. The outline of the badges of his rank and various insignia remained, but the patches themselves had been removed.

A canvas knapsack was provided … again by the generosity of the Richter's. The military issue knapsack of unknown origin served as a good replacement for his survival vest and makeshift parachute-silk backpack. Helga had placed a loaf of bread, two turnips, and four potatoes inside the pack, and the woolen blanket that had warned him for these many weeks was rolled up and bound to the back of it. His .45 caliber pistol was in the waist band of his trousers. He wore one of Helga's scarfs over his head and tied it under his chin. Perched on his head was a peasant cap of the type worn by men and boys throughout that region.

Suddenly a loud banging on the door above him announced the presence of two German men uniformed in black and wearing the double lightning bolt emblems of Hitler's SS. Gus heard Albert answer, "Ein moment."

Hurriedly, he scrambled up the coal chute and out into the cold snowy night. Beneath the canopy of falling snow, and under cover of darkness, he scurried to the tree line no more than 150 yds distant. Out of breath and concerned, Gus hunkered down behind a tree where he could see the house. Beyond the range of their voices, the night seemed quiet, even peaceful. …But that illusion was ended with the "crack-crack!" of two rifle reports.

Albert and Helga Richter had given their lives for him on this day!

Gus couldn't control the heart-breaking flood of grief that overcame him. His knees buckled, and he dropped to the ground. He wept as if he had lost two members of his own family. Indeed, they were true guardian angels. The memory of their love and service would stay with Gus the rest of his life.

Gus noted that his footprints were quickly fading beneath the new fallen snow. In the next ten minutes or so they would be completely obscured. He forced himself to stand and headed northeast in hopes of finding other AK members … resistance fighters, who, like Helga and Albert, fought against Nazi oppression with the courage of the bravest of soldiers. By day Gus traveled through the woods and over streams. His progress was slow, averaging only four to five kilometers per day. Fallen trees, boulders, and other natural obstacles were often so obscured by snowpack that they became a dangerous risk. Gus knew that if he should suffer another fall, like the one that broke his ankle five months earlier, he would be as good as dead.

Every breath pumped steam into the air. Gus' lungs ached from sucking in freezing air and the exertion of pushing oxygen into blood vessels and arteries of a depleted body that had been denied necessary life-giving nutrition. His meager food supplies ran out days earlier, and he was again left with scrounging for any "food" he could find bugs, lichens, fungi … some of which made him so sick that he lay in the snow retching and enduring severe abdominal and muscle cramps. He came across one variety of mushroom which was edible, but mushrooms boiled in snow water wasn't enough.

Late in the afternoon of December 17, Gus saw a narrow column of smoke rising above the tree line about two kilometers to the east. If his compass was correct, he had been travelling roughly northeast in the direction of Schwedt, a small town about 200 kilometers from Stettin near the border of occupied Poland. Desperately malnourished, he changed course slightly and headed for the source of the smoke thinking it might be a place where he could scavenge for food.

Ahh, there's a working farm. I need to get inside that barn. Gus stayed hidden in the trees … positioned so the barn was between him and the house. He waited for any sign of activity. The lowing of a cow from inside the barn caught his ear. Against one wall was a wagon with some sort of cultivating equipment used for working the ground for planting. After half an hour of watching and waiting, he emerged from the forest and scrambled toward the side wall of the barn. He held his breath, so no one would see it in the cold air, and moved to the front of the barn. A three-foot long two-by-six board secured the door in place, but there was no lock attached. The board had a length of rope attached to an eyebolt at one end and was threaded through an opening in the wall. The other end was hinged; it was obviously meant as a means of opening the door from the inside of the barn. Gus lifted the board from its support brackets and swung open the door. He entered, closed the door, then used the rope to lower the board back onto its brackets.

He was shivering uncontrollably and had been awake and on the run for over 14 hrs. He hadn't had any food for nearly two days and drank melted snow to keep himself hydrated. Stomach cramps were constantly trying to empty his already empty bowels. What would have been diarrhea was only discolored water. Dehydration and starvation were double-teaming to bring about the end of his life. In the dim light remaining inside the barn, Gus started looking around for any items he could use. There were two draft horses in stalls on one side of the barn, and a cow was in a stall across the floor on the other side. A stool and milk bucket occupied a space against the outer wall of the stall nearest the cow.

Never having milked a cow before, he found desperation to be good motivation to learn. On further investigation, Gus came across a good supply of hay and bagged oats and barley … no doubt, the cow's winter feed. The loft was full of loose hay, and more hay was piled up in a stall-sized enclosure at one end of the barn.

Gus was about to make his first attempt at milking a cow when he heard the rattling of the board being lifted from the door.

Crouched low inside the cow's stall, Gus peered between the slats of wood that formed the low walls separating the three stalls. He drew his service weapon and chambered a round.

The barn door was closed quietly. Someone was inside. The figure was that of a shorter person, well under six feet, he estimated. Gus couldn't tell if he was armed. He watched as the intruder filled a wheelbarrow with alfalfa hay. Adding a half-empty bag of grain to the heap, he pushed the loaded wheelbarrow over to the horse stalls

Good. It's only the farmer coming to feed the stock, Gus thought.

After feeding the horses, the farmer walked over to the cow. "Und jetzt bist du dran, mein Haustier." ("And now, it is your turn, my pet.")

Gus had worked his way into a dark corner with the cow between himself and the young man. He holstered his pistol and waited.

The fellow placed the milk bucket beneath the cow's udder and pulled a stool in place to sit on while he milked the animal.

For a moment Gus thought the man would leave the barn without noticing that an American pilot was hiding in the shadows, but then the farmer started to sing a familiar song in English! … *There is a green hill, far away* … from the book of hymns at his church back home. Gus was taken by such complete surprise that he found himself in a momentary fugue state. Visions of countless church meetings as a youth scrolled through his memory … picture-book pages of his life growing up in Utah Valley. Gus was compelled to step into view of the farmer.

Upon seeing a shadow in the corner of the stall that moved and took on human form, the frightened farmer armed himself with a pitchfork that was leaning against the wall.

"Halt! Wer bist du? Warum bist du in meiner Scheune?" the farmer demanded.

"Ich spreche kein Deutsch. Ich bin ein Amerikaner. I mean no harm to you. Do you speak English?"

"Ja … er, yes. I speak English … ein bisschen."

"This is good. You just heard all of the German language I know. This is your farm? If you are going to turn me over to the Gestapo, I will leave you. I am hungry and tired. I need rest to recover my strength. Can you help me?"

"This is good, Gus. I am Luca Brunholdt. My wife is in the house. You can come in and eat with us, then you must return to the barn to rest. I will come here before the sun rises to see that you are gone, ja?

The Nazis come here often. They were here yesterday asking to know of any men walking alone near my farm. …Come."

Gus followed Luca to the house. The aroma of cooking caused Gus' stomach to sit up and beg to be fed … *like Highway.* The thought brought a smile to Gus' heart.

On seeing Gus, Adelheid Brunholdt's otherwise cheerful countenance changed to a look of suspicion. "Luca, wen hast du in unser Haus gebracht?"

"Speak English, Adelheid. He is American. Gus is fleeing capture. I have told him he may eat and rest, but he must leave before sunrise. He will rest in the barn," Luca explained, and then added, "He is a Christian, like us."

They talked about the war and of how the Nazis allowed his church to conduct their meetings under close supervision by the ruling National Socialist government. They grew up together in the town of Schwedt not more than 17 km south of their farm. Because theirs was a working farm, the government allowed them to keep it. In turn they were required to produce grains, potatoes, beets, turnips and legumes for the German Reich. Luca and Adelheid were allowed only meager 2000 calories per day each. During the dormant winters after the final harvest, laborers were returned to camps and prisons from whence they came to work on the farms. Luca was told that if he wished to keep his farm, he must consent to obeying the punitive rules of forced labor imposed by the German Reich. Consequently, regular visits by local Nazi party government leaders were used to keep an eye on the shrinking domestic farming industry and ensure compliance with the law. They paid particular attention to any signs of resistance efforts involving trafficking of enemy airmen and soldiers who were trying to find their way back to allied territory.

With a watchful eye, Luca brought Gus into the house to warm him while Adelheid finished cooking the evening meal. The bowl of *eintopf,* a stew of potatoes and late-season vegetables boiled in bouillon thickened with flour, and served with warm bread, had been carefully proportioned. Gus' hunger abated, but he knew that the young farmers had denied themselves their full portion to feed him. The meal over, and with a grateful heart, Gus returned to the barn where he made a bed of hay in the loft. He set aside a burlap bag of stored beets, turnips, and potatoes, courtesy of Adelheid; a smaller bag of oats was placed inside the larger one. In all, Gus figured he could stretch out the supplies for six days or so. He estimated approximately another week to reach Poland, some 60 kilometers to the northeast, on the eastern banks of the Oder River. He hoped to find help from the AK (Polish Resistance) in the area of Gryfino, about 40 kilometers south of the city of Stettin on a tributary of the Oder River. He wanted to avoid getting too close to Stettin because of the strong Wehrmacht (German Army) presence.

CHAPTER 24

DECEMBER 4, 1944 / PROVO, UTAH

Addie Russo-Bodine and her sister-in-law Catherine carried down the last of the boxes containing Christmas tree decorations from the top shelf of one of the upstairs closets.

Addie started pulling the strings of red, yellow, green, and blue lights from one large box that Gerry Bodine brought up from the basement. He had tested the lights to make sure they were functioning correctly, so when Addie and Catherine strung them around the tree and plugged the end into the wall receptacle, the lights flashed on with a flip of the wall switch.

"Oh, this is going to be such fun. Are we going to string popcorn this year?" Catherine asked.

"I know Gus would have enjoyed that if he were here. Let's do the rest of the tree and string the Garland of popcorn as the crowning glory of the season," Addie suggested.

An hour later the Bodine family Christmas tree stood in glory in front of the large living room window ready to be brought to life. Catherine reached toward the light switch just as her mother entered the living room.

"Hold on there. Have you forgotten? We must all toast the

Christmas season by turning on the lights and holding our eggnog mugs high. Then we shall all gather together in front of our tree in a chorus of 'Silent Night.' Catherine, come help with the eggnog, won't you?" asked Mother Bodine.

While Catherine and her mom busied themselves in the kitchen, Addie laid three-month-old Gus Bodine, Jr., on the sofa and tucked pillows around him. Highway curled up on the floor next to the sofa. This would be the first Christmas shared together for Addie, Highway, and baby Gus, but Addie's heart ached for her husband to be there to complete their little family. Meanwhile, it was their baby boy that strengthened her and gave her purpose. Her faith that Gus was alive had not faltered, but the loneliness still brought with it a darkness that never quite allowed peace to take hold.

Catherine brought a tray loaded with cups of steaming eggnog and placed it on the coffee table.

"All right, everyone. Gather around. I have a special surprise this year." Addie's mother handed each person in the room a five-inch-wide roll of paper tied together with a red ribbon. Everyone removed the ribbon from the paper, and unrolled it.

"You have before you the lyrics to the new popular Christmas season song, 'White Christmas.' Catherine and I copied it for each of you, and in case you don't remember how the song goes, I have a surprise for you to help with joining in chorus. Gerry, if you please."

Gerry Bodine lifted the lid on the Victrola record player and placed a new 78 rpm record on the turntable. They all sang "White Christmas" accompanied by the slightly scratchy voice of Bing Crosby.

Anna Bodine ended the brief tree lighting ceremony with gratitude and love. "And if this evening could be any more joyful, it would be if our boy, Gus, could be here with us. In our hearts, we know he is out there somewhere and pray that he will be joining us on the next white Christmas."

CHAPTER 25

GERMAN SOLDIERS

It was now December 23, 1944, but Gus' thoughts were not on Christmas. His legs were burning from the exertion of lifting one foot at a time over the top of the knee-high snowpack. Every joint, tendon, and muscle ached as if he had been running one marathon after another for the past four days. Suddenly, Gus stopped at the sound of voices echoing through the trees. As he moved stealthily in that direction, he could hear laughter and the clinking together of metal utensils. *A group of men stopping for a chow break? Wehrmacht! How many?* He adjusted his course, thinking to parallel the activity and work his way past it. He walked on, fighting the snow and trying to be quiet at the same time. The voices were now directly to his right no more than 30 or 40 yds away. Then he heard it … more voices of men approaching from his left. *Oh, no. I can't move or they'll see me.* Gus crouched low and tried to slow his breathing … he was pumping steam like a locomotive.

———

Seventeen-year-old Franz Schmidt pointed toward the trees. "Was ist das? Es sieht aus, als würde jemand hinter diesem Baum sitzen." The young German soldier hardly knew one end of his rifle from the other. Like so many other young men, he had been pressed into service to protect the fatherland in a desperate attempt to boost the numbers of the badly depleted Wehrmacht who were fighting on two fronts: the west where the Allies were approaching, and the east where they were losing ground to the Russians.

Raising his rifle, Franz took one step forward and was stopped by the strong hand of his sergeant.

"Wait. Don't rush into something you're not certain of. We will spread out and approach from both sides."

Gus knew he was caught. The German soldiers surrounded him, and if he were to run from them, he would likely be shot. He had no choice. He stood up and stepped into the open with his hands raised high.

Gus' back pack, his few possessions, and his weapon were taken from him. He was manhandled to a troop-carrying truck where he was forced to sit on the bed rather than on the bench which was occupied by a ragtag bunch of local German "soldiers. These were all older men who were too old to join the ranks of the regular army who fought on the front lines, or they were too young and inexperienced to be exposed to the horrors of war. Gus suspected that most, if not all, of them didn't want to be there any more than he did.

The sergeant commanding the squad of misfits wanted to get Gus into the hands of the Gestapo as quickly as possible and return to his duties of patrolling the main roads and byways around Schwedt. He ordered the small convoy of vehicles to move out.

Gus could see that they were headed toward Schwedt back in the general direction of the farm of Luca and Adelheid Brunholdt. What he didn't know was that Schwedt was a rail stop on a line that traveled northeast into Poland, terminating at Gross Tychow.

CHAPTER 25

INTERROGATION

Gus was offloaded in front of a three-story brick building that looked as though it was a local government office before it became a resident Gestapo headquarters for the area. Selected for its central location, the building housed not only Gestapo officials, but a 25-man platoon of elite, black-uniformed SS troops.

Gus' escorts were instructed to take him to an interrogation room. An SS guard was posted outside the door. The space on the wall once occupied by a window was now a four-foot by five-foot brick addition. He was encouraged to sit on a wooden folding chair across from a cushioned office chair on the opposite side of a small utilitarian-looking desk. A four drawer filing cabinet stood next to the door. An hour passed. Gus' eyes were heavy from the lack of sleep since he left Luca's farm, and he began to nod off.

"Stand up!" said the man who had suddenly appeared in the room.

Gus stood. Fully alert, he took note of the man's demeanor and appearance: early thirties; a suit of clothes (grey, with a white dress shirt and a necktie; polished black shoes); neat, closely cut hair; and grey eyes as cold as ice. His countenance was one of indifference: flat and without expression.

"Name?"

Gus cleared his throat. "Bodine, Gus, Captain, United States Army Air Force. My serial number is zero-nine-seven-three-five-three-eight-one."

"Complete this form." Gus was handed a form with blank lines for home address and next of kin. "I will provide you with no further information than I have already given you."

The Gestapo agent consulted some papers contained inside a manila folder, jotted down some notes, and closed the folder. "Captain Bodine, you are now a guest of the Third Reich. Your status as a *kriegsgefangener* (POW) entitles you to a place of shelter. You will not be taken to the camp at Colditz Castle, where many of your officer associates are enjoying the hospitality of the Reich, but we can't get you there. The only transportation available is a train which will depart for Keifeide in one hour's time."

The man left the room. A burly Wehrmacht NCO stepped in. "Do you have need of a toilet?" he asked flatly.

"Yes," Gus replied, also flatly. He would offer no social niceties, gratitude, handshakes, etc. He was in the hands of a sworn enemy, not a business retreat for Spartan Air. *Good heavens. Where did that memory come from?* he thought. The recall of Spartan Aircraft's "meet and greet" of students and faculty back in 1942 brought a hint of a smile despite his circumstances.

He was unceremoniously escorted by his guard to a lavatory. Gus relieved himself and was returned to the interrogation room.

CHAPTER 26

WESTERN UNION

The International Red Cross was periodically provided with a list of newly interred prisoners of war who, in turn, submitted a copy of the new names with rank and serial number to the proper allied authority. In the case of American servicemen who were interred in the one hundred Stammlager (Stalags or base camps), the authority was the Director of the POW Information Center. Once received, the airman's status was reported to the next of kin.

On January 15, 1945, two weeks after Gus' capture, a Western Union messenger rang the doorbell of the Bodine house.

"I'll get it," Addie shouted, and walked to the front door.

Addie had moved back in with Anna and Gerry Bodine just before Christmas with her parent's blessing. She needed to be with Gus' parents in the house where Gus spent his childhood. Somehow, she found comfort in those surroundings.

Addie opened the door to a Western Union messenger.

"Oh! Hello there. I … I wasn't expecting Western Union."

"Are you Mrs. Adelle Bodine?"

"Yes … yes I am," she said with a quivering voice.

"Sign here, please." The young man handed Addie a clipboard

with a receipt confirmation, which Addie quickly signed and returned to the man.

Trembling with fear, she carried the unopened telegram into the living room.

Gus' mother entered the room and noticed Addie's troubled affect.

"Addie, dear. What is it?" She noticed the telltale envelope in her daughter-in-law's hand. Her heart, like Addie's, revved up to a staccato beat as she sat down on the sofa next to her daughter-in-law. Gently, she pulled the envelope from Addie's hand. "Here, I'll read it."

Gus' mother opened the telegram and began …

The Secretary of War desires that I convey the following update of the status of your husband, Captain Gus Bodine: as of January 15, 1945, Captain Bodine's status has changed from Missing in Action to Prisoner of War. He is interred at Stalag Luft IV, a Luftwaffe prison camp for American and Allied Airmen captured by forces of the Third Reich. He is reported to be in fair health, after having survived the loss of his aircraft and his crew on 18 July 1944 and evading capture for five months in the forests of eastern Germany. Further information will come to you via the Director, Prisoner of War Information Bureau.

Sincerely yours,
Colonel Howard F. Bresee
POW Information Center

"He's alive, Addie, our Gus is alive!" Anna and Addie threw their arms around each other and wept tears of joy. They read the telegram twice more, crying and hugging anew.

Addie emitted a soul-deep sigh of relief, and with it, a flood of tears. A confused Highway lay at her feet.

CHAPTER 27

INHUMANITY

Gus was taken to the railyard in Schwedt. He was forced to stand as a train pulled into the station bearing the flags of the Third Reich, one on either side of the massive cattle catcher, with the emblems of the black swastika on a white roundel and red background. In place of passenger cars with comfortable seats and windows through which a passenger might admire the vistas of the German countryside, the train Gus was about to board was pulling several of what looked like cattle cars. Already, Gus caught a stomach-turning rancid scent of urine and human feces emanating from the cars. When the sliding door was pulled back to admit him, even the armed guards were forced to turn their heads and cover their noses at the stench. Gus noted that he was pushed toward the door by the same soldier who guarded him in the district Gestapo headquarters.

"Schnell! Schnell!" the man commanded while jabbing the muzzle of his rifle into Gus' back.

Gus was pulled into the cattle car by the helping hand of a young U.S. Army Air Force staff sergeant whose uniform was soiled, and he looked to be 20 lbs underweight. His face, though, appeared freshly washed, and his blonde hair was practically glowing. His penetrating blue-grey eyes shone a light that was iridescent. Gus found himself standing in the midst of what must have been 80 men, all prisoners of war, crammed into a space barely big enough for 20 men. He looked for the young NCO to thank him for his help but could see no sign of the good Samaritan.

The prisoners were so tightly packed that there was no room to sit … let alone lie down. A few metal buckets were emptied into a large tank on the bed of a military truck when the train stopped in Schwedt then returned to the cattle car. The military contingent assigned to guard the prisoners adhered to the idea that ruling from a distance kept the leaders safe and breathing fresh air. Gus surmised that they were riding in the luxury of passenger coaches.

The allied invasion of Normandy began shrinking the Wehrmacht front lines as they were pushed back into Germany itself. The German High Command, in an effort to increase the numbers of troops on the Western Front, decided to evacuate Stalag Luft camps and build camps in northern Poland, thus relieving the forces needed to guard and care for the prisoners so they could be reassigned to combat units.

One such newly constructed camp, Stalag Luft IV, was built in a field outside Gross Tychow in German-occupied Poland northeast of Stettin. Designed to house 640 prisoners, the International Red Cross reported a population over *11 times* that at 7,389 in October with groups of 100 to 150 arriving every few days!

The Reich was in violation of most of the 71 articles of the Geneva Convention regarding treatment of prisoners including housing, feeding (quantity, lack of nutritional balance), sanitary and hygiene facilities, protection against torture and physical harm, and the list went on. Mail exchange was inadequate with mail arriving infrequently as was the delivery of Red Cross packages. Evidence of malnutrition, starvation, and hypothermia could be found within all four camps. Building of new facilities stopped as the POW situation overwhelmed the supply chain of essential goods and supplies. Tensions grew as the Wehrmacht disallowed prisoners direct access to Red Cross parcels. They would have to make do with whatever the guards stingily doled out while keeping the larger part for themselves.

———

The train ride to Luft Stalag IV was a six-hour trip. The men Gus joined had all boarded the train from Stalag Luft camps in west Germany. After three hours of standing with no opportunity to do more than shift his weight from one foot to the other, Gus managed to squeeze between the legs of a pair of men and sit on his heels with his back against the wall next to the door. He caught a whiff of fresh air blowing in through a space between the wall and the sliding door. It helped his queasy stomach.

"Hey, buddy, how long have you been on this train?" Gus asked an American tech. sergeant.

"Some of us Air Force guys were sent from Stalag III-A by train to Berlin to board this ride. We've been on the road for going on two days. Nothing to eat but a cup of some boiled beets and potatoes. What about you? You look Air Force."

"Yeah, Fifteenth Air Force. Lost my Fort and my crew back in July. Been on the run ever since," Gus replied.

"On the run since July? You must have had some help along the way."

"I did … don't care to talk about it, though." Gus looked around and wondered if any German ears were listening.

"I get that. Well, sir, I hope things get better soon for all of us. Say, I haven't seen any officers but you." The sergeant made it sound like an accusation. It wasn't the reaction Gus expected. The men on that train lacked leadership, but Gus would wait until they reached Stalag Luft IV before he made any move at building a command structure. Gus needed some sort of purpose … goals to work toward. He found it in the 80 souls wasting away underneath the weight of hopelessness inside that cattle car. He would do his best to help them get through the rest of the war as American POWs.

CHAPTER 28

STALAG LUFT IV

The train pulled up to a platform in the town of Keifeide. A blinding burst of sunlight accompanied the rattle of the steel rollers on the sliding door as it opened. Squinting, Gus caught a glimpse of a line of a dozen German soldiers, all armed with either a Mauser bolt-action rifle or an MP40 9 x19 mm submachine gun. He stepped aside and did what he could to get the men moving. A few were struggling, one lost his balance and fell. Gus reached out and lifted him to his feet. He could feel the man's ribs through the woolen blanket issued to all POWs by the Wehrmacht.

"I've got you, pal."

With a raspy voice, weakened by hunger and neglect, the staff sergeant replied, "Thanks."

When Gus exited the cattle car, he noticed many of the men being formed into columns of four by guards who were too free with their bayonets and boots as they jabbed and kicked the new prisoners.

"Captain Gustavus Bodine!" A voice shouted in a thick German accent. Gus turned toward the source of the voice and immediately spotted Luftwaffe Oberst Leutnant (Lt. Col.) Aribert Bombach, the camp Commandant.

Gus raised his hand, feeling much like a schoolboy about to be called upon to answer a question he was unprepared to answer. A gruff armed guard prodded Gus, jabbing at him with his bayonet.

"AUGH! Okay, I'm going." He allowed himself to be led to the officer, and saluted the commandant as a show of respect.

"Captain, walk with me, please," Bombach said in an inviting tone.

Gus was led to a Luftwaffe staff car and was invited to get in. He didn't move.

"Are my men riding the rest of the way to the camp, sir?" he asked.

"Unfortunately, there are no vehicles available. They will be escorted on foot. It is not far. I assure you, they will be unharmed."

"I'll march with the men." Gus started walking toward the columns of prisoners. A guard stepped in front of him, holding his Mauser rifle at the ready. Gus stopped and waited.

"Schnell!" The guard's rifle was aiming directly at Gus' gut. The man, holding his right forefinger on the trigger, was rock steady.

"Sergeant, let the captain walk. Bring him to me when they arrive at the camp."

The guard stepped aside. Gus joined the group of NCOs and began the four kilometer walk to the camp.

The man in charge of the guards, Gus learned later, was Feldwebel (Sergeant) Reinhard Fahnert. He ordered the American column to follow the route through the center of Keifeide. The shorter route would have skirted the city, but Fahnert had something else in mind. Under orders from his boss, the Camp Security Officer, Hauptmann (Captain) Walther Pickhardt, Fahnert and his squad of guards had made certain that the townspeople knew about each trainload of prisoners.

At first, when Gus saw the large number of civilians lining the streets, he thought nothing more than a little name calling and profanities would be thrown at them. But, to stir up the people, Capt. Pickhardt stood up in the staff car and began shouting, "Lassen Sie diese Amerikaner es haben!" (Let these American have it!) He shook his fist and yelled, "Schweine" (pigs) and "böse" (evil ones), and then gave the order to make the prisoners double-time it all the way to the camp. A few of the inflamed citizens ran up and spat on the POWs. One man threw a bottle striking one of them on the shoulder. They were kicked and prodded by bayonets. Still, they ran.

Gus was afraid the guards would shoot stragglers. *I need to do something … but what?* Suddenly, Gus broke ranks and sprinted to the front of the column. He matched their speed and began calling cadence, "Hup, two, three, four. Let's show these grey-uniformed cretins who we are, men! In cadence, on me!" Gus set the pace, slower than what the guards wanted, but he figured there wasn't much they could do about it without causing a major incident. They slowed to a walk three times and then ran again for another mile. Each beleaguered man in the column was further hampered by the weight of his own meager possessions: blanket, mess kit, old letters (if they had any), cigarettes, coats and gloves. Whatever they could load onto their bodies, they were allowed to possess … if they could keep up.

The barbed wire compound with its guard towers came into view as the four columns of men rounded a curve and got their first look at Stalag Luft IV. Gus summoned every ounce of energy he had and continued to lead the men the rest of the way to the guard post at the main entrance. "Stay on your feet, men."

Limping and taking short, halting steps toward the staff car carrying the senior officers, Gus addressed the commandant, "I demand that these men be given proper food. Many of them are suffering from malnutrition, disease, and need medical attention."

Oberst Leutnant Aribert Baumbach called from his staff car, "Bring the American captain to my office!"

Gus was manhandled by two guards to the commandant's office. He was not allowed to place his personal belongings on the floor and had to stand at attention for 15 min before the commandant took his seat behind his desk.

"Well, Capt. Bodine, you made quite an impression on the prisoners. Do I assume that you believe you have taken command of Stalag Luft IV? Do you feel that Germany has lost the war, and the likes of you can bomb our cities and murder our women, children, and old men, then act the part of conquering heroes? I would love to take you on a grand tour of our generous treatment of you American assassins, however, that will have to wait. You are about to get all of the rest you need … in solitary confinement. Your personal possessions will be returned to you in seven days. You may keep your blanket and the clothes on your back.

Captain, we will talk again. Perhaps then you will show proper respect to the honorable men who fight for the Reich. Take him away."

The guards poked and prodded Gus along to what he guessed was their jail. Judging from the distance between the doors, he estimated the width of each cell at less than five feet. He hoped the length was much longer. One of the guards opened the third cell. The second guard jammed the butt of his rifle into Gus' back sending him reeling inside against the wall. He fought to stay on his feet despite a wave of dizziness that nearly overtook him. The cell door slammed closed.

Gus began to explore his surroundings. His cell received sunlight through a barred opening set high on one wall about seven feet from the floor. A filthy mattress with what looked like rat droppings scattered on and around it sat in one corner, and a bucket, about the size of the one in Luca and Adelheid Brunholdt's barn, occupied the opposite corner. It was empty, but the odor that arose from it defined its purpose.

Twilight fell over the camp, but it came as the dark of night to the men in solitary confinement. The light in a cell, at its best, was not much better than a late afternoon overcast winter day in Provo: good enough to see details of one's surroundings, but not enough to drive a car without headlights to light the way. There was nothing here to light the way to any destination—here Gus was, and here he would stay, for the next week.

Every prisoner of war goes through a period of disorientation as to time, place, and incident. Days go by repeating the same routine, mostly boring, unfulfilling and repetitious, sometimes painful and sickening … nothing changes. The angry gnawing at the ribs of a bloated starving gut that drives a man to near madness, is part of life in a POW camp.

Gus wondered if there was any spirit left inside him that would offer the gift of hope to the men he met and walked with. *Can I find the dignity and faith to help them?* Gus pondered. He from his father, early in life, that a person's character is defined by the good he has done to raise up another in need. ...There, in the seemingly hopeless environs of Stalag Luft IV, Gus Bodine was reminded of that most valuable lesson: a generous heart rewards the giver with even greater gifts than those that are given.

A steel panel about four inches high and ten inches wide opened, and a bowl was placed on the flat surface. Gus hadn't eaten in over two days, and he hurriedly grabbed the bowl. A tin cup of water appeared, and he took that as well. The bowl contained a half of a boiled potato in a brown tasteless broth and a chunk of stale bread. Gus estimated six ounces of water and three ounces of broth. He forced himself to chew and suck every calorie that he could from the bland meal.

On his third night of confinement, Gus lay on the soiled mattress wrapped tightly in the thin, grey, woolen blanket. The nighttime temperature dropped to 12 °F. No heat was provided for the prisoners in the entire blockhouse of 12 cells. Coiled in the fetal position for warmth, his head nodded briefly, but he was shaken awake by a shuddering spasm of chills.

A squeaking sound came from near the bucket. A rat had decided to pay him a visit.

"Scram! Get out!" He wrapped himself in the blanket even more tightly.

The sensory deprivation was maddening. He had not heard a human voice since his solitary confinement. On his seventh day, the guards returned. The door swung open just in time for Gus to see two more guards remove another prisoner ... on a stretcher. He didn't need to get any closer to see that the fellow was dead. The faded name over his right breast pocket read "Wayland."

Gus was escorted to "Compound C." Men were lying or sitting on their beds or the few chairs the Reich provided.

"Welcome the newest resident of your pig wallow," the Wehrmacht guard announced. He struck Gus in the back with his rifle and sent him sprawling to the floor.

"Here, let me help you." An Air Force tech. sergeant helped Gus to his feet. "I'm Sergeant Dick Chapman, camp leader for Lager (camp) C.' Do you mind answering a few questions, Captain?"

Gus sat down on the nearest bunk. The man that was lying on it left to join a few other men on the opposite side of the narrow hallway between the two rows of bunk beds stacked three-deep.

"Fire away, Sergeant Chapman."

The sergeant engaged Gus with an unflinching pair of hazel eyes set below heavy brows that joined above the bridge of his nose in a natural scowl, giving Gus the feeling of being stared down by a hungry bald eagle.

"Why aren't you at Oflag IV-C, Captain? Only NCO's are here at Stalag Luft IV."

"Colditz Castle? My Gestapo interrogator told me that the only transport was on a train to this place."

Sgt. Chapman asked Gus about the Memmingen mission, his unit designation, the Fifth Wing logo on the vertical stabilizer of the B-17s, and questions going back to MacDill USAAF Base. They talked about Gus' family and Provo. Finally, satisfied that Gus wasn't a Nazi plant sent to ferret out any escape plans, Sgt. Chapman extended his hand.

"Sorry about the grilling, sir. We need to be careful about prying eyes.

"For the last few weeks we have been getting POWs in from other camps along the western front. We know that the allies have the Germans flanked by the Russians coming down from the east and the American and Brits from the west. The sound of artillery is getting closer almost daily. Our feeling is that many of the camps are being evacuated because of the advances of our guys."

Gus nodded in agreement. "I've seen a lot of troop movement since I've been on the run. You would expect it closer to the front lines, but not in the vicinity of downtown Berlin and Munich. The Nazis are in full retreat. I think what's happening with the camps is that the Nazis can't afford the manpower to guard the numbers of prisoners in the one thousand or so camps throughout Germany and Poland. Look around you. You guys don't have enough bunk beds to go around. Your latrines, well … And what about the food? I just spent a week in solitary confinement, and all I got was a bowl of soup, if you can call it that, and some water once a day. Are you guys doing any better?"

"No, sir, we're not. Look around you. You'll see where our boys are stacked three high. These huts were designed to house sixteen men with eight sets of bunk beds. The whole camp is overcrowded. From what we can tell, there are over ten thousand of us inside the barbed wire. This camp was designed to hold a little over six thousand. There have been escape attempts, but the commandant has ordered his guards to shoot any prisoners who attempt to breach the inside fence line or are caught with escape paraphernalia.

"Three months ago, we were getting regular Red Cross packages and some letters from the states. Now, we are not even allowed to *handle* the boxes from the Red Cross. The guards have been seen loading them up on trucks and taking them out of the camp … obviously for their own use. What does that tell you, Captain?"

"It tells me that their supply chain is breaking down. Distribution of goods from the Red Cross, letters from home, food consignments from private parties, clothing … everything needed to sustain life in keeping with the Geneva Convention, is being denied. I see men who are sick, many of which should be hospitalized. What are your medical facilities here? Do you even have the opportunity to go on sick call?" Gus asked, shaking his head as the full impact of their condition was being impressed upon him.

"We have two doctors to treat ten thousand men: one American and a Brit. There are only one hundred thirty-two beds in the infirmary. A medical staff of fourteen personnel—all prisoners themselves—are all that is allowed by the camp commandant."

Gus shook his head in disdain at what he was hearing, though it didn't surprise him.

"I saw a lot of mistreatments that were, in my opinion, in direct violation of the standard of care outlined in the Geneva Convention. How would you say the prisoners are being treated by the guards day-to-day?"

Sgt. Chapman laughed. "Sir, with all due respect. I have complained about prisoner treatment on numerous occasions since September. I personally interviewed over one hundred prisoners who have come here from other stalags in the system. To a number, their response to your question was affirmative as to the violations and 'less than poor' as to the quality of care. The guards do not allow prisoners to handle Red Cross packages. They organize raiding parties where they line us up outside and then ransack the huts, searching through the personal belongings of prisoners and taking whatever they like: watches, rings, photos, clothing items. Every day when we are lined up for roll call, men are kicked, slapped, jabbed at with bayonets or struck with the butts of their rifles. The camp's so-called "Chief of Security" condones the behavior of the guards under his command. His excuse to me was that these measures were taken to prevent any prisoners from trying to escape.

"A case in point is the story of Sergeant Sean Riley. A little man, he was a turret gunner in a Fortress. He was singled out by one particular guard … last name of Fahnert, as I recall. It happened one day during the roll call about a month ago. Sergeant Riley refused to fall out for roll call. He simply could not take any more hitting, jabbing, kicking, name-calling. …He'd had enough. Riley climbed out of the window at the back of his hut and ran for the inside perimeter fence. He managed to maneuver his body through the barbed wire and into 'no man's land' (the space between the inside perimeter and the main outside perimeter), until, with no warning whatsoever, Fahnert shot him in the back. Then he laughed, sir! … He laughed in our faces."

Gus had written only one letter to Addie since his arrival at the camp. He doubted it would ever get to her. Like all outgoing mail from prisoners, only letters describing the best conditions and lauding the fairness of their treatment by the guards and officers, were allowed to be sent. For Addie's sake, Gus felt the less she knew about the truth, the easier it would be on her. He had no way of knowing if his letter was even given to the Red Cross to be mailed—another denial of reasonable rights by the likes of Baumbach, Fahnert, and Pickhardt.

By February, conditions at Stalag Luft IV had deteriorated to an inhumane level. The greatest culprit was lack of food. Trucks with the Wehrmacht cross stenciled in black paint on their grey doors, commonplace a few weeks earlier bearing food and medical supplies, trickled down to a slow drip. The rations were arriving only sporadically now, and were used primarily to feed the German overseers. The calorie count for prisoners had dropped from an already paltry 1100 to fewer than 800 calories per day. There was not a man in the camp who was not showing signs of ill health: weight loss, scurvy, diarrhea, peptic ulcers, dysentery, typhoid, pellagra, tuberculosis, etc.

On February 5, the final roll call at Stalag Luft IV was held. It came as a surprise to no one. The sound of Russian artillery had become louder and more frequent. The influx of more prisoners increased to the point that there was not a single available bed in Camp C. Nineteen hundred men were sleeping on the floor and a third of them had no mattress. Each new prisoner was given two blankets. In the entire camp of nearly 10,000 prisoners, there were only five small iron stoves to provide heat. The waste disposal facilities (latrines) consisted of two open air latrines for each of the four camps. Each hut had a two-seat latrine to be used at night. Fleas and lice were at near pandemic levels. There was no soap for washing or showering, and the camp had only one coal-heated water tank with a capacity of 100 liters for 1,000 men. Stalag Luft IV was literally bursting at the seams.

Sgt. Fahnert called for the prisoners to come to attention. Although it was difficult and even painful for some, all of the prisoners managed to stay on their feet despite standing ankle-deep in a mix of mud and snow in below-freezing temperatures,

The camp commandant, Col. Baumbach, stood on a wooden pallet. With his riding crop tucked firmly under his left arm, he addressed the prisoners.

"Tomorrow, you will leave Stalag Luft IV. You will march for three days to a stalag near Stettin. This transfer is necessary to protect your lives and is required by the Geneva Convention. You may carry as much as you can manage. All remaining food will be parceled out among the four lagers. Those of you who are unable to walk, and have been examined by the medical staff, will depart today on trucks equipped with cots for the most infirm among you."

On the morning of February 6, 1945, the American Airmen of Stalag Luft IV marched through the gates in groups of 250-300 men. Each group marched out in columns of four.

Within an hour they had marched, or more precisely … slogged, out of view of the prison camp. The road was not paved but had been used regularly and was preferrable to going cross-country. Barely hanging on, they were forced to march for six hours.

What little food could be scavenged from Red Cross parcels was seized by the guards and placed in trucks. The prisoners were each given a meager third-of-a-loaf of bread when they left Stalag Luft IV. There were a few parcels of Red Cross food, but it was consumed in the first three days. There wasn't a man among them that hadn't lost 15 to 20 lbs or more in the camp, leaving many without the physical stamina to complete the march. What was to be a three-day march, was now in its fourth day with no sign of their destination.

Gus was in a group of about 200 prisoners headed toward the village of Stolzenberg when he heard an outburst of angry shouting behind him. A prisoner was on the ground, doubled into a fetal position, trying to fend off the kicking he was being subjected to by one of Fahnert's guards. Gus didn't think twice. He sloshed through the mud and slush as fast as he could.

"Hey, you! Stop kicking that man!" he shouted as he placed himself between the guard and the fallen man. "This man is finished. I demand he be placed on a truck."

"No, I …I can make it." The prisoner stood and began walking, staggering through muck and mire, hardly able to keep his balance.

"You! Get back to your place. Schnell!" The guard prodded Gus with the bayonet of his rifle. Gus yelped at the sudden jab of pain. He turned and walked away while gently exploring the spot where the bayonet pierced his German issued overcoat. Reaching inside, he checked his shirt for a tear in the fabric and probed for more damage. *Hurts. …No blood. …Hard to inhale.*

The column left the road and marched toward a farm on the outskirts of the village of Greifenberg where a Wehrmacht truck was parked. The guards herded the men to the barn that served as the first roof over their heads in four nights. Gus scooped some straw together and covered it with a blanket. He stretched out and wrapped himself in his other blanket. Not more than ten minutes later, a guard ordered the prisoners to line up for some chow.

"Now, maybe we'll find out what the Nazis have done with our Red Cross parcels that they've been hoarding," said a fellow POW.

Gus turned toward the sound of the voice and recognized the ball turret gunner he had helped that day.

"It's you. My name's Wilkins … Reggie Wilkins. I'm glad I found you in this crowd. I wanted to thank you for intervening with the guards earlier. I was just about done in when you put me back on my feet"

"I'm Gus Bodine, Reggie. Bring your cup, and let's grab some chow, such as it is." Gus noticed Reggie looked unsteady on his feet. The man's face was waxy looking, and the whites of his eyes had a yellowish tint. Critically underweight, Reggie had been losing muscle. There was no fat left on his body to burn.

They took their turn in the chow line. They each were given a cup of weak broth of some sort with a half of a boiled potato floating in the brownish liquid.

"C'mon, Reggie, I've got a spot staked out for a good long nap," Gus offered.

"Good. I'm so cold, I can barely walk." Reggie offered a wan smile. He tried to laugh, but what came out was a paroxysm of coughing. Gus had to hold him up to keep him from falling until the coughing spasm stopped.

"How long has that been going on, pal? Sounds like it could be pneumonia."

"A couple of weeks … worse since we started marching. I was hoping we'd find some help by now. Three nights sleeping out under the trees in the freezing temperatures sure hasn't helped."

Gus lent a hand to get Reggie settled and noticed that the man had only one blanket. "Where's your other blanket, Reg?"

"Stollen a couple of weeks ago. Never found out who."

Gus wrapped his second blanket around Reggie. "Here. …Go to sleep. You need to get some strength back by morning." Gus sat with his back against the wall and gathered some loose straw. He stuffed as much of it next to him as he was able and wrapped his remaining blanket around himself. He tried to ignore the constant shivering, and finally drifted into a restless sleep.

The yelling voices of the German guards brought the prisoners to their feet. There was a lot of groaning, cursing, and mumbling as they filed out of the barn into the freezing morning air.

"C'mon, Reg, we need to …" Reggie didn't move. "Reggie?" Gus shook Reggie's shoulder … nothing. He checked closer, but it was clear —Reggie Wilkins was dead.

Reggie's body was thrown into the back of the sick truck, the only vehicle dedicated to the treatment of the dead and infirm. In Reggie's case, his body and those of two other men ended in a common, shallow grave dug in the woods out of sight of the column of POWs.

The march continued. It was now six days into their journey, February 12, 1945. Walking 14 hrs per day, the men were beset with rugged terrain, miserably cold and wet winter weather, and by burying sometimes 20 or more whose suffering had ended. Digging the graves was one the hardest tasks they endured, not as much because the labor was so demanding on the body, but because of the emotional toll it worked on the soul. Friends who were one day helping the weakest, became weak themselves and died along the way.

Distance was measured by the delays not by kilometers. Some days they walked 30 or more kilometers, yet other days their progress lagged as the stronger men slowed their pace to help the growing cadre of the less abled among them. Gus wondered if he would make it home, or if he would be marched into the woods to take a bullet in his brain. That scenario had repeated itself with horrifying regularity. Men were "eliminated" when they could no longer keep up with the march by succumbing to starvation, disease or just plain exhaustion.

The men were given one cup of boiled beets or potatoes per day. Drinking water came from creeks and streams, but the water from those sources had become tainted from use by other groups of prisoners. Often times, it smelled of urine. Men took to sucking on handfuls of snow while they walked. At night, fires were built to boil the snow water, but it wasn't enough to prevent the inevitable cases of diarrhea, dysentery, cholera, and parasites. Progress was painfully difficult and slow They were being herded like cattle toward the next forsaken place of refuge … perhaps the luxury of a barn belonging to one of hundreds of German peasant farmers who eked out their living plowing, planting, and harvesting their scant crops of various tubers. The freezing cold interior of those oversized barns presented themselves only rarely.

With over 200 men to feed, the death toll continued to rise.

Starvation and exposure were the main culprits. The daily lack of nutrition had added to their desperation and that of the German troops as well. The last night Gus spent bedded down in a barn, a couple of fellows trapped two rats. Somebody in the group had a shoehorn that he had ground to a sharp edge on a flat rock he picked up in the yard of the prison camp. (This he did, not so much to arm himself, but simply to pass the time; the more they found to do to distract themselves from their situation, the faster time seemed to pass.) He used the shoehorn to skin and gut the rats. The rats were a welcome source of protein, added to the cooking pot only rarely, whenever providence afforded it.

Ten kilometers from the Oder River crossing at Swinemünde, the guards called a halt. A small truck with the logo of the International Red Cross pulled off the road and parked near another barn where they were allowed to rest for a few hours. Food parcels, cigarettes, butter, and even chocolate were doled out sparingly. For the first time in several months, the prisoners had full access to the Red Cross parcels. Most certainly, it made the German guards and their handlers look good to the world news outlets, but the 200 empty stomachs desperate for food couldn't care less about the optics. The prisoners all received a generous portion of a soup made from Red Cross rations combined with potatoes gathered from a local farm. A much-welcomed surprise came when two dozen loaves of bread, the first bread in over a month, were off-loaded from the truck.

The Oder River followed a winding course through and beyond the town of Swinemünde before draining into the Baltic Sea. As they arrived, the prisoners were loaded onto barges and ferried across. They marched 20 kilometers until they came to a paved road leading into Neubrandenburg. The American prisoners were welcomed by the locals in what was a distinctly pleasant change from some of the towns where they were cursed, spat upon, and struck by anything the citizens could throw from empty bottles to horse manure and mud.

The column stopped for a two-day rest. The men were told that more prisoners would join them from Stalag Luft II-A. Meanwhile, another local farmer offered the prisoners everything they could dig up after the final harvest the previous November. Many spent their time digging in the muddy fields for the priceless food: potatoes and kohlrabi. The sick among them slept in a barn much of the two days … those were the men who suffered from starvation (and associated diseases), and injuries of all sorts: sprains, fractures, trench foot, hypothermia, pneumonia, and tuberculosis. Influenza took a terrible toll. There was always the relentless specter of death threatening to take any stragglers. All too often the infirm would be marched off into the forest and shot.

———

By the second day of their bivouac on the farm near Neubrandenburg, on the 32nd day of their trek, Gus had developed a fever and a cough. He was sitting on an empty, rusted, 40-gallon drum, with his back against the west wall of the barn, trying to drink down a last bit of watered-down potato soup, but his stomach fought against it with wrenching spasms and vomiting. He set down his cup and buried his face in his hands. Seventy POWs from Stalag Luft II-A had joined them earlier in the day, and they were about to move out. Destination? ...No one asked, and no one offered to say.

A guard, one whom Gus didn't recognize, climbed into a wagon with a plow attachment of some kind hooked onto the rear. The guard stood up and called out:

"Prisoners of the Reich! We will not be walking today. There are Red Cross parcels coming to us and we must wait for them. You will rest here at the barn. Do not attempt to walk beyond the perimeter of our soldiers or you will be shot!"

"Red Cross, eh? Maybe we can get some decent chow. I haven't eaten in going on three days."

"By the looks of you, you haven't eaten in a while either, Skipper."

Gus turned in the direction of the American voice. With an immediate flash of recognition, his attention was drawn away from his fever and focused on SSgt Carpenter. At first, Gus was disoriented and thought he might be hallucinating. The last thing he thought possible was that he would ever see a member of his crew alive.

"Sergeant Carpenter? Woody? I ... I can't believe it! How ...?"

The two men embraced as if they were long lost brothers.

"After *Addie* was hit, Dink and I, and Sykes, hit the silk when you gave the 'bail out' order. When my chute deployed, I looked around to see if there were any other chutes. I spotted Sykes' and Dink's, then way off in the distance I saw our Fort hit the ground. She sent up a ball of flames and black smoke. I thought I saw another chute just before she exploded, but I couldn't tell for sure."

"That would have been me alright. Go on," Gus prompted. He didn't explain the tears in his eyes ... three found, six dead.

"Well, we all landed pretty close together ... only about a hundred yards apart ... but the bad news was that a German patrol was on the road bordering the field where we landed. Ten of them came at us with fixed bayonets looking to skewer us like hot dogs at a weenie roast. We all raised our hands and dropped to our knees. We were taken to Stalag Luft XX-A, but "Dink" and I were moved to Stalag Luft II-A a few weeks later. We lost track of Sykes. He was pretty banged up when the Krauts got to us. I figured they took him to a field hospital.

"Yeah, you're probably right. Where's Dink?" Is he with you?"

"He sure is. He's not well, though, Skipper. I need to bring him some chow. That's why I headed over in this direction for the Red Cross parcels."

"I've never pulled rank on anybody, Al, but I'm going to make an exception. Can you get by the guards one more time?"

"I think so. Most of them hate this marching crap as much as we do."

"Good. Bring Dink over here. I'm going to round up a couple more fellas who are on their last legs, and we're going to get some of that food ... medical supplies, too, if we can."

Some of the old energy, lost by weeks of starvation, freezing temperatures, unrelenting sickness, and physical exertion that had sapped Gus of his strength, was returning. He had purpose again—to help the sickest among them.

Gus, Dink, Woody, and five men from Gus' column huddled together and planned their strategy. The target was the Red Cross truck parked next to a Wehrmacht 6x6 troop vehicle. The soldiers were in the process of offloading the Red Cross parcels. Several were already stacked neatly in the German army truck.

"We're starting right there." Gus said pointing in the direction of the trucks. "Follow me." Two of the men helped Sgt. Dinkleman, while Gus with four of the other POWs walked over to the man who appeared to be in charge. The German non-com was supervising the theft of food and supplies by transferring packets to the military truck.

Gus wasted no time. He squared off against the man. "Stop what you're doing. You are violating the laws of the Geneva Convention."

The man leveled his Mauser at Gus. "And you will be shot if you don't return to your place."

"I demand to speak to your commanding officer. …Now!" Gus persisted.

"Treten Sie ein, Stabsfeldwebel." (Stand down, Sergeant Major).

The order came from a Wehrmacht lieutenant who had been standing across the road next to a parked staff car. Upon hearing the raised voices coming from the group of men, the man occupying the back seat of the vehicle stepped down to the ground and joined his subordinate. They both approached the POWs who were contending with the German sergeant. The sergeant, on seeing the major and lieutenant, immediately came to attention and snapped a "Heil Hitler" salute.

"Who is responsible for these men?" The major demanded in perfect English with only a slight German accent.

"These men are acting under my orders, Heir Major (pronounced *Mi-yor*)," Gus answered. He saluted the man with an American-style salute: right forearm straight, fingers extended and touching the brow above his right eye. "I'm Captain Gus Bodine, United States Army Air Force. These men and I are simply acting within the Geneva Convention articles governing the treatment of Prisoners of War."

"Show me your papers. If you are what you claim to be, we will talk." The German officer drew his sidearm from its holster. The barrel of the Luger was pointed directly at Gus' stomach. "If not, I will shoot you myself."

Gus handed the man his ID. He wanted to appear calm and confident, but his heart was racing. He forced his breathing to slow. He recognized the signs of hyperventilation and needed to get in control of himself before he passed out.

The Luftwaffe major returned them to Gus and holstered his weapon. “Order your men to stand down. Come with me to my car. We can talk there.”

“Sergeant Carpenter, you’re in charge. I’ll be right back.” Gus followed the major.

As they walked toward the staff car, the German officer glanced furtively about before speaking as if not wanting to be overheard. His countenance suddenly softened as he began, “I attended university in the United States:Yale. I found it curiously interesting. The environment supporting open dialogue among faculty and students was … intriguing. I received a degree in European History and Political Systems and graduated in 1937. When I returned home to Germany in 1938, the Fuhrer’s Reich invaded Poland, and I was pressed into service.”

Gus was taken off balance by the German officer’s open willingness to talk about his personal history. He wondered, *Why is he telling me this?*

“I am on my way to Berlin. I will most likely not be able to help you and your men beyond today. I need for you to understand that my education in America created an understanding within me—an appreciation of how your way of life in America’s Democratic Republic is based on the assumed rights of its citizens. Captain, I sense within you a respect for … no … rather a *love* for your men. …I have said enough. Perhaps we will meet again sometime. Let us work together to resolve the more pressing issue at hand.” He turned to his lieutenant.

“The Red Cross packets are to be given to the prisoners … all of them!”

The next day, when the prisoners of Stalag Luft IIA left the main column, Woody and Dink were among them.

“So long, Skipper. God willing, we’ll see each other again one day.” They both saluted their aircraft commander.

“One day …” Gus returned the salute and watched them march until they were just part of the gray, indefinable morass of the mist covered landscape.

THE ELBE RIVER ... AGAIN

The next 16 days were made marginally more tolerable by the sharing of the food parcels. The two American doctors from Stalag Luft IV were able to treat some of the more serious cases of trench foot and dysentery. Two men died from typhus, and countless others needed hospitalization, or they, too, would run up the death toll.

On March 25, the 48th day of the march, they were approaching the Elbe River near Ahrensburg just northeast of Hamburg and two kilometers south of their first crossing of the Elbe. The column's numbers had been reduced by 83 men. A few had been taken to various hospitals in nearby towns and cities they had passed through, but the death rate had slowly increased as the living conditions declined. The need for more and better health care grew under the burden of increasing privation from even the least of provisions demanded by humanity. Decimation of the human bodies sky rocketed.

They halted along the heavily forested shores of the Elbe. Heavy storm clouds threatened, and by late afternoon a fierce snowstorm hit. Two local farmers crowded as many of the sick prisoners as they could manage into their barns, but the majority of the men had to hunker down beneath the canopy of trees in the freezing wet snow. That night the temperature dropped to -3° F. During the night, Gus' fever spiked to 104°. His sleep was all but non-existent. Hallucinations overcame him as faces of the dead paraded across his mind's eye. Reggie Wilkins and many others, whose names he never knew, drifted in and out. Their voices, carried by the freezing wind, created by Gus' own fevered mind, drifted into the swirling snow. The howling wind was their cry.

DELIRIUM

Every step was an act of physical labor. Gus was only vaguely aware that he was running a fever as his body continued to move forward in a robotic, mindless rhythm. He stopped, and in his delirium, he was vexed by images of the thick mud pulling at his feet as if to hold him in the depths of its sodden bosom … to claim him as its own; some growing *thing* like so many others growing in this sad excuse of farmland: beets, potatoes a few carrots passed by in the final harvest. He saw himself as not a mere vegetable which had assumed human traits … no, nothing quite so benign as that. These malevolent mud creatures wanted to feed on him as if *he* were the vegetable … to drag him down to be dined upon. A semblance of a chuckle escaped his clenched teeth. With an audible grunt and a slurping "pop," one mud-caked boot after the other pulled the roots free from ankle-deep mire that passed for soil in that part of Germany. The ogre's meaty claws clung to his feet, wanting to pull him down. Each laboring step was, in its own way, a victory over the *real*, gray-coated ogres … the rifle packing kind: German soldiers herding him and 200 others with the butts of their weapons prodding at the POWs. At least that's how Captain Gus Bodine felt. Was it just his fevered thoughts? Maybe, but a victory over the dark specter of death, notwithstanding.

"Schnell!" one of them grunted.

The sharp voice lifted the American aviator from his fever-fueled dreams. He had fallen asleep during a brief halt for food. Potato soup was the fare today. No bread to add substance to the meager meal. Bread was a rarity on this march to unknown places. Gus sat among a group of POWs awaiting their turn to join the line of men slogging their way to nowhere. He clenched his teeth, forced himself to his feet, and pried a boot from another grasping tendril of muck.

Gus found himself looking forward to a night in a barn and some dry hay to lie in to insulate his body against the numbing chill. The alternative, most often, was another endless wet, freezing night beneath the "shelter" of a tree that afforded little respite for those who were still strong enough to continue. The farmers frowned on the use of their barns as a camping venue for the sad lot of POWs, claiming that the hay stored in those barns was rendered useless as feed for the farm animals … useless because of the filth they left behind. There were plenty of farms dotting the landscape, but the prisoners were most often ordered to bed down outside where they would lie shivering and wet until the earliest rays of sunlight.

On March 26, 1945, as Gus laid chilling beneath the snow laden branches of a pine tree, the sun had not yet appeared over the east hills. A heavy overcast promised yet another snowstorm moving down from the north. *I wouldn't want to be flying a mission in that weather.* Just as his mind finished the thought, the drone of countless aircraft engines approaching from the south caught his attention. He turned and looked up to see what must've been over a hundred B-17s trailing contrails through a generous break in the cloud cover at about 20,000 ft. His spirits soared at the sight. Gus knew that the column was close to Hanover. Enemy fighters were engaging the escort of P-51 Mustangs. Bursts of ack-ack from German 88 mm cannons pocked the sky. One of the Forts broke from the formation … a thick line of smoke marking his decent.

"Hurry … Bail out! Bail out!" Gus yelled. The effort threw him into a coughing spasm. As quickly as it began, the sky quieted, and the clouds resumed their silent game of tag.

They prisoners marched most of the day, every day. The aggregate numbers of POWs continued to decline. Their malnourished and emaciated bodies dropped like flies. Disease, frostbite turning to gangrene, and hypothermia took no small number of them. Many of them didn't carry the necessary clothing to survive the freezing nights. Lying exhausted on the wet ground, they were no better off than if they had been locked inside a freezing meat locker in their skivvies. As for Gus, survival's one enduring mechanism was at once simple and as complex as life itself—the soul's very life blood—his faith. The Lord's gentle mercies had preserved him thus far, and he grew more certain every day … every agonizing step … that there was purpose to his survival. He often thought that his staying alive was meant to benefit the men whose efforts to survive were flagging by falling victim to the aforementioned maladies … and then there was Addie. It was at those times he drew renewed strength to stay the hand of death's dark angel. Someone much greater than he knew why he had managed to keep his crippled bomber airborne while some of his crew were able to bail out and escape just before it cork-screwed into an unpopulated mountain meadow, and why he ended up here instead of dead in some field in Vienna among the ruins of *Addie's Armor.*

On March 27, the fiftieth day of the forced march, they were approaching the Elbe River near Langenburg, just northeast of Hamburg, just two kilometers south of their first crossing of the Elbe. Gus overheard a couple of prisoners saying, "Where are we going? We've already crossed the Elbe River, and now were going to cross it again!" It looked like they were reversing course back toward Stalag Luft IV, toward columns of black smoke rising from distant booms of artillery. Russians to the northeast, allies coming up from the southwest. *Our guys have them on the run,* Gus cheered to himself. As for POWs, those ragged remnants of a war recklessly conceived and selfishly brought to life by a madman … *what of us?* All that was left was the mud and the bone-numbing cold that invites sweet rest and sleep. In Gus' delirium, the growing despair among them had a voice … *Just stop, lie down and close your eyes from this torture. Peace awaits.* His mind snapped into focus, and his hands reflexively reached out to prevent the fall when he tripped over a dead tree branch. Too late. Gus went face-first into a puddle of mud.

"Come, let me help you."

Gus looked up into the tired but youthful eyes of a German soldier. The voice was not imagined … no invention of a fevered mind. Strong hands lifted Gus to his feet. Something about this German stirred a distant memory. *I know that face. … Where?*

"Danke." Gus whispered throatily as his hands wiped thick muck from his eyes. *Who are you? Do I know you?* They were questions left unspoken … the young man with blonde hair and penetrating gray-blue eyes was gone. There was no sign of him. It was as if he had been an apparition. Gus was left alone once more to blend with the others of his kind, the detritus of battles fought, and prisoners all. *Lord, I'm so tired.*

Signs of frostbite sent nerve jangling stabs of pain to the switchboard in his brain. *Got to keep moving.* Twilight blanketed the quilted patches of farm acreage. *There, off in the distance, a barn. It looks like the Krauts are herding us there. I can make it that far.* Gus walked on.

What's that up ahead? Somebody is down … I must help him. He pulled harder at his boots. The added effort to quicken his pace sent his heart racing and ears ringing.

"No! Please don't!" he called out to the German soldier, in a voice surprisingly strong, his mind suddenly alert. "Please don't. …I'll help him."

In a flash, the Wehrmacht guard turned his rifle toward the impudent POW. "Halt!" His rifle was steady and pointed directly at Gus' midsection. "Get on your knees, American!" Unlike the young soldier who helped him earlier, this man spat out the word *American* as though it were something vile.

Gus was certain his life was at an end. "I only wanted…" he started to say.

"Silence!" The guard paused and hesitated. First looking down at the man fallen in the mud and then at Gus, he gestured with his rifle and spoke in English with a thick, guttural accent. "Get him on his feet. If he falls again, I will shoot him … and you as well."

Blue eyes gazed up through a mud-caked countenance. Gus, while hardly able to help himself, took the soldier's raised hand and pulled him to his feet. With one arm around his waist, he pulled the man's his left arm over his shoulder, and together, they made their way arduously nearer the barn. Their progress could have been measured in inches. Stumbling over plowed ruts, they barely avoided pitching face-first into the mud. Behind them, the metal-on-metal *click-click* of the slide on the guard's Gewehr-43 semi-automatic rifle, reminded them that he was a man of his word: "I will shoot him … and you as well." They wouldn't be the first. Every day, the familiar *crack!* of a rifle was heard from somewhere along the edge of the woods near their line of march. Stragglers were shot and left to molder in those woods. Even after nearly two months of the mind-numbing horrors endured by the POWs, the thought of being that close to death every minute of every day, still sent shivers through Gus.

The two bedraggled men quickened their pace toward the barn, now a scant 70 yds farther. "We're among the last. I hope we can find a cozy corner to lie in," Gus whispered to his new friend. As they and the remaining POWs entered the tree line, the guards brought them to a halt. The lot of them were ordered to sit. The sound of a truck approaching from behind caught Gus' attention. He turned to look, half-expecting to see a machine gun in the bed ready to fire, but there was no machine gun … just boxes, some with a tell-tale red cross emblazoned on them. A few of the prisoners were ordered to offload and distribute bags of eating utensils: an assortment of spoons, metal plates, bowls, and canteens. Then, several bags of potatoes, mostly covered with dark mold, were offloaded.

A small stream meandered its way through this part of the forest. It was there that the guards led the prisoners to obtain water for boiling the potatoes and to fill the canteens. The water appeared clear, but the steam rising from the pots hanging over makeshift fire pits gave off a familiar unpleasant odor … no doubt from various farm animals and the many POWs that had occupied these same wooded forests over the months from late September when the evacuation of the stalags began, to now at the end of March.

The barn filled up quickly. The remaining men were herded to the leeward side of the structure that offered some slight respite from the chill of the winter wind that prevailed in that clime during late winter. However, it meant yet another night huddling, shivering on the muddy ground. At least the forest's canopy gave them some protection from the falling snow. Gus huddled against the trunk of a tree and wrapped himself in his now tattered woolen blanket to face the long night ahead. *When will this end? It can't be long before we're liberated.* Worry deepened the lines in his brow. His strength weakened along with his resolve.

How many more nights must we all lie here starving, freezing cold, dysenteric, toes and feet blackening from frostbite. If only we can survive the night. His thoughts and prayers were directed heavenward. Gus' eyes closed as his body curled itself into a fetal position … too weak to fight off the freezing chill. As he drifted off into a fevered, fitful sleep, his last lucid thoughts took him back to Addie and the child he had never seen.

CHAPTER 29

"Highway! Here, boy!" Gus tossed the dog's favorite chew toy into the meadow grass. Highway chased after it, subdued it, and trotted over to Gus. He placed the toy at Gus' feet as if it were a solemn offering. He sat on his haunches and patiently waited for his master's voice to send him on his next search and recovery mission.

"Gus, honey, the picnic is laid out. We have cold chicken, potato salad, lemon cheesecake, and sparkling grape juice."

Gus stood and walked toward Addie. Oddly, he didn't seem to be getting any closer to her. The baby was lying in a baby carriage but was turned away from Gus, so he couldn't see his child's face. He was struck with a sudden fear that he wouldn't reach them in time … *in time for what? Hurry, Gus. Run!*

Gus stumbled and fell. When he recovered his balance, he felt the grip of hypothermia. *Strange, it's the middle of summer. I shouldn't be freezing.*

"Gus, where are you?" Addie called. Her voice was a receding echo as his mind reclaimed the harsh reality of the freezing winter. He tried to stand but faltered dropping to his knees.

A pair of strong hands reached down and lifted him to his feet. Gus looked into the eyes of the same young German soldier with the kind face that projected peace and renewed hope, who helped him once before. Before Gus could ask his name, the young man turned away from him and called back over his shoulder, "She's waiting for you!," then disappeared into a flurry of snow.

Gus' felt his legs tingling as blood flowed into them invigorating his tired muscles. His limbs experienced a feeling of renewed energy, and he was surprised to find that he was able to walk without stumbling to the ground. He felt as though he had been visited by a ministering angel. "Thank you," he whispered.

STALAG XI-B

The column prepared to move out on the following day for Bad Fallingbostel and Stalag XI-B, a 71-km march of four days. Prior to starting out, however, two International Red Cross trucks were being off-loaded by several German guards. Instead of helping themselves to the provisions intended for the prisoners, the guards began handing out boxes full of socks, blankets, food items, cigarettes, chocolate bars, and sundry medical supplies. Gus removed his boots and took off his hole-worn socks and replaced them with a brand new pair of French Army woolen socks. Rather than throw them away, he pulled the older pair over his hands. That extra pair of socks had no doubt saved his feet and hands from limb-threatening frostbite. Before they left, he made a point of acquiring and delivering over 40 pairs of the same Red Cross woolen socks to several of the men who showed the greatest need.

April 1, 1945, another Stalag with the familiar guard towers and barbed wire enclosures came into view. They had arrived at the site of Stalag XI-B and its companion camp, Stalag XI-D/357. Both camps were overflowing with detainees forced to leave a half-dozen other camps. North and east of there, the Red Cross had run out of food, clothing, and medical supplies, leaving nothing for the added population.

On April 6, the American airmen of Stalag Luft IV were ordered to evacuate Camp 357 after bivouacking there for only five days. Additionally, they were joined by 12,000 British troops and airmen, leaving just 1500 of the original camp compliment of POWs. With the Allies only 30 miles to the south, and the sky filled with the smoke of battle drawing closer to Fallingbostel, Commandant Oberst Hermann Ostmann directed the burgeoning column of nearly 20,000 POWs to march, under guard, to Griese in the Ludwigslust-Parchim district, near the North Sea in the northernmost region of Germany, a distance of 117 kilometers.

Before continuing their journey northward, Gus and the prisoners of Stalag Luft IV were treated to a shower and delousing. Gus couldn't help but believe that the recent acts of benevolence shown them by the German Wehrmacht were no more than desperate acts of feigned concern on the part of German officers and men to gain favor from a too-late show of appeasement by the same men who had so brutally abused the stalag prisoners.

After four days' rest, Gus' fever finally broke. Surprisingly still alive, he continued to weaken for want of nourishment … living on only a cup of watery potato soup and a chunk of bread, about the size of a child's fist, per day.

Fighting continued around the columns of prisoners as they proceeded on a northwesterly path. On April 8 and 9, they had to stop because of the battles that were flaring up around them. British Typhoon fighters were attacking German hot spots by strafing artillery and machine gun emplacements. Spitfires and Typhoons were seen every day. To the German guards' credit, they kept the column moving, while taking advantage of lulls in the fighting to quicken the pace of the prisoners.

When they arrived in Griese on April 18, the prisoners were ordered to march on for four more days to Lübeck. The Allies were closing in on the Wehrmacht, and the fighting became intense in the area. The German army was in a state of disarray and were in full retreat.

Red Cross parcels were being dispatched to the struggling POWs, and four of their trucks bearing the bright red crosses of the International Red Cross met head-on with the evacuees. In spite of the fierce battles going on all around them, the trucks pulled off onto a dirt road leading to a farm. Grateful for the respite, the prisoners were fed a much needed hot meal of meat and potatoes, bread, and coffee. The life-saving Red Cross vehicles continued south, leaving behind parcels of food and medicine.

Two days before arriving at Lübeck, the column had been marching at a quick pace when a flight of three British Typhoon low altitude interceptors dropped out of the sky turning toward the large mass of prisoners. Mistaking them for German soldiers, the Typhoon's four each 20 mm autocannons opened fire on the column of prisoners. The guards returned fire with their rifles, but to no avail. Finally, two men unfurled a 20-foot-long, white banner with "POW" etched in black paint. The fighters waggled their wings and veered away leaving behind 60 fatalities and over 100 wounded. The Wehrmacht guards ordered that the wounded be carried. The dead were left on the side of the road—but not before Gus assumed the responsibility of collecting the personal IDs of every deceased prisoner.

Ten days after leaving Fallingbostel and Stalag XI-B, on 22nd of April 22, the POWs of Stalag Luft IV arrived at Oflag X-C in Lübeck. Red Cross trucks were ordered to supply the Allied POWs with some of the items that they had been denied since they began their march nearly two and a half months before on February 6. Anticipating their arrival, prisoners of the camp had been ordered to erect a tent community to house the new tenants. Over 20,000 POWs had marched northward from Fallingbostel.

On April 16, an emaciated and very sick Captain Gus Bodine was taken to a camp hospital suffering from the effects of endemic typhus, dysentery, trench foot, starvation, and scurvy.

The International Red Cross doctors and nurses were few in number but were allowed access to antibiotic medications. Chief among them was penicillin. Under close supervision by a German physician, Gus was placed on a heavy regimen of the new antibiotic. With an 1800 calorie per day diet of boiled potatoes, lentils, animal meat-based protein, and the German winter staple of kohlrabi, augmented by an occasional can of American "Spam" that would find its way into the infirmary food locker, Gus slowly began to regain his strength and weight.

The Wehrmacht troops who ruled over Oflag X-C were ordered to keep a close watch on the allied prisoners. The commandant, Oberst

Franz Gerhardt, governed the camp based on a two-pronged paradigm: security against escape, and appeasement of American and British officers. Heir Gerhardt's instinct for surviving a war-crimes trial was his prime motive for the approach.

Toward the end of April, when the British Sixth Army and General Patton's Seventh Army tanks were within the sound of distant artillery fire, Oberst Gerhardt decided a change of plans was called for. He determined, like many perpetrators of mayhem, that a time-worn solution to avoiding punishment when the "jig is up," was to "get out of Dodge." His family's Villa on the shore of the Baltic Sea was waiting for him, and he knew that was likely his only hope of seeing his wife and two sons again.

The morning of April 30, Gus was awakened by a great commotion. A Red Cross Nurse ran past his bed to the entrance of the infirmary. She opened the door and gasped, momentarily speechless.

"They're gone!" she cried when she found her voice. "The German soldiers are gone!

The German guards, under cover of night, had abandoned their posts amid rumors that General George Patton's Seventh Army was approaching. However, it wasn't General Patton's tanks of the Third Army that liberated Oflag X-C. A platoon of paratroopers from Britain's Sixth Army, under the command of Major General Sir Richard Nelson Gale, was first to arrive at the camp, and it was they who threw open the gates of Oflag X-C without a German combatant to be seen. The platoon was marched in by Regimental Sergeant Major (RSM) John C. Lord of the Third Parachute Brigade.

CHAPTER 30

OPERATION MAGIC CARPET

On VE (Victory in Europe) Day, May 8, 1945, the war in Europe ended. Then began the logistical challenge of assembling together three million United States Army personnel and transporting them out of war-torn Europe to debarkation points in England and Italy. Through the efforts of the WSA (War Shipping Administration), over 700 ships were brought into service, each carrying as few as 300 to a maximum of 3,500 American servicemen and women. Aircraft carriers such as the *USS Saratoga* and the *USS Lake Champlain*, battleships, commercial luxury ocean liners, including the *Queen Mary*, and 300 converted liberty ships including the *USNS Aiken Victory* were activated to return four 435,000 soldiers per month. By February 1946, there were fewer than 7,000 American servicemen and women in the ETO (European Theatre of Operations).

MAGIC CARPET

Back at the American air bases in England, the plan to airlift all American and British POWs out of Germany was spelled out and put into action as part of Operation "Magic Carpet."

The first item on the agenda of the massive repatriation effort was to centralize a base of operation and communication to handle the deployment of an armada of aircraft to bring the former POWs to England. RAF Alconbury was selected because of their two 6000 ft paved runways, and they were the home of the 435th Troop Carrier Group. The existing cadre of C-47 Skytrains and C-54s would be augmented by an air group-sized array of B-24s and B-17s from the Eighth and Fifteenth Air Forces. Planes were stripped of their bomb racks and guns, and their crews were trimmed to include at most a pilot and co-pilot, flight engineer, radioman, and navigator. Only a handful of American servicemen, mostly POWs, flew home from England aboard the converted bombers. The individuals who were in good enough health to endure the seven-day trip, returned home aboard any one of the ships leaving from either Plymouth, England or Pisa, Italy.

On May 15, after two weeks of being poked, prodded, stuffed with protein-rich high-calorie food, and participating in a muscle building exercise program that would be the envy of any boot camp drill instructor, Gus had gained back 10 lbs of the 40 lbs he lost during his internment as a guest of the Third Reich. Still weak, Gus turned more and more of his attention to Addie. He had written to her every day since the German surrender. As a matter fact, among the first items he acquired from the International Red Cross, were two pencils and a composition tablet of lined paper. He knew that it would probably be a couple of weeks before Addie received any of his letters, but writing to her eased the hurt of their separation during the last year. He had just finished a letter, and was about to ask a nurse for an envelope, when a USAAF officer, dressed in a flight suit and sheepskin-lined flight jacket, approached Gus' hospital bed.

"Are you Captain Gus Bodine?"

"Yes. Yes I am. What can I do for you, Major?" Gus had never met the man before and wondered why he had singled out Gus. He suspected it might have something to do with military intelligence and his own internment as a POW in Stalag Luft IV. *Oh well, I guess I'll find out soon enough.*

"I'm Major Donald Mallard, 483rd Bomb Group. Do you know a Captain Sandy Plunkett of the 483rd Bomb Group?"

"The 483rd, did you say? That's my outfit … at least it was. Yes, Sandy was in my squadron … the 816th. What in heaven's name brings you here, Major."

"Captain Plunkett has been keeping an eye on the MIA list that comes into the group intelligence officer every couple of weeks. Ever since you didn't return from the bombing sortie on Memmingen, he has been trying to find out if you were dead or alive. In all this time, he has not let up on his efforts to find the truth. He told me a story about you both agreeing to stick together and get back to the states in one piece. You promised each other that you would get in touch and stay connected after the war. Well, since you were declared missing, he has taken it on himself to pin down your status so that he could contact your family after the war. The last notification of your whereabouts came in a POW report from the Red Cross. Your name was mentioned as one of the new arrivals to Stalag Luft IV way back in November."

"But, why … how is it that you came here? You're a long way from Sterparone."

"We lost track of you when the camp was evacuated back in February. We knew that you were headed for Fallingbostel, but we lost you again until you showed up here two weeks ago. The International Red Cross bookkeeping expertise came to the rescue, and your name appeared on a list of patients admitted to the hospital following the abandonment of Oflag X-C and the arrival of the British paratroopers. Oh, here's the good part: the 483rd is being deactivated soon, so some of our planes have been converted to passenger planes. Can you believe it? With the bomb racks and guns removed, our Forts can carry up to 35 passengers. A dozen of us have been deployed to Lübeck airport to ferry some of the POWs from Stalag Luft IV to England, thanks in part to you and Sandy. You have been on the mind of group command ever since you dropped off the face of the earth. I suspect they were able to pull some strings. All of the flight crews here are volunteers from the 483rd. …So, would you like a ride?"

It took two days for Gus to be processed out of the hospital at Lübeck. He was re-issued his uniform, rank insignia, wings, and awarded ribbons as they were stated on his DD Form 214 service record. After packing his duffel bag and signing his hospital discharge papers, Gus rang up Maj. Mallard and 10 minutes later the good major, with a staff sergeant as driver, pulled their Jeep up to the front doors of the hospital. Gus tossed his duffel bag into the back seat and climbed in beside it. During the drive to the flight line, Gus was struck suddenly by the fact that he was leaving. The heartache, pain, torture and interminable cold would be gone … but not ever forgotten. The lost friends and crewmates … brothers all, would live in his mind until he breathed his last breath on earth.

Captain Sandy Plunkett was conducting a walk around preflight inspection of his converted B-17G, *Montana Cowgirl.* They were scheduled for wheels up in a little less than an hour. He turned toward the sound of approaching voices and recognized Gus immediately.

"Gus Bodine! God in heaven has blessed us all. Here you are looking all dapper and rejuvenated." He quick-stepped to Gus and embraced him in a spine cracking bearhug. "I can't tell you how happy I am to see you, my old friend."

"Old friend, eh? Need I remind you we're still in our twenties, pal? I've missed you too, Sandy. I didn't think I would see any of the gang ever again, but you … well, you and I go way back. If I were given the chance to see only one person after the nightmare of this war, it would be you, Sandy. What can I do to help?"

Sandy clapped his hand on Gus' shoulder. "You can climb aboard. The next time you step down on the tarmac will be in Reykjavik. I understand the officers' club there has a very nice dining facility. I figure we'll refuel there, let the passengers grab a bite, and head for Bluie West-One in Greenland then onto Goose Bay. The final leg of the northern ferry route will take us into Godfrey Army Airfield (Bangor, Maine). You'll want to stop by base ops when you get there.

They have travel vouchers for rides on commercial airlines to various cities. You'll have to find your own way to Provo from Salt Lake. Plan on 16 hours enroute to Godfrey. Tell you what, I think I can manage some time at the controls for you. My co-pilot, First Lieutenant Mike McFarland would probably appreciate some shuteye in the back. We've turned the tail gunner position into a semi-reclined couch. It's a squeeze getting in and out of it, but it has a great view." They both had a good laugh at the thought.

On May 18, 1945, the main wheels of the Fortress lifted from the concrete runway at Lübeck, Germany on the first leg of Gus' return to the waiting embrace of Addie's loving arms.

For Gus, the vibration coming up through the seat of his pants, combined with the steady drone of the four radial engines brought back a flood of memories of the missions he flew in *Addie's Armor* … flak, attacking German fighters, the ordeal of the countless days and weeks of his survival odyssey. For a minute, he was overtaken by the memories and became disoriented to the point that he was unsure if he was actually sitting there in *Montana Cowgirl* … or was he still delirious with fever, huddled inside a freezing barn?

"Hey there, Captain, Are you okay?" The rich baritone voice of a USAAF tech. sergeant brought Gus' mind back into focus. The "thousand-yard stare" on his face disappeared.

"Yes … I'm fine. This whole liberation thing is happening so fast, it doesn't seem real. You know what I mean?" Gus asked.

"Yes, sir, I do. I remember you from the walk out of Stalag Luft IV. You were the only officer in the column. You helped me when I stumbled and fell into a mud puddle. The guard almost shot us both ….

"That was you? I'm really glad to see you again. I never got your name, but I remember now what bad shape you were in. You looked like death warmed over. I wondered if you would make it."

Gus offered his hand, which his new, old friend gladly took. "We should try to keep in touch."

Shaking hands vigorously, the non-com introduced himself as SSgt Mark Heimlich, nose gunner with the 99th Bomb Group. "And you?"

"I'm Gus Bodine, on my way back home to Provo, Utah!"

Talking to someone else who shared the ordeal of what became known as "The Black March" had a settling effect on Gus. He was eventually able to get himself into a somewhat comfortable position in the "seats" installed inside the bomb bay. The crisscross nylon straps stretched over aluminum frames conformed to his body, and Gus allowed himself to doze off.

CHAPTER 31

THE MAIL

On the same day that Gus left Germany for Iceland, Addie Bodine walked to the mailbox as she had done many times before. She had noticed the mailman earlier when she happened to look down to the street from her bedroom window. The last Western Union telegraph she received from the Adjutant General's office informed her that Gus was in the hospital at Lübeck, Germany where he was recuperating from his time spent as a POW. Addie knew that Gus would write to her. The only question was how long it would take for his letters to reach her.

She pulled down the lid of the mailbox, and her eyes immediately fell on the envelope with a red, white, and blue sticker and the phrase "VIA AIR MAIL" printed on the white line.

"Gus" she whispered with a gasp of air caught in her lungs and a smile on her lips. She sprinted back to the house and sat down at the kitchen table. Savoring the moment, Addie lightly caressed Gus' handwriting on the envelope. With her hand trembling from the excitement of the moment, she reached for a butter knife, slid the blade underneath the flap of the envelope, and withdrew the treasured letter.

My darling Addie,

At last I am in a safe place where I can write to you. For nearly nine months I have not been able to tell you that I'm still alive, and that your presence in my mind has buoyed me up and seen me through the most difficult trials of my life. I am writing this letter from my hospital bed in Lübeck, Germany. Not to worry, I have not been wounded. I am simply recovering from the illnesses and maladies of malnutrition and exposure to the elements. I will tell you more about that when I get home. Yes, that's right, HOME! Sometime in the next three or four weeks I should be in a situation where I can board a ship and return to the states. I know things seem vague now, but there are well over a million servicemen and women who will be coming back over the next few months. I intend to write to you every day and keep you updated on my well-being and of the plans the Air Force is making to get me home. Rumor has it that former POWs will be given preferential consideration for the earliest possible departure dates.

Addie, I love you. There were several times in the last few months that I did not know whether I would survive to keep my promise to you, but today I can say with blessed assurance that I WILL return to you and to our baby. Our dream of raising a family and being together forever is alive and well. I want those things as much is I ever did. All of my dreams and all of my hopes for the future rest within the bands of love that I feel for you..

Gosh! As I read over what I've written, it sounds like I'm giving a talk in church. How do I express the immeasurable joy in my heart at the realization that I will soon be home?

All of my love,

Gus.

Gus was true to his word. A letter to Addie was in her mailbox the next day and the day after.

GOING HOME

Sandy taxied *Montana Cowgirl* to the passenger terminal of Old Town Municipal Airport in Bangor, Maine. One of the waist-gunner openings was made larger and fitted with a door through which passengers could board and deplane. Sandy and Gus walked together into the small passenger terminal.

"Well, old man, I'd best get over to USAAF operations and see what's on the manifest for tomorrow's return trip. Gus, I hope you'll keep in touch, and I'll do the same."

"You've got it, Sandy. I have your address. As soon as Addie, the baby, and I are settled I'll get in touch with you. Until then …" Sandy clasped Gus' hand, shook it briskly, and with a final salute, they turned different directions and walked away.

Gus was able to get a flight out to Chicago aboard a Pan Am DC-4. After a three-hour layover in Chicago, he boarded a DC-3 United Airlines flight to Denver and flew on to Salt Lake City on the same plane. At 2 a.m. he walked out of the passenger terminal at the Salt Lake municipal airport. At 3:45 a.m., he boarded a bus for *home*.

Addie had risen abruptly from a pleasant dream to change an impatient Gus Jr.'s diaper. She laid him back down and started to close his bedroom door, when Highway, ever on guard, jumped to his feet and began wagging his tail making an excited staccato thumping against the wall. Suddenly he turned, bounded down the stairs, and sat down facing the front door. It was still dark outside - clearly, something was going on. Highway let out an impatient bark as the headlights of a car cast splashes of light into the foyer. A moment later the lights disappeared. After cautiously descending the stairway and tiptoeing to the door, Addie decided to take a peek outside. Just as she turned the latch and opened the door a few inches, Highway squeezed in front of her and raced outside. He dashed down the flagstone walk in what seemed like a single stride to give Gus his very best doggie greeting of paws and slobber—almost knocking him over in the process.

"Gus … it's you! Oh, my dear Gussy!" Addie cried as she ran into her husband's outstretched arms. Highway joined the hug fest and ended up getting tangled in their feet. Gus' service cap tumbled to the lawn, followed by the three of them … still hugging … rolling around on the grass, giddy with happiness and love. In Gus' mind, everything he had been through to get back to his family was all worth it for this moment!

Tears streaming down her face, Addie gazed into her husband's eyes still hoping this wasn't a dream. "You're really here, Gus. You kept your promise, my love. …Come, let's go inside … there's someone very special who's been waiting to meet you.

THE END

ABOUT THE AUTHOR

Spencer Anderson is a U.S. Air Force Vietnam war veteran, former pilot, teacher and counselor, and an honorary Colonel in the Commemorative Air Force. His passion for aviation and aviation history is clearly seen in his writing. Spencer is dedicated to keeping alive the legacy of the patriots who chose to fly and fight for our grateful nation in its most trying times.

His latest novel, *Survive the Night*, recalls the tragedy of the German death march of more than 10,000 American and allied POWs through 900 miles of mountainous forests and war-torn lowlands of Germany. Though the march was a tragic stain on our world's history, *Survive the Night* is full of tender moments, happy outcomes, and the antics of Highway the dog.

Spencer is also the author of the popular warbird trilogy of historical-fiction aviation novels featuring Carl Bridger, the son of a Montana cattle rancher. *The Last Raider*, *Avenging Angel*, and *Mission Critical* chronicle Carl's adventures as a WWII pilot, a spy-plane test pilot and CIA operative, and a grandpa on a daring rescue mission.

Spencer is married to the love of his life Carole. Together they have seven children and live in St. George, Utah. For more information on Spencer's books, visit www.warbirdtales.com.

ACKNOWLEDGMENTS

To my wife Carole who got me unstuck when I couldn't get through a particular scene for want of a woman's point of view and who spent countless hours editing out the typos, grammar errors, and continuity goofs. She is my true and eternal love and my partner in all good things.

To Chris Schafer and the kind folks at Tactical 16 Publishing who took on this project and gave it life.

To Paul Bryner whose father, Faye Bryner, survived the nights of the forced march from Stalag Luft IV across Germany in the brutal winter of 1944-45 and to whom this story is dedicated.

ABOUT THE PUBLISHER

TACTICAL 16

Tactical 16 Publishing is an unconventional publisher that understands the therapeutic value inherent in writing. We help veterans, first responders, and their families and friends to tell their stories using their words.

We are on a mission to capture the history of America's heroes: stories about sacrifices during chaos, humor amid tragedy, and victories learned from experiences not readily recreated—*real stories from real people.*

Tactical16 has published books in leadership, business, fiction, and children's genres. We produce all types of works, from self-help to memoirs that preserve unique stories not yet told.

You don't have to be a polished author to join our ranks. If you can write with passion and be unapologetic, we want to talk. Go to Tactical16.com to contact us and to learn more.

All of Tactical 16's books are available on our online bookstore, T16Books.com. Visit it today to see more books from our selection of authors and to find a new adventure to read!

Printed in the USA
CPSIA information can be obtained
at www.ICGtesting.com
JSHW012028031023
49387JS00007B/21